SENSATION

For my brother Neil, who left us too soon, too young—
You would have loved this one . . .

For Karen . . . so many memories . . .

And, as always, for John, ever patient,
and for Mike, Tom, and now, Mom

Prologue

London, at a session of Parliament
Early March 1897

"There he is." The voice was barely above a whisper.

The Sicarian nodded. He didn't need to look; he knew the man. He knew everything about the man who was generally considered the logical successor to the prime minister.

The man was Anthony Venable, a charismatic young man who had all the perfect attributes of an up-and-coming leader: youth, recklessness, a fresh voice, and a superlative and majestic confidence that could even have been called autocratic; there was not a jot of humility marring his moral stance—he knew exactly what was right for everyone and who could provide it.

He was so very good looking women fell all over him, dowagers and debutantes alike; and he was as plumed and polished as only a man can be who has the kind of inherited wealth with which to indulge himself.

In addition to that, he had gotten major monetary support from some very prominent politicians who saw in him the future of the country and had pushed him right up into the House of Commons where he performed with a deceptive ease as if he had been standing for years. No one questioned why such a minor player had garnered such impressive backing.

It didn't matter; his impact was immediate and absolute.

They immediately nicknamed him *the musketeer* because of the sweeping philosophy of change he continually advocated in his rich, urgent, persuasive, and sometimes haranguing voice: control of everything in the hands of the few, and control of the country in the hands of one elected leader.

He would be the overseer of it all. It wasn't something said out loud. It was tacitly understood what he wanted, and that he was the one who had all the answers; they had only to elect him to make the decisions, elect him to take control, and all the freedoms they coveted would be theirs.

No one saw that under that mask of elegance, wealth and charm, there was a charismatic zealot running amok, seducing the adoring crowds who hung on his every word.

They were listening intently now as he spoke from the podium in the House of Commons in his deep, hypnotic, compelling voice.

They loved him. Everyone loved him. Devoured every snippet of gossip about him. Followed every line in the paper that bore his name. Thought they were his next best friend, that he had their best interests at heart, that he wanted only to give them a perfect life in a perfect world.

Look at how he had formed a consulting party, to give the populace a forum to express their opinions and make them feel they counted. That was Tony Venable. He had a way of making everyone feel that he was listening, that he heard.

He was the right man for the moment: he would listen, he would act, he would lead.

He was special, extraordinary, the kind of political creature who comes along once in a lifetime.

He had the crowd in the palm of his hand. Anything he wanted, and he wanted much, they roared their approval.

But he did not have the approval of two, the watcher and the Sicarian, who were seated in the shadows of the viewing boxes that day.

And that was most important of all.

"He has gone beyond," the watcher said.

The Sicarian nodded. "He will be stopped. Soon."

Nothing more needed to be said. Their doctrine demanded it. Their discipline was to obey.

Two days later, Tony Venable was found dead on the floor in his library, a bloody little cut in the shape of a fishhook on his bare chest, and his fingers curled around a letter opener, as if he had tried, with just this puny object, to fight off his murderer.

The public was outraged. It couldn't be true. They wouldn't believe it. The murderer must be caught. Soon. Now.

And it was the watcher and the Sicarian who were the first, most public and most vocal, in demanding that justice must be done . . .

Chapter One

Sometimes a man had to live between yesterday and tomorrow, because in the present, he had no future. Sometimes he had just to let himself go and immerse himself in sex, submerge himself in sin, and submit to every base instinct he had kept suppressed in the name of civility, restraint and common decency.

Sometimes, it felt really good to just surrender his body to the pure physical demand that he had ruthlessly kept in check every day of his life.

And that was just one reason why Kyger Galliard found himself sprawled naked on an ermine-covered platform, wallowing in the carnal excesses of Bullhead Manor, a tight rubber ring around the base of his ramrod penis while one after the other, beautiful naked sirens slithered in, just as he had ordered, and mounted him. Just one hot, tight tunnel after the other in which to subsume his desire and his pent-up, inexhaustible lust.

He had turned into Lujan, he thought suddenly.

The thought jolted him. The unholy irony of it. Given the right circumstances, he had become his brother, after years of being his brother's keeper. Only he wasn't feckless, reckless or dissolute. All this dissipation had a purpose, and it wasn't just pleasure.

Even though pleasure definitely was at the top of the list of reasons why he was at Bullhead Manor.

Except, he was getting bored stiff with all these bouts of fucking in hot holes with no faces, and nothing to distinguish any of the women but their willingness to spread their legs.

That just had never been his way, and with nothing to restrain him or contain him, he still found it hard to conceive of how Lujan had spent years similarly occupied to no avail.

Yet here he was at Bullhead Manor, naked and willing, his penis raring to go.

And Lujan had put him here.

Good God.

The door opened.

Goddamn—not another one.

Absolutely another one, just as he had ordered. He wondered if someone was keeping score. He wondered what the women talked about after they left him, after they left any of the patrons upon fulfilling all their perverse desires.

But he shouldn't be thinking about these things when a ripe naked woman was crawling into the room, her backside undulating with each movement, her breasts swinging, her nipples tight, her desire to please him thickening the air like smoke.

He should be thinking about the gnawing need in his groin, and the almost instant gratification that would take all of five minutes. No need to please the ladies. Just the need to fuck and spew and ready himself for the next one.

He felt her now, hot and close, her breathing steady, heavy, simulating the need and desire that neither of them felt.

Up onto the sumptuous platform she came, sliding her body up over his like a piece of fine silk, draping herself over his hips, his belly, and angling herself for the optimum penetration of her hot pulsating core onto his staff.

He braced himself for the hot slide of her wetness encompassing him. And just like every other time, the initial excitement, the lure of free, unfettered sex caromed wildly down his consciousness into an almost mechanical pumping response where his penis took over, his mind disengaged, and the race to culmination became primal, instinctual, and tinged, in the end, with a body-suffusing disappointment.

His penis was all there, as if it had a mind of its own, and had given itself over to as much hard fucking as it could stand in the wake of years of denial. He calculated he had spilled enough semen to fill a punch bowl, to fill as many women as could fill this room for two dozen days, enough to spawn a half dozen devils in hell.

But these women weren't *the* woman. The one who was mistress of Waybury House, the one who now nurtured the son she had spawned by his brother's seed. The one with whom he was still hopelessly, futilely in love.

Goddamn . . .

Jesus . . . Jancie . . . He had to stop thinking about Jancie. A year and a thousand miles' distance from her hadn't cooled his fire. And now he was fifty miles too near, with an amorphous mission too close to home that was not nearly distraction enough to keep her far from his thoughts.

And drowning in sex was not the antidote for him.

He supposed that Lujan had thought it would be. He'd been away too long, but he never thought he had any other choice but to leave.

He had needed to get away from Jancie, from the tentacles of the past, from the betrayals of their fathers that left both men dead, the mystery of his baby brother's disappearance solved, and a fortune in diamonds in his, Jancie's, and Lujan's hands.

After that, there just was nothing to do but leave. Trying to make things work was fruitless. He ran—from the past, from unrequited desire, from responsibility, and from a love that couldn't be. Jancie had made her choice, and Lujan wanted her, with all that entailed, after a lifetime of indiscriminate debauchery spent in part at Bullhead Manor.

And Jancie had forgiven Lujan everything and taken him back, in spite of all that.

What an irony that he'd wound up here, in Lujan's stead. *Lujan, only better*—words he'd heard all his life, laughable now. Not that much better when you got to the bottom line. Sex was sex, and no man, no matter how principled and austere, could withstand it. Not even he was immune, and it was God's joke that he had always thought he was.

And over and above that, there was the blasphemy of thinking about his brother's wife instead of this luscious piece of tail riding him like a champion steeplechaser; he had no more feeling about it, or her, than he did about the next stranger on the street.

But his penis was rampant with the building, engorging feeling of letting go, yielding to a force all on its own, pushing and pumping to reach exaltation.

It took no little time—no need to hold back, to need, to feel, to care. Just get it out, get it over and get on to the next one.

She rode him high, arching her back, cupping her breasts. Her nipples were hard, tight, luscious little buttons that she pulled and tweaked with her whore's expertise whenever she caught him looking at them.

Did she feel? Did she care? No, she wanted only to arouse him, ride him and bring him to a frothing flood of come.

No time at all to accomplish that now. It didn't take more than just the thought . . . immediately, he felt his lower torso seizing, lifting, all his energy gathering for that one last hot hard drive to oblivion.

It came like a gunshot, one hot gut-wrenching blast that left him boneless, breathless, and as uncorked as a bottle of champagne. And it was so unexpected, he almost spun out of control.

Not quite, though. He was a man who prided himself on being *in* control. And even in the wake of that cataclysmic spending, where he felt every last eddying swirl of pleasure down to that tight rubber ring, there was still a part of him standing outside and watching everything, a little amazed, wholly detached and analyzing it all.

The whore was waiting, still astride his penis, with his penis—she had made certain of this—still as deeply embedded within her as when she first mounted him.

There was more to come.

She smiled at him knowingly, her fingers still busy squeezing and playing with her nipples, watching his expression, seeking his eyes, shimmying her hips to arouse him all over again.

Just what he was paying for. A hot body to make him come any which way she could. But for one moment, he had felt something else, something deeper, something outside himself, and inside, simultaneously.

He ruthlessly pushed it away. This was something he didn't

want to feel when he was pounding away inside a body he'd paid to occupy.

Because he knew it for what it was—that shocking moment of recognition that he could lose himself in someone he loved.

It was not a gift to be given to a whore.

"My lord," she whispered. Her voice was husky as fog, on the edge of impatience.

"Come again," he invited, because that was his mission, his message.

She smiled again, that smug knowing whore smile, and lifted her hips, and began her whore's dance all up and down his iron bar of a pole.

Up and down and around and down . . . too easy to get lost in sensation and want nothing more.

Just now, just now—it was enough. This was a most experienced courtesan, whose hands were everywhere on her body, enticing, arousing, fondling and feeling every place he would want to, if she would let him.

And as he raced toward the finish, she slapped his flanks, and tweaked his nipples, and pumped him ferociously in and out of her bottomless sex, and he had no choice at all but to submit, succumb, and surrender.

It was not the same. It just was what it was. The spume, the pumping aftershocks of semen releasing. The feeling of deflation. The sense of the whore sinking down deep against his chest for a moment, her hands moving over his breast, her finger tracing lightly against his skin.

He felt depleted at last. The air was thick with sex and scent. He felt foggy and groggy with this last release; there was something sweet in the air, something seductive, that he could sink into with much more abandon than a wanton's body.

So perhaps he was imagining things—he didn't know precisely when she removed herself from his penis; he thought he felt her fingers sliding off the ring because there was a sense of relief from the constriction; he thought he heard her whisper something sibilant . . . something that sounded like the word *seven*. For certain he felt her fingers drawing on his skin—circles, lines, numbers?—all over his chest, around his nipples, and down his belly.

. . . *Seven* . . . Seven hours? Seven minutes? Seven days? No, he'd dreamt it in the aftermath of all this hotbox sex, his penis finally drained and sapped of all desire, all need, all primal response, and him wholly asleep before she even removed herself from the saddle of his hips.

. . . *seven* . . .

As many days as he had been at Bullhead Manor. As many orgasms as he had in a hour. As many years as it would take to forget the thing he most wanted to remember.

The scent was luscious; it permeated everywhere. It smelled like roses and something matte and familiar. It crept over him like a blanket, and he felt comforted and sublime.

He was done here for now, he thought in that netherworld where he was skirting the edge of a deep unconscious sleep and yet awake enough to have a cogent thought. The death of a minor but coming member of Parliament just didn't seem to have anything to do with sin, sex and the perversions of Bullhead Manor.

He was free . . . untethered, floating free, finally free—of responsibility, duty, penury, pestilence, possibilities, pretenses, perverseness. *His* seven deadly sins released into the heavens like so many hot air balloons . . . drifting away from him, leaving him wholly and completely free . . . and alone, suddenly . . . for how long he didn't know—the whore had vanished like fog, leaving him alone . . . him, his sins, his conscience—alone . . . oh, good Lord, please—

"I want him."

The three words blasted into his consciousness, the voice seductively feminine with an unrecognizable accent so patently out of place at Bullhead that it was as jarring as a headache, and worse, it was too close and very adamant.

"I want him."

"Madam—" Soothing tones, leading her away, explaining he was a privileged customer whom one did not demand to fuck out of hand.

"But I *want* him . . ."

"Yes, madam . . ." Conciliating tones. Everything and anything was possible at Bullhead. Everybody knew that, especially the spoiled bitchy women of wealth who had the wherewithal to buy anything in their world.

But this was a dream, of course.

Immediately there was a knock on the door, and a shadowy figure slipped in. "My lord." Hushed tones. "If I may—the lady would like to try you. She says *she* will pay."

Kyger levered himself up onto one elbow and eyed himself. He wasn't wholly at half-staff, it seemed. But since it was a dream, of course he could get primed and potent in a minute—for money.

Nice dream.

He shrugged. "Send the body in."

"Most accommodating."

"Definitely my strong suit," he murmured. Who was this unctuous dream-person—the ringmaster directing the circus? God, it *was* a circus, and he was the lion tamer, the tightrope walker, the clown . . .

He fell back onto the bed and closed his eyes. Another sweet scent came wafting at him. A rustle of skirts. A presence in the room, a body sinking down on the platform next to him.

A woman's hand stroking the ermine, brushing up against his flanks, her fingers tentative but firm—too real to be a dream, but what else could it be?

Then he felt that hand on him, grasping his hip compellingly, shaking him a little. "Who are you?"

Yes, that same accented voice, not unpleasant up close. Slurred and soft like a down feather pillow.

And she was quite beautiful peering at him through the fog like that. Which of course she had to be, in his dream. All women were beautiful in men's dreams; otherwise, what was the point?

Strange dream.

He considered for a moment what to say. Why say anything important—it was a dream. "I'm the second son of an itinerant diamond miner who made a fortune in South Africa. Who are you?"

"Excellent. Just what I want. Second sons always need money. I'll just pay you to do the deed, and we'll be done."

He blinked. Levered himself onto his elbow so he could see her more clearly. "The deed . . . ?"

"I need your help." Now her voice was urgent. "I need to lose my maidenhead. Today. Now. And you're going to do it. I'll pay you to do it."

"Excuse me?" This was a fantasy in a million—a beautiful woman begging to be deflowered—? This was crazy . . .

"Right this minute, tonight. Name your price . . ."

"I will *not* marry that man."

"YES, YOU WILL!"

Angilee Rosslyn crossed her arms and stamped across the commodious hotel sitting room and whirled to face her father. "I will NOT."

Zabel Rosslyn reined in his temper. They sounded like a couple of three-year-olds having at each other, he thought furiously, and this conversation, this argument, this battle, had been ongoing since day one of their arrival in London and his daughter's first meeting with the titled gentleman to whom he had engaged her to be married.

Except she didn't want to be married altogether, not yet, and their shouting matches to and fro on the subject were already the talk of Claridge's, and they hadn't even been settled in there a week.

Today was starting out to be no exception.

"I will not discuss this any further. We've talked enough. Three days' worth. And I will not change the plan. You will marry Wroth, it's all arranged, and that is the end of it. I'm going out."

Angilee leapt on his words. "With Wroth?" How like her father, to just lay down the law and then abandon her for his own pleasure. She felt strangled with fury.

"Not your business, my dear. Men's business. Your business is to make yourself agreeable to Wroth tomorrow when he calls."

She felt murderous. "I will NOT."

Zabel grasped her shoulders. "Listen to me, you stubborn, ungrateful girl. A beautiful young virgin with a wealthy father is a hard commodity to come by these days. Wroth offers a title, an estate, entrée into the highest society, and association with the most influential people in the land. It is not inconceivable you might be presented at court either. These are things that would have astronomical monetary value if one could even afford them. Things any father would want for his daughter."

"You're selling my virginity for a title and a curtsey?"

"Put it any way you wish, daughter, but this marriage will come off. We post the banns next week, irrespective of what you think you want, and you might just as well give in and give over, and let it happen."

"Wroth is a pig."

"Wroth is a gentleman. And you are not a lady. At minimum, your marriage will raise you *that* high."

"I'd kill him as soon as marry him," Angilee spat.

"I don't care," Zabel said. "The thing is done."

No, it wasn't, Angilee thought fiercely. The idea had been to come to England to *find* a husband, not have one handed to her on a silver salver. And it still wasn't clear to her just when her father had made this arrangement. It had been presented to her practically the moment they settled in at the hotel.

She took a deep breath, trying to calm down. She had to try to make him understand one more time, although every conversation for the past three days had deteriorated after about three minutes just like this into a shouting match.

"Let me try to make you understand my position. I really, really don't want to get married right now," she said, enunciating her words as if she were speaking to a child.

"Of course you want that," Zabel countered with the arrogant assurance of a man who knew everything.

Especially, apparently, what was right for her. Angilee grit her teeth, clenched her fists, and bit back her anger which came to the boil immediately with his next patronizing words.

"Every woman wants that," Zabel went on, absolutely secure in his position. "If your mother had lived . . . well, I've tried, by God, to be to you what your mother would have been. If she had lived, she'd be appalled, horrified, that you talk like this about a perfectly eligible gentleman and a most auspicious marriage."

His voice rose. "You don't even know what you want. What *do* you want? It isn't as if you needed to work in a factory or . . . or—" His imagination could not go beyond that; his control was sadly slipping to the side of belligerence at her stubbornness.

"Why do I need to do anything?"

"Everyone has to do *something*. Babies. Running a house,

keeping a husband happy—that's what women do. You need a husband. I've found you a husband."

No, he wanted her to marry *his* choice of a husband. His version of the kind of man she wanted. And Angilee hated that man. Despised him. Choked every time she uttered his name. The pig name.

"No, you haven't."

"Yes, I have. I've committed you—us—to this marriage." Zabel stamped his foot.

"I *won't.*"

"You *will.*"

"You can't make me." The whole thing was degenerating again. It always came down to this fine line of who had power over whom. Always in the past, Zabel had given in, because nothing had ever been so important that he wanted to test the limits of what his spoiled Angilee might do if he put his foot down on an issue.

But this was different. This terrified him, but this was the one thing he had ever wanted of her, and this was what she must do.

"You think not, my girl?" He sounded so confident, but deep inside, Zabel knew that he couldn't issue threats—and the moment all the wrangling came down to this, he felt helpless to make her conform, and furious that he, her father, and a *man,* couldn't.

"You will find yourself walking willingly down the aisle in the end, I promise you that," he said, finally out of patience, and there was something in his tone that made Angilee look at him warily.

"You are a prize—a virgin, an acknowledged beauty, from a wealthy Southern family who is as eligible as any of those heiresses from questionable money and the merchant class. Believe me, their antecedents aren't as important as their assets. American money is the magic incentive, I'll tell you that. They have ancestry enough for everyone here, and I swear, there's a titled aristocrat for every last heiress who desires one. And I have found the one for you."

And that he had, after a fruitless foray to New York, trying to crack the Four Hundred, all of whom had known each other from the cradle, had gone to the same schools, parties, churches since they were born; and all of whom were inbred, insular, and, as he'd discovered, habitually married their own.

The doors had been locked to anyone from Outside long before they even rang the bell.

No wonder England seemed like the gates of heaven opened. All one had to do was throw enough incentive at an impoverished aristocrat, offer him an exquisite virgin, an open purse, and he immediately came to point.

It had taken no time at all to come to terms with Wroth.

And now Angilee must come to terms with this marriage.

She was too quiet. Zabel was too tired; he wanted to leave. These arguments drained him beyond all measure, and nothing ever got accomplished anyway.

"You're selling me," she accused suddenly. "You're selling my purity—and I can't even figure out for what."

Her perception stunned him. "It doesn't matter," he said bluntly, bluffing through his teeth. "It's men's business, my business. Besides, I know what's best. It's my God-given duty to make sure you marry well. I want you to be happy, and I want you to have every comfort and nicety in life . . ."

He had said that all before; it still sounded practiced, false.

"And you think *that man*—?" That cold, ascetic pig. She shuddered even thinking of him. It was all in his eyes—the greedy glitter of a man who wanted a living doll that he could manipulate and maneuver any which way he would, with no one to stop him. There was a cruelty in him, in the thin line of his mouth, and in the slightly porcine appearance of his body. This man—this pig—would mount her and give her babies while he ramped through her father's money like a raging bull.

NEVER.

"I *will* walk you down the aisle," Zabel said, and his voice was deadly quiet. No shouting now. He meant it. Nothing would stop it.

Angilee felt a coldness seeping right down to her toes.

"And you won't walk anywhere outside this room until you come to your senses."

It was pretty much the best Zabel could do with her right now. The thing was done: Viscount Wroth was willing to marry her and take the money that came wrapped up with her purity and give as good as he got in return.

Blood money. Coffers full of money. After all, what had he worked for all his life? This was a synchronistic fusing of need and greed. And it was no small bargain he'd made either, and not one to be reneged upon. There were some benefits to this union that just weren't quantifiable in dollars.

Everyone horse-traded something, Zabel thought irritably. But Angilee refused even to barter. Well, everyone did at some point.

So if he had to lock Rapunzel in the tower for yet another night, with a guard stationed right outside as usual, and another in the lobby as a precaution . . . so be it. It was getting damned expensive to teach his daughter her place, but as far as he was concerned, it would be worth it in the end.

Out with Wroth, was he? Selling her virginity, to that pig, was he?

Telling her it was none of her business . . .

Oh, her father had sadly underestimated her, Angilee thought venomously. He always had; he always regarded her as his prize investment. And now someone wanted in on that investment, wanted to run the venture for him, and for some reason, he was perfectly willing to hand over that much power to a perfect stranger, with tangible assets exchanged in return.

Her fury knew no bounds, nor her desire to thwart his stubborn decision to give her to Wroth no matter what her feelings.

Well, she had had lots of time to think about what to do about that—and she had come up with the perfect solution . . . it didn't take five minutes to conceive the plan—but it was so bold and so destructive in a far-reaching way that she had to be firm in her convictions.

The stunning thing was how easy it had been.

Money could buy you anything, and Zabel had always made sure she had plenty of money. It bought the waitress's uniform who delivered her evening meal which enabled her easy escape from her guards.

It bought information. Transportation.

It shocked her, it sent her every preconception of what wealth and influence could buy reeling, but it didn't deter her from her course: she had fury, determination and the driving need to outmaneuver her father propelling her, and the deed was going to be done.

Her plan was buck simple: if she wasn't a virgin, she wouldn't have to marry the pig. It seemed a crystal clear equation to her. And she didn't care what she had to do to accomplish that. And so the only remaining question was, where did a *woman* go to have mindless, emotionless sex.

Money had bought that information, too, and entrée to the most famous whorehouse in the whole of London.

And a well-muscled, well-hung man for the night.

And so now here she was, deep in the hushed, thickly carpeted, dimly lit hallways of the notorious Bullhead Manor, with a menu of penises laid out before her like a banquet, and she had chosen one.

And he was quite a one. She had taken a very long time—too long given she had such limited time—to settle on him, as the enormity of what she had done and what she had yet to do suddenly shook her to her bones.

She would literally be asking a stranger to ram his penis through her maidenhead. A mindless, naked body would punch away at the barrier until he had penetrated, taken his pleasure, and he'd be gone. Someone she'd never see again. A faceless, nameless penis, occupying the most private, most intimate part of her body . . .

And suddenly it seemed much more important than that, and that whoever she chose to do it would have to at least *seem* to have some humanity.

But the men—or women, for that matter—who frequented the Bullhead didn't offer themselves up to be genteel lovers. They wanted sex, unlimited, unfettered, undiluted, unadulterated, fast, hard fucking; they were machines, pumping away, and the game was gratification, any which way they could get it.

It would be a sorry way to lose her virginity.

There wasn't a man among them, a penis that she was shown that looked remotely as though she could stand to have it within a foot of her body.

Her naked body. She knew what the thing entailed. Her father had been a dirt farmer, before he'd begun buying up the decimated plantations of her childhood for pennies on the dollar and selling off the land for profit. She knew how animals mated. She knew what that part of a man's body was.

"Madam . . ." The hushed voice of her guide wafted through the silence. "Is there no choice that would satisfy you?"

"Not yet," she said imperiously. What did women who patronized this place do? Say?

Feeling desperate, she thrust open the next nearest door, and she saw him. He was lying flat on his back on a fur-covered platform, his arms and legs splayed, his penis poking out and angled downward from his thick thatch of pubic hair.

His face in repose was impassive, his cheekbones high, his mouth carved, his hair just this side of too long, his eyebrows beautifully shaped, his eyes closed. His hands were large, his chest broad and overlaid with just enough hair. His belly was flat, and his legs long, and his penis and scrotum of more than ample size. The line of his body was arresting, powerful; she couldn't stop looking at him.

Even though his wasn't a kind face. Rather, it was remote, removed, austere, even in repose. It did not look like the face of a man who was profligate—in his emotions—or his appetites.

Really? You can tell all that about a naked man sprawled out in an exclusive brothel bedroom? Are you crazy?

She *was* crazy. This was a bad idea. And she felt trapped. The guide waited, judging her, she thought. She had either to go through with it or leave, and she didn't know which was the lesser of the evils: giving her precious virginity to a stranger or giving it to the pig.

Not the pig. *Never the pig.*

She made a quick decision.

"I want that one."

"But madam—he's not . . ."

"Ask him." She didn't know where she got the nerve; she was shaking so much.

"As madam wishes . . ."

Everything was for sale at the Bullhead. Everything was for sale everywhere. She'd learned that lesson at her father's knee.

And time was flying, and soon it might be too late. She felt the press of time in her bones as she divested herself of her cloak.

The guide returned. The man had agreed—the penis—had agreed. A weight fell on her shoulders. *Oh, God . . .* She had to go through with it now. She had to walk into that room and get on that platform naked and just let him do the deed. With *that*— you wouldn't think an appendage of muscle, veins and blood could be so big and thick and be able to . . .

She had to stop this. Make it business. Make it as remote and removed as he seemed to be. A second son. Diamond mines. A nobody, really, just like her.

So get out of the dress—entice him a little. Make him give her a monetary amount so she had the power.

"How much?" she demanded again, her voice harsh to subdue the tremor. Awake, groggy, and close-up, he was even more striking.

What on earth was a man like this doing here?

The same thing a woman like her was doing here . . .

Forget that. Maybe this wouldn't be as bad as she feared. "Time is short. We have to get going." She pulled at the bows and hooks of her corset.

Kyger shook his head as if he weren't hearing right. It was the accent. That was how he knew it was a dream. *Hao* much . . . that odd pronunciation—how much ought he sell himself for? In the dream?

Surely a thick, hard penis with an hour's worth of stamina was worth more than a high-priced whore . . .

"Two thousand." That seemed over the moon, but it was *his* dream. He could ask what he wanted.

"Dollars or pounds?" she asked briskly.

His head snapped up.

"I have dollars . . ." *Ah have dollahs . . .*

What the hell . . . ?

"Here—" She took a fistful out of a pocketbook she had girdled around her waist and unfastened that and tossed it on the floor. "Now . . ."

Naow . . .

"Wait a minute . . ."

"*Now . . .*"

Jesus . . . what the hell kind of dream—

Off came the corset. Down went the delicate stockings, the

lacy drawers divested with a kick. Her camisole gone with the shrug of her shoulders.

She was luscious, a bonbon of femininity, all creamy skin, chocolaty hair, and hard pointed raspberry nipples, a body full of fascinating peaks and valleys limned in the soft sensual light.

Edible. All of her. Where did a man start?

She sat back down on the platform, wholly naked, feeling cold, bereft and stupid. "How do we start?"

Good God. *How do we start????* Just how innocent was she? This was an act; it had to be. He pushed himself into a sitting position. "Now, just wait a minute . . ."

"Are you going to help me or not?" Bravado always worked. Another lesson from her esteemed father.

She had a slurred accent, American, Southern perhaps? . . . and her dark eyes were fierce, determined—and nakedly afraid, her body shimmering with apprehension in the dim light.

Shit. No one came to a brothel and paid this kind of money without meaning to get fucked. She meant to get fucked—or someone would fuck her over. She was such an innocent. Such a princess. Such perfection.

And for some incomprehensible reason, she wanted to lose her maidenhead—now, tonight. With just any random person. Except for some reason, she'd chosen him.

Shit. No. A dream. No. She was real, as real as hot bare skin and real hot money could make her, and she was six inches away from him on the platform and ready and willing to go.

Why not him?

"Give me a minute," he said brusquely because she didn't want mercy or pity. Not from someone like him. Or the someone she thought he was.

"I shouldn't think you'd need a minute," she said, goading him. "You're all there. Just get it in and get it over with." She eased down onto the fur. "I believe I lie like this, spread my legs, and you—"

This dream could not be better . . . Why was he resisting it? His penis wasn't. It had already thickened to a jutting hardness in response to her nudity and to her words, and it was just aching for penetration.

He climbed over her prone body. "It will hurt."

"I don't care."

Defiant, too. What was this about? Did he care? A beautiful innocent wanted him to take her virginity, and he was rationalizing reasons why he shouldn't or she shouldn't?

Some dream.

He braced himself on one arm and looked down at her. God, she was beautiful, her eyes wide open and glazed with fear and behind that, a glittering expectation. Her mouth, her chin, her neck, her breasts, her—

A body made for ramping and nothing more. She was a young, bored, wealthy virgin who wanted to spend her money on the thrill of a male whore's penis spending inside her while he took her innocence.

That was all it was, pure and simple.

She didn't want to be coaxed. She wanted cocking. She didn't want a judge. She wanted jism. She wanted jam.

Or was it some kind of game?

Whichever it was, she'd come to the right man.

He spread her legs farther apart. "Brace yourself."

She grabbed the edges of the platform as he positioned himself between her legs. Her pubic hair was thick, dark, mysterious, and he nosed his penis directly into her hairy bush, and into her slit, and she bucked.

Virgin territory. For real. No games here. She had never been touched, never been plumbed. Never been . . . all of her . . . *never*—

His excitement escalated in spite of his determination to keep this on the most impersonal level possible. Ram and bam. That was what he meant to do, and collect his two thousand *dollahs* for the fastest, easiest fuck of his life.

"Not there yet," he murmured, holding himself and stroking her labia with the tip of his penis.

She made a sound. He kept stroking, watching her face as she accommodated her body to the unaccustomed sensations of a penis pushing and stroking her between her legs.

"That's better." It was a mere whisper. Her body was reacting, moistening just a little. She was stiff and wary. So beautiful. Too innocent. How had this happened?

It was a dream, he could and would pretend it was a dream,

and he was not getting involved. Five minutes he'd give her, and over. It was about all he had in him anyway, and he couldn't really take the time to soften her body, to make her ripe and ready to receive him.

This was a business deal, right down to the bones. He had what she wanted, she was willing to pay, and he was going to give it to her.

Except—he was not that merciless. He had some sympathy for her, and for whatever the reason was she was taking this desperate step.

He wanted to know—he didn't want to know . . .

Damn . . . hell and blast and back . . .

"Why are you doing this?" He had to ask because he was certain as the night that she'd find someone else to do it if he didn't. It was Solomon's choice for him—

Or maybe not. Maybe it just was.

Angilee looked up at that cool, calm face above her. Looked down at the intersecting line of their naked bodies with his penis nosed in between her legs, rooting, seeking, pushing as he shimmied his hips bit by bit against all her barriers. Couldn't believe she was lying naked with a man's penis between her legs and not in utter hysterics. Couldn't believe her courage or her insanity . . . and didn't know what to answer this man who was a paid penis and wanted to know too much.

"I want control over my own virtue," she said finally, her voice neutral, emotionless. "And that's all you need to know."

He pushed again, a little deeper, and she writhed at the sensation of him filling, stretching her just a little more.

"You are so tight."

"Too tight for you?" she whispered a little breathlessly. It wasn't such an unpleasant thing to have a man's penis forcing its way into the center of your being. Not yet anyway. She didn't feel overwhelmed, not yet. And he wasn't being coarse about it, or contemptuous.

It would be fine. Maybe it would be . . . fine . . .

"For you," he said, rearing back and driving a little deeper.

"OH!" Her whole body seized up in response. Now he was *really* there, his penis head butting up against her precious barrier;

she could feel it pressuring her, pushing her, and she wanted to scramble out from under the suddenly overpowering invasion of her body by this huge, hot filling *thing*.

Mutely, she pushed frantically against him, and he pushed more forcefully inside of her.

"Yes or no?" Kyger asked plainly.

She caught her breath. It was as if he didn't care one way or another. Why should he?

What was she doing?

She was escaping the carnal possession of the pig was what, and that superseded every fear, all propriety, and what would happen tomorrow.

"Yes," she whispered. Her body was shaking; she could barely get out the word.

"Are you sure?"

She wasn't sure of anything except she did not want to be sold to the pig. "Yes."

"Hold on then . . ."

At least he warned her, but nothing could have prepared her for the ultimate moment: that scary tearing drive deep into her body with that one forceful, hard, unbending part of him.

He reared back, and he took her, took her maidenhead and her innocence, and gave her back control of her life.

Chapter Two

So now she knew.

What did she know?

Losing one's virginity was incredibly painful.

The dark invasion and the heft of man's penis not only occupied a woman's body but her mind, too, taking over every inch of space in her consciousness and her thoughts.

There was an awful lot of sticky fluid seeping out between her legs.

And, a man's body, after it was spent, was damned heavy.

And with that, she understood she knew nothing.

She had to get back to the hotel . . . time was flying. Her father would return in the wee hours, expecting to find her in bed.

She was in bed. Was this a bed?

A wave of panic suffused her bruised body. Oh God—dear God—what had she done? No, no. Calm down. It was almost over. And it didn't matter now; it *was* done, it hadn't taken all that long to accomplish really, and the pig would have to withdraw his offer to marry her, and she would finally be free of all constraints—for now.

It was worth every last dollar she had spent.

He was spent, this second son of a diamond miner with his questions and his strange attempt to steer her from her course.

Well, no one told Angilee Rosslyn what to do. The loss of that hidden part of her body was a minor thing compared to the end result of a disastrous marriage to the pig.

No one would ever have seen her maidenhead anyway. No one would ever know, except Zabel, when she triumphantly announced his defeat.

Good. She was feeling so much better already just thinking about that. She'd won. She'd outmaneuvered her father and vanquished the pig.

So, the next thing was to get out from under the hired penis and get out of this place.

And the rest she'd think about later.

It was a dream. Sometime, deep in the night, when he awakened from a deep luxurious sleep, Kyger found her gone.

If she'd ever existed anyway.

Except that there were drops of the evidence on the platform. There was a stack of American dollars on the floor.

But for that, he would have fully believed it really had been a dream.

She'd chosen well, he thought mordantly. She'd found the exact fool who could get it up one last time, and who ultimately was so milked of all his energy and will that he had collapsed into unconsciousness after he'd done the deed, and allowed her to get away.

Perfect. No strings. No connections.

WHAT??

What was that last thought? *Allowed* her . . . ??

It struck him suddenly that in the forty-five minutes between his agreeing to *host* her and his falling asleep, he hadn't once thought about Jancie.

Not think about Jancie? *Unthinkable.*

And yet, there it was. His whole focus had been on the edible virgin who had now gone forth into the world to allow any number of indiscriminate, hungry men to devour her, occupy her.

Shit.

Time to get out of this place. It must be morning. God, he

hoped it was morning—he couldn't face another night of mind-less, formless fornication.

There was something about the taking of a virgin . . . he couldn't get her out of his mind. Who the hell was she? How many Americans were in London anyway?

Hundreds . . . it was goddamned invasion . . .

Shit all over again.

It was time to see Wyland. Wyland made sense, even if he *was* a friend of Lujan's. It actually went against the grain to think Lujan had any friends among men of sense, intellect and discrim-ination. Men in important government posts who seemed not to regard him as a screw-up and who made it their business to be in-terested in mysterious things like the death of Tony Venable.

And that, in fact, was the one thing that had roused him from the torpor of depression and boredom that had engulfed him on his return to England after two years of aimless wandering around the world.

Anthony Venable. Possibly the most mourned and lamented death in the recent history of the country. You couldn't avoid him: thousands had attended the funeral, weeping, wailing, col-lapsing, rending their clothes in ostentatious displays of grief, and then visited his grave and wept on his tombstone after he was fi-nally laid to rest.

Wherever you turned in the weeks following the burial, there would be something about Venable's death. The sensational cir-cumstances. The shock of it. How young he was. How admired, adored, feared, loved, trusted, maligned he'd been.

The loss. The waste. The unfairness. The utter bleak finality of it all.

There was something about this man that roused all those pas-sions in the common man, and not one of them could stop talking about it, in newspapers, on street corners, in pubs, or even in churches.

Or at Waybury. It was the first thing Lujan had said to him when he walked in the door on his unexpected, unannounced re-turn. Not even a hello. Not even surprise at seeing him. Merely, "Did you hear? Venable's dead."

"Who the hell was he?" He'd thumped his suitcase on the floor and shaken Lujan's hand.

"Big up and comer, Tony Venable. Deep into socialist politics. Said to be on track for prime minister. It's like the whole country's in mourning. You wouldn't think the thing would raise such a row after a couple of weeks, but they won't let it go." He led the way into the parlor. "Jancie's on a walk with the tot. Oh, how are you anyway, baby brother? Nice to see you."

He rang for tea.

"God, you're domesticated."

"I'm happy," Lujan said, motioning to a chair. "Really, how *are* you?"

"Confused by the furor over Venable," Kyger admitted. "It's all over Town. You can't move an inch one way or the other without hearing about it."

"Ummm. Ah. Here's our new man—Phillips. Set out tea, will you? And something for the tot as well."

Phillips withdrew, and Lujan took a long hard look at Kyger. "Too thin, brother mine. I'm thinking this time away hasn't been all that beneficial."

"I didn't find anything if that's what you mean. Saw a lot of the world and wound up back where I started, which is as good as anywhere else, I suppose, but doesn't seem to have much of a future."

"So you'll stay here for a few days."

Kyger shook off that suggestion. "Not wise. Nothing's changed."

Lujan's eyebrows shot up. "Really. Well, we need to find you something to play with."

"Or someone," Kyger said dourly.

Phillips entered, carrying the tea tray.

"Right there—" Lujan indicated a table beside Kyger's chair. "Phillips, this my brother—my *young* brother—Kyger. Have Mrs. Ancrum make up a room just in case he'll be staying."

Mrs. Ancrum. Still faithful and loyal to Lujan. No, to Jancie. Who wouldn't be loyal to Jancie? Wasn't *he*, still?

"As you wish, Mr. Lujan." Phillips bowed in Kyger's direction. "Pleased to meet you, sir." He was so correct. Kyger's lips actually quirked as he watched Phillips leave the room.

"We are ever so proper now," he murmured. "Such changes."

"Who would have thought?" Lujan said whimsically, as he reached over the table and poured. "But then—there's Jancie."

"Exactly," Kyger said, taking a sip from the delicate cup that Lujan had handed him. He looked around the room. There had been a happy hand at work in this room and, he would wager, all over the house. All traces of what had happened here, all the echoes of deaths, confessions and recriminations were gone. Everything was new, fresh, light, comfortable, more reflective of Jancie, it was obvious, than his brother.

And, he thought, if it had been him with Jancie at his side, he could have been happy here, too.

Mrrrrrow. And here came Emily, Jancie's cat, pacing into the room curiously, nosing around him and rubbing against him as if she remembered him, warning him, with that ferocious tone, that his thoughts and needs were to be contained, constrained, and forever his own.

He reached down to pet her. *Owww.* Approval. Maybe.

"She keeps us all in line," Lujan murmured. "I married that cat as well as Jancie, it turns out."

"I don't doubt it." Kyger rubbed her ears, and she nudged her nose up into his palm.

"When you're here at Waybury," Lujan said with an unaccustomed reflectiveness, "it's as if the outside world doesn't exist."

"Is that good or bad?" Emily had jumped up onto Kyger's lap, and he ran his hand down her arched back.

Lujan sent him a look. "I don't think I need to answer that, old son. But still the Venable thing invades everything, even here. The servants. The farmers. It's amazing. But then, by all accounts, *he* was amazing."

"Or not, depending on who you talk to, and what you read."

"True enough."

A silence fell. The thing they hadn't yet talked about was as palpable in the room as the mystery of Tony Venable's death.

Jancie. It was as if they were both waiting to hear her step. Her voice.

Maybe, Kyger thought, he was waiting to see some sign that Lujan was mistreating her, that she was unhappy, that he could comfort her and hold her hand.

Sweep her up and take her away . . .

"Kyger!!!!" He heard the joyous shriek behind him, and he bolted out of his chair just as Jancie threw herself into his arms.

"Oh, my God, oh, my God, where did you come from? How did you get here, how long can you stay . . . ?"

Kyger swung her around. The world tipped up on its axis, and everything suddenly made sense.

"Momma—?"

Oh, that tentative, heartbreaking little boy voice . . .

Kyger set Jancie down, and there was Gaunt. A little over a year old, standing on wobbly legs and reaching for his mother, who was disentangling herself from some strange man's arms.

Gaunt. Not his own little brother Gaunt, dead by the hand of his rapacious and amoral father; no, Lujan's Gaunt, born of his love for and redemption by Jancie.

Jancie bent down and picked him up, and he promptly buried his head shyly in her shoulder. She looked at Kyger, her eyes suddenly damp. "This is Gaunt, your nephew."

Kyger nodded, swallowing the lump in his throat. He reached out and touched Gaunt's dark curly hair. He was as real as the baby brother they'd lost, and every bit as precious. Not a replacement. Just a little boy with a soul all his own.

A boy that could have been *his* son, had Jancie fallen in love with *him*.

"I'll put him down for his nap now," Jancie said, aware of his rampant emotions. "You—*are* staying with us for the time being. Don't say no." She was gone in an instant, and Kyger turned to Lujan, whose expression was still bemused, as if he couldn't yet believe he had this extraordinary wife and beautiful child.

It had only been two years.

"Madonna," Kyger said.

"Close to," Lujan whispered. "She's a damned saint." He seemed lost in some netherworld of thought, and then suddenly he shook himself. "I have an idea."

"Oh, God—no ideas, big brother . . ."

"No—this is a good idea."

"Never in your life have you ever—"

"I swear to God, old son, this is a damned good idea. You'll thank me."

"I'll probably curse you before I thank you, brother mine. What's the idea?"

"Wyland."

"Hell, what's a wyland?"

"It's a top level government official who's been looking for a way to tone down the furor of Tony Venable's death without calling attention to the fact they're doing it."

"I'm sorry—would you like to repeat that?"

"Which part?"

"The top level government official part."

Lujan let out a deep, appreciative laugh. "This is a great idea. What else have you got to do anyway?"

"How the hell do *you* have anything to do with top level government officials?"

Lujan laughed again. "My dear boy, don't be naïve. A man's a man, no matter what his position in life. You find them in the strangest, most unlikely places."

"Obviously," Kyger said dryly. "Like on their knees in a brothel, I presume."

Lujan laughed again. "My lips are sealed, baby brother. But trust me, this is a truly great idea."

What it was, Kyger decided later, was the confluence of need, his and Wyland's, overlaid with Lujan's desire to get him away from Waybury as quickly as he could.

He hadn't thought fifty miles would be distance enough, but after this dreamlike night with the delectable virgin, he wasn't so sure.

Because he now had something to think about rather than Jancie. He had a mission that was meaningful and, although this simmered deep beneath the surface, he had a quest all his own.

His first meeting with Wyland was indelibly impressed in Kyger's memory. Wyland was nothing like he'd imagined—and everything that the quintessential bred-in-the-bone aristocratic Englishman was supposed to be.

And Wyland was worried. The outcry over Anthony Venable's death was almost fanatical in its intensity, and it was growing every day instead of diminishing with time. It had already been two weeks since it had happened.

"They want answers, and I don't mind telling you, there are no answers. Not the press. Not the general public. Nothing. The man was found alone in his house, dead, after apparently spending the night—or nights—at Bullhead Manor. No one has pried that out yet, because no one would swear to it. There's some kind of code of honor among those who patronize the—establishment. And someone like Venable . . . Well, no one will talk to anyone official, you can be sure of that. But that is the first place you must start.

"This is the point: that man had a grip on the soul of the country and it won't let go, even in death. We need this to die down. Quickly. And all our efforts to contain it have only exacerbated the problem.

"So we need someone unattached and unencumbered who can move about more freely than a government agent or a Scotland Yard investigator; in other words, someone not known in the usual circles to infiltrate and investigate certain aspects of Tony Venable's life to find the thing that will push this death out of the public consciousness so we can bury the bastard for once and for all.

"Someone like *you,* Mr. Galliard."

Someone like *him,* a well-heeled itinerant second son of a thieving diamond miner, who had nothing to lose and nothing to gain by sifting through the detritus of Anthony Venable's life to find anything that would make his loyal public despise him. That, in sum, was what Wyland was really saying in his circumspect way. Find the idol's feet of clay and chop them out from under his memory.

Simple.

And the first thing was to spend a few nights in lubricious splendor at the Bullhead and try to root out some proof Venable had even been there. That alone might make a difference in the public perception of him, but it seemed so unlikely that a man like Venable would have been so careless, or so utterly indifferent to his public image and the expectations of those who revered him.

Or would he?

But in the end, Kyger discovered nothing at the Bullhead except an unexpected appetite for sex that diminished rapidly after the third day, and an edible virgin who had vanished into his dreams.

Thank you, Lujan.

"So there it is." He was seated in Wyland's office, giving his report, except there wasn't much to report. "No one admits to seeing Venable anytime anywhere at Bullhead that I could discover. Ever."

Wyland steepled his fingers. "And yet—and yet, our best information is that he was there. Well, my boy, it needs more investigation. Witnesses can be reticent with strangers. They can tell you things without telling you things. They can seem to be telling you the truth while they are actually leading you astray. I understand you are, as a novice in the game, feeling your way into Venable's life and circle. Just keep in mind, this death is a case like no other. The reverence for him grows, it's nearly of religious proportions already, and they'll be venerating him like a saint before you can blink an eye. So find the thing that will stop it, Galliard. *Anything* that will stop it."

Anything that would smear and sully Venable and diminish the zeal of those who would make him a martyr. Anything that would vilify him, slander him, and bring him down to the ground, like the idols of old.

That was the mandate, nothing more, nothing less.

And if there was another side to the story? He didn't care.

The money was too good. The mystery was too intriguing. And the memory of the edible virgin was seared in his soul. Definitely the man for the mission.

Zabel was suspicious. Angilee hadn't said a word about Wroth which was highly unusual, and she was too quiet as she drank her tea, ate her breakfast, and sat wrapped in thought.

"Well," he said finally.

Angilee looked up. "Did you say something?"

This was very unlike Angilee. Her silence was unnerving. Her calm demeanor raised Zabel's hackles. Something was up, he could feel it in his bones. "I just wanted to say—we'll be having luncheon with the Vandermarks this afternoon, and then tomorrow evening, we will pay our respects at a memorial gathering for Anthony Venable."

"Really? We're not lunching with Wroth today?"

"We'll see him at the memorial. Everyone will be there."

"And just why are we attending a service for a man we didn't know?"

"It's the right thing to do," Zabel said.

"In other words, Wroth will be there."

"And if he is?"

"My sentiments haven't changed."

"Nor have mine," Zabel said sharply. "There will be no further discussion. Wroth will obtain the license, and the marriage will take place as planned."

Angilee slanted a shimmering look at him, and Zabel immediately became even more wary.

"Well," Angilee murmured, "here I am, shelved, so much merchandise to be disposed of as my owner sees fit."

Zabel fidgeted. Disaster was coming, he felt it in his bones.

Angilee took another sip of her tea and went back to staring out the window.

He couldn't stand it. "My dear girl . . . I want only the best for you."

Angilee turned her head to look at him. "You want what is easiest for *you*. Somehow, sometime, you made this arrangement. When or how I cannot determine, but you are obdurate about proceeding with it. Fine. You have sold me as a commodity, in perfect condition. Fine. So I ask you, dear father—"

She paused for effect, and Zabel felt a cold chill go down his spine.

"What if the merchandise is not perfect?"

He absorbed those words slowly, taking them in like pieces of nougat candy, to be chewed over and swallowed one by one, and then finding what had been a delicious confection had turned sour and clogged his throat.

"I'm sorry, daughter. I'm certain I misunderstood what you said."

"You didn't," Angilee said. "But I'll repeat what I said, slowly. I said, what . . . if . . . the merchandise is no longer . . . perfect?"

He was having a heart attack, he was certain of it; every atom of his body constricted, his heart stopped, his breathing heightened as if he had been running, and the details of the previous night flashed before his eyes—the argument, his ultimatum, his leaving her, the guards, the certainty she would come to her senses . . .

And instead—

Instead—

HOW???

He grabbed his chest. She couldn't mean what he thought she meant. She couldn't. There was no way she could have gotten out of the room and away from the hotel.

So if she meant what he thought she meant, it had to have been one of the hired guards taking advantage of her, of her innocence, of her anger, and her determination to spite him.

But he couldn't believe it. He wouldn't.

He took in enough breath to bark, "WHAT DO YOU MEAN?"

Angilee smiled a knowing, triumphant little smile that he wanted to rip from her firm perfect lips—*his daughter!*—and his heart took a hard, heart-stopping dive to his feet.

She meant what he thought she meant. Goddamn her, goddamn her—he had no doubt she'd known exactly what she was goddamned doing . . . just to spite him, just to keep him from getting what *he* wanted for a change . . . and he didn't want to hear what she'd done, but he needed to hear it from her own lips.

And Angilee was glad to oblige. She waited, watching him, examining every emotion as he absorbed and comprehended what she said, what she meant, and then she dropped the leaded words one by one: "I mean, Father dear, that the thorns of your pure and precious Southern rose have been stripped away. I am no longer as I was."

Her tone was jubilant, victorious. She thought she'd won.

He stopped breathing again. . . . *no longer as I was* . . . He would never breathe again until he killed the blackguard who had taken her innocence.

"*WHO?*"

Angilee set down her teacup and smiled. "A faceless, nameless man, Father dear, to whom I am forever grateful for giving me back my freedom."

But he wasn't faceless—she had only to close her eyes to see his impassive face hovering over hers, asking those too probing questions, holding himself back, giving her the control, the decision, and making the moment more meaningful than it had needed to be.

Not faceless. And never to be forgotten either.

This was the end of it, she thought giddily. There was nothing her father could do about *this,* and surely Wroth would terminate the engagement, things would come back to normal, and she could finally start enjoying this sojourn to England.

Surely . . . ? She looked at Zabel's face and felt a fulminating moment of terror. His expression had gone rock hard, his eyes glittery as ice, and he was looking at her as if she were a stranger, as if he had no more feeling for her than a stone.

"So . . . you've played your little trick, my girl, and got yourself pierced, pricked and pummeled, God knows where and with whom, and you thought you'd get around me. Well, let me disabuse you of that notion right now. It was all for nothing, your little insurrection. Nothing will change. I'll see to that. There are ways and means to get around it, but you never thought of that. You never thought your dense old father knew about things like that. All *you* cared about was disobeying my wishes.

"Well, so you did it. And it's your loss, my girl. You'll never be able to get it back, but that's no skin off my hide. The marriage will go forward, just as we planned, only now I will make certain that you are contained and controlled and under my thumb until it does."

Angilee's stomach lurched. This wasn't quite the scenario she'd imagined; it was a disaster, and he didn't care, and she'd suffered all that pain and humiliation for nothing. Oh, God, dear God . . .

And Zabel wasn't done with her either. He was looking at her speculatively, as one would eye a bug, almost as if he were ruminating on a further punishment for this disruptive and disrespectful insubordination.

And found it.

He smiled, unpleasantly, Angilee thought, horrified. And his words made her skin crawl.

"From this moment forward, you will have no more money at your disposal. You will never leave this room but that you are in my company, or Wroth's. And when I must attend to business, I'm afraid, my dear girl, that I'm going to have to chain you to the bed and lock you in your room."

She was so stunned, she shrieked, "WHAT?"

"You will be chained up. Nothing onerous, my dear. I wouldn't want to damage the . . . uh—merchandise. Just a cuff around your wrist, attached to something you can't wriggle out of. I'll provide you with everything you need in the event I must see to business out of the hotel, and it won't be that uncomfortable. And at night, well, I'll figure that out."

She flew at him with her fists pummeling him. "Are you crazy? Why? Why? I'm your daughter, for God's sake."

Zabel held her off, feeling smug and in control for the first time in years. "No, you're not. You're chattel, my dear. Inanimate, inhuman, without feelings to consider, and mine to dispose of as I will."

"Father—?"

"The thing is done," Zabel said. He picked up the call indicator. "We'll cancel that luncheon. I've lost my appetite anyway, and so it will be much more profitable to take care of the arrangements to contain you here. And I must think about tomorrow night since you've so high-handedly destroyed the trust between us. It will put a crimp in my plans for the moment, but in the end, it will be for the best. And it may very well turn out that you won't leave this room until the very day of your wedding . . ."

Tony Venable was everywhere. Storefronts festooned with mourning and his black framed photograph; letters to and stories in the newspapers; random citizens on street corners demanding answers to the cause of his blasphemous death; posters on telegraph poles hawking rewards; church services devoted to eulogizing him, and mourning and grief everywhere still, after weeks of unrelenting demands for his murderer to hang.

What was it about this man? Kyger mingled with the crowds, listening, observing, asking questions.

"God, he was so . . . magnetic."

"He listened."

"He wanted to help us all."

"He was going to make the decisions so we wouldn't have to."

"He knew what was best for the country, for certain."

"He was as good as God . . ."

"He . . . He . . . perfect, he was for the little people. . . He was one of us . . . He was going to rein them in . . . make the country benevolent for everyone . . ."

"Did you ever hear him speak?"

"He was mesmerizing. You couldn't not listen to him . . ."

"His ideas were phenomenal, and included everyone—"

And more . . .

"The son of a bitch wanted to take over the country."

"Did any of you *really* listen to what he was saying? He was a damned demagogue."

"No, no—you're wrong—get him away . . . Tony Venable wasn't like that—" The merest dissent roused the crowd to a fever pitch. They ran the heretic down, pummeled him, kicked him, left him writhing in pain. Refused to hear anything but their own version of what Tony Venable was to them and could have been to the world.

It was a fascinating thing to watch, terrifying to be in the midst of such frenetic devotion to just such a man.

Tony Venable, even in death, was that powerful.

And the speculation over the murder was ongoing and constant.

"Who—?"

"Why—?"

"Did you hear . . . ?"

"I heard . . ."

". . . new information . . ."

". . . from a friend of someone high up at Scotland Yard . . ."

"—found with a weapon in his hands . . ."

"No, found with—the *death mark* . . ."

". . . the *sign* . . ."

"—the *sign* . . ."

Whispers about the *sign* . . . barely audible—the *sign* . . .

The sign, the death mark. Found with the death mark . . . the sign, carved in his chest . . .

Palpable fear . . . some of them knew about the sign.

What sign? What was the sign?

Shhhh . . . don't breathe a word of it. Don't. They wanted to stop him; they wanted to kill whoever got in their way. He was on his way to overstepping their influence, their control.

They found him with the *sign* . . .

. . . *it was a number . . . a slash . . . a fish hook . . . check mark . . . the death mark . . . Carved in his chest . . . You don't talk about the sign—everybody knows, nobody talks . . .*

Somebody talked, breathing it in Kyger's ear as he hunkered behind him, hidden in the threshold of a shop on a worn little street back behind all the expensive shops where the gentry spent their money. *Shhhh* . . . The sibilant sound was barely audible in his ear because his informant could be murdered just for knowing that much.

What, what did he know? He knew the one thing Kyger's money would buy—lots of money, the only reason he'd risk his life and reveal what was always simmering under the skin . . . the *sign* . . .

Shhhh . . . sacred seven . . . shhhhhh—he could die and a thousand pounds wouldn't save him—*shhhhhhh*—he never said the words . . . or God couldn't save him . . .

A hard shove at Kyger's back—and Kyger pitched forward onto his knees—a kick to his ribs—*seven* blows . . . *did he hear it, feel it, count it—did he imagine it—had he heard it someplace before* . . . ?

. . . he'd never know. He descended into a fog of semi-consciousness before his informant was even gone . . .

There was to be a private memorial for Anthony Venable the next night. This was something the public was not to be privy to or the sanctuary where the service was to be held would have been stormed by thousands.

Only those of a certain level of influence had been invited to attend.

Wyland had got all the particulars and everything Kyger needed for legitimate entrée. The invitation was waiting at his rooms in Cauldwell Gardens, which he had taken immediately after leaving Waybury House that first night of his return, and before his initial contact with Wyland.

They were serviceable enough rooms in a part of Town that was not too pricey and all he needed for the moment. He had a bedroom, a sitting room, a bath, and the wherewithal to make a pot of tea, toast some bread, or heat a tin of soup. It was enough.

The invitation, which he'd propped up against the mirror on his dresser, was engraved on thick vellum:

> *Join us in a solemn memorial in remembrance of Anthony Venable, who passed from this life so tragically on . . . at the Sacred Sanctuary, 7 P.M.*

Seven. And *Sacred.*

All mentioned within the invitation to the event: The Tony Venable Event.

He stared at the name. Venable. Immediately this jumped out at him: Venable's name was composed of seven letters . . .

. . . *seven* again . . . no—*sacred* seven. Surrounded by sevens. Where had he heard *seven* before this?

And the death mark. What *was* the death mark? The *number* seven? No, that was too simple. Was it that simple? Did it herald a coming death, or was it a symbol of the one who committed the murder?

Seven.

He began dressing for the event. Too many sevens all in the course of a day. *Where* had he heard *seven?*

You'll want the invitation, Wyland wrote in his instructions, *and you'll want to watch and see if there's any other kind of sign or identification required. I shouldn't think so. But it's best to be wary and observant.*

Sign . . . he was surrounded by signs and sevens.

He took a hansom cab to the Sanctuary, which was an ornate edifice attached to an unobtrusive church just over the bridge on the outskirts of Town. The amazing thing was, there wasn't a crush of carriages or anything overt to indicate there was anything momentous going on behind those ornate brass doors.

Rather, there was a cadre of police personnel stationed several blocks away, in all directions, halting traffic, vetting the guests, and sending each carriage forward to the Sanctuary one at a time, so as not to call any attention to the building.

The backup wasn't noticeable: the arrival hour had to have been staggered. Just that much attention to the small details was impressive.

Kyger disembarked before the cab was stopped and proceeded

on foot to the Sanctuary. It was a covert kind of building—highly decorated with carving and moldings, one double brass door and few windows.

There were three people, two men, one older, and a woman, at the door ahead of him, and he watched with interest as they gave their invitation to the sentry. He spoke, they spoke—answering questions? Giving a secret password? Was there some kind of sign . . . ?

He was making a mountain out of an ant hill, but everything surrounding the death of Tony Venable seemed that elusive, that eerie.

The three were admitted into the Sanctuary.

His turn. He approached the sentry, a man in a gold-braided unidentifiable uniform, as stiff as a board. There would be no getting around him if just his invitation were not enough to get him in.

"Your invitation, sir."

He gave it over, and the sentry examined it. "Very good, sir. I welcome a guest of the government. You may enter."

Too easy. He wondered if there was some kind of code on the invitation that segregated the guest list. Or was he inventing the details of a penny dreadful?

He stepped up into the anteroom, where it was immediately apparent that question would never be answered. It was a crush, everyone from the highest strata of society: government officials, lords and their ladies dressed in black and dripping diamonds, and foreign dignitaries; it was an exclusive assemblage—no one could have gotten entrée who had not been specifically invited.

Except him. How did Wyland do those things?

He edged his way up into the Sanctuary. There were windows, actually, stained-glass windows, fitted into the ceiling where, during the day, sunlight poured through them and made the jewel-toned panes into a dancing collage of color along the bare walls.

And there were doors—into other rooms—anterooms, interior rooms, the vestry, the church. And those milling around and conversing obviously seemed to know each other.

Ahead of him were the three who had entered just before he had—he recognized the woman's dress, which was a deep bronze silk rather than the elegant black most of the women were wearing. She walked close and tight next to the two gentlemen, and it seemed almost as if they were nudging her along between them. There wasn't an inch of space between her and them, and the set of her shoulders looked distinctly uncomfortable.

Which was odd. Although why he even had noticed it was another question for consideration. Maybe because it almost looked as if she were being pulled along against her will.

Maybe he should . . . but then she turned and looked over her shoulder for one startled instant, and he recognized *her*.

Holy shit.

The edible *virgin*. He could think of her as nothing else, despite the fact he had ruthlessly taken her maidenhead. There was still an innocence about her, and she was as beautiful and delicious as he remembered; and how he remembered—every minute, every thrust, every painful jolt of her body . . . her luscious raspberry-tipped naked body—

Goddamn—now what the goddamned hell . . . ?

She recognized him, too, her eyes widening as she caught sight of him.

Or maybe that was wishful thinking.

Just what was the correct etiquette in a social situation with a woman whose virginity you'd just ravaged?

She turned away abruptly, or perhaps she was pulled back to the moment at hand by the strong arm of the gentleman by her side, because a moment later, they pushed forward and melted into the crowd.

He felt stunned. Disoriented. This was the last place—except, given her wealth and where she had chosen to be defiled, it should not surprise him at all she'd be among Tony Venable's friends and followers. Well, it was good to know; it meant he needn't devote any more time to thinking about her than he had already, and he could focus his attention on the matter at hand.

Twenty minutes later, everyone was properly seated in the chapel, and the memorial began. Whispers like a wave swept over the crowd, a buzzing undercurrent to each eulogy extolling Tony Venable's seemingly inexhaustible list of virtues.

That's how it was.

That was Tony.

Yes, yes—so sympathetic, so caring . . . yes . . .
Oh, Tony . . .
If they could have resurrected him, they would have. They would have chanted incantations and blasphemed themselves to bring that man back from the dead.

It was just a little sickening. Venable just could not have been that much of a saint. He was much more a man with a magic touch, a silver tongue, and a golden vision that appealed on the surface to a constituency that was as broad as it was exclusive.

How, then, had he become so revered? That was what Wyland wanted to know—how—and what could be done to neutralize his growing influence in death.

It had to be experienced to be believed. Most everyone there seemed to have known him. He seemed to have touched them each individually. Made them part of him, his life, his hopes, his dreams, made them feel as though they were the bedrock on which he would build the new national order that would encompass them all.

It was too persuasive, even from beyond the grave. How could one man mesmerize a nation like that?

It would be in his speeches, and how he voted in Parliament. What he'd said, what he meant. What was in the death report. What he'd done at Bullhead in the hours before his death . . . What—?

He caught something: *seven . . .*

The eulogist was saying, "The seven precepts of Tony's moral code embraced everyone . . . Honor, Loyalty, Faith, Respect, Trust, Belief, Acceptance. . . ."

. . . *Seven* . . . Kyger counted them off as the eulogist listed them. Precepts. Principles? No, precepts. Treacherous. Calculating. Insidious . . . *seven* of them . . . *seven*—it tickled him right at the back of his mind, on the tip of his consciousness—the Bullhead floated into his mind—yes . . .

Seven . . . what moral code? Damn he couldn't get sidetracked. *Seven* . . . where had he heard *seven?*

. . . Wait—at the Bullhead—he got it: the whore—at the brothel . . . *seven* . . . she'd whispered *seven* as she traced circles and lines all over his body. *Seven—*

Sevens everywhere. Seven letters in Venable's name, seven precepts to inculcate his followers, sacred seven, whore seven . . .
seven days and seven nights at the Bullhead—biblical . . . seven—
. . . and one edible virgin in the last place he'd ever expected to
find her . . . *seven* . . .

How? Why?

Holy shit . . .

After what he'd seen at the memorial service, Kyger found it
easy to imagine the impact of Venable's speeches. They were easy
to access—the papers had reported them in depth, and reprinted
them whole. Everything, aptly, was available in the morgue,
where he spent the next morning deep in newsprint.

He could hardly credit what he was reading. Tony Venable espoused pure out-and-out monomania, disguised in altruism. All
for the country, for the good of the country—one man, one voice
over all, and unprecedented freedoms under the protection of
their chosen overlord. Everyone taken care of, everyone prosper-
ous, everyone equal under the law.

Tony Venable comprehended their pain. He felt it, took it into
himself, he wore it with pride, displayed it with honor, and he
vowed to change the very notion of the monarchy to reflect the
new freedom, the new philosophy that encompassed everyone
under one umbrella over all.

His followers could not have wholly understood exactly what
he meant. It was too socialistic under the skin, too insidiously fanatical, and too dangerous for one man to have even suggested
such sweeping changes; he espoused nothing short of overthrow-
ing the monarchy, couched in humanistic patriarchal terms.

And he had done it, out loud, in public, converting thousands
to his beliefs, which was an unbelievable testament to his magic:
he'd convinced a legion of tenacious and devoted adherents that
his way was the only right way, and that they must carry his message forward—even in the event of his death.

Kyger would be striking down a god. Nothing less. And a
movement that must never get a foothold in England.

There was no other choice. It was a daunting challenge, much
more than he'd imagined when he agreed to take it on.

He couldn't let anything get in the way—not Jancie, not the virgin, not the past and or any regrets, past, present or future.

This was the thing he'd been searching for all around the world—the thing in which he could immerse himself to the exclusion of everything else.

This was a holy crusade, nothing more, nothing less, and it would be the crucible from which he'd emerge purified and—finally—whole.

Chapter Three

Her father had spared no expense. The cuff around her wrist was exquisitely decorated with ornate chasing and fastened with a tongue-in-box closure, almost like a bracelet, except that it locked and there was a key.

And the links of the chain that appended it to one of the three iron rings Zabel had had installed in the room were thick, gold and as unobtrusive as a chain and ring set low on the wall could be.

Which meant, not much. And hardly anything that would pacify her.

The humiliation was complete. She sat mutinous and silent in her elaborate, pillow-laden bed, her father and Wroth surveying her, Wroth with a look in his eye that she did not like.

But she liked nothing about him altogether.

"I do believe this is the proper way to train a wife," Wroth murmured to Zabel. "I do like a woman bound in her place. I clearly see how our future will be because of your courageous decision to punish your daughter properly."

"It's true," Zabel said, clapping him on the shoulder. "There are just some things a father, or a husband, should not hesitate to do to show a daughter or a wife that he means business."

"And his wife-to-be in chains is a beautiful thing to see," Wroth said. "It opens up such realms of possibility . . ."

"While training a daughter—or wife—to become as biddable as a father—or husband—could ever wish."

"Exactly," Wroth agreed, with nauseating enthusiasm.

They were salivating, Angilee thought, positively drooling over the thought of her wrapped in chains and Wroth locking the cuffs.

"Although, you might have started her off with a shortened chain and both wrists encased in cuffs," Wroth mused as he paced around the bed observing her from every angle. "Then, when she became more compliant, you could have rewarded her by lengthening the chain, and eventually removing one of the two cuffs."

Zabel considered this for a moment, and nodded. "You're exactly right. I have been too lenient with my property. But I would be hard put to constrict her further when my intent was solely to inhibit her freedom of movement within this room. However, when you are married, and starting off a new life together—then, you might implement binding her more constrictively to suit your taste."

"Yes. In fact, I'm thinking even now of all the ways we will do that. The first night in particular when a woman is most prone to hysteria as she approaches the moment of physical penetration. If she were chained and splayed, it would be that much easier to ram the penis head right past the barrier into heaven. My dear father-in-law-to-be—you have opened up vistas I hadn't thought to consider with my new virgin bride."

"My pleasure," Zabel said.

"*My* pleasure—tonight," Wroth countered, gesturing toward the bedroom door. "So let the pleasure begin . . ."

"Good night, daughter."

Angilee spat.

"Good night, my bound virgin goddess . . ."

Angilee gagged, choked, wretched against her dry throat. But they didn't care—they just left her there, happily steeped in their male superiority and plans for the evening. Left her alone, cuffed to a long length of chain, for God's sake, and neither of them cared.

She couldn't stop choking. How had this happened?

Dear God, her father had as good as abandoned her tonight to be with Wroth, and she couldn't pinpoint when he'd started putting his own interests before hers. That, and when Wroth had entered the picture. Where had Wroth come from? It was as if her father had conjured him up just to torture her.

How could her father abandon her to that pig? And now the bastard was rubbing his hands over the sadistic nuances of chaining her up as well?

Ohhhhh, *NEVER!* She punched the mattress in frustration and anger.

There had to be a way out of this, there had to be. She *was* a beautiful woman, and Zabel was wealthy enough for three fathers—and even he had said those were commodities prized in this country. There had to be some other eligible man who would marry her out of hand for both those considerations.

It was the only way she could see to mitigate this disaster, but even that passing idea was fraught with difficulties—not least, getting away from her father and Wroth, who between them had pinioned her like a prisoner at that memorial service the other night.

She'd felt like a felon, for God's sake . . . she'd felt like—

Her breath caught. Wait—wait . . .

Oh, dear God—*him* . . .

She'd forgotten about *him*. The Bullhead man. The Bullhead bull . . . she'd call him, in preference to the *hired man*. Or the hired—other part of him . . .

She swallowed hard. Hard. That was on her mind, too. Wroth hard—between her legs on their wedding night—doing the things the Bullhead . . . bull had . . .

NOOOOOO . . . oh, good God, she couldn't even bring herself to envision it; her stomach lurched at the thought of it.

And now, with Wroth's unholy idea he was going to keep her in chains until she was biddable—

No. NO. Anyone else was preferable; the bull man would do. He had ravaged her; now he could redeem himself by becoming her savior. Simple. Perfect. Biblical, even.

The man needed money, obviously. A second son . . . ? Anyone, anything could be bought. She'd bought him—she'd buy him again.

But first she had to find him.

She had to think. She couldn't think. A thousand ideas and thoughts went scattershot through her brain, to which the blood flow was undoubtedly constricted by the god-awful cuff and length of chain.

And the thought of Wroth with her in bed on their wedding night.

She gagged again.

Zabel just wasn't that cruel.

Yes, he was. The chain was proof of that, even if it was a good ten feet long so she had purchase to move around the room and to the bathroom if necessary. And he'd fixed it low on the wall so that she wouldn't look so much like a prisoner as . . . as what?

How did someone look chained to the wall?

Like a prisoner in chains, for God's sake . . .

She buried her head on her drawn-up knees. She didn't even want to contemplate the thought of any of it.

Better to think about the bull man. A man definitely as arresting dressed as he was naked.

She'd caught just the barest glimpse of him before Zabel and Wroth propelled her into the crowd, but she knew it was he, and she had been shocked to see him among London's elite, in the least likely of places.

She supposed that the how and why of his attendance was hardly important now. The main thing it proved was that he traveled in these elevated circles. She hadn't expected that. She hadn't expected ever to see him again. She thought of him as a pirate, plundering her virtue and stealing the treasure away.

And there he had been, not a dozen steps behind her, looking like some elegant lord of the manor, staring at her intently, recognizing her instantly. Remembering—what?

Oh, God. When she remembered—she didn't want to remember. She needed to concentrate on this one thing: there was hope.

They could get licenses, they could keep her contained, Wroth could talk all he wished about molding her and making her his compliant mistress, but now she knew there was hope that she could get away from him—and her father.

But how? She had to think.

It was clear that if she kept on her course of rebelling against the marriage, she would never see the outside of her room again until the day she walked down the aisle to Wroth. So the best strategy would be to let her father and Wroth believe that she had come to heel.

It meant suppressing every instinct, every willful thought, every rebellious inclination. It meant acting like the mewling virginal miss they both so ardently desired her to be. Batting her eyelashes, saying yes to everything. Suborning her nature to their dictates. Telling Wroth how strong and wonderful he was.

She choked again. God. No. She couldn't do it.

She wrenched at the cuff, pulling and twisting and only injuring her wrist in the process.

She had to do it. She had to gird herself and just do it. Act. Pretend. She could do that. Women did that all the time.

Look at her father, so loving, treating her like a princess for so many years. Like his prized possession, if you really looked at it closely. And now suddenly he'd turned into a devil, and she'd never had any inkling that he would ever come down on her this hard for flouting his wishes.

This was a revelation. There had been the two of them for so long, dependent on each other, scrapping with each other, goading each other. It was like a marriage in so many respects, but there was something about *this* proposed marriage that had changed Zabel into someone she did not know.

Someone who was willing to go to any lengths to get what he wanted and didn't care whom he trampled in the process. Even his own daughter.

Well, if that indeed was the way he wanted it, then she would have no compunction about her course of action, and anything she could devise to escape them both was fair game.

Including involving the Bullhead bull.

So . . . *him* . . . since he already knew everything about her he needed to know.

Dear God—don't think about that.

And that he could have no question about her past or why she was not whole and pure. *Don't think about that.*

Although, it could be said that was a good thing. It could be said she was *accustomed* to him already.

Yes. So that couldn't be a bad thing.

One hurdle down.

Convincing him to marry her—well, she'd think about how to accomplish that when the moment was at hand.

First she had to get past the real obstacle, convincing Zabel and Wroth that she was properly chastised and could be allowed out—properly chaperoned and in their company, of course.

That wouldn't be easy. That would take a week perhaps under lock and key, and a show of repentance and humility that she wasn't sure she had in her.

But she would do it. It was the only way. Convince them, those two fatuous, know-it-all, sadistic sons of bitches, that she was properly disciplined and that Zabel's unconscionable punishment had worked.

And the rest she would figure out later.

"Awful thing, Venable's death." One didn't have to say anything more to any stranger on the street to evoke a ten-minute discussion, tirade or argument.

Time was flying. It had been two days since the memorial service. Since then, he'd read the speeches and read the coroner's report, which had come to no conclusion as to the cause of death, and the only anomaly noted was the strange bloody little cut on Venable's chest that looked like a check.

As in—off the list?

Whose list?

Or was that the death mark they talked about in whispers.

He was groping in the dark, and he wasn't yet ready to go back to the Bullhead. There had to be something in the public record with which he could work.

It was as if everyone knew, and nobody would tell.

He had to dig something up, even with those amorphous clues. The Sacred Seven. The number seven. Seven precepts. The death mark. The death of a political fascist who was that close to becoming canonized.

How could Kyger take him down?

The virgin at the Bullhead. Could she have been—?

No. She was too innocent, too real, too scared.

Yes. Really? Because if he really wanted to push the thing to the extreme—when he rearranged the letters of the word *scared*, they spelled *sacred* . . .

Holy shit.

Nothing was exempt from consideration. The raspberry virgin could have been part of the whole, sent to him to distract him from discovering what was there to be found.

No—it was too far-fetched to believe that they kept a cache of virgins to offer to anyone who seemed unduly curious about who patronized the Bullhead.

There is nothing too far beyond to be considered.

He read in the newspaper that morning that a committee had been organized to raise money to turn Tony Venable's flat in Park Lane into a museum. Visitation was available from noon to three, three days a week, entrée with the requested, not required, offering of a pound note.

The very thing. Kyger was in Park Lane—*Seven* Park Lane, more sevens—on the dot of twelve, only to find a line of visitors already snaking down the street from the building's entrance.

This was getting worse and worse, but there was no point not to wait.

The crowd was hushed, reverent. There was a brochure passed around detailing the plans of the Venable Museum Committee, which—with the proceeds from the admission fee—intended to buy the building, relocate the two other tenants, and turn the entire three floors into a shrine to Tony Venable's life and work.

He felt the danger lurking in those plans, subtle and shadowy. He saw everything in a flash: if they owned the building, there could be no questions about anything that went on there; and so it could become a place for Venable's followers to meet, to plan, to conceive doctrine, and perhaps print and distribute propaganda; and it would become the temple where they kept the flame of Venable's ideology alive.

And no one could stop them.

He had to stop them.

The crowd shuffled along, whispering about Venable's death, about Venable's life. Venable's promises. Venable's lies. Watching intently as each visitor exited, each face suffused with exaltation.

Kyger stepped into the building an hour later with some trepidation.

It was hushed, dark, cool, elegant, all dark wood and soft suf-

fused gaslight, and a thick carpet winding up the second-floor flat
that had been Tony Venable's.

He wondered what he'd expected to see. It was an apartment
like any other. Two bedrooms, a bathroom and kitchen, a sitting
room, the library room where he'd died, and a parlor were all elegantly outfitted as befitting Tony Venable's status: all rich, thick,
dark—satins, brocades, Persian carpets, walnut furniture, soft,
diffused light.

In the library, there was a secretary desk by a window where
you could imagine Venable sitting, thinking about his last speech,
his last meeting where he listened to those he wanted so badly to
represent, thinking about how to help them, what to do about
their needs, their burdens, their pain.

A whisper: "Look . . . the notebook on the desk—what do
you think he wrote in there . . . ?"

A subtle movement to look. Just the date, written in a close,
tight, masculine hand. The date was a month ago. *A month.*

"He's been gone a month?" Another whisper.

"I don't believe it."

Another voice, rising in religious fervor: "He's here in this
room, I feel it. This is where he died. He hasn't left us—he's here,
he's here . . ."

"Madam—" The docent coming discreetly into the room, taking the woman's arm, leading her out the door into the hallway.
"Madam . . ." A whisper, whatever said to the woman lost in the
hush beyond the door.

This was where Tony Venable had been attacked and died.
They looked for blood. They looked for some sign of death, some
sign he'd survived. The mood was reverent, hushed, sacred as
they tiptoed through the room. It was as if he had stepped out,
had gone to Parliament, or out to dinner, as if he'd return at the
moment.

"She's right. I feel his presence so strongly . . ." Another whisper, sibilant, ghostly, unidentifiable, and they all could imagine
him sitting at the desk in that plush upholstered chair, his back to
the door, thinking of them, their good, their welfare, and his as-
sassin moving into the room silent as air, wielding his silent
weapon, taking Venable's not-so-silent life.

Sobs behind him as the realization hit the crowd that this was the place of death, a memorial to contrition.

There was no sign anywhere of blood or death.

They moved as slowly as if they were marching to a dirge, through the library, and into the sitting room where there was another desk, where they could imagine Tony Venable working hard, thinking about them and how to help them, and into the parlor with its ornate walnut fireplace surround, lavish plasterwork, comfortable sofas and chairs. On the table behind the sofa, a pile of papers, Parliament concerns, right there, right where everyone could see how hard Tony Venable was always working for them.

The carpet, soft and thick under their feet. Into the first bedroom, with its curved and molded walnut bed frame that dominated the room.

"Tony Venable slept here . . ." Awe in the voice of the speaker as if she could see the imprint of his body on the bedcover. A dresser, an armoire, a dressing room, faintly redolent of his scent. Papers piled neatly on a small slant-topped desk. Another place, less ornate. Brocade curtains. A view to the front of the building.

The second bedroom was at the rear, as neat and meticulous as the rest of the flat, and the bathroom and kitchen situated side by side next to that.

"I heard he had someone to do for him," someone whispered. "How fortunate can you be—to work for Tony Venable, to ease the everyday cares of his life so he could concentrate on the important things—like helping us."

They peered into the kitchen, where there was a sink, a nickel-plated stove shiny with assiduous care, a large white porcelain icebox, a bank of cabinets covering one wall, and a well-scrubbed worktable.

Someone wanted to look into the cabinets to see what Tony Venable ate. Someone else discouraged her.

Back into the parlor, where now they noticed there was also a small dining area in one corner with a small round pedestal table and two upholstered chairs. There were more papers piled on this table as well.

This time, not even Kyger could resist peeking at what was on the top page. It was blank with the exception of a check mark in the upper right-hand corner.

Something checked off . . . on a blank page? Strange.

The docent ushered them out. The line outside had grown longer, crowding up the stairwell now, to make room on the street.

Expectant faces looking at him, at the others emerging, seeking to find what, on his face and in his eyes? That seeing Venable's home and touching the objects that he'd lived with was some kind of transforming experience?

Oh, he was transformed all right, and more determined than ever to bring Tony Venable—

Wait—

Down the respectful line of visitors waiting to go into Venable's home he saw her. No, he saw *them*. The two men and his recalcitrant virgin. The same two men he'd seen with her at the memorial service, one of them older, the other not much younger, now he could see their faces.

This time she was wedged tightly between them, she was dressed in a deep mink brown suit, collared up to her chin, the sleeves pulled well down over her wrists, and she looked stoic, unhappy and resigned, her gaze focused downward—or perhaps away from the two men.

He slowed his step because there was no way he could approach her, and it once again looked to him as if they were prodding her along. The men were too close to her, too encroaching, and her demeanor was too stiff.

What the hell was going on? He stared at her, willing her to lift her head, to see him, to know him.

She would know him.

Did she feel the intensity of his gaze?

She looked up suddenly as she felt the pull of his presence. She saw him instantly and turned her eyes away, looking quickly to her left and then to her right almost as if she were assuring herself the men, the *guards*, he thought of them, weren't watching what she was doing, that they were solely intent on moving with the crowd, and, as they pushed her forward, she shot him a quick anguished look and mouthed the words, *Help me.*

* * *

It hadn't even taken a day.

"They are opening Tony Venable's flat to the public," Zabel announced conversationally at breakfast the next day. "Wroth feels it is necessary to pay our respects. It's the right thing to do. So, as loath as I am to have you leave this hotel room, we must accede to his wishes. However, there will be some safeguards. You will be chained to Wroth, for one thing, so you will choose your clothing accordingly so that it will be your little secret. And Wroth's."

Angilee swallowed bile. "As you wish, Father."

"Oh my, aren't we compliant today. Very good, even if it is an act. You do comprehend what is expected of you, and that's the first step toward your becoming the kind of wife Wroth expects. The other little problem, well—we will take care of that as well."

What??? How did you mend damaged merchandise? Oh, she just couldn't even summon the energy to think about it. It was enough to know she would be bound to Wroth for the duration of their visit to the putative shrine to Tony Venable.

"I don't like being chained up," Angilee said stonily.

"Well, I rather like it. And Wroth was in transports over the thought of it, so—we'll just keep you constrained for the moment. After all, it's very few weeks before you'll be married. You need to learn to be obedient and submissive in any event. You've had your head your whole life. Wroth is absolutely correct about that: I've spoiled you beyond anything proper and ruined you forever. No man wants to take on a willful bride with a mind and opinions all her own. I should have applied discipline long before this. We are exceedingly fortunate that a man of Wroth's stature and influence is willing to marry you despite those negatives."

"And you're saying we'd never have found another willing groom?" Angilee asked coyly, swallowing the venom in her voice. "Anywhere, in the whole of England? Ever?"

"Well, look at how it went in New York. Not a nibble. Every door slammed in our face. I had thought it was due to our lineage. Now I see it could equally have had to do with your high-handed ways. It was the best decision I ever made to come to England, and lo and behold, we found Wroth. So all has worked out exactly as I would have wished, and the only stumbling stones—your defilement and your intractable nature—are both remedial with time and a little coaching. So rest easy, my dear. I'm not going to be a hard taskmaster. I leave that to your husband-to-be. We will make the visit today, and we'll see how that goes as to how much latitude a deeply suspicious father can allow."

This was how it went: Zabel specified exactly what she should wear, and when Wroth arrived, her wrist was chained to his on a shorter length of links, and he had whole control of her movements by virtue of his arm tucked against hers.

She had to walk at their pace, with them crowding her on either side. She had to bear the feeling of Wroth's body squeezed tightly against hers. Allow him to maneuver her and press against her, listen to him slaver over the increasing list of ways he had thought up to constrain her.

In the hansom cab: "What do you think about a thrall collar for my lovely? With rings all around it so I can chain her in any position that strikes my fancy, or lead her wherever I may wish. I've been ruminating about that all night. What do you think, my dear?"

Angilee swallowed her fury. "Whatever would make you happy," she murmured, pushing the words out through her dry throat.

"Oh my, here's a change of attitude—so quickly? No, I think not."

"Nor I," Zabel said, "but Angilee is pragmatic, if nothing else. She will come to heel because she knows this is the best course, that the marriage is the best thing for her, and she will become as obedient as any man could wish in a very short time."

"I will hold you to that, Zabel, because I *am* anxious to claim my beautiful, *submissive* bride."

"And so you shall, won't he, Angilee?"

She licked her dry lips. "I will endeavor to become all that Wroth could wish," she said finally.

"Very good," Zabel said. "You see?"

"Ummm," Wroth murmured. "I still think you are too lenient with her. But that will change. It wants only that she comes to me willingly when the time arrives."

"She will. Won't she?" Zabel nudged her, hard.

56 / *Thea Devine*

"I only hope I can meet the high standard you've set for your wife," Angilee muttered viciously, nearly choking on the ironic words.

Pig. Bastard. Sadist . . . DIE . . . !

Wroth turned to her and suddenly cupped her breast. She couldn't help it, she flinched.

He nodded, satisfied. "Yes, I like that fear, that cowering innocence in a woman. One has to test these things now and again. My wife must be the purest of the pure, and come to me lily white and begging me to impose my will on hers.

"I don't believe I have actually spelled out what my expectations are, so perhaps this is as good a time as any, on the heels of your properly disciplining Angilee for her insubordination.

"There will be no such thing in my house. I expect my dictates and desires to be followed to the letter. My wife—is me, totally immersed in me and my wants, needs, dreams, wishes. She will come to know, even before I do, what I want and how she can provide it. I will train her, of course—a woman isn't born knowing what a man's needs are—and I will teach her the level of obedience I demand by virtue of gentle, loving, corrective discipline when she veers from my course. And in return, I will provide for her everything she could possibly want, from clothes to jewels, a level of luxury, attention and love that is beyond anything she can imagine.

"That is what I expect from Angilee and what she can expect from me."

"It sounds like everything a woman could want," Zabel said. "Angilee?"

"I cannot wait until the day I put myself in your hands," Angilee ground out, her voice thin and reedy.

Wroth smiled, not a particularly pleasant sight. "She learns."

"She is very intelligent."

"A man doesn't want intelligence, Zabel. He wants obedience."

"Oh, I absolutely agree with you there," Zabel said hastily.

"Then we are all in agreement," Wroth said complacently. "Just in time, for now we are here."

"Here," however, was rather daunting—fifty, perhaps more,

people already lined up, waiting patiently to be admitted to the holy sanctuary of Tony Venable's flat.

It did not deter Wroth. He was perfectly willing to take his place in line, and he propelled Angilee right by his side.

And then it was a most deadly wait. Quiet. Strange. Reverent. Angilee felt faint. There was no way out of this. She was doomed, and Wroth would be the agent of her demise. Her father had sold her, for what recompense she couldn't begin to imagine. And all that was left for her was a life of servitude to Wroth's demands.

She couldn't play this out. She couldn't—he was too powerful and too dangerous. She couldn't change her personality that drastically that he would believe she had come willingly to submission and obedience, and she had nothing with which to fight him otherwise. He'd bury her, with every legality on his side, and walk away with every ha'penny of the money Zabel promised him in the bargain.

She looked down at Wroth's arm intertwined with hers. It was like iron, like the chains with which he would soon shackle her.

The line moved forward. She looked up to see where Wroth was guiding her, and she saw *him*.

She was hallucinating because she wanted a way out of this so badly. It couldn't be *him*. She slanted a glance quickly each way—Zabel and Wroth were too engrossed watching the crowd, thank heaven—but she was almost past him, almost. It might be too late.

But she could try. Even imprisoned as she was and being propelled forward so forcefully, she could . . . just . . . try—

She raised her chin defiantly, shot the Bullhead man a quick look, and mouthed the words, *Help me.*

But it was too late—she had already moved past him, and the one chance she had to get his attention was gone.

Help me . . . Good God—the last goddamned thing he needed—a *needy*, edible virgin. Shit. He stood staring after the slowly moving line, not able now to even pick her out of the crowd.

Who *was* she?

No. No—this wasn't the time to get caught up in someone else's story. But then, what was she doing at these public events memorializing Tony Venable? And those two men with her . . . looked as though they meant business—whose business?

It wasn't *his* business.

For certain. Which was why he couldn't leave it alone. If there was one thing he'd discovered about himself in the time he'd been away from England, it was his well-submerged need to be a knight-errant. To the rescue, that was him, first his undeserving father, then his reprobate brother, then the innocent and too seductive Jancie who hadn't wanted rescuing at all, and now . . .

Her . . . the unknown delectable *her* whose body he had penetrated, and whose life he had to leave alone.

That *her*, the one stiff with resentment and resistance and needing help, possible rescue—needing *him*.

The one other irresistible thing in his life besides his mission to save England . . .

Jesus . . .

Where did he go to escape his conscience? He didn't know how he could leave her there, imprisoned between those two men. But the line had moved forward appreciably, and none of them were visible, and for all he knew, the three were already in the flat wandering around and poking among the pristine fragments of Tony Venable's life.

Likely the crowds would grow less respectful as time wore on, too, and as their insatiable curiosity prodded them to be the one who discovered the secret of the enigma that was Venable.

Except Kyger fully intended to be that one.

A seemingly insurmountable task still, and he was no closer to any idea as to how to accomplish it. Venable was a thing unto himself, and, like a top, the idea of him kept spinning, his vortex drawing the unwary and the worshipful into his orbit.

But what was he really? A witch doctor with a sorcerer's tongue, weaving words and wizardry, wishes and schemes, mirroring back his constituents' needs and dreams and couching them in a smoky autocratic doctrine that seemed to speak to every man, rich or poor.

Except when you examined his ideas and his philosophy word by word, line by line under a microscope, because otherwise, the overall effect of his speeches was mesmerizing.

Utterly Machiavellian. So he had to neutralize the ghost of

Tony Venable as well. It was like trying to put out a conflagration with a cup of water.

And on top of everything, on a personal level, Tony Venable seemed too good to be true. Not a blemish to be found. Not a salacious or questionable misstep anywhere. No mistresses, lovers, public sexual escapades. Nothing except for Wyland's covert information that he had been at Bullhead Manor the night before his death.

That, and the whispers about a *death mark*. And the inexplicable cut on his chest. And the mystery of the recurring sevens.

Sevens everywhere. *Seven Park Lane. Sacred Seven.*

Seven Cups Tavern and Divan. He saw the sign out of the corner of his eye and stopped dead. *Seven* again.

Nonsense. The whole of London was not in some conspiracy of sevens.

Nevertheless, he turned from his course and traced his steps back to the tavern. There was nothing unusual about the tavern. He saw that instantly.

There was a bar to the one side when he entered, already crowded with habitual drinkers. There was a bank of divans already occupied by smokers and chess players deep into their games. There was a scattering of empty tables and luncheon available for the nominal amount of 2/6d, your choice—steak and kidney pudding or a cut of roast mutton with Yorkshire pudding.

He took a table and chose the steak. The smoke was thick and sweet, reminding him of the thick, sweet scent that night at the Bullhead.

The talk rumbled around politics, jobs, the cost of living, Venable's death. Nothing that wasn't discussed in every coffeehouse and tavern on a daily basis. He stoically ate his steak, along with a pewter of stout, listening to the strands of conversation.

". . . a man can't make a living these days . . ."

". . . what are they going to do about replacing Venable? We need someone like Venable—someone strong, take-charge . . . knew what was best . . ."

". . . appoint . . ."

"—no, not yet, not until there's something definite about—"

"—meeting in Kensington Park today—"

"—right—"

". . . no rabble-rousing this time—"

"No—I'll pass the word . . ."

"—deliver a message—"

"—it's the seventh day . . ."

". . . in the park, I told you. . . . At the Seven Sisters—spread the word—"

". . . they killed him, certain as stones . . ."

"—who *they?* It's the Bolshies . . . it's always the socialists—"

"No, it's government—he was getting too powerful, too many people listening to him . . . make changes . . . no more queen and country—"

". . . right, Tony Venable and country—"

Kyger's head jerked up. . . . *Wait*—He'd almost missed something in the rumble of typical talk you'd fully expect to hear from a luncheon crowd at a working-class tavern. Nothing new. Just what Wyland had told him: everyone wanted answers, and there were no answers.

Just sevens, floating around in the least likely places.

What had they said?

He couldn't pin it down in his mind. Wait. Something seven. Something about sisters. Shit. And now people were paying for their food and drifting out the door and away. Who had said that?

He grabbed a waiter, paid for his lunch and bolted out the door. The sun glared so brightly in his eyes after the dense darkness of the restaurant that it was almost painful. He dove into the usual crowds heading this way and that, the busy street, disoriented by the normalcy of everything around him, so stunning when there were sevens in the air.

This was what Wyland had warned him about—the elusiveness of the thing he was chasing. A reputation, an ideology—as intangible as the wind, and just as destructive.

Seven. Something about a park and sisters.

What park? What sisters?

He felt a moment of confusion—it was the smoke, it was in his head, in the air, the foggy density of the air in the tavern . . . which was *seven*. Cups. Seven Cups.

He felt dizzy, everything spun, and suddenly he was on the ground, pinned by a body, someone's fists punching him, pummeling him, more than one person, and fierce, hard guttural whispers in his ear, in his head, in the fog: *don't come around again, you fucking lob-cock, you sack of shit—stay away—don't come back . . . kill you if we ever see you here again—*

Blackness. Fog. Cotton. Aching. Dark—Cold.

Awake? *Awake.* Not dead. And aware, suddenly, of sounds and cold and . . . time. Time . . . He bolted into full consciousness, his heart pounding erratically.

No. Still daylight. It was him, tumbled over and curled up in a dark doorway, not unlike the one where his unknown informant had whispered the profane words, *sacred seven,* in his ear.

He moved, painfully unwinding himself from the urine-soaked stoop of the doorway, and crawled into the piercing sunlight.

Everything ached—his ribs, hips, belly, arms. His eyes. He could barely get himself upright. He didn't know where he was either—far from *Seven Cups,* that was certain.

He limped down the odd, filthy, little back street. *Seventh Lane.* Jesus.

He had no idea where he was. And his money was gone as well. They'd rifled his pockets, taken everything. Nothing made sense. He didn't know anyone there. There was no connection to anything he was involved in except the random fact of the number seven.

It had to be random. It just couldn't be a conspiracy of that magnitude that every *seven* in the whole of London was connected to . . .

Connected to what? *Sacred seven . . . ?*

Nothing is exempt from consideration.

Where *was* he?

He was getting dizzy again. Passersby eyed him warily, thinking him drunk. He sagged against a nearby building and took some deep breaths. This would pass. Give him a minute. Give him—

Someone touched him. "Are you all right?"

"I'm not drunk." His voice was as thick as if he had downed a half dozen quarts of bitters.

"Oh, all right, then." Rank skepticism, and then a closer look. "Can I help?"

"I don't know where I am."

"Cheapside."

He swallowed hard, fighting for air. They'd gotten him in the lungs, too. "I have to get to Cauldwell Gardens."

"That'd cost a bit, mate."

"I'd pay you back."

"Sure you would." The man pulled out a handful of notes and thrust them at him.

"Tell me where." He could barely speak.

"Come find me at the Seven Sisters, mate. See if you're good as your word."

What? The words stunned him. He pulled himself up to try to get a look at his Good Samaritan, but the man had vanished.

A moment later, a hansom came rumbling down the narrow street.

What?

Kyger waved him down, just barely, and crawled into the backseat.

Seven Sisters, he'd said?

Holy shit.

"Cauldwell Gardens," he managed to whisper, and then he passed out.

Chapter Four

Meekness did not become her. Angilee was restless with the need to take action. To move, to seek, to find. Because even if the hired man hadn't seen her plea, the possibility still remained that their paths would cross somewhere else sometime again.

But she would never see him at this rate if she was kept cooped up in this hotel room chained to the bed.

Zabel, however, was very content with the arrangement. It meant he didn't have to worry about her, where she was, what she was doing.

What she had done.

He still had yet to deal with what she had done, but until Wroth obtained a license, he did not wish to think about it at all.

Meantime, he had thoughtfully provided Angilee with all manner of novels and fashion magazines for when he went on his nightly forays with Wroth, and he did his duty and kept her company during the day as much as he could stand. So he really thought she ought to be reasonably content and spending her time seriously contemplating the changes she must make in her nature to accommodate herself to the needs of her future husband.

It was the second day after their visit to Tony Venable's flat.

They were at breakfast, Zabel immersed in the morning paper, and the table drawn up to the bed so that Angilee could easily take her tea and toast.

Angilee felt fidgety and irritable, she was tearing her toast to crumbs, and she had to clamp down on her impatience to broach Zabel about getting out of the hotel. But she knew very well, in this new order of obedience, the suggestion must come from her father, who had no compelling reason to want to do anything for her right now.

On the other hand, she had been deliberately less combative the last few days as part of her plan to convince him she was coming to accept the terms of the marriage.

You would think he'd notice, she thought wrathfully. *You'd think he'd show some appreciation of the effort.* Instead, he was complacent, smug, and certain that the punishment was working, and he ought just to keep on doing it.

Her plan just wasn't working. At least as fast as she had hoped. And time was running out.

"Oh, my God—look at this—there are going to be simultaneous séances all over the city tomorrow to try to contact Tony Venable."

"*What?* Where? I want to go—" Angilee caught herself. "I mean—my goodness . . . how—where?"

"All over the city. How astonishing. There's a list of places, dozens, where a séance can be attended." He scanned the newspaper story and began reading the details: "Each of the mediums has agreed to use one method, which will be spirit writing. Each of the sessions is limited to a dozen attendees around the table, and as many as the room will accommodate, to bear witness. Each medium has agreed to begin the séance at the dot of seven. Each room will be prepared exactly the same, with every extraneous piece of furniture and all decorative objects removed, and all drawers emptied of contents. All windows are to be sealed. And some substance like flour or cornstarch sifted around the table and the threshold of the door and windowsills so there can be no question that someone is manipulating the séance in any way."

Zabel stared at Angilee. "By God, this is extraordinary."

"Oh, we must attend one of the séances," Angilee said in her most coaxing manner. "Isn't there one being held near the hotel?"

"By heaven—" He looked down at the list. "There will be three sessions in each of the hotels in Town. You wouldn't think there were that many psychics in the whole of London."

"I wouldn't suppose the medium would need to be psychic— just receptive," Angilee said. "We must attend one. It would be something to tell my children—don't you think?"

Her children? Hers and Wroth's, Zabel thought with some complacency. She was coming to accept the idea of marrying Wroth. She was thinking about children. Grandchildren. The future. He was very pleased with her. "I expect we can try."

He looked back down at the announcement in the paper. "Hmm. Yes, well, it appears to be highly organized. This won't be a random thing. There are actually specifications as to where interested parties in different sections of the city should go."

"And we would be . . . ?"

"In the hotel here, and there will be someone coordinating things at each location," Zabel paraphrased as he read. "Gathering will begin two hours before so that everyone is assured of being accommodated in one of the locations. We have four choices within the hotel: Rooms seven, seventeen, twenty-seven or thirty-seven. How odd. Every location has the number seven. Seven Cups, Seven Regents Park, Seven Swans . . . Well, we don't have to leave the hotel, of course: we're closest to room thirty-seven, and I'm just intrigued enough that I think we'll go."

Kyger was in consultation with Wyland. He was back to himself now, after that vicious attack, but the events of the previous day had sounded him a warning. Someone was suspicious of what he was about. Someone connected to Venable, possibly.

And now this mass séance on the heels of the huge positive response to the public admission to Tony Venable's flat, and the large attendance at that private memorial.

"A bold stroke," Wyland said. "Impressive. Hit them, hit them, hit them. Never let awareness of him out of the news, out of the public consciousness. There's genius behind this, my boy, and that makes everything that much harder."

"Which of the locations should I try to get in?"

"Not the likely one. If they indeed have some suspicion of you, then cross off the taverns and the flat. I'd choose one of the hotels. Someplace where Venable's contributors might come together over this. It might be interesting to watch them during the thing. It's pure hokum, of course, but they've been primed to want it, and they are raw with grief and ripe to want to believe in it."

Kyger chose Claridge's, giving the proper address to the Venable acolyte that would gain him admittance to the hotel. Everything was orderly, everyone quiet, prayerful, respectful, hoping that something extraordinary would occur that night.

It was astonishing to watch it. But everything concerning Tony Venable was astonishing. And impenetrable.

The devotion. The adoration.

The sevens. More sevens. All the room numbers, sevens. The participants didn't have a choice of which room to go to. Kyger was sent to room seventeen, located on the first floor.

There, everything was in readiness, probably since the morning. The medium was already at the table, there was a blank writing tablet, as large as a sketch pad, before her, and she sat with her eyes closed, while the awed audience entered quietly and those who were to sit around the table were randomly picked from among them.

To his surprise, Kyger was one of those chosen, and he warily took his seat across from the medium so he could watch everything closely.

The excitement was palpable but subdued. There was no sense of impatience, no move to hurry things along. Everything was precise and deliberate as if it were being executed according to a plan.

It was eerie.

The lights were low in the room, and it was empty of any furniture, as the news stories reporting the event had detailed. Those who would be in the audience had to stand because, practically, the room would accommodate many more if they weren't seated.

No one complained.

The windows were tightly closed, and at five minutes before the hour, the door would be locked and flour shaken around the room at the specified points.

At seven, the acolyte told them, those who had been chosen to sit at the table would join hands, and he would initiate the summoning. All around London, the presiding acolyte would perform the same ritual, would say the same words. Everything was synchronized; everything would be happening simultaneously.

He then locked the door and walked around the room with a sifter, shaking flour around the door, the windows, the table. At his signal, the medium displayed a planchette with a pencil attached to everyone in the room.

"This is the method by which Tony Venable will speak with us," the acolyte explained. "It slips onto her hand with that rubber band you see stretched across the upper side. She will now put on the implement. It wants but two minutes to the hour. Let us say a silent prayer, and when Big Ben strikes . . ."

Time never moved so slowly. It thickened around them as if it had a life of its own. The silence was like a dense cloud, rolling around them, enfolding them like fog.

The tolling of the hour sounded. *Bong, bong, bong . . .*

"Join hands," the acolyte whispered, taking his place three persons to the right of the medium.

They joined hands. Hot hands, heated breaths, a jumpiness, a nervousness as if they could sense something there, something—a throbbing, an anticipating. *Someone . . .*

The acolyte intoned, "We are gathered here to beseech the beloved spirit of Anthony Venable, departed from this life one month and five days ago, to honor us with its presence. We entreat you, we who mourn your untimely loss, we beg you to make yourself known to those who revere you, those who love you, through the medium of this blessed woman's hand."

The silence was thick, deafening. The medium's body slumped back in her chair, her free hand with the planchette still on the pad.

Everyone jumped.

The acolyte whispered, "Is the spirit present?"

Nothing happened. There was a pulsing in the room as if every heart was beating furiously in unison.

"Is the beloved spirit present?" the acolyte asked again, his voice hushed.

The medium's hand moved; the planchette moved across the

paper making wide slashing scribbles, then circles. Then a big swooping Y, which could be seen all around the table, appeared on the page.

"Is this Anthony Venable, our beloved soul?"

More scribbling. Another big swooping Y.

"Tell what you wish for us to know."

The medium's hand went into a frenzied movement. More scribbling strokes, and then four grotesquely shaped words appeared: TELL THEM I LIVE.

Everyone's blood ran cold. Everyone froze. Someone shrieked.

"Tell what you wish for us to know," the acolyte repeated firmly.

The medium's hand moved again, furiously up and down and sideways, crosshatching scribbles that were meaningless, as if Venable's spirit were fighting to get out the words.

And then: I WILL RETURN.

The medium's hand slid from the table, the planchette knocking against the table leg; her hand slipped from the grasp of the woman next to her, the circle was broken, but the message was left, written large and clear where everyone could see it.

I WILL RETURN.

Everyone looked at each other, stunned. No one could move. No one could breathe.

No one had expected this: a message, a promise.

A resurrection.

But on the surface, it was nothing less than that.

Still, the verification had yet to be accomplished. The acolyte chose a gentleman from the audience at random, and he painstakingly went around the room and ascertained that the windows were still closed, the door was still locked, and that there were no footprints or unusual marks in the flour.

"All is as it was when the séance began," the gentleman confirmed in a shaky whisper. "It happened."

A buzz rose. *It happened.* They had seen it. Witnessed it. Tony Venable had been there. He lived, he would return . . .

The acolyte unlocked the door. "You're free to leave."

No one moved. The medium came to slowly and levered herself upright. She glanced at the page on the table and drew in a quick, shocked breath. Shook off the planchette as if it could bite her.

"I hate this," she whispered, but even she was rooted in place. No one wanted to leave. No one spoke. It was as if they thought Tony Venable was still in the room and any sound would disrupt the moment.

The feeling was so powerful, so pervasive, Kyger almost believed it himself. They really thought Venable had spoken through the planchette. It was the most unconscionable mass hypnosis. Or something like that. Because there was no other answer. And Wyland was right—the thing was escalating exponentially. It was a marvel to behold, and it had to be stopped.

He made a decisive movement and got to his feet. Everyone looked at him, appalled. They would stay there all night, he thought grimly, moving purposefully around the table. He wanted to look at the spirit writing. He wanted to understand how, with all that scribbling, the medium had found space enough to write those words so large on the page.

The words looked like the lettering of a five-year-old. Or someone who couldn't quite see what she was writing and was doing it by feel. By gut. Did it matter? As long as the mystery was maintained and the message came across?

All over the city, the message would have been gotten across.

It was the most heinous deceit.

He strode from the hotel room and into the corridor and down the steps, finding a crush of visitants who were just exiting from the upstairs rooms, in various emotional states. In tears, in whispers, exaltation, discussion, argument, prayer . . .

Shit—it had even come to that? Every last page in every last room all over the city—the same message at the same time?

He had to know. He wheeled abruptly and raced back up the steps. Up one flight, he couldn't believe the need to know was so compelling that he was racing to get to room twenty-seven on the second floor before anyone left.

Too late—it was empty except for the acolyte who was just picking up the page on which the message was written.

LIVE . . . RETURN—he saw the words, similarly written by the medium in this séance, similarly disjointed, large, scraggly—

and he whipped around and ran up to the third-floor séance room.

But this room was empty, too, and it felt as if the air were sucked out, and a different kind of thickness hovered in the atmosphere.

There was no remnant of what had occurred there except for the blank pad on the table at the place where the medium had sat.

He didn't have a pencil. Shit. He ripped off the top page and folded it into his pocket. Raced out into the hall, looking for another stairwell to take downstairs.

Looking, looking—too many doors, too many choices—he didn't need choices now; he needed a pencil. He needed to shake the eerie feeling that pounded within him—

He could have believed, he thought. He'd been that close to succumbing to the atmosphere, to the will, the need of those around him.

He was too susceptible—and maybe he wasn't the right man for—

—*what*—? He stopped short. Down the hall, far ahead of him, he saw her—at the least likely moment when every nerve, every sense needed to be focused elsewhere—he saw her.

Or he was dreaming . . . no—he saw her, just a glimpse of her beautiful face, her chocolaty hair in a loose rolled bun, as she disappeared into a room on the arm of just one man this time; as she looked back into the hallway over her shoulder, just before the door closed, he saw her.

His delectable, edible virgin whom he couldn't get out of his mind.

The goddamned virgin who was as elusive as Tony Venable's ghost.

Help me . . .

Save the world.

He raced the hallway, too late—by the time he reached the door into which she might have gone, he couldn't remember which of the three or four it was along that wall.

He took note of the numbers—32, 34, 36, 38.

He didn't have time for this. He didn't need a slippery virgin haunting him, tiptoeing around the edges of his consciousness, complicating his life.

He needed a pencil.

He knocked on the first door. A man answered, not the man he had seen with his virgin. Not her room. He gathered his wits. "Could I borrow a pencil?"

"Oh, for Christ's sake—" The man slammed the door.

Thirty-two eliminated. Now what?

He didn't have time for this.

How long would it take to knock on three other doors. Shit. Damn.

The paper crackled in his pocket, the proof, the key?

He needed a pencil.

He had to see Wyland.

Help me . . .

He felt her pull.

Help me . . .

England needed him.

His needy, mysterious virgin would have to wait.

"I'm damned." Wyland stared at the sheet, which they had covered with pencil scrawl to bring up some of the indented impressions of the letters from the medium's spirit message.

He didn't need to see much.

. . . LIVE . . . RETURN . . .

"How does one stop such a thing?" he murmured. "And they wanted it. There was no way to stop it from happening." He ran a hand over his chin and shook his head. "It's the damnedest thing . . ."

"Hypnosis," Kyger said.

"Do you think so? Everyone susceptible to the same controls? Even you?"

"It's possible." Was it?

Wyland was skeptical. But the evidence was there. At dozens of locations around London, hundreds of people had received the same message at the same time in the same words through the same mechanism.

Some kind of mesmerism had to be in play: it was the only answer.

Except there had to have been cynics among them, and how could they, too, have been so receptive?

They had been, they were, and Kyger was proof of that, and it galled him that he had been drawn in like all the believers. He had been stunned, and chilled by the words as the medium scrawled them on the page. Which made it more imperative than ever that he find something to countervent this growing movement to make Tony Venable into a martyr, a saint.

"There's been nothing else?" Wyland asked.

"Nothing concrete. The coincidence of the sevens—you can't build a case against him on that." And Wyland didn't even know about the whore at the Bullhead.

If he even remembered what he thought had happened. At this point, he was questioning all his senses and whether he could even be effective.

Wyland seemed to think so. So it would be back to the Bullhead as soon as could be. It was the one tangible bit of information they had. The one place he might uncover a saint's dark side.

Kyger was pacing the room. "This is where I've come to in the month I've been involved in this. I've found that the common man thinks Tony Venable was as common as he is; the elite celebrate his life and mourn what he could have done for them; and the man on the street is perfectly willing to discuss and defend his every last word and action of the past five years.

"The fact that sevens seem to be a recurring motif surrounding him . . . or that they whisper in the streets about a death mark that was found on his body—there's nothing to take public there. There's no proof, nothing concrete. Just whispers. There's nothing negative, nothing against him, really. Nothing that would bring him down from his pedestal to where he will be renounced and reviled.

"It will not be his theories. Much as it is clear to you and me what he was about, too many people don't really understand the fanatical nature of his philosophy, and it's no use explaining it. He got to them first, and nothing will sway them from their devotion. It's as simple as that.

"And now we've had this séance, which only proves how well organized and determined his followers are, and which has promised nothing more than he—or whoever takes his place and bears his message— will come back to life."

Wyland was nodding as he went through each point.

"So it seems to me, I'm continually trying to grab hold of smoke. It's a funny comparison actually, because of course you *can* make something of smoke. You can inhale a mouthful and blow rings. And he has us jumping through them, even from beyond the grave."

"Exactly. We have nothing. We have smoke and evanescence."

"So—" Kyger said, pausing delicately.

"Exactly . . . you have to go back to the Bullhead."

"I thought tomorrow as soon as I can make ready."

"That would be best. It's really our only lead. The money you need will be made available tomorrow afternoon, just as previously," Wyland said, holding out his hand. "Good luck then, I'm counting on you."

There was just one thing more he needed to do before he returned home. It was by then around eleven o'clock, because he'd gone straight to Wyland's office from the hotel. It was too late to do much, if anything, about the edible virgin, but, he thought, with some subtle bribery and a little charm, he might possibly find out her name.

She was hallucinating again; she *thought* she'd caught a glimpse of her hired bull in the hallway just before her father hustled her into the room.

She felt a consuming fury that she was so powerless, and that her father had had her under lock and key even to attend the séance.

And worse, that could have been the Bullhead man within a dozen yards of her, and he hadn't seen her, and he didn't know she was even there.

He couldn't help her now, here anyway. And how on earth would she ever find him if things went on this way?

She had to do something. Her father just wasn't responding to the coaxing and cooing Angilee, and she was choking on the gall every time she opened her mouth.

She watched in frustration as her father shut the hotel room door firmly behind them. That was the end of that. The sideshow was over, the message had been imparted, and Angilee must go back into her golden cage like some performing monkey.

"Here we are," Zabel said jovially, handing her onto the bed. "Wasn't that something? What do you make of it?"

Oh, and he wanted her opinions now, too? Ha. "It was a big fake," she said trenchantly, hoisting herself up as best she could onto the side of the bed.

Zabel looked shocked, and regretful he'd even asked her. And then he thought she ought to be thinking what he did. "Really? It was so real."

"It was a side show, Father, nothing more, nothing less. Nothing, in fact, that I would boast about having been part of with any child of mine."

So much for obedience, Zabel thought. "I cannot wait to hear what Wroth thought. He must have attended one of the sessions, being as loyal to Venable's memory as he is."

Angilee barely heard him. She was thinking about escape, and how to get hold of some money and the key to the lock. "I'm certain he must have," she said abruptly as she absorbed what he had said. She had to think, and thinking about Wroth was just too taxing right now.

"Well . . ." Zabel rumbled, whatever he might have said petering off as she seemed irresponsive. "*I* thought it was really powerful." And she should, too, he thought irritably.

She looked up at him, hearing the petulant tone that said she wasn't paying attention to him the way he expected, and she schooled her expression into one of complete agreement. "Oh, yes—powerful—and mysterious. Everyone believed it. How did they do it, really?"

And all the while she was thinking, planning. Tonight, she had to get out of there tonight. Maybe the hired man was actually somewhere in the hotel. Maybe someone knew him.

She needed money, too, because if it came to that, the next step was she would seek him out where she had first encountered him. It wasn't that unlikely that he'd be there; maybe he was there every night. Maybe she could just hide out there until he came.

That was better, Zabel thought. "Very powerful. People believed it. I almost believed it."

" . . . yes, it was very convincing," Angilee said, furiously marshalling the points of her plan. Zabel slept in the other bedroom, which meant unless she could keep him from cuffing her wrist, she would never get out of the room or get hold of any money. "Almost . . . spiritual." How could she convince him to take off the cuff?

"Exactly." Zabel liked that assessment, which dovetailed nicely with what he had thought but couldn't express. "Spiritual. Tony Venable was very spiritual." With that, he retreated to the sitting room, and Angilee almost screamed.

She examined her wrist instead. Not too badly scraped by the cuff. Yet. It could be worse. She could make it worse. Maybe it wouldn't be a bad thing to make Zabel feel guilty about it. She began twisting the cuff against her bare skin. How desperate was she? That really hurt. It didn't matter. She'd take care of the injury later.

"Wroth will be here soon," Zabel called from the outside room.

Angilee's heart dropped. Never tonight. It HAD to be tonight—she couldn't stand it one minute longer. *Come into my parlor, Father dear.* But you didn't pray for the moment you could deceive your father, especially if you were planning to prowl around a whorehouse looking for a male . . . a male *what* . . . ? A male *bull* . . . to bribe into marrying you . . .

Don't think about it.

She kept rubbing the cuff against her wrist. It hurt now. She gritted her teeth. This was too drastic; no one should have to resort to such tactics. She made a sound as she dug the edge of the cuff into an already angry-looking red welt.

Zabel appeared suddenly at the bedroom door, and she dropped her arm guiltily. "Something wrong?"

She pouted. "This cuff is chafing my wrist. I've been wearing it day and night now for several days, and it really hurts. You need to give me some respite from this, you really do. Even for an hour."

Zabel eyed her warily, and she felt that fulminating impatience. Now she must beg. Fine, she'd beg. "I'll be good, I promise. I won't do anything out of line. I'll just sit here quietly, and when Wroth comes, you can fasten the thing back on again."

So she'd lied. She had no compunction about lying. Not now. Maybe later, if she thought about it.

He examined her wrist. There were two angry-looking red welts, just as she said. He looked into her eyes. They were shiny with tears. She was hurting. She was going to marry Wroth; she had been much more compliant in the last few days. Was there really a reason to punish her more than was necessary?

"All right. All right," he agreed gruffly. "An hour." He kept the key in his pocket. How would she get the key from his pocket, locked up this way? He removed the key, unfastened the cuff, and it fell onto the bed. "But I'm locking you in your room," he added. "Just as a precaution."

She didn't care; she pushed herself back onto the bed as Zabel left her, as she heard the click of the lock. She had an hour. A precious little hour to discover how she could impair the cuff so he couldn't lock her up again. And then, after he returned from his late night of carousing with Wroth, she had the rest of the wee hours of the morning to figure out the rest.

Chapter Five

He was in a similar room at the Bullhead, similarly furnished, lit low with flickering candle sconces, and that sweet, head-fogging fragrance clogging his senses. It was almost as if he had never left. He'd been here perhaps five hours, but in this place, night was day and day was night, and he felt as if he'd been there forever.

Nothing had changed, not the whores, not their practiced caresses, not his boredom. He was alone now, taking a break so he could gather his thoughts and figure out what to do now that he was here.

The Bullhead provided everything. There was fruit and wine on a shelf near the platform, easily reachable whether one was on one's back or one's knees. There were thick towels piled on the floor beside a ewer of hot water.

What would they provide their special customers?

A place like the Bullhead had its secrets. And they would be buried, deeper than a pharaoh's tomb. If someone like Venable frequented a brothel, any brothel, he would never risk his reputation and losing his followers by being seen publicly in such a place.

Even so, a man did have needs. A man who set himself up as

someone who knew what was best for everyone couldn't fuck a common whore in a common walk-up.

For Venable, and others like him, there had to be some special arrangement in a house like this, something luxuriously decadent specifically created and appointed.

It was a house of accommodation, after all, and now he thought of it, Lujan had even hinted at it, the day he conceived of the idea of referring him to Wyland.

... *A man's a man,* he'd said, *no matter what his position in life. You find them in the strangest, most unlikely places* ...

Like Bullhead Manor . . .

Maybe especially Bullhead Manor, which catered to men of wealth, influence and substance. This was a palace of pleasure that could easily render invisible a man who needed isolation, security, protection, discretion, loyalty, and wholehearted allegiance to him and his needs.

Where in the Bullhead would they quarter men like Venable, who were accustomed to the best, who wanted their sins to vanish like words on a magic slate . . .

Somewhere in Bullhead Manor there must exist a suite of rooms in which those men spent untold hours humping and pumping and indulging their every secret perversion.

And maybe Venable had been one of them, and he *had* been here the night before he died.

It was a theory as to why things seemed so insubstantial, and it was more than he'd had when he came here today.

But all the sex was life-sapping. It was automatic, on call. The whores wanted too much from his reluctant body. The memory of the delectable virgin exerted too strong a pull—she still occupied his thoughts, his energy, another ghost haunting him, and he had nothing in him for the whores.

And because he needed to be here now, he couldn't help her; he couldn't even find out who she was: all the bribes he'd offered yesterday got him nothing more than a half dozen surnames of the occupants of the suites on that side of the third floor of the hotel.

No help there. No virgins floating around the lobby looking to be rescued. He had even waited, spending the time before the bank opened in the hotel restaurant drinking tea and scribbling on a napkin the thing that most occupied his mind.

. . . I . . . LIVE.

. . . WILL RETURN.

The words were bone-chilling, even written in his own hand. They were meant to incite and arouse. To rally people, to infuse them with the longing to have what had been, to relinquish everything to what was, to believe the cryptic promise . . .

. . . I LIVE—he checked off the words . . .

. . . so that when someone would eventually step up and offer it to them, they would be primed and ready to receive it with open arms . . .

I WILL RETURN . . .

He checked that off.

Another Venable. What else could it be? Waiting in the wings somewhere was a strong, charismatic man through whom Venable's words and ideology would live. And a country waiting, hoping, praying for it to come to pass—that was the most ingenious thing.

It was such a disturbing thought on this bright spring morning that he deliberately crossed out the words in bold black strokes.

Check check check . . . no matter where he looked, Tony Venable was there. Because nobody knew who the next Venable was. He could be the man across the room at the window table. Check.

He could be the waiter. Check.

He could be the elegant elderly gentleman who had just paused at the restaurant door. Check.

He could be Wyland, for all Kyger knew. Check.

He had better stop this—he scrawled STOP in large letters—check.

He sipped his tea, now cold. No virgins. Close to the time the bank would open and he could access the money Wyland had arranged for him.

Check.

He looked at the napkin, covered with slashes, scribbles, words, checks.

. . . checks . . . Where had he seen checks?

He turned the napkin around. The check marks looked like

sevens turned backward. What? Sevens again? He was getting delusional.

Enough of that. He crumpled the napkin, paid for his tea, pushed the notion of sevens from his thoughts, and went to the bank. It was all the time he could spend on it. Any of it, given what he had to gird himself to spend at the Bullhead.

Maybe the virgin had been a dream, anyway. Sometimes he thought so.

Help me . . .

It was too easy to think none of it was real, and everything was a figment of his imagination.

Even Venable . . .

He now felt as if he were invisible, as if he were drifting off on his silky soft ermine-covered bed. It was the scent in the room, in the air, in his head. More bodies entered, sliding all over him, pushing, prodding, pumping.

His quiescent body was not immune. He got lost in sensation, his penis spouting like a geyser once, twice, and again. They climbed onto him then, the experienced and well-schooled whores, one mounting him, one between his legs, one at his mouth. There was no getting away from them at the Bullhead. They were everywhere, pulling out his pleasure, drowning him in sensation.

There was nothing to do but lie back and let it happen.

They just couldn't let a vigorous man rest.

She got out of the hotel by noon, and it was no small feat, with her father snoring away in his bedroom and Wroth due for high tea.

Her heart was pounding so hard she thought it would come out of her chest. Every nightmare pursued her—the worst, that her father had seen her rooting around his room looking for his money.

If he ever—

Well, he'd discover her perfidy soon enough.

Besides, he had more money than he could spend in his lifetime and hers put together. It was her one consolation. She wasn't stealing anything that he couldn't easily replace.

And he shouldn't have done this to her, shouldn't have just sold her off to Wroth. She had firm justification for this rank rebellion. Let *him* experience the sensation of losing something precious like he had taken her freedom.

She'd set her course, her determination was rock hard, and she wouldn't look back.

Defeating the lock had actually been easier than she'd thought. It was a matter of plugging the mechanism with a little piece of cotton. And thankfully, Zabel was in a hurry with Wroth due to call for him, and him wanting Angilee to be greeted in her proper submissive place.

So he was more careless than usual in fastening the cuff around her wrist. The tongue slid in but didn't click shut as it butted up against the tiny wad of cotton she'd pushed into the opening with the thin crochet hook she sometimes used to fasten tiny loops and buttons.

Zabel, thankfully, didn't notice, and Angilee made sure she held the cuff closed and tight against her body until Wroth had paid his visit and he and her father left for the night.

Even then, she stayed immobile for hours to assure herself they were gone, and only then did she unclasp the cuff and cautiously search the suite for anything she could use in her quest.

She had hours, she knew, but even so, they would eventually return, and Zabel would check on her to make sure she was still locked up, still firmly in place. The guard would still be outside the door. Her dinner would still be delivered, and the attendant would expect to see her properly chained to her bed.

Her father had paid everyone to spy on her. She comprehended that the day he'd inaugurated the system of chains and rings.

Yet another reason for her to revolt.

And this was the last step: she'd waited patiently for Zabel's return, for his requisite bed check, waited for him to dismiss the guard, to prepare himself for bed, waited, waited, waited, until she thought her nerves would explode, and then she waited some more.

And then, when she was certain he was in a sound drunken sleep, and that a bomb wouldn't awaken him, she'd ransacked his room, stolen his money, and she was well on her way to the place where she'd sacrificed her virginity to find the Bullhead bull who had taken it and to beg him to marry her.

* * *

Kyger was finally alone in the room, waiting for a precise moment which he didn't know when it would be, but he would know when the time was right.

It was a nerve-wracking wait. The whores had left him to his own devices at his request, but he couldn't count on another trio not being sent to him, by his reckoning, within the next half hour.

The Bullhead staff was punctiliously prudent with their clients' money and stamina. If a client could pay the price, the client was assured of twenty-four-hour cycles of unadulterated fucking pleasure based on his wont, his need, his price and his virility, all of which was precisely parceled out and automatically provided.

It made any kind of reconnaissance almost impossible. It meant he had very little time at all to implement the next phase of his plan, which involved dressing in dark, loose clothing and scavenging the hallways to see what he could discover.

Not now. No time now. There was a commotion somewhere in the house, at this late hour. And it sounded so close, too close, maybe even right outside his door. Shit. No reconnoitering, not now.

And the voice sounded familiar; it was a woman, and, as he listened more closely, he recognized that slurred accented voice, loud, aggressive, out of place. She sounded imperious in her demands—and to him, a little desperate.

She was looking for *him*.

"I want this particular man. He is the only one who will satisfy my . . . my particular . . . er—needs. I paid for his . . . services . . . not two weeks ago. I assume he's still here. That is the . . . bull that I want."

Damn and blast. *Her* . . . ? Here? Now?

Dammit, not *now* . . . he didn't need this complication right now.

Help me . . .

"You must know who I mean—I bought his services for a substantial amount of money not two weeks ago . . ."

". . . name . . . ?"

"It wasn't necessary to know his name," she said haughtily. "I think of him as—the *bull.*"

Kyger choked.

"Madam . . ." The guide's voice was soothing. He was paid well to be soothing.

"I want what I want—" *Ah want what Ah want* . . . It was the edible virgin pure and plain, and Kyger was torn about what to do about her causing an uproar in the hallway of the Bullhead, demanding to see *him*.

"Madam, if you only could—"

"Well, I can't. I haven't been here for a couple of weeks, and, well, you don't ask a penis its name . . ."

Enough—Kyger grabbed his trousers and jumped into them.

". . . and that was all I was interested in—"

She was bluffing, he thought, but she was making such a commotion it would be impossible for him to accomplish anything tonight if he didn't stop her . . . now.

"Madam . . . if you would just . . ."

"—and if you people in this—this—establishment don't even know who your own . . . bulls . . . are . . ."

Kyger opened the door to his room. "What's the problem?"

"Sir—" the guide said, his tone apologetic.

Her head snapped up. "You—"

"Me?" he murmured, mimicking her tone.

She whirled on the guide. "He was right here all along and you—you—"

"Madam . . ."

"I'll—" Kyger said simultaneously, yanking her arm. Useless to try to calm a virago.

"But, sir, you shouldn't—" the guide began, but it was obvious he preferred that Kyger did.

"I'm not . . . busy . . . at the moment," Kyger said easily. "It's obvious the lady has cherished whatever experience she had here. I'll just give her some time to collect herself, and then we'll see if there's anything we can do."

Angilee stamped her foot. "I paid you quite generously for your services. And I fully expect . . ."

"Of course you do," Kyger said gently. "And perhaps we will, if that's your preference. But let's be civilized, shall we?"

The guide held up his hand. "But, sir—"

Kyger shook him off. "It will be fine. Whatever the lady wants . . . I can handle her, if she will just step into the room."

He motioned to the open door.

"That's better," Angilee said haughtily. "That's all I wanted."

Kyger closed the door behind them. "Not hardly, my lady. Jesus. You couldn't have made more noise if you were a pregnant cat."

"*What?*"

"Keep your voice down. Get on the bed. Let's get this done, and then you can go back to your other . . . companions."

"You don't understand—" Angilee began furiously.

"I certainly do. You have dollars. You're willing to pay. I'm willing to fuck." He looked down at himself. The sun was rising, hot and vital. "Absolutely willing. And for some reason, you've—"

She barged into his diatribe. "Help me."

Shit. The one plea a knight-errant couldn't resist.

He pulled her close to him and whispered in her ear: "You don't understand. They're watching. Somebody's always watching. Voyeurs who get their jollies from surveillance. Wardens who vet everyone to make sure only the right people are given entrée. The people who make sure nobody is here who means to upset the system. So, pretend you're trying to seduce me, take off your clothes, get on the bed, and then we'll talk."

"You have to help me." Was she as desperate as she sounded, after all her bravado both in getting into the manor and then even finding him?

Her hands shook as she unfastened the few buttons on her dress, which she'd chosen purposely for ease of movement and, maybe unconsciously, the possibility of having to disrobe.

Everyone disrobed at the Bullhead.

He watched her warily as she began taking off her clothes. Her movements were innocent, artless even, because he still thought of her as a virgin; everything about her was chaste, restrained. She didn't like this undressing in front of him; she bit her lips as she dropped each piece of clothing to the floor with a little moue of distaste.

It was the most arousing sight, the peaks and curves of her naked body against the soft sensual light as she climbed onto the platform and positioned herself on her back. The smooth roundness of buttocks, her chocolaty bush, her ivory skin, her raspberry nipples—he wanted to feed and feast on every inch of the mystery of her. Take her down, devour her between her legs, root at her nipples all through the night and into eternity.

He couldn't touch her. He must not touch her, or he'd be lost forever.

He aligned his body tight against hers. Not a good idea. Too close. Too hot. Too hard.

Shit. *Shove all that out of your mind.*

Fine. Ignore the call of the flesh. He could do that. He'd done it for years. All he needed right now was to find out what she wanted him to do and do it. Quickly. Tonight.

He knew what he hoped she wanted him to do, but that was not in the realm of possibility. Or was it?

She was breathless, her skin hot, flushed, her heart pounding. His body was tight as a drum, his penis reverberating with the hot physical need to penetrate.

Ask the penetrating question, for God's sake. Get this over with and get her out of here.

Exactly. This was too dangerous, lying here side by side with an edible virgin who was trembling on the brink. A man had to be made of stone . . . and he wasn't. Not by any measurable standard. And right now he felt a yard long and ten inches thick, with no furrows to plow.

He was losing perspective. Losing his head. When had that last happened? Back to the business at hand.

His hand. He clenched his hand tight because the temptation to caress her glowing naked skin was almost too much to bear.

God. *Just find out why she's hunted you down. Ask her what she wants.*

He was going to say, *talk,* and just ignore his senses and his body, which felt much more urgent, needed much more than that from her.

Instead he whispered, "Kiss me."

She drew in her breath sharply. Shook her head imperceptibly.

And he knew he was going to blackmail her to get that kiss. He *needed* that kiss. "They're watching. You made the row. Everybody heard you. You wanted . . . the *bull* . . . here I am . . . they're waiting—kiss me."

He was right. She couldn't refute any of that. She'd come pre-pared to give up something; a kiss seemed little enough for what she was going to ask.

She turned her body reluctantly toward his, so that her nipples were hard against his bare chest, she turned her head toward his, so that her mouth was right there, invitingly there, and she turned her determination and desperation into this seduction, because if he had accepted money for taking her virtue, then maybe, just maybe he wasn't that virtuous and he would consider . . . help-ing—

He kissed her, and her mind went blank.

In a fever, he crushed her lips with his, and in that five sec-onds, he knew her, wholly and completely, knew her innocence, her reluctance, her taste, the way she could yield, could submit, could—love . . .

He pulled away roughly. It was too much. All that innocence. It could drown a man. It could swamp him. Make him blow just from the touch of her tongue. Make him pearl up with a kind of longing he hadn't felt with any other woman in at least two years.

Damn. Damn. Damn.

"*Talk*," he growled. "I have to touch you; it would look damned strange if I didn't touch you."

"All right," she breathed, but she didn't want him to touch her because she could almost feel the ache of his rampant penis, because she knew he wanted to, because she sensed for the first time ever how much power she could wield. Because if he wanted to sink himself into her again so urgently, then maybe, just maybe, he would—

She caught her breath as he placed his palm flat against the curve of her hip and began a thorough exploration of her but-tocks.

"They're watching," he whispered, and for one insane mo-ment, she thought he was lying, that this was his way to get what every man wanted, and she would never ever know if somewhere behind the curtains, someone *was* really watching.

And then it didn't matter. His hand was magic, stroking and probing and persuasively, forcefully teaching her the pleasures of a man's fingers inserted in private and intimate places that were so arousing, she made no protest and just let herself drown in the sensation.

And he kissed her. Concurrent with the voluptuous stroking of her body, he expertly stroked her lips and her tongue with his own, showing her, teaching her, arousing her still more.

This wasn't quite how she'd planned it. This wasn't nearly what she expected to feel after his raw plundering of her maidenhead.

She didn't know what to think. She couldn't think. The sensations swamping her body were too powerful, too compelling, and older than time. Her body knew things she did not know. How to move, to entice his further exploration of the hollows and holes of her femininity. How to respond to his kisses, what to feel, how to ask for more.

To ask for what she wanted.

No, not yet, not yet. Just let him keep feeling her naked body this way. She needed nothing else tonight, just this glorious descent into pure decadent pleasure. This was a man's secret, and a woman's downfall. All she needed was this, a willing man, an expert hand, and she would debauch herself forever.

If she gave him all this, how could she ask him to marry her?

And then it didn't matter. Somehow, he had removed his trousers; somehow he was between her legs, his hands cupping her face, delving deep into her mouth, nosing himself into her bush, pushing into her slowly, slowly, slowly.

She spread her legs, she grabbed his arms, she canted her hips all with a woman's instinct to invite that first forceful, penetrating thrust.

Not yet. Not yet. He gyrated his hips, insinuating his rock of penis into her by degrees, slow, slow, slow. Her body melted against the heat and hardness of him, her woman flesh liquefying as he pushed deeper, deeper, deeper.

He was there, he wasn't, not yet, not fully, and yet she felt every inch of him that fit and filled her with a fullness that took her breath away.

He pushed again, undulating patiently, slowly, gradually; there wasn't a word for all the sensations she felt as he worked himself into the tight, hot wetness of her.

Time stopped; there were no barriers. There was only the naked heat of their bodies, and the hot, urgent press and push of his penis to penetrate her wholly and completely.

And suddenly, shockingly, he was there, fully occupying her, thrust tightly against her hips and deep between her legs.

She couldn't breathe. She couldn't move. This was real. This was naked; this was what everything was all about—this—a man's need to do it, a woman's need to comply.

How bad was it really? It was strange. It was . . . too raw, too encroaching—overpowering, even. A woman could get lost in it. Come to want it beyond all reason.

Oh, God, no. All she wanted was a solution, a way to escape her father. He could marry her and divorce her in the space of a month, and she would give him pots of money, Zabel's money, if only he would save her from having to marry Wroth.

This didn't have to enter into it at all.

Except—they were watching . . .

If THEY were watching . . . them, together, their naked bodies fused in this voluptuous, primitive joining . . .

. . . with whose eyes watching . . . ?

Oh, dear God . . . she ought to just marry Wroth and give up . . . This was crazy, being invaded, penetrated, and occupied by a strange man whose name she didn't even know, in the best known brothel in the whole of England.

What did she think she was doing?

This was a really bad idea. She had to get away. The money she had taken from her father was probably enough to book passage back to America. She could travel steerage—if she had to. She could parcel out a sufficient amount from that to support herself once she got there. She could get a job, find a good man, have a decent marriage, a nice, if not luxurious life . . . but she could take care of the details later . . .

But think—she could be on her own, alone . . . *don't be scared*—she was so scared . . . she could—

He moved. She died. No, she didn't die, she swooned, the pleasure was so intense, so all-enveloping, so sharp that she felt as if she might explode, from the center of her being, like a firecracker.

He moved again, twice, three times in, out, in, out, and the sharp, hard feeling coalesced, peaked, and sent her suddenly, shockingly jolting over the edge.

Her body rocked with the aftershocks, one two three. She felt him folding her into his arms, taking the pounding movement with her, absorbing her pleasure.

What was that? What was *that*? Dear heaven, why did no one ever warn a woman about *that*?

"What was *that*?" That was *her* unrecognizable voice, a sibilant whisper, shaking and shocked with the new comprehension of the knowledge of Eve.

He moved again, a gentle back and forth as if there were no urgency; he had all the time in the world. For all of three minutes . . . and then his body seized, his hips ground against hers, and she felt his body stretch out tightly and pitch into the same kind of churning culmination.

This she remembered from the first time. His hot spew and the sticky flow of his come seeping between her legs.

And someone was watching all of this—this, which should be the most private and intimate congress between two people . . . someone, in this house of indiscriminate fornication, was watching.

It was an abomination. It was a different kind of violation.

"Shhh . . ." Kyger murmured against her lips.

"I know," she whispered back trenchantly, "they're watching."

He didn't respond. His face was buried in her chocolate hair. He wondered if he even wanted to know who she was, or whether she just ought to remain the edible virgin to him.

Because he fully intended to eat her before they left this room. Eat her and nibble and suck on those hard pointed nipples that were so tight against his chest, and just devour every last inch of her and mark her with his tongue.

His penis, still wedged deep in her deliciously tight vagina, immediately ramped up. His penis liked the idea of him gnawing on her perfect skin, sliding his tongue all over her raspberry nipples and rooting deep between her legs.

Oh, yes. Before he left this room, he would cover those tight hard nipples with his hot saliva and suck hard on those firm tips until she melted and broke all over him again.

Most definitely.

He shifted his weight so that he was slightly above her. He nudged one of her perfect breasts.

Immediately she pushed against his bare chest to stop him. "Wait a minute."

"There's a part of me that can't wait a minute. It hasn't forgotten it's a bull . . . and it knows exactly what a bull does."

The insufferable fool. Another lesson. A man was too full of himself after . . . well, *after* . . .

She took a deep breath. This was such a stupid idea, but she was here, she had found him, and she was in for much more than two thousand dollars this time.

She was in for her life.

"You have to help me," she whispered urgently.

"Anything you want."

"You don't even know my name."

"Oh, I *know* you . . ."

She bucked against him. "I have to leave."

"I wouldn't dream of letting you."

"This is a waste of time."

"Not after the commotion you made. Everyone knows you're here. Someone is watching. You can't just walk away. They won't let you. They'll come after you. No, you have to play this through, and then we'll talk."

He was scaring her, badly. She summoned up some bravado; she really was her father's daughter to the core. "Oh, I see. I'm trading . . . this . . . for your help . . . ?"

Was she? There had been a different kind of urgency in the air before she barged into the room. He'd been suffused with another purpose, a different pressing mission. And now everything had shifted in one direction—upward—and all he cared about was fucking her. Every which way he could think of. And he was thinking . . . hard—his body, his mind, his senses suffused solely with the sexual sense and scent of her.

What was it about this woman?

He wanted to stay embedded in her body forever. She was the embodiment of Eve, pure unadulterated temptation, made to be fucked, to be sucked, to be devoured by . . .

By him—no one else. And she was still so virginal in so many ways. That was the sticking point. He couldn't conceive of letting her—

Letting her *what?*

What the hell was she doing here anyway?

This was crazy. She needed his help. He needed to get on with what he had come here to do.

He couldn't move. Didn't want to move. Didn't care who was watching or what was thought behind the curtains, or in the minds of the miscreant perverts who had created this place and watched over it like Olympian gods.

He wanted this woman. No one else. Period.

And he had always thought himself immune to those emotions.

"You don't understand," he whispered finally, taking control of his impulses, but keeping himself firmly planted in her. "There are other things at work here. You can't make a commotion, demand a penis, and then say, 'Sorry—didn't want to fuck after all.' This is a flesh factory plain and simple. There are too many secrets and there are tight controls. So if you've paid out the money, you are expected to fuck until forever or they want to know why."

"All right," she breathed. "You can do it. What's one more time after . . . ?"

Jesus. Like it meant nothing?

He wanted to shake her, his overwhelming desire to *do* it again warring with his more pressing need to get her away from here altogether.

"You want help," he asked finally, barely mouthing the words and feeling paranoid beyond reason suddenly. "What kind of help?"

Finally. The point of it all. Angilee felt a wash of relief. He would listen at least. He might be mercenary, but he wasn't a bastard, and he was tolerable altogether in . . . other ways.

Like kissing. And . . . the pleasure she felt so keenly between her legs . . .

"I have money . . ."

"What do you want?"

They were almost mouth to mouth, so tightly wedged together because *they* were watching, but because of that, she couldn't really see his face clearly. Couldn't gauge his response, or his reaction to anything except the primal thing.

He wanted that. No question about that.

The real question was, would he even consider the other?

She wouldn't know unless she asked for what she wanted. She'd given away a lot in order to circumvent her marriage to Wroth, and this man was her first and last chance to escape him.

And now, she needed something, and she was at point with the . . . *bull* . . . who was still bull-nosed tightly between her legs, which made it hard for her to think clearly at this most important moment of the whole misadventure.

Maybe the best thing was to just say it, she thought. Another lesson learned from her father. Ask for what you want. Plain-speaking. A good old Southern virtue.

All she had to do was make it clear to the bull exactly what she wanted. He could only say no, after all, and then she would come up with another plan.

Later.

But why would he refuse if there was a willing body and lots of money on the table? She swallowed hard. He must not say no. The time to ask was now; he was listening and, she sensed, even willing to help her if he could.

"I want you to marry me," she whispered finally. "I have money. It wouldn't be forever. But right now, I need your help—I need you to marry me."

Chapter Six

. . . marry me . . .

The words sat there, perched on the edge of his consciousness.
. . . Help me . . . She meant *that* kind of help?

Holy shit. No.

No. He wanted to say it. He didn't say it. No.

"I will not marry the pig," Angilee whispered fiercely. "My father doesn't care that I'm not pure anymore. All he cares about is influence and connections. He doesn't care about *me* anymore. So I have to find someone to marry, and then he can't force me to marry . . . that . . . that . . ."

No. The edible virgin was not going to seduce him that way. Never. *No.*

She pushed away from him. "If you're not going to help me, I have to find someone who will—tonight."

"Now, just a minute—" Kyger pulled her back.

She bucked against the pressure of his arms. "I'll pay you. It doesn't have to be for the rest of your life. It just has to be long enough to convince my father that I'm married to someone else and he can't marry me to the pig . . . And I thought—I thought . . ."

"For God's sake . . . would you just—?"

"I can't—I don't have time." She kept fighting him, feeling too open, too naked, too vulnerable with a strange man who was nothing more than a hired penis in a brothel. She should have known. What was wrong with her? How could she ever have thought . . . ?

He wasn't going to help; she'd been naïve to even think it was possible. Her desperation escalated. "If you won't do it . . . then—"

"I know . . . I know—you have to find someone . . ." He tucked her into his arms with some difficulty, but he had to calm her down. ". . . just stop—right now. Stop—"

"I can't—I have to go . . ."

"Shhhh!"

She wilted suddenly, defeated. He was too strong, and she'd given away too much already. Her ill-conceived gamble had not paid off. Nor did she have guts enough to approach another stranger, despite what she'd said. It was just too risky.

She had no time anyway. It was over. Zabel had won.

And the stranger was staring at her too intently. She averted her eyes; she blinked back tears.

Kyger saw them trickling out from under her long lashes.

Damn and hellfire. He felt time seeping away, felt the press of her need and the urgency of his commission intersecting in a way that was going to blow them both to kingdom come.

He couldn't allow her to get away. He couldn't marry her. He couldn't take her with him where he needed to go. He couldn't . . . he couldn't . . . he couldn't—

What *could* he do to keep the edible virgin tight in his arms?

"Now . . . tell me . . ."

She sniffled and swallowed hard and whispered in a soggy voice, "We were coming to England because my father wanted to find a husband for me who was worthy of his wealth and position. But he had already arranged this very strange and unexpected marriage to Viscount Wroth before we even arrived. Without my consent or my even meeting him. And there's no getting out of it, as far as my father is concerned."

"You're American—from where?"

"Georgia."

The accent. The money. A buccaneer. Of course. Shit.

"And so you thought . . ." he prompted in a whisper.

"He put such a price on purity, I thought—" She didn't need to elaborate further. The picture was clear.

"Well, I thought wrong. He chained me to the bed, to keep me from doing anything else to spoil his plans. So—well, what else could I do but run away and try to find someone else to marry me?"

Of course. What else indeed? And—the words, *chained me to the bed,* suddenly registered. Holy hell. Now he was aware, he noticed the welts on her wrists. Dark, red . . . who the hell was this barbarian?

No, he didn't want to know—he'd kill him, and he couldn't afford the luxury of those emotions. And while the edible virgin would probably love that, such a drastic measure would present a hundred more complications he didn't need.

Jesus holy hell—what was he going to do—because for certain, he couldn't allow her out of his sight now. She'd scavenge room to room auctioning her body for the price of a marriage license and kicking up a new commotion, and his whole mission would go to hell in a handcart.

Just what he needed, a spoiled, wealthy Southern buccaneer calling attention to him. God almighty, how the hell had he gotten this involved with her?

Help me . . .

The magic words. He had no help. He had no words. "You could just say you're married."

"You don't know my father—he would check it out thoroughly. He'd find the clerk who issued the marriage license, and the minister who married me, before he'd believe it was even possible. No, it has to be real, this marriage, even if it's just an arrangement."

She sounded so forlorn, it raised every protective instinct in him. He couldn't afford that. He couldn't afford her, on so many levels, even if she paid for it.

How would she pay for it?

She'd run away, she said. She'd offered him money to marry her. She couldn't go back, she said. There was an arranged marriage in the offing that was so repugnant to her, she'd taken the desperate measure of hunting him down here.

How could she have even known I'd be here?

He pushed away from her this time. Forcibly. Away and out and apart from the temptation of rooting in the moist enveloping heat of her luscious body. It was too distracting. It was too seductive in a place where seduction was used as currency for things outside the realm of sex, things like influence and alliances.

Things she said her father hungered after.

Not a coincidence.

He had to get away from her. He couldn't think, and now he was thinking things he didn't want to think—

Like this was a Banbury story and he was a gullible fool. That nothing about it or her was true, and that the whole thing was a ruse to keep him embedded in her needy innocence and far away from the secrets of Bullhead Manor.

Shit. He jackknifed himself into a sitting position.

"Who the hell are you?"

She looked shocked, bereft even. She was a terrific actress.

"Who are you?" she retorted.

They stared at each other. He couldn't believe this was a betrayal. Her emotion was too real. Her bewilderment.

Nothing is exempt from consideration.

"You first." His voice was guttural, harsher than he'd meant it to be.

She scrambled to the edge of the bed, rooting around for something to cover herself with. This was the last thing she envisioned happening, this sudden volte-face as if she had transformed into something distasteful and disposable.

Especially after—*that* . . . all that . . . bone-melting sensation—

But that was a man for you—all in a night's work for him—pleasure and play for a hired penis. That was the point, wasn't it?

But it was the price of admission for her.

Already paid.

And where was her damned skirt anyway? Anything to drape over her nakedness . . . She grabbed a handful of material and hauled it up onto the bed and wound it around her upper body.

There, now she could face him. Fabric was like armor, and she felt as though she was charging into battle. She'd done something royally stupid, and she had to gird herself to pay the price for that as well.

Only she wasn't certain what it was. Something had shifted;

the bull was uncertain of her. Didn't believe her or trust her—or something.

Something had made him wary. Something she'd said . . . ? But how strange that was. The bull for hire in the brothel. Why had she thought he was somehow different?

She stared at him, conscious all over again just how striking he was. How austere his features, how strong and lean his body. Nothing about him, naked or dressed, seemed dissipated. He looked as if he was keenly in control of all his senses and wholly in charge of himself.

She'd thought that about him the first time. He *was* different.

So what was a man like this doing in a place like this? It begged an answer, defied all logic.

Or perhaps *he* wasn't what he seemed?

"Well?"

She hated him just then. For all his talk about mysterious watchers, here he was treating her as if she was being questioned at the Yard.

"They're still watching," she retorted. "Or doesn't that matter now?"

"Your name," he said implacably.

She stared at him mutinously.

"If you want help," he added as an inducement. He knew exactly the kind of help he would give her—right out the door and let her fend for herself from this moment forward.

No matter who she sold herself to after.

If her story was even remotely true.

It couldn't be true.

"Your name . . ."

She squared her shoulders. He wasn't going to help her, she knew that. "I'll just leave you alone, let you get on with whatever you were doing when I interrupted you." There, her best-mannered voice, reducing all that soaking soul-rending pleasure to nothing more than a passing intrusion. As if she'd entered the wrong room and seen something she shouldn't.

Exactly what it had been like for her.

No, it wasn't.

Damn. She couldn't look at him. She didn't know what she was going to do, and bluffing it out didn't seem the right solution.

His eyes bored into her; she could feel the intensity and the heat of him. She was suddenly aware of how formidable he was.

What is he doing here?

She slanted a look at him. Still waiting. Patient as sin. Getting more irritated by the minute. And he would just let her walk out of the room to her doom if she pushed a minute further. This was the place between the hardness of a rock and the hardness of him.

He wasn't going to help her—not the way she wanted anyway—but she had nothing to barter, with anyone, if money couldn't buy him.

"Angilee," she whispered finally. "Angilee Rosslyn."

Seven. It jumped out at him immediately. In her name. Both names. More sevens. Shit. Not here. Not her.

"Who the hell are you?"

"I told you. My father is an investor who made an arranged marriage for me to a most repulsive viscount. Why don't you believe me?"

"I don't believe you."

His answer was so stark, it shook her. It was as if there had been no intimacy, no pleasure, no connection. He'd used the threat of some mysterious *watchers* solely to get to her. To seduce her. To root in her and take his pleasure.

Never mind what she had felt. She'd felt something, but the naked sensation of their joining wasn't really anything more than primal instinct—and she was ashamed of having felt anything for him at all.

All she felt now was a deep searing humiliation, and she had to get out of there.

She rolled off the platform onto the floor and scrabbled up her clothes and pulled them on haphazardly as she lay on the floor.

He hauled her up onto the platform before she was even done.

"You could confirm everything I've told you," she spat, wrenching her arm away.

"Oh, for sure. You people are damned thorough," he hissed back. "You're not going anywhere. Sit still."

"No."

"Yes."

"You can't make me . . ."

"Son of a bitch—you're not a two-year-old. What man would marry a goddamned two-year-old? SIT THE HELL STILL!"

She flopped down onto the platform, fuming. There was a point where it just didn't pay to antagonize him further. And this was the moment. He was as furious as she, and feeling as duped and taken in by her. And he was a lot taller and stronger than she, so how far and fast could she run?

And how was it that everything came down to *paying,* anyway?

She turned her head away; she couldn't bear to look at him.

His face was impassive as he dressed. This was hell—a virago on his hands, and Venable on his mind, and no time to implement his plans.

He couldn't waste this visit to the Bullhead. He'd just have to work around the virgin. Blindfold her or tie a gag around her runaway mouth.

. . . her runaway body . . .

Stop that.

He paced around the room for a moment. She was dressed in that mink brown suit she'd been wearing that day at Venable's flat. He was dressed all in black in preparation for his stealthy exploration of the Bullhead.

The question was . . . he didn't know what the question was. He couldn't leave her here. He'd never find her again if he did. He couldn't take her with him—it was too dangerous, two people creeping down the forbidden hallways of the Bullhead in tandem.

Shit.

He had to take the chance, even if she was the enemy. He climbed onto the platform next to her and pulled her close enough so he could whisper in her ear. "We're getting out of here." Maybe that was all she needed to know. "You have to trust me."

"Like you trust me?" she shot back.

He pushed her away. He had no patience for this. She could be his downfall, either as part of the Tony Venable faction, or just as the temptation of a lifetime to which he could not succumb. It didn't matter. He didn't have time for her antics. Barely had time to accomplish anything with her on his hands. Better to just let her go.

"Fine. Then leave."

That obdurate line settled around her lovely lips. She didn't like that either.

"You have to behave. You have to be silent. We can hash this out when we get out of here. If you can't, I'll be happy to leave you to the watchers."

Her head snapped around. "What does that mean?"

"You thought that was a piece of fiction? I promise you, Angilee Rosslyn, they do exist, and you don't want to know any more than that."

He was scaring her again. And it occurred to her, hearing her name on his lips, that she didn't yet know his. He was still the bull, the penis, the hired man.

Her savior, if only he would take her hand and keep her away from Wroth. Take her hand and lead her out of this god-awful place where ominous watchers observed whatever they would.

He was still her only chance to circumvent Wroth, to make it out of the Bullhead come to that, no matter what he thought she was.

"I'll do what you ask," she whispered.

He doubted it. But he had to take the chance. He got off the platform and snuffed out the candle sconces. Somewhere deep in the manor house, a clock struck, mellow chimes barely noticeable unless you were about to descend into the impenetrable depths of the forbidden.

Three in the morning. *Bong, bong, bong . . .* the sound reverberated in his bones. It was too late, too late for this, too late for him.

He opened the door a crack. The dim light from the hallway sliced right to her feet.

He was a shadow at the door, he moved, and he motioned for her to follow, then stepped out into the hall.

Zabel slept. He didn't know how long he slept. He barely remembered falling into his bed the night before, after all the rabbling and revelry . . . it was all mixed up in his mind, but it was everything he had ever dreamt of. The inclusion. The camaraderie. There was nothing like it. And it was all because of Wroth.

How much he owed the man. And giving him Angilee was such a small price to pay. She ought to be grateful to him, actually. Wroth was a man of substance and ideals. He would curb Angilee's natural inclination to get her own way. He would mold her and instruct her, and make her into a fine English lady with a big house and a life she could only have imagined in America.

It *was* a fair exchange.

And it was only days until they would marry. Wroth had got the license, he'd found a church and a minister, and it wanted only that he, Zabel, prepare Angilee for her wedding with the appropriate clothing and obedient attitude.

Her mother would have been so proud . . .

Zabel slept, his dreams infused with visions of his lovely, tragic young wife. Angilee was the very picture of her. She'd died so young, but he'd had Angilee, and that was in no small way like having Mary Lee.

She had been from a fine old, proud family who had lost everything in *that* war. He had been the brash land-grabber who had bought their plantation and fallen in love with their lily-pure daughter.

Mary Lee hadn't resisted him the way her parents had. They hated him. They saw him as one of the carpetbaggers, as a man who had betrayed his country by selling it off to foreigners.

They had disowned Mary Lee. But she didn't care.

Angilee was so much like her, with the same stubborn heart, the same obdurate will, the same breathtaking beauty.

He knew how Mary Lee had seen him: he was her savior. He had rescued her from poverty and given her the life she should have had.

And all he'd asked of her was sons and obedience.

She'd given him a daughter the mirror image of herself, and then she'd died. He'd been inconsolable for months because all his dreams for dynasty and acceptance had died with her.

But then, for him, Angilee became enough. As much like Mary Lee as she was, she was also his, cast from his clay, his seed. She would obey. Eventually, she would obey.

And she'd give him grandsons from another man's seed. He could live with that. The right man. The right time. He'd spent his life earning and investing for Angilee. For Mary Lee, too, to show her parents that he hadn't betrayed them, that he'd meant all along to reinstate them to their elegant life, too.

That part hadn't worked. All the money in the world could not buy the approbation and goodwill of Mary Lee's family.

That part, Zabel cut away like a limb off a tree.

Angilee was not to know them, ever, and they would never know her, or that she was the living image of their dead and eternally mourned daughter.

Zabel believed in righteous revenge. It was enough that they would never see Angilee. And as far as Angilee knew, everyone on her mother's side of the family was dead.

And so now that her marriage was imminent and grandsons would follow, Zabel would finally take his place among men of influence and power.

It was perfect; it was what he had worked for and striven for—yearned for, even—all his life. Just a place at the table . . .

In his dream, he was seated at the table, and shockingly, Mary Lee and all her family were there. All of them there, in his big, beautiful brick house in Atlanta, Georgia, around his elegantly appointed table that was set with a real lace tablecloth, and fine china and utensils of gold.

All of them there, sitting and talking and ignoring him, the paterfamilias, at the head of the table, as his paid servants brought in the first course of a six course dinner, and his attendants poured wine, free-flowing, expensive wine, and still they ignored him.

Him, Zabel, at the head of the table, the head of *his* family—and they paid no attention to him whatsoever.

Blast them all, blast them to hell—Zabel stood up, banging his fist on the table so furiously that the plates rattled and wine spilled on the expensive Alençon lace tablecloth.

Everyone looked at him, startled, but worse, Mary Lee looked at him with reproach in her eyes. And then, in her soft sweet voice, *What can you be thinking, dear Zabel? We have another guest . . .*

He turned, and there was Wroth, grabbing his arm urgently. *Where is Angilee? I've come to see Angilee, and she's nowhere to be found . . .*

Zabel looked down the table, and Angilee was not there; she

was not at the table at all, and Wroth was shaking him and demanding to know where was Angilee . . .

And he jolted awake to find Wroth kneeling on his bed, shaking him violently, trying to wake him up, mouthing the same words as in his dream—*Angilee is gone, where is Angilee* . . .

This is a dream . . .

"Dammit, man—get your wits together. Angilee is gone."

What? What—? What was real, what was the dream—dazed, Zabel elbowed himself to a sitting position. Wait, wait—this was his room, the sun was pouring in, high and bright, flooding the walls with aching light, and there was Wroth, pacing back and forth, waiting for him to collect himself before he launched into another tirade.

"ZABEL—"

Oh, that man had a hammer of a voice when he wanted to use it and a hammer of a fist that he was using to emphasize his words.

"I hear you . . ." Zabel muttered.

"She's gone. You heard me say that? Angilee is not in her bed." *Bam* on the dresser. "Not in the hotel." *Bam*. "Not anywhere on the premises." *Bam*. "Nowhere." *Bam*. "And believe me, I searched."

Zabel shook his head to clear it. He couldn't get the vision of Mary Lee's sorrowful gaze out of his mind. It was almost more real than Wroth pounding on his dresser in a fit of pique.

"Nonsense," he managed finally. "I chained her up again . . ." Uh—bad choice of words. Wroth didn't need to know she'd been free of restraints for that hour last night. And of course he comprehended what was meant, exactly, by *again*.

Wroth's expression changed. *"Again? Again?"* His voice went dangerously silky. "Tell me, Zabel, assure me, swear by God, that you did not take off the cuff. Tell me you weren't that gullible."

He had been that gullible, and there was no way to get around it.

Wroth's fury was amazing to behold. "You have raised that girl for twenty years, and you don't think she's cunning enough to try to find a way to slip out of her restraints. *You* uncuffed her wrist? You ACTUALLY unlocked the cuff? Left it . . ." his voice was rising . . . "so the brazen bitch could tamper with it? Are you terminally STUPID?? Did you learn nothing from the story of

Eve? It's the first lesson in the Bible for a reason: how else could man learn that a woman is not to be trusted, that she is full of deceit and guile and only wishes to trick and topple him to his knees.

"And you willingly unlocked the cuff that kept her constrained . . ."

He spat disgustedly. "It is not to be believed that you could be that naïve. You should have cuffed her wrists behind her, wrapped her legs in chains, and then encircled the bed, *twice,* and then perhaps you could have been assured of the fact she would not betray you. Probably not, though. She is a most defiant and intractable girl, and you are arrogant beyond permission to think she had even remotely changed, that she'd come to heel. No, she wanted only to trick you and humiliate *me*—and so she has done, and she will be punished for this insubordination. She will not get away with it, I promise you. I will hunt her down like a dog, and I will marry her wrapped like a mummy, chained to my wrist and my ankles, if I must, in order to make her obey my will.

"And she will. She will come to obey, and then our bargain will be met."

Zabel struggled out of bed. "I must see . . ."

"There's nothing to see . . ."

Zabel hobbled through the parlor and into Angilee's empty room. *Gone* . . . the cuff displayed prominently, cheekily, defiantly, on a mound of pillows where it could not be missed when one stepped into the room.

Damn damn damn damn . . . damn her to hell . . . He saw all his aspirations disintegrating like smoke.

He plucked up the cuff. "How—?"

"She is a woman—scheming, crafty, sly"—Wroth's voice behind him—"who will not rest until she savages a man no matter what it costs her . . ."

Zabel ignored him. "How did she do this?" He pushed the tongue of the lock into its slot. There—*there* . . . something obstructing it . . . oh, the duplicity, the wiliness of her . . . and he'd believed her. His own daughter, damn her, he'd believed her hurt, her anguish, her willingness to change . . .

You couldn't believe anything a woman ever said . . . Wroth

was right. She must be contained and controlled. A willful spirit like hers—it was the only way for her to be happy.

"Where can she be?" he whispered, still holding the cuff.

"I'll find her," Wroth said firmly.

"How?" Zabel sounded lost for a moment. He still couldn't believe . . .

"I have ways." Wroth dug into his coat pocket and produced a pocket knife encased in ebony. He pulled out one blade.

"Let me see that." He took the cuff and pressed the knife blade into the slot. "There's something in there. She put something in there, Zabel. Deliberately, and with intent to deceive you, she put something in that slot to compromise the lock. Now do you believe me?"

He worked the blade for a couple of minutes and removed a scrap of cotton. "Probably from her nightgown—or a pillow . . . that shifty, sneaking, lying bitch. Treacherous. Disloyal. Unscrupulous—ah, thy name is woman, but you won't escape *me*.

"Zabel!" He barked Zabel's name, and Zabel jumped. "I will find her, you know, and we together will mete out a punishment that will bring her in line and in consonance with my ideal of the perfect wife. You need have no worries about that. I still want the bitch, and I will contain her and constrain her to my specifications. I took the precaution of obtaining a special license, and I could marry her tonight if my sources find her.

"So be of good cheer. All is not lost. I relish the challenge of remaking your lying, wayward daughter into a compliant and obedient woman who is worthy of my name. Put down the cuff for now, although I would keep it as a symbol of the perfidy of woman once we are wed.

"But—that . . . is for later . . ." He was at the door, in command and ready for action. "We have other considerations right now."

Zabel stared at the cuff, then set it on the pillow as if it were a crown jewel instead of the symbol of disaster.

How could she? How could she do this to me?

"Zabel!" Wroth's voice cracked over him like a whip. "Get dressed. Others will find her. Leave it to them. They know what they're doing and where to look."

There was no other choice. Zabel recognized that immediately; he had never been able to contain Angilee, never been able to mold or shape her or rid her of her independent streak.

And by this traitorous act, she could ruin everything. It was only by the grace of Wroth's stubborn determination to subdue her, and to tame her, that he would be saved. He couldn't take much more in any event.

And why should he, he wondered irritably. When did he get to pursue all those possibilities that had always loomed over the horizon just out of reach?

All that he had set aside because of Angilee; all his ambition he had suborned to his duty to his daughter.

Well, thanks to her unyielding need to disdain his authority, he'd be damned grateful to hand her off in marriage to Wroth. And then, and only then, he'd be free to plunge his fingers into all the pies that would be spread like a banquet before him in the aftermath.

Leave it to Wroth . . . little did the man know—and maybe he shouldn't ever know, Zabel thought craftily—that had been *his* plan all along.

It had just been a matter of determining what it was that motivated Wroth. And that had been so easy to see. Domination. Power. Obedience. Let him lead. Let him take control.

So easy for a man like him who had learned to sell near-worthless bottom land to Northern speculators for a flagrant profit.

Learn what they want; give what they want.

Let him wield the whip. He was positively salivating over all the ways he would punish Angilee.

Let him do it. Wash his own hands of complicity. Take what was offered. Easy. So easy. Unleash the beast that was Wroth. Why not? He was set; he was still outside—it wouldn't hurt *him* . . .

"Yes," Zabel whispered, stroking the cuff and smiling to himself.

Give him what he wants. Let him take control.

"You're so right, Wroth," he murmured in his most fawning tone. "We have other considerations right now. I completely agree. I will—I'll be most happy to leave it *all* in your most capable hands."

Chapter Seven

Kyger eased out into the hallway, pulling Angilee after him. It was preternaturally quiet—dead quiet—as if there were no sentient beings in the manor house, as if he were chasing ghosts.

But the Bullhead was never empty. Ever. And he knew that better than most.

They crept down the hallway in tandem, the thick carpeting muffling every footstep the way the house muffled every vice.

It seemed to him that it was important to take note of the details: the way the walls appeared to be one endless slab of mahogany, lit to a warm, glossy sheen by the banked flame of the gas lamps hanging intermittently from the ceiling; the way the doors fit flush floor to ceiling into the walls, barely noticeable except for the dull brass ring pulls. There were six pulls, six doors, including the door from which they had just exited.

And he noticed that when he looked closely, there were seams in the wall, subtle, like paneling, but nearly hidden in the grain, and that all the rooms were on one side of the building.

That in itself was strange. It meant the rooms all faced the inside of the house. But the opposite wall, also a long slab of glossy mahogany with those same incised seams, had no windows at all.

The hallway seemed to go on forever, but they were almost at the end, where there was a window and an intersecting corridor.

It was so quiet. The silence had an eerie quality to it; it felt ominous, disquieting. There was not a single sound. Kyger couldn't even hear his own breathing, and he knew it was coming fast because everything felt so flat and deadly, as though there were ghostly eyes everywhere.

Why were there no windows on that long hallway wall?

There were no answers here, not tonight, not for him, not with the added burden of *her;* he'd been a fool to even try, and his wisest course was to get the intractable virgin out of this place and figure out the rest later.

Easier decided than done. The intersecting corridor provided no answers. One way looked the same as the other, except that now he could see there were door handles along the interior walls on either side of the corridor.

All rooms facing inward. And not a sound anywhere. No conversation. No moans of ecstasy. No cries of rapture, no screams of pleasure. No sense of anyone anywhere.

And then . . . suddenly—

The sound of a door opening, and voices, in the distance.

He pushed Angilee around the corner to the left, into the intersecting corridor, and down on the floor, and then he folded himself over her.

Voices, closer, coming from the direction they had just come.

The guide's plummy voice—did he never sleep?—"This way, sir."

Closer, closer, closer—

They could never lie flat enough on the floor not to be noticed. The guide would trip over them first.

"Here we are, sir."

He was so close. Right around the corner from where they were crouched. One extra step, and he'd hit Kyger's knee.

The sound of a door sliding open. The guide again: "I'll send someone momentarily to help you prepare for your guests."

"Much obliged." A similarly plummy tone in response. The door slid closed.

And—silence. They listened for footsteps, but there would be none with that thick muffling carpet.

A moment, two, three—the suspense was killing—still on his knees, Kyger peered around the corner into the hallway. Empty. Immediately, he levered himself upright, grasped Angilee's hand, pulled her to her feet, and turned and pulled her down the corridor.

They ran. Around another corner, and another, turning here, a long hallway there—racing through a labyrinth of hallways—and getting nowhere . . .

Kyger stopped short suddenly, and Angilee pitched into him.

How was this possible, that there was no end to these hallways, and every last one of them led someplace else, and none of them led anywhere?

Anything is possible. Nothing is improbable in a house of secrets . . .

The rampant skeptic in him took over: the house turned on an axis so that the hallway from which you entered a room was not the one into which you exited. Rooms with more than one door leading into other corridors. Walls that were movable . . .

Shift things around, and every perception changed.

Moving walls?

Make a room smaller, larger, make a place of confinement, make it a haven. Change the perspective. Confuse things.

Moving walls . . . ?

He ran his hand over the glossy smoothness of the mahogany. The incised seaming. Could have hinges. Push on one and it might collapse into itself.

He pushed. It gave slightly.

Moving walls . . .

He looked at Angilee. Her eyes were wide, wary. Her whole body was tense; her hands were icy cold. She opened her mouth, and he motioned for her not to speak. It was too risky. What they were doing was more than risky—it was an invitation to disaster.

He should never have taken her along.

If there really were watchers . . .

Following their every move. Knowing that strangers who should not be there were prowling the hallways of the Bullhead . . . What wouldn't they do to keep their enemies from uncovering their secrets?

Cut them off. Confuse them. Send them in the wrong direction. Lead them away from the mysteries. Confound them with mirrors.

Direct them where *they* wanted them to go.

Corner them.

Kill them.

Moving walls.

Goddamn.

He had to test the theory. Dangerous to test the theory when he was hampered by the burden of the virgin's life in his hands.

Hell. He took Angilee's hand once again and motioned her to follow him. Now he walked slowly, down a hallway no different from the half dozen other hallways they had followed.

Deadly silence. Flat, hushed, eerie . . .

Flickering gaslight shooting shadows well ahead of them down the hall. Not a sound. Not a breath, not a moan, not a sigh . . .

Slow, slow, slow—passing a doorway, looking for a seam . . . and suddenly, he turned and shoved his body hard into the wall.

It collapsed inward, and part of the succeeding wall went with it. A woman screamed as a dozen yards of wall toppled flat down on the floor, revealing two rooms, both with the occupants naked, and heavily entwined and pumping hard, one into the other.

Screams, shouts, scrambling for clothes and coherence. Kyger jumped into the closest room, pulling the stunned Angilee after him, and made for the door on the opposite wall.

How many doors? It didn't matter—moving walls, moving doors, moving motives—

It was as if the house were a living entity, watching them, surrounding them, swallowing them . . .

Out the door into another corridor, quick down that hallway to the end, where they could only turn right. Running, running, running in circles, squares, running toward nothing and everything—running around yet another corner—

And—flat out of anywhere to run. Walls. Moving walls, cutting them off like an executioner's blade.

No windows. No doors. Just the wall. And distant shouts and loud voices and the sense of the enemy coming closer. *They* were the enemy, whoever was operating those moving walls with such vicious accuracy.

Kyger took the measure of the wall, gauging that it was some three feet wide. He ran his hand over the surface, finding the seam.

"Now what?" Angilee whispered, hazarding the question in spite of instructions. She hated this: rejected by him, depending on him. This whole thing had been a disaster. She wanted out of this ridiculous place, she wanted to get started finding that husband, and she wanted never to see the hired bull again.

Not likely, not yet. It was too apparent she'd never get clear of the Bullhead without him. Damn it.

"We do what we've been doing," Kyger said grimly, "—we *push* . . ." And he pushed, leaning his body into the seam, and the wall gave, folding to a narrow *vee,* just enough so that there was a space at one end, and they could squeeze through.

He pushed Angilee through first—"It's dark . . ." her whisper, barely a breath of air, came back to him. Dark. But they had no choice. There were no bells and horns sounding, even though the effect was as if they were breaking out of prison, but there had to be other alarms, other protections that came into play when security was breached like this.

He couldn't get in through that slice of opening fast enough, the rough edge of the wall scraping his chest through his shirt as he wriggled his way into the pure bone-chilling darkness.

There was just a sliver of light from the hallway in that instant, but it illuminated nothing. And they couldn't afford to crack the wall open further.

"I'm scared," Angilee whispered. She was terrified. All this silence, all this mystery, and she was supposed to trust him? Still? In the dark, groping around, walking into who knew what?

"Me, too."

The fact he said that was momentarily reassuring. Until he pushed the wall back into place and immersed them in the unutterable evil blackness.

It was as palpable as a touch. Pure wickedness, surrounding them. A blank nothingness, no beginning, no end, what it must be like to tumble into hell.

Except the Bullhead was such a paradise of profligate promiscuity, there had to be a way out for a sinner or a saint.

Kyger took a deep breath, groped for Angilee's frozen hand, and reached out into the darkness of nothingness, looking for something to hold on to, something to guide them.

But the underworld would have no markers. For a long, dark pulsing moment, he felt paralyzed, dispirited, disoriented, and he didn't know quite which way to turn. It would be like stepping into emptiness, falling into oblivion.

Or—the skeptic in him rose up again: maybe he was meant to feel that way. Maybe everything had been manipulated to make an infiltrator feel off balance and as if he was losing perspective, losing life. As if death was close, and he was powerless to stop it.

Power. Yes. It was all about power: the power of influence, greed, sex, secrecy, persuasion, corruption, and control.

All that power. Seven powerful things . . .

The power of seven . . .

Sevens everywhere . . .

Whoever managed the Bullhead made it seem as if they were invincible. But whoever they were, they were only men, with enough money, or access to it, to move mountains, politicians, policy, and Parliament.

To make a murdered demagogue into a saint.

There was nothing supernatural or surreal about them except the mystery with which they surrounded themselves.

There was nothing inexplicable about the Bullhead. It was the trappings, the silence, the exclusivity. The unholy covenant with those who paid to be invisible.

There *was* a way out. This wasn't a priest's hole. They were encased in a little prison of moving walls. And if one wall moved, then other walls must move. He had only to find the perpendicular wall and follow that and see where it led.

He reached behind him to feel just where the entry wall was. Right there. Very close. Something substantial, real. And Angilee— she was inches away, rigid as a stone statue, shaking as though they were in a windstorm.

He folded her against his body to give her some warmth. The scrapes on his chest ached. Angilee in his arms made him ache.

But there was no time for that—now or ever. They had to get out of there. And that was as much help as he could give her.

He reached for the wall, turned to his right, and with his out-stretched hand as ballast, and his other arm around Angilee, he moved into the darkness.

She felt as if the blackness were devouring them. As if they could step into a void and be lost forever. The only real thing was the warmth of the bull's arm around her shoulders, the pulsing of his breath, the firmness of his step.

He seemed absolutely certain as he moved forward, even though they were stumbling over each other in the darkness.

"Shhh," it was barely a breath against her ear, his body was solid against hers as they inched forward, but she hardly felt reassured.

How could she when the bull wouldn't even consider marrying her. It was a wonder he hadn't left her to her fate in that room.

Dear heaven, what was she going to do? Once they got out of this hell, once they were away from the salacious spell of the Bullhead, then what? Maybe it was best to keep her focus on that rather than the dark and the mystery of this place, and the stupidity of her chosen course altogether.

She couldn't afford to keep looking for a husband in brothels. Bulls in brothels were totally undependable.

On top of that, by now, her father would have discovered she was gone, and found that she'd taken—borrowed?—a whole lot of money. So it was imperative she find a way to simultaneously stay out of sight and find a likely candidate to marry her.

Or buy one. There had to be men who would marry for money.

Or she *could* go back to America.

Except, she couldn't count on anything once she got back there. Her father had sold everything and put all his assets into cash when he first determined they would go to New York to try to find her a husband.

And then, after that resulted in his failure to crack the upper echelons, he had conceived this misbegotten trip to England and somehow, sometime, contracted this improbable alliance for her with Wroth.

Well, that had obviously given him entrée to connections he could not attain either by himself or in New York. And the price, apparently, had been *her*, because he'd made it too obvious he wanted that more than he cared about who she married. It was clear now that he had financed this trip for reasons that had nothing to do with her, and she would never feel any guilt again about what she had done to circumvent his plans.

But if she went back to the States, she would use up a good portion of the money she had, and there were no guarantees she would find a husband, or that she wouldn't wind up working in a mill or something.

That was *not* for her, especially with her pedigree and her father's wealth. It would be far more efficient to find rooms here, perhaps hire a chaperone who could introduce her to the right people. Could one hire a chaperone for that purpose? It didn't matter: if money could buy anything, it could buy a chaperone, and then she could continue to pursue her plan to find a convenient husband.

It was another way out. It was a plan. And it was one for which she didn't have to depend on the hired penis for one minute more than it took for him to find a way out of this yawning oblivion of wickedness.

She felt galvanized, impatient now, her hands no longer cold, her body heated and humming with the need to take action.

Kyger felt the change in her instantly; her body was no longer slack against him. The virgin was nothing if not determined, he thought, as she shook off his arm, grabbed his hand, and matched her step to his. Nothing kept this one down for long. Not a bad trait in a situation like this.

He was walking very slowly as he felt the wall. There seemed to be no end to it. And it was smooth, without a seam. That worried him, because it might mean this was a stationary wall, and that the other walls in this enclosure were as well, and that they were trapped despite all his efforts to save them.

Hellfire. *No.*

. . . wait . . .

He groped around. No, a corner. He pulled Angilee toward him as he rounded it. Hell. This was pure hell. Blankness. A feeling of emptiness, futility, with no awareness of time at all. Every step forward could have taken hours, for all he knew. In an abyss of nothingness, time had no meaning.

They inched forward. The silence was like a feather bed, enfolding, suffocating, hot, breathing . . .

Or was it them . . . ?

Shit. Where the hell was the end of this thing? He was starting to feel manipulated again. Pushed and pulled *their* way . . .

Not their way, damn them all to hell—

. . . wait—another seam. He stopped short, and Angilee bumped into him. No—not a seam—

He ran his hand up and down—and there it was—the ring pull.

He pulled Angilee close and whispered, "It's a door."

She made a relieved sound.

"Shhh . . ."

He went very still, listening for any sound, anything discordant in the air. There was nothing. Just the flat dead silence.

He grasped the ring. A slight eeking sound, barely audible, that still seemed to squeak a little too loudly in the silence.

Angilee nudged him impatiently. But he couldn't risk sliding open the door just yet. He listened. Not a sound beyond the wall.

Maybe he couldn't *not* risk opening the door . . . He inched it open a crack.

Another hallway was what he saw. Of course. And low lights. Long glossy walls. Jesus. No end to the goddamned walls—

Slowly, he eased the door open just enough so they both could slip through.

No—not just another hallway. There was a bank of windows at one end of this one and an archway at the other, over which there was what looked like some kind of circular symbol suspended.

They crept closer, keeping their bodies flattened against the wall. The thing was dark, like shiny dark gray onyx, large, reflective, and perfectly round. Like an eye, watching them.

They are always watching. It played into the mystique of omnipotence. You couldn't help but believe it.

He believed it.

That circle symbol was eerie. It was nothing like an eye, and yet, the feeling that someone was watching was palpable.

Nevertheless, they had to move. They edged under it cautiously and found that the archway gave on to a low-lit balcony which overlooked a winding stairwell. Nothing else was visible except a faint glow below, and the ever-present darkness.

There was only one way to go from here, and that was down. "Come." Again, a breath of a word.

Hand in hand they dashed down the steps, halted at the bottom, again flattening themselves against the wall, holding and waiting.

Silence.

A faint, deep, resonant musical note in the distance. Where?

The glossy circle was suspended here as well, over another arched opening that was shrouded by brocade curtains and lit on either side by gas sconces.

Kyger nodded, and they edged their way forward until they were just to one side of the arch. He pulled the curtain a fraction away from the molding that framed the arch.

Directly opposite was a brass double door incised with indecipherable symbols all over the surface, over which was hung the same dark glossy circle symbol. In the distance, they could hear a low hum. A faint, deep musical sound.

There was a pulsing sense of something imminent. Kyger motioned Angilee to the opposite side of the arch so she could watch, too, and he mimed wrapping himself in the curtain in case someone should come.

It was such a chancey strategy, but it was something. In case. Because there was nowhere to run if anyone should come down those steps or into that hallway beyond the curtain.

Something was happening. It was in the air. The humming sound pulsed, like a heartbeat.

The deep resonant note sounded again. The brass doors cracked open. From either side of the brass doorway, figures approached, and paused, two from either side, each swathed in long, enveloping hooded robes that totally obscured their bodies, their faces, their identities.

A rustling from above, from the stairwell landing.

Shit, hell. Kyger motioned to Angilee. He should have known: there *was* nowhere to hide, and the curtains were no protection at all; the figures on the other side would see the movement of the brocade and know someone was spying on them.

Angilee's heart swooped to her toes. No other hiding place. No protection anywhere.

Seconds now to dive on the floor or throw themselves on the mercy of whoever was beyond those curtains . . .

And then suddenly, silently—a seemingly disembodied pair of hands parted the curtains in concert with a humming sound from above.

Kyger motioned to her urgently; they had seconds now to enfold themselves in the rustled curtains. Seconds to conceal themselves flat against the archway molding and hope no one noticed.

Seconds as the humming came closer and closer and a line of three shrouded figures, the first carrying the circular symbol on a pole, came marching down the stairs.

They didn't dare breathe, so tightly wrapped were they, each against the archway molding. If she so much as drew a breath, they'd find her. Angilee was sure of it, her body was boneless with terror because of it.

But even so, she was so much more slender than the bull— they would see him instantly, and they would kill him. That large a man could not squeeze himself that flat against the molding. He just couldn't. He'd be obvious. He'd be dead, and then what would she do?

She didn't know how she could stand it, listening to the hum, feeling the sense of bodies close to her, passing her, and not knowing if they had found him.

How could she not peek?

It was impossible not to look. She had to know. Keeping the fold of curtain wrapped around her, she eased herself downward by increments, until she was just lower than eye level where any movement would be less likely to be noticed.

Now she could risk it—she didn't know if she could risk it— she had to risk it. She eased the edge of the curtain back from the molding.

Just a peek . . .

A quick glance—

She froze.

There were seven figures—three lined up between the curtains, two on either side of the brass door. A low, golden glow from beyond the open doors, and limned in the entrance, an ornately decorated bier. No coffin, just the bier.

And the pulsing hum. The deep musical note that resonated in her vitals each time it was struck.

And eerie, amorphous, anonymous figures, moving—floating—slowly, the figure with the symbol leading the way, moving through the curtains, and pushing the bier through the brass doors, followed by the others in slow, sonorous steps, each of them intent on the ceremony, not in the least looking for intruders and infidels.

Who was the infidel after all? It was not the bull, still safely hidden.

Her heart pounded painfully. She knew. She would never tell.

She watched with increasing apprehension as the last of the figures turned and pulled the curtains together, and then vanished beyond the brass doors, which then closed emphatically behind him.

The low musical note sounded again.

And then silence. That flat, dead silence of the damned.

She didn't know if she should move. If some other one of the hooded robed figures might still be on the stairs or guarding the doors, keeping the secrets somewhere that she couldn't see.

And where was *he*?

Who was he?

Minutes ticked by. Not a sound. Not a breath.

And then suddenly—a touch—she jumped; she stifled a shriek—he was right there, his hand on her arm, pulling her out from her hiding place and motioning her to be quiet.

She hated not being able to talk, not being able to try to make sense of what had happened, what they'd seen, what they thought, but perhaps it was better this way. It was still too spooky, unnatural, macabre.

She nodded, and he motioned for her to follow him. He did not go through the curtain. Or perhaps it was too dangerous to chance it.

Rather, he led her into the dark shadows under the curve of

the stairway, pulled her close against the wall, and whispered tightly, "Doorway over there. Just found it. Not safe upstairs . . ."

She nodded, and he moved her aside, and there magically, was a small arched doorway. He took a deep breath and opened it, and they stepped onto a small landing leading to a narrow, metal circular staircase.

Circles again. Circles and sevens. What the hell had that all been about?

"No moving walls," Kyger whispered. "Maybe storerooms . . ."

Or maybe a coal chute or door out where stores were delivered . . . an exit from which no one could find them or follow them.

He could only hope.

Especially after seeing those grown men dressing in costumes, playing boys' games and pushing around a bier in the most expensive whorehouse in the country. Surely this wasn't one of the sacrosanct secrets of Bullhead Manor. God, he hoped not.

There wasn't any way to investigate that now in any event. And his time had run out: he had to get the intractable virgin out of there and fast.

He started down the steps with her following carefully behind. They heard that low, sonorous musical note sounding in the distance above them as they went downward toward yet another low flickering light.

The basement storerooms, but in which part of the house Kyger couldn't tell. Stone walls. Dirt floor. Icy cold. Bins and storage areas as far as they could see in the dim low light which petered out a couple dozen yards farther down.

"Talk?" Angilee mouthed.

He shook his head. "Come . . ."

Swiftly, toward the dark, and beyond, they followed the wooden supports, toward the cold air seeping in toward them, blowing colder as they got closer to a different kind of oblivion.

What if there were no way out?

There was always a way out.

Was there?

What if every which way you could escape was designed to confuse and confound? What if someone were waiting for them on the outside?

It was so cold, there was no light; there was only the blowing air and the wooden supports and Kyger's certainty that they would eventually get out of there.

No wavering now.

Angilee followed blindly, tripping over her skirts, so exhausted she felt like crying. This was not how this adventure was supposed to have ended. She was supposed to have left by the front door with the hired bull in tow, a willing accomplice to her scheme to marry him.

If she ever got out of this . . . but that was for consideration later. The reality was the cold, the damp, the dark. Always the dark. And the mystery and the hovering sense of danger, and the underlying terror of the watching eyes.

And the endless hallways and basements of Bullhead Manor.

Closer and closer they came to the spewing air, moving carefully and cautiously, wooden post by wooden post.

It was a curiously empty section of basement and storage rooms. Nothing was kept here, not food, fuel, or fodder.

Because . . . ?

Kyger's step quickened.

. . . *because it was the entrance for that concealed stairway into the house . . . ?*

It had to be . . . he started running . . . but he didn't know what it meant; he didn't care . . . it had to be, and it meant that somewhere farther down in this maze of an empty basement there was a way to get outside—

Angilee sprinted after him as he ran toward the blowing air. And so, they nearly crashed into a rustic door in a far wall that was just slightly ajar. The wind was whistling through almost as if it were human, and he had a moment's pause before he yanked it open all the way, and they burst through the doorway into the safe night air.

They ran into the wind, and they didn't stop running until they were far and away from the house, away from the danger and the eyes and entryways that were made for sin and secrecy.

Angilee collapsed first, and Kyger followed, burying his face in the freezing dirt of the field, both of them panting, gasping for breath.

"Oh, my God," Angilee whispered. "Oh, my God."

Kyger levered himself to his feet. "We don't have time. We have to get off the grounds and get back to London somehow."

Oh, God—how insurmountable a task was that?

Only Kyger knew. He turned and looked at the gleaming lights of the Bullhead. As innocent as sin. A fine family could have lived there. Lives could have played out there, happy and moral. Instead it was a monument to vice and voluptuaries. And duplicity and intrigues that had yet to be laid bare.

"Let's go," he said brusquely, holding out his hand.

"I can't."

"You have to."

"I'm cold." She felt as if the wind was cutting through her clothes.

Cold and windy in the fields, and she had no cloak or cape, and her boots were in no way made for walking. And yet she knew he would make her walk no matter what she wanted or how she felt.

And then he'd just abandon her.

"Take my coat, then. We need to get farther away from here." He stripped off his frock coat and put it around her shoulders.

"But you'll be cold . . ." she protested faintly, but she put her arms through the sleeves and was immediately suffused with the residual heat from his body.

"That's of no consequence. Come, we'll go as far as we can, whatever that will be."

She looked up at him even though she couldn't really see him. He was a dark bulk standing over her. He was such an odd lot of contradictions—greedy and considerate, aloof and kind—but he represented safety for the moment, and she wished he would take her hand in marriage as well because she just might feel safe with him.

But those were stupid things to be thinking right now. They could freeze in the early morning wind, and probably it was better to keep moving even if they did not progress all that far.

She took his hand, got to her feet, and they began walking.

The only vestige of light was behind them, coming from the house. Before them, dead darkness. No sense of any direction. No road. Thick, hard frozen dirt under their feet.

Angilee stumbled now and again as she stubbed her toes

against a rock, an odd branch, and Kyger ruthlessly hauled her up and pushed her forward.

He was so strong, so certain. Almost superhuman in that he didn't feel the cold, and he had the stamina to keep going.

The stamina to—

Don't think about that . . .

Where were they going? It seemed to Angilee that the darkness outside was every bit a void of nothingness as it had been inside. And she couldn't take much more. And she was weighted down by the money, which she had so cleverly inserted into the lining of her skirt.

She was so tired. She wanted to stop, to rest. He was holding her hand, pulling her after him, and she wanted to protest, but she didn't because, it came to her again, she didn't even know his name.

Exactly. All of a piece in this god-awful adventure. She didn't know his name. Why should she know the name of a hired penis who didn't think she was good enough to marry?

It was too much he knew hers.

She never wanted to see him again if and after . . . after—

A sound. Her heart leapt. It was a thick, dull sound coming from behind them. It sounded like horses racing through the fields. It sounded like escape was what it sounded like.

She yanked on his hand, signaling him to stop. He turned and looked into the wind, saw what she saw: movement coming toward them, the bulk of what could have been a carriage, horses, making toward them, targeting them—knowing they were there.

Goddamn.

He turned and started to run, pulling her after him, knowing full well there was nowhere to run because whoever was driving that carriage at that ferocious clip knew they were there.

Someone was coming after them. And there was nowhere to run. They were out in the open, with no bushes, copses, haystacks to hide behind. They were too out in the open. It was futile to run.

Finally, he slowed, he stopped, and caught Angilee as she pitched into him. They stood and watched as a carriage came barreling toward them in the dimming shadow of light from the house.

Watched as it slowed, as it stopped precisely in front of them. As the coachman leaned down, tipped his hat, and said, "Do you care for a ride, mate?"

Kyger opened the carriage door so that Angilee could climb in. This was something he couldn't fight, couldn't win.

And he knew that voice. He knew it.

How?

"Where to, mate?"

Not back to the Bullhead? This was passing strange—God, he knew that voice.

"Going back to Town, are you?"

He knew that voice. His own voice was rusty as he answered, "Yes," and climbed in beside Angilee.

"As you wish."

Kyger closed the door. He felt exhausted and outmaneuvered. For the moment at least, the forces he was fighting had won.

Why had they let them go?

The rock and roll of the carriage as it bumped its way through the field and onto the road was lulling. Angilee slumped against him, utterly fatigued. He closed his eyes—just for a little while— while he tried to unknot the problem of where he had heard that voice.

Whose voice?

He slept.

And then suddenly, he jolted awake, and he wasn't certain if it was because the carriage was curiously still or because he remembered.

He remembered: the informant all those days ago, the beating, being left in Cheapside.

Oh, God—the Good Samaritan. A wad of pound notes—he could almost feel them in his hand. Promising to repay the man's skepticism, in his delirium.

And he hadn't gone back; he'd totally forgotten.

Where had he said to go? Seven? Seven . . . *Goddamn always sevens* . . . Swans—? S . . . ters . . . Sisters—

Right. And then that coach suddenly appearing out of nowhere.

Not this coach which, strangely, wasn't moving now—

But that coach, suddenly looming down the street like the Samaritan had conjured it, or signaled to it?

No, he had to have dreamt that. He had been half conscious that night; he wasn't remembering things right—

But he was nearly certain about this: the coachman that night had been the same coachman as tonight, their most accommodating driver . . .

Chapter Eight

He erupted out of the coach into the dead flat nothingness of a soupy gray fog, with barely the flicker of street lamp visible. But this much he could see: the coach was parked by the side of a road, and their driver and the horses were gone.

Hellfire. He whirled around. He couldn't see a foot in front of him. They could be in Cheapside for all he knew, or, but for the little flick of light, stranded on Brompton Moor.

Shit—and if they were in Cheapside—?

They'd get a cab at daylight. That couldn't be far off. Except he couldn't tell what hour it might be, and he couldn't wait for a solution to present itself.

He felt his way around to the opposite side of the coach, and then he cautiously started forward.

Wait—his boot nudged into a curb. Curbs were in the city. Curbs presumed walkways. They weren't in the center of London because there was no traffic, no noise.

So—The Gardens? Why not? The driver knew exactly where to take him . . .

To hell and over. Damn. Shit. He inched up over the curb, his hands out, reaching through the fog for something to grasp on to.

A fence. Ah, more like it. He inched along the fence until he came to the gate. Everything familiar. Goddamn. He wasn't steps away from his own flat.

Why had he been returned home?

He made his way back to the carriage, hoisted himself inside, and roused Angilee.

"Come."

She awakened with a jolt. "What? Where?"

"My flat," he said flatly. "It's the best I can do right now."

She was aware enough to know she didn't want that. "No—no—tell them to take me to . . ." She peered out the window. Oh, God. It was hell all over again, all foggy smoke, and there was no exit and they were doomed.

"Shhh—" He wrapped his arm around her. She was shivering; his coat was still on the seat, and he reached to retrieve it. "Come."

She came, blindly holding on to him, clambering awkwardly out of the carriage because she was still half asleep and disoriented, and because his arm was so warm around her shoulders and he just compelled her to move forward when she hit the ground.

The fog was so dense, it seemed to swallow them; he moved her gently around the carriage—something about the carriage wasn't quite right, she thought dimly—up onto a walkway, edging forward slowly, slowly, slowly, not a thing visible, everything fuzzy, and with big and bulky things rising up suddenly like ghosts out of the fog—

And then—a turn, the faint glow of gaslight, stone under her feet, and up a small stoop, and into—oh, blessed warmth. A hallway, lit by a banister lamp, dark woodwork, wainscoting, papered walls, a runner up a flight of steps, a door opening, and into a room. A parlor kind of room, she saw fuzzily, when Kyger turned up the gaslight just a flick.

"Come." Into a bedroom—oh, no, no no no—"shhhh . . ." onto the bed, his bed?

She wasn't going to be bedded ever again unless there was marriage in the offing, and really, she needed to get to that hotel and make her arrangements and find that chaperone—she resisted even as she toppled into it—but oh, the bed was so soft, so comfortable, and suddenly there was a blanket being tucked around her so gently—

Maybe she could stay—just for a while, until she rested and the cold seeped out of her bones and . . . and—

She was sound asleep, almost instantly, looking as innocent as a child. Not a child, Kyger thought mordantly. Not quite a woman, perhaps, but as sensual, alluring, and fascinating as the moon.

Help me . . .

He had to withstand her plea. He could watch over her tonight, he thought. He could get her wherever she wanted to go tomorrow. He couldn't do anything else for her, though God knew—no.

No. He wasn't ready. There were other considerations. And there was that distant memory of another woman, which had been relegated to a place in his heart where he could keep it warm and safe . . .

Don't think about it—

He pulled a chair close to the bed. Got a spare blanket and pillow from the armoire. Turned out the light. Folded himself into the chair.

Now he could take the time to try to make sense of what happened today. Except nothing made sense—not her appearance, not what they had seen at the Bullhead, not the circles and sevens, or the moving walls, not the reappearance of the ghostly driver . . .

None of it—

SHIT—

He jumped out of the chair and dove for the parlor window which overlooked the street.

Shit. Damn. Hell. He should have known; he should have kept watch—it was all of a piece, and he should have known, but it was too late now . . .

In those few minutes that he'd gotten her settled, when his mind was preoccupied and his back was to the window wall—in those few minutes, just enough time had passed that the fog had lifted slightly, and what was there was what he should have foreseen: the street was empty, and the coach was gone.

What the hell . . . ?

He was too tired to think, too disoriented to make sense of anything, let alone the mysteries of the Bullhead or how a bloody coach, horses, and driver could disappear into thin air.

But the edible virgin—she was the biggest mystery of all, coming out of the fog and into his world in ways that were too intrusive, distracting, and maybe deliberate.

What was he going to do with her?

She was so beautiful and more intriguing than she ought to be. She was limp as a rag doll lying sprawled on his bed, her hair flowing like melted chocolate all over his pillows. *His* pillows. His place, marking his territory the way he had marked her.

He felt his gut tighten. Immediately, he wanted her. Instantly, he remembered mounting her, pushing into her, breaching all her barriers, being enveloped by her, held by her, worn by her . . .

Hell and damn . . .

She was the personification of Eve, as tempting as sin, as disturbing as fire, sent to make him burn, to melt him to ashes.

Shit. He got up and started pacing. He didn't know quite where to go from here. He was so tired and so galvanized. He wanted to sleep, but he couldn't, because he was certain as stones in the morning he'd find her gone.

But that's what you want . . .

No, what he wanted was *her*.

NOW.

What he needed was another day—to think, to plan, to comprehend what was happening, to make sense of everything, to make sense of *her*.

But how could he spare another day, when he was so tired and so gut-bustingly aroused, and he couldn't be sure she wouldn't sneak away when he was asleep?

What did he have that she wanted, now that he'd taken her virginity and her money, and rejected her plea for his help while blackmailing her into letting him fuck her a second time?

Hard question. Hard him. He couldn't think straight. The walls, the danger, the robed men, the chocolate virgin who could be his enemy, mysterious coachmen, sevens and circles . . .

God . . . so tired—

He dropped onto the bed. If he were lying beside her, he'd

sense her movements; he'd know if she left the bed, left the room, left him.

That made sense, in that hard rock moment, as much as anything else made sense this night. The carriage was gone; there would be no answers about that until later. Later today. He could wait till later.

And besides, he needed time and he needed sleep. But most of all, for reasons he didn't want to examine, he needed *her*.

Angilee was not that deeply asleep that she didn't feel him easing himself into bed beside her. Her heart leapt, her body tensed, and she waited for him to move toward her, for something to happen.

Nothing happened.

Why was nothing happening?

No . . . why did she *want* something to happen? She was adamantly against something happening given that he wouldn't help her and she had devised this whole new plan that didn't include him.

Because—because—it might be a very good thing if something happened, she thought suddenly. Because she really didn't want to go out hunting for a ready-made husband. The thought of it paralyzed her, scared her, made her body run cold and shivers skitter down her spine.

To take someone strange and vile as her husband for a while? It made her skin crawl to even imagine it. Not to say she wouldn't do it. She was perfectly prepared to do it.

What if she didn't have to do it?

What if something happened here, now, and it turned out that he *could* be enticed by having sex with her again? It would save her days of frustration trying to find a suitable chaperone and that elusive husband she could even stand to be in the same room with.

Lord, she wanted the solution to be that simple. Absolutely. She wanted it to be *him* because he was already a known commodity, he wasn't strange to her, and maybe because she knew his touch, his sex, and his body, and he knew exactly how to extract that unexpected bone-melting pleasure from her still virginal nakedness.

Those really were all good reasons to try to seduce him into changing his mind about helping her.

If only he would move.

WHY DIDN'T HE MOVE?

Well, maybe he was tired. She herself was exhausted, and wholly unnerved by his refusal to help her and by their experience at the Bullhead.

He must be utterly sapped. So there. That was why. It *wasn't* her.

And besides, she was here in his bed, where she had least expected to ever be. There was still time. It couldn't be but very early in the morning. It was still dark in the room; there was hardly any light but that shed by the sconces. The fog seemed wispier, what she could see of it out the window, as if the rising sun was trying to burn it off.

He looked pretty close to rising and burning it off; there was something hot and ferocious about him, at close glance. And she was close as an eyelash now, and she could see, in the flicker of the dim gaslight, every line in his face, the grizzle on his cheeks, and feel the radiating heat of his body.

He was as benign as he could be as he slept, and she still felt the knife-edge of danger in him. If he was a seething voluptuary by night, he had it well under control. But he was a man who must need money if these quarters were anything to judge by.

Or . . . maybe this was where he brought his many conquests so they wouldn't think he was a man of means who really had the wherewithal to offer them everything they had ever hoped for.

But he didn't really seem like either kind of man to her. Yet here was where he brought her, and she must assume this was the level at which he lived his life.

And if this was the truth about him, then why would he refuse to help her? He must need money, and she had money, and she wasn't asking for more than the time it took for her to present the proof of their marriage to her father so that Wroth would be out of her life forever.

After that, he'd be free, with a substantial remuneration to fuel all the endless debauchery he could ever want.

Why would he turn that down?

A man who lived like this and squandered his income at the Bullhead could have no pride. He must be pretending, and she had misread him totally.

She had to try again, it was simple as that. She was here, and he was, and had been, her last hope, really. Her nebulous plan of finding a chaperone was as wispy as the fog outside and just as substantial.

This was still a much better solution, even from the moment she'd first thought of it. He had no right turning her down, really.

Well, her tenacity was more than a match for his determination. Yet another lesson learned at Zabel's knee. It was merely a matter of figuring out how she could accomplish it.

She was ever her father's daughter, she thought ruefully; there was no getting away from him, no matter how hard she tried. Everything she'd ever learned from him was always in the forefront of how she acted upon her decisions.

The answer was simple: all she had to do was put the problem into business terms, as her father would, and the answer became perfectly clear:

Make the bull a different kind of offer—and make it one he can't refuse . . .

Kyger jolted awake. . . . *What?*

Something was strange, out of place. The pillow was over his head, and he was hanging on to it for dear life; beneath the edges, he could just see dull dreary light suffusing the room. Daylight, still adrift in fog. And concurrently, the sound of hooves and carriages on the street. Movement in the house. Movement on the bed beside him . . .

What?

He threw off the pillow and was nearly blinded by the dull sun-glazed light of a fog-shrouded morning. Shit. What?

Why was he feeling so confused?

Because . . . there was a naked woman lying on the bed next to him.

Hellfire—the chocolate virgin, in all her edible glory.

Shit. Damn. Hell. He jackknifed out of the bed.

Don't look at her.

As if he could help it. The virgin was playing havoc with his mission and his life, deliberately and intentionally presenting her most edible self to delay and distract him, and he wasn't immune.

And he hated it. He despised her for it.

Goddamn it, he, who thought he was invulnerable, controlled and with every sexual impulse held severely in check, felt about as contained as a rampant bull at this moment, and just about as ready to rut.

And why the goddamned hell not? She'd undressed herself sometime during the early morning hours while he slept. The message, her intention, was clear, in every curvy line of her body, in just the way she'd positioned herself on the bed: the chocolate virgin was melting hot for him to pour his seed into her.

He hated that she had stooped to that. It made her just an everyday whore, not a wealthy man's daughter with an evil fiancé. It was a good story, though, even if it was wholly unbelievable. Even with her throwing around the kind of money she had offered him to take her virginity.

She was so gorgeous, a man might easily believe her.

But he just wasn't that gullible. And she was no different from the rest of them at the Bullhead. Just a vessel. A receptacle for a man's lust. Offering him the perfect paradise, because she thought another round in bed with him would bring him to his knees, begging to give her whatever help she really wanted.

He couldn't help her. He could only help himself to her tight hot cunt as she was so blatantly inviting him to do. Why not? She was here, and he was most definitely *there*.

He yanked the curtains to further darken the room, and then he unceremoniously ripped off his clothes. He felt no compunction about it. She'd been clothed to her neck when he brought her back here, and now she was naked. There was no misconstruing her intent—or his, for that matter: one look at her naked body and he had descended into nerve endings, impulses and lust.

He climbed back into the bed with her, aligning his rampant nakedness next to hers, giving himself a moment to feast on the naked whole of her that still beguiled him, in spite of the reality of what she was, and in spite of all the lies.

Maybe it was a reverse thing with her, and the way she got

aroused was to troll for men and pay for them. She certainly had come looking for him tonight.

Well, she'd gotten him. He was ready, she was primed, and it wanted only to wake her and get the games started.

He didn't quite want to do that yet, and he didn't know why. For some reason, he felt obsessed by her. He wanted to bite her, to devour her, to cram her so full of his penis and his cream that she would never want another man ever again.

Why? What was it about her? That thick chocolaty hair? That milky skin? That innocence, real or feigned? Her responsive body? Her neediness?

Her? Needy? She was as needy as a piece of iron. And just as hard and unbreakable.

But that was the thing: he knew it, he felt it in his bones, in his craw, in his gut, in his heart, and he still felt protective of her.

Was he crazy? He wanted to prong her *and* protect her?

God, she was making him crazy. And he had to touch her. He couldn't wait a minute longer to touch her.

He stroked her hip with a feather touch. Her skin was silky, baby soft, so caressable and tactile, he almost came then.

And then he lusted to come, to pour his cream all over her luscious body. He wanted to rub it into her skin, her breasts, her slit; he wanted to taste her and lick her, and burrow his tongue into the chocolate between her legs.

As he surrendered into the grip of that overpowering desire, she awakened, slowly and sinuously moving and stretching like a cat right into his questing hand.

She opened her eyes, and closed them again. Perfect. She had him right where she wanted him. His touch was soft, subtle, arousing. She saw in that glance that he was utterly captivated by her body. It couldn't be better—whatever he wanted to do . . . anything—as long as he said yes at the end.

She caught her breath as he insinuated his fingers between her legs. There was no more naked feeling than that, being parted and prodded by a man's fingers. Her body responded instantly, canting upward to pull him deeper, undulating to the rhythm of his pumping.

Everything liquefied inside her. Her nipples tightened, her desire heightened. She couldn't spread them wide enough to accommodate his magic fingers pushing and playing with her labia, with her cunt, and deep between her legs.

He made her wet, made her melt. If he could just—just what? She couldn't put a name to what she wanted, just more of it, more from him, more of the pleasure and the swamping feeling of losing herself, of drowning in sensation, in lust, in unimaginable pleasure.

This was what the Bullhead was about. This was what men paid for, the power women wielded. This pleasure, this full unfettered access to their bodies. Anything he wanted, anything . . .

She was climbing the mountain again, step by step, soaring up the mountain, up toward the heat, the crackle of the sun. It was so simple, so natural, just go to the sun, and let the rays dance all over your body and slide between your legs and—

. . . and . . .

—explode in your body, a hot shower of crackling sun and stars and the cool moon taking the sensation down down down . . . until his fingers stopped pumping and she could just burrow down on that hardness and rest.

"*Oh* . . . !" she whispered, she breathed, she thought, she felt—

Her body felt boneless, suffused with heat and well-being. She felt him kissing her at the hip, the valley of her belly, licking her navel, sucking it, her body shivering at every touch, twitching as he nipped and sucked his way all the way up to her breasts still with his fingers inserted between her legs.

Her nipples were hard, constricted, flushed an even darker berry color, ripe, succulent. Ready for a man's tongue to swirl and taste and manipulate erotically with hot, wet little flicks back and forth, back and forth.

She bucked her hips at the first fluttering of his hot wet tongue on her luscious nipple. Hard, raspberry, virgin nipples . . . a man could come for days feasting on them, and he intended to eat at them without surcease. They were made for him, these hot tight teats, his tongue, his lips would be the first to lick and suck at them, and after that, no one else could have them.

No one.

He felt her body go soft, and she spread her legs wider as he pushed yet another finger into her and pulled hard at her one hard, pointed, succulent nipple just with his lips, just the nipple. Just . . .

His penis spurted. He sucked harder; he came harder, his cream spurting like a geyser as he rubbed himself against her silken hip, as he fondled her deep in her cunt, and deeper still, as she arched her back, lifted her hips, and begged for more.

More was not a problem.

He covered her body as he sought her other breast and took the other ripe virgin nipple into his mouth and lapped at it with his tongue.

Just that—that one little movement and her whole body twisted beneath him, writhing and undulating to meet the sensations he created by just flicking his tongue over the hot hard tip of her nipple.

They were moving together all of a sudden in rhythm and unison, his penis against her hip and thigh, his mouth on her nipple, his fingers between her legs, moving with delicious little sounds of pleasure from the back of her throat, moving with intensity and purpose, knowing what the full-blown culmination would be of all that naked sucking, pumping and licking and fucking.

It hovered, like a balloon, floating tantalizingly above them, swelling and expanding until it was nearly impossible to contain it—and still it hovered, so distended, so stretched and inflated, it had to burst.

It burst.

It detonated.

It sent everything spinning out of control so that the solidity of him, the heat and heft of him, was the only thing in her world.

And then, as the sensation scaled downward to the rock-hard extension of his fingers, he removed his fingers, he mounted her, and he plowed his penis into her, burrowed forcefully into her heat and wet and the enfolding softness of her, and planted himself there.

The moment was transcending. Neither moved, both intent on the rock-hard feeling of him occupying her. She wore him with the familiarity of an old lover, the way her body received him, enfolded him, enabled him to root deep between her legs. It was enough, in those lingering eddies of the pleasure, enough for him just to be coupled with her, joined with her, wholly encompassed by her . . .

Embedded in her. The first, the only, the always. That was her thought. *Him.* Simple. This was the way it was meant to be. She had offered, he'd taken, and for his part of the bargain, he must, must, must marry her, and then, she was never going to let him go.

And neither of them had to give up anything. They both would get what they wanted.

His head was buried in her neck. Her eyes were closed, her whole being concentrated on the feeling of him inside her, mounted on her, rocking against her in that primitive unconscious way, as if he, as if his penis, were seeking, reaching, elongating still more to root deeper, tighter, harder.

It couldn't be hard enough for her. His ever-lengthening penis pressed deep down inside her. The nestling, nuzzling and nipping enchanted her. The feel of him rutting between her legs made her nearly faint with excitement.

Her body responded involuntarily, her legs widened, her hips moved in a primal dance of invitation. She knew these things. She didn't know how or why, but she knew them, and she knew instinctively what pleased him: her cunt tight and wet, and welcoming the forceful penetration of his penis.

She didn't feel raw from his using her—she felt as thick and rich as honey, her whole body sweet like molasses, every nerve tuned, primed, creamy with anticipation.

He moved.

An indescribable wave of pleasure undulated through her, poured through her as he felt her response and began the rhythmic pump of his primal possession of her.

This, this, this—there was nothing ever in life like this, this pleasure, the feeling of being joined and utterly enveloped and beyond herself.

How—*how* she could ever do this with anyone else, she just couldn't conceive—well, she wouldn't—it had to be him. He *had* to marry her, he *must*—and that was . . . was—

Was—is . . .

Her body seized. Her mind went blank under the lush surging

pleasure of him hard and driving between her legs. It billowed like a rolling wave; it caught her in the undertow and quickly broke over pure hard rock as she bore down onto his penis and let him carry her away.

He pounded harder, taking her response, pulling it up and out and into himself so that he felt the crackling body-scoring pleasure of her taking him and her cunt soaking in every thick creamy ounce of him that he poured deep and unceasingly into the very feminine essence of her.

Silence. A thick, sex-suffused rolling silence. The weight of him covering her body. The curiously enfolding twilight in the room. The street noise outside, reassuring, faraway, a backdrop to the permeating pleasure of him holding her, possessing her.

It was perfect. He was perfect. She didn't know how, but somehow fate had put him in her path, and he was meant to help her and save her from Wroth.

But he was so wrung out, he couldn't even save himself from himself.

The chocolate virgin was too delectable, too responsive, and far too confounding. He had no time to spend on figuring her out, he didn't know what to do with her, or about her, and he didn't want to let her go.

She had to stay with him until he could sort through everything. Everything. Her strange and unbelievable story about needing to get married. Why she'd come to the Bullhead—twice. Why she had been at the Venable funeral and flat, and who those men had been. If there were any connection between her and his mission. And all those coincidences involving sevens.

She had to stay—just for this day, because he had to pursue the clue of the Good Samaritan and the ghost coachman. He couldn't wait another day, another hour. He needed just this afternoon, if it even was afternoon—time seemed suspended and unreal when he was burrowed this deep inside her—just this afternoon to track down the Good Samaritan at the Seven Sisters and find some answers.

Which he would already be doing if he hadn't got sidetracked by—his lust for her.

It was a good plan. She would be shielded from the ghastly fiancé, if indeed he wasn't a fiction, and she would be *here* where he could protect her, where he could . . . feast on her, suck on her, devour her . . .

Oh, God—he didn't want to move. Everything concerning Tony Venable seemed to recede into the fog beside the fact of her here in his rooms. This was beyond anything he ever expected, and he didn't know how to cope with it. It was playing havoc with his mission. It was disloyal to old loves. And it disproved his imperviousness to the lure of the flesh.

Goddamnit, he was NOT like his brother, Lujan.

Except . . .

He was. About *her*.

Goddamn. Caught wholly and fully where a man is most vulnerable . . . that was the other thing—he couldn't afford this; he couldn't get involved with her, as luscious and enticing as she was.

And it was going to take every ounce of willpower to remove himself from her. To leave the heat, the wet, the pleasure, the searing sense of self divided and conquered . . .

Shit and hell.

He moved . . . and she immediately reached to bring him back.

He broke the joining between them, and he broke the silence; he had to as he lifted himself off of her. "No, listen. Angilee . . ."

Her body tensed. That tone of voice did not bode well. She didn't like him right then. How could he just unceremoniously leave her like that?

"What?"

"I have to—"

Of course, all men had to. She knew that. Every time a man left a woman, *he had to* . . . She couldn't believe *he*—the perfect *he*—was giving this putrid excuse to her—after all *that*. *He had to.*

"Me, too," she said stonily. "I have to also."

"Have to what?"

"Whatever you have to do."

"Angilee . . ."

She decided to give it one last try. "I still need your help."

He said nothing.

She girded herself, because she could see by the set of his face what the answer would be. "I need you to marry me."

He hated this. He felt a surge of need and lust. He wanted to, he couldn't. There was Jancie, always, deep in his heart. And there was Tony Venable, hovering like a malevolent ghost, haunting him, mocking his impotence.

And there was the fact he still didn't know if he could trust her . . .

"I have the money," she reiterated. "I can pay you. Just for a month, two. No more. I need a husband. *Now.*"

She sounded so true, so sincere. A woman like that, for a month, two, just his, all alone, in the sacred bond of marriage . . . forsaking all others—

All others. And his quest and his mission. His cause.

"I can't."

Even after all that pleasure? After . . . everything? She went very, very still. All right, then. She'd find that chaperone; she'd go into hiding until she found that other man. Somewhere. Somehow. There would be another man, someone she could stand. They didn't have to do *that*. She'd make certain he understood that, this other husband man.

"All right," she said.

He hated that *all right*. It was a dead, dull, flat, horrendous disappointment; he'd failed her, and for some reason he hated that, too. But there was no other course. None. Except that she stay here.

"No, it's not all right. It's just . . . there are things . . ."

There were always things. How much she had learned from her father. He always had things. Didn't he have things from the moment they arrived in London? *Men* things that women just couldn't understand?

"You have to stay here."

"I do?" *Not for another five minutes,* she thought furiously.

"You'll be safe here. No one could find you here. I need to go out for a couple of hours. Only a couple of hours, and then we can . . ."

A couple of hours when he could be with another woman doing all the things he'd done to her? After all, by all the evidence she had seen, he was exactly that kind of man.

What a fool she was.

"What—do *that* all over again?" she said bleakly.

"Angilee—I'll help you however I can. I just can't marry you."

It made sense to him, she could see that. The knight-errant who was the habitue of a brothel, who looked like a prince and behaved like a libertine—what had she expected if she lay herself bare for him in his own lair? Of course he'd devour her and spit her out.

She was such a naïve simpleton—maybe she deserved nothing better than a life of servitude with Wroth.

"You have to stay here. It's the only thing you can do right now."

Surely he was jesting. *Oh, fine, I'll stay, I'll be waiting, I can't wait for you to come back and do all that naked pleasure again and then give* me *nothing in return.*

Well, she was a quick learner—Zabel always said that sometimes a man had to fail in order to succeed, and that if you got nothing from the bargain, it was no bargain. She was the living example of the truth of that.

So what did you do? You lied. "All right. I'll stay."

"You have to."

He was so sincere, an absolute prince among men with a relentless penis-for-hire to prove it . . . and he expected to furrow between her legs as much he wanted just because *he* thought she needed him? Ha. She needed NO ONE. Not him, not her father. Not Wroth.

She had her own good common sense, foolish as she could be, she had money, she had a plan, and now she knew all about *that* experience that would come in mighty handy when she found that next man who would willingly marry her.

She smiled her best Southern lady smile. The one she'd used when Zabel was entertaining business associates, the one she used when they got a little too frisky.

"You're right," she murmured. Men loved to be right. She knew that from dealing with Zabel. "I'll stay right here until you can figure something out."

"Good." Maybe. He didn't like that smile. Maybe not.

Maybe she'd capitulated too quickly. How did he know he could trust her? Lust did not equal trust.

Damn. This all was spinning so far out of control, he couldn't think straight. But that coachman . . . he couldn't set that aside for another day. He had to find that Samaritan. He had to know.

He scrambled for his clothes, aware of her gaze following his every move. Aware that there was still something skeptical in her eyes, something he shouldn't take on faith, but he had to.

He should take her clothes, he thought suddenly. He should just take her clothes and dump them somewhere, and then she couldn't possibly get out of the flat at all.

She saw that look in his eye, saw him glance at the pile of her clothing near the bed, saw a muscle tighten in his jaw, saw that flash of determination, and she knew what he was thinking instantly—he'd grab her clothes, and she'd never get away from him.

Oh, dear God—and the money—he'd know exactly where it was, and he wouldn't need her anymore—

And she was lying there as submissive as an odalisque.

Dear heaven, now what? Stupid. *She* had done this to herself, put herself in this horrible position, and she had to get herself out. Had to wait for the right moment to get herself out. Not look as though she knew exactly what he was thinking.

She held her breath, and she looked away only so far as she could watch him from the corner of her eye. He was still slowly getting into his shirt. Hadn't reached for his trousers yet. That would be the moment—she thought—when he was putting on his trousers . . . he'd be neutralized for mere seconds . . . the moment to pounce— .

She was certain he could hear the pounding of her heart.

. . . Taking a damned long time to get to his trousers. Watching her like a cat, as if he didn't trust her, as he shouldn't, but she didn't trust him either—what would she do if he got to her clothing before she could? He was so much stronger than she . . . so determined—

No more than she . . . she purposefully softened her body, turned, twisted, soft subtle movements to distract him as he reached for his trousers, his eyes still on her, watching her, wanting her—

That was her key, the thing that gave her control: he wanted her; he wanted her to stay, to be with him, to have sex with him— he just didn't want to marry her . . .

He shook out his trousers, both hands on the waistband, his gaze intensely fixed on her.

But that one moment, when he was stepping in, when his whole concentration would be on balancing himself—almost . . . almost—he was looking at her suspiciously—

He didn't trust her; she didn't trust him . . .

He had to get those trousers on . . .

. . . He wasn't sure he wanted to put those trousers on . . . he was torn, she could see it. Things were warring inside him—whether to grab the clothing or continue dressing, to stay to go to succumb to lust and longing—

Lifting his leg . . .

. . . lifting . . .

She dove, grabbing her shirtwaist, her skirt, especially her skirt, the money in the skirt, the thing he didn't need to know. "Oh—" she said in her best sugar-coated voice, as his foot thumped down heavily on the floor. "I am so cold . . . you'll excuse me, I'm sure, while I dress?"

Another moment . . . everything inside him knew he should get hold of those clothes. Every instinct screamed it was the only way to keep her here. But now it meant grabbing her, forcing her, tearing the garments away from her.

And there he was, with one leg in his trousers, the other bare, and how effective could he be, hopping after her like a lusty hare?

It was too late. She'd slipped into the other room, slipped into hiding, slipped away from him altogether.

Another moment later and he was clothed, but she hadn't come back into the bedroom.

Damn. Fuck. Hell. Trust a lying bitch like that—

He sprinted for the sitting room.

Son of a bitch—she was gone.

Not that long gone either . . .

He raced down the steps and out the door—into the smoky pall of a still-hovering fog.

No one there. No one running, no one walking. Not a soul on the street. How could she disappear so completely and thoroughly in the space of five minutes?

Goddammit—was everyone in his life a ghost?

Where the hell—?

He raced down the street, the fog wisping by his face like the touch of ghostly fingers.

Hellfire.

"Hey, mate—need a cab?"

The hansom had rumbled up behind him like a phantom from the fog. He hadn't heard it; he hadn't seen it. He felt as though he were operating in a dream.

Of course, in the dream, the driver would be the ghost coachman, and every question would be answered. But he wasn't. He was just a grizzled old man with a cap over his eyes and a mean-looking whip who couldn't answer anything except where he might want to go.

"Did you see a woman running down the street?"

"Can't say as I did."

Of course. She'd just vanished. Right into the fog. It was all of a piece. Hell and gone. Now what? No point to returning to his rooms.

Shit. Get back to business. Stop being haunted by the damned coachman and *her*. Time to find the Samaritan. Time to root out Tony Venable's weaknesses. Time to stop rooting in the chocolate virgin's excesses.

She was the one thing in his life that could wait.

He climbed into the cab.

"Where to?"

Where? To? He didn't know. He said the first thing that came into his head: "The Seven Sisters."

"Eh? The park?"

A park? "The park."

"Here we go."

Drab, dreary day. As the cab got over the bridge, the fog thickened, got grayer, more ominous, hovering so that the only thing visible was the road and, just barely, what was just ahead of them.

"Not going to be fast," the coachman shouted to him as they came to a standstill just over the bridge.

Everything was fog-shrouded, dark, gloomy.

"I'll walk. Where am I going?"

"Over toward Shoreditch."

Kyger threw him a pound note and vaulted out of the carriage.

The city was curiously still, as if the fog had utterly paralyzed everything and everybody. Objects loomed, buildings, street lamps, people, coming out of the gray smokiness like ghosts, like smoke.

Maybe it wasn't the fog. He started to see that people were gathered on street corners, huddling in storefronts. Traffic wasn't moving. Not an inch. Everything was at a standstill. Everything was hushed.

What—?

He felt as if he were the only one moving and it *was* the dream.

He crossed the broad boulevard in the company of two or three others who looked as disoriented as he. But no one said a word. No one made a comment. So strange. Eerie.

Something was going on, but it seemed almost sacrilegious to break the silence, to ask.

. . . Holy shit . . . This was so odd, almost spooky.

And when he finally approached a small knot of people on the corner, he found himself whispering. Goddamn, he was *whispering* . . . into the silence and the hush, in the eerie straining afternoon of stillness and fog.

"What's happening?"

"Oh, my God, oh, my God—you haven't heard?" They couldn't believe it. They turned, all of them, to face him, their eyes hollow, their faces pale.

"What? I haven't heard. What? What happened?"

They all looked at each other and then at him. And then the eldest among them whispered, "They took him. The heathens. The infidels. The skeptics. They took him. Tony Venable. They dug up his grave in the dead of night—his body is gone . . ."

Chapter Nine

She was a woman alone. For the first time ever in her life, she had no one to depend on, to lean on, to tell her what to do. *He* would have, the brothel house bull, had she let him, had she stayed, but what good would that have done?

She didn't know his name, still. She didn't know where she was, even. She had dashed down the staircase half-dressed and crouched in the shadows of the first-floor hallway, terrified he would find her, terrified that he wouldn't.

But then he was gone. And he didn't come back. He thought she'd taken to the street, expected she'd found someone to take her on almost immediately because he thought she was that kind of woman.

It was good he was gone. He didn't trust her; she surely didn't trust him, especially now that he had refused to help her. She didn't need him, she *didn't*.

She waited a very long time before she emerged from the shadows in the hallway, and that was after she finished pulling on the remainder of her clothes and made certain her money was still intact in her skirt lining.

Only then did she tiptoe out the front door. And into the soupy fog. It seemed more oppressive even than the previous night. It felt as though it was a living entity, as if it was moving of its own volition, low to the ground and predatory, subsuming everything in its path.

It scared her half to death—it would swallow her whole, and no one would ever know where she'd gone.

She grabbed on to the iron fence that fronted the house to have something real and substantial in her hand. She sensed that if she let go, she'd be letting go of everything that had anything to do with who she had been, and everything to do with *him*. She'd never be able to find her way back here again. She didn't know the street, the number of the house, the section of London, didn't know his name . . .

Didn't even know if this episode was real or a dream. If Wroth was a bogeyman she'd invented. Maybe she was still back in her featherbed in the house in Georgia.

Maybe this had been a nightmare, and she would wake up, a virgin again . . .

No, this was too real. She could feel the rusted iron biting into her palms as she held on to the fence like a lifeline. This was real: everything else—the brothel, their escape, the vanishing coachman, her stupid attempt to try to seduce him into marrying her, every last wrenching moment of her orgasms, the feel, the touch, the heft and the presence of *him* deep inside her—all of that was as amorphous as the fog and just as evanescent.

It felt like a fog of death, and she was alone, and she would be consumed by it if she didn't move.

Where to move? Hang on to the fence. Hope something presented itself. As she had waited in the shadows of the hallway, she had begun to methodically figure out each next step: She'd need money; she extracted some banknotes from the lining of her skirt. She'd need transportation. That was random, on the street. She'd need to *look* as if she were a traveler, because a lady would never approach a hotel without luggage, a maid, and a chaperone.

She didn't have the chaperone or the maid, but she certainly could have a trunk and story about her people arriving later.

She needed to find a department store and outfit herself accordingly.

She needed to find out where she was and how to get where she needed to be. She didn't need the most expensive hotel in the city. And probably, they were booked full with all the husband-seeking heiresses her father had told her swarmed all over London.

And actually, she didn't need a hotel at all: a nice, respectable rooming house would do, since she planned to stay in one place for a fair amount of time. Someplace her father would never think to look.

His rooms would have been perfect . . .

She banished the thought. What could he have done for her otherwise? She could have stayed there and spread her legs for him for months, wallowing in the pleasure, and then what? Would her father have given up the hunt for her, or Wroth given up the quest to obtain what had been promised him?

She didn't think so.

No. She had to forget the libertine prince and his bull of a penis, solve the problem, divorce the solution, and finally get her life in order.

This wasn't a very promising way to begin, hanging on to a fence and walking hand over hand into oblivion. But this was all she could do right now, so this she would do.

She was nothing if not determined.

And the rest she'd figure out later.

It was a city of ghosts, stupefied, walking ghosts, sliding in and out of the fog, followed by sibilant whispers that floated in the air like ashes.

. . . He's gone . . .

Grave robbers. Desecraters. Infidels. Curse them, damn them send them to hell—

No, he never died . . .

He died. They murdered him, and they took him from us . . .

No, don't you see—it was a plot, a plan; he's alive, he's been waiting, he's coming back . . .

Kyger heard the buzzing whispers, almost as if they were imprinted on his consciousness and not the slivers of conversation floating around him as he made his way among the human statues huddling publicly in shock and horror.

He's gone.

We have to find who did this . . .

He's alive—

Sobs, murmurs of consolation, anger—
He's—
. . . don't say it . . .
. . . we know, we're waiting . . .
Rabble-rousing, rage, fury, and then calm voices in the fog toning down the hotheads, the voices of reason, the voices of Tony Venable's followers reassuring those who loved him that the miscreants, the defilers, the murderers would be caught, punished, drawn and quartered and hung in the Tower.
. . . don't say it . . .
Kyger was chilled to the bone. They were saying it without saying it. Resurrection. Return. Secrets and lies. That Tony Venable had faked his death and he was coming back to them—
They hadn't seen his bloody body; at the funeral all those weeks ago, they had seen the sanitized, living-in-death body, cleaned up, dressed up, theatrically made up, perfect, as if he were sleeping, suspended in life.
Of course they thought revivification was possible, they thought he was testing them, they thought he could do anything, even return from the dead.
The buzzing whispers grew louder; he felt as though he needed armor to protect himself from the anguish and turmoil. The city was in agony; the fog wept because it could not.
He felt as if he were the only one moving, the only one with a purpose, but in actuality the fog had slowed everything down to movements in increments.
And not everyone was devastated. Not when you looked closely. Not everyone was feeling fraught and lost. It just seemed that way.
But as Kyger moved away from the bridge, the knots of people, and the clotted traffic, the pall in the air, and the sense of doom and denial that seemed concurrent with the menace of the hovering fog dissipated bit by bit.
It wasn't that the fog was any thinner. It was that there were fewer people clustered together, because those who mourned had chosen for some reason to congregate nearby the bridge, and so the atmosphere of grief and denial wasn't so cloying here.
Good. He needed a fresh breath of air. He needed to get to Shoreditch, which was to the east. He headed toward Aldgate, asking directions as he went until a kind passerby pointed him to-

ward Liverpool Street Station and the Shoreditch Road, where he would find what he was seeking—Seven Sisters Park.

It was faster to walk at this point. The oppressive fog and slow movement of the passersby and traffic only heightened his sense of urgency. And yet, it was the kind of day where no one would go to a park, least of all his putative Good Samaritan.

He wondered how he expected to find any of the answers he sought when he didn't know the questions. It didn't seem to matter. His instinct was to go, and he was not far away now. He'd passed the railroad station, and moments later, he came to Shoreditch Road, at the intersection of Bethnel Green. Suddenly the fog swirled away, and there was the park.

He couldn't see much of it: just low stone walls, interspersed with tall stone pillars, two of them supporting a tall iron gate with ornate triangular designs all over it. It was closed tight, surely a sign no one could possibly be within.

But then suddenly, the gate swung wide open as if it were inviting him in, one elongated triangle just at chest level noticeably dividing into what looked like the number seven on the right, and its mirror image on the left.

No. Yes. He wasn't imagining it. It definitely was a seven. *Two* sevens, one reversed. No other place on the fence did the triangles divide in just that way. But when you looked, there were sevens. Part of every triangular shape on that fence.

Hellfire.

And there was nothing beyond the threshold of the park but ominous gray rolling fog. Sevens and fog. Symbols of—what? He felt as if a biding evil was reaching out to him, teasing him, playing with him, toying with him, goading him to come in.

Sevens.

Enter the park and you enter the abyss. He could see nothing beyond the fog, and it pulsed like a living thing, waiting for him, watching him.

Watching, always watching.

He shook himself. This was crazy.

It knows what I'm thinking . . .

Crazy.

It knows about the sevens . . .

Insane.

But he couldn't make himself take the first step over the threshold of the gate with the reverse sevens.

I'm waiting . . .

He knew it was waiting. He felt it in his gut, in his craw. Something evil was in the park, and if he put one foot past that gate . . .

Better to leave. Get out. Fast. And forget it. There was nothing beyond the gate that he needed to know. No clues. No answers.

He turned abruptly, and pitched right into a man who was standing directly behind him. A man he hadn't seen, heard, or been aware of.

A man he recognized instantly despite the fact he'd been half dead when the man came to his rescue.

The Samaritan. "Well, it's about time you got here," he murmured.

"Why is that?" Kyger couldn't keep the grit out of his voice.

"Because you said you would."

He was so tense he thought he'd explode. "I did, didn't I?" There was something so preternatural about the Samaritan, and yet there was nothing distinctive about him at all.

What could he have to do with the supernatural fog, or the design of the sevens in the gate?

"We like a man who keeps his word," the Samaritan said smoothly. "We've been waiting. Come."

We? We . . . *Who* was *we?* And come where? Into the gate with the mirror-image sevens? Into the fog? Into oblivion?

The Samaritan took his arm and propelled him forward forcefully. Past the gate with the sevens, into the fog.

And as they seemed to be swallowed up into the smoky gray, it suddenly opened up, and they were in a clearing around which were seven statues, and some small stone tables and benches.

"The Seven Sisters," the Samaritan said, gesturing.

It was like a little Stonehenge—the statues were shapeless, faceless. They could have been anything, gods, men, monsters, symbols. Or they could be nothing. They just were, tall, formless, and menacing, and they dominated the space.

Kyger whirled on him. "The coachman."

"There's no coachman," the Samaritan said from behind him.

Kyger whipped around. "The coachman who came right after you found me . . . where is he?"

"There was no coachman," the Samaritan reiterated, and now he sounded as if he had moved farther away.

Kyger whirled again. The Samaritan was nowhere to be seen. He heard the sound of hoofbeats, the rumbling of a carriage. He saw the shadow of a coach moving behind the fog, coming at him and at him—the face of the coachman, the face of death, coming at him relentlessly—close, close, close—running him down—God almighty—

He fell forward as the death sound of coach wheels rumbled over his head . . .

The fog closed in around him, swarming with fizzy whispers.

SSSSSSSS . . .

. . . seven . . .

. . . seek seven . . .

. . . dead and alive—

SSSSSSS—

Sacred . . . sssssss—

. . . sacrosanct . . . sacrilege . . . sacrifice . . . sacrament . . .

Sacred . . .

Seven—

Buzzing bees of sound swarming around his head, infiltrating his consciousness. He didn't know where he was—he was on the ground, the death's head coachman was coming . . . coming—*what?* Sacred seven . . . again—?

Bzzz, bzz, bzz . . . hissing sevens . . . *zzzz's* like bees, like sevens upside down, right side up . . . all in his ears. He couldn't get rid of the sound of the bees in his ears . . .

And then he was rolling on the ground, as if he'd been tossed down an incline. All the way down, no way to stop, no way to save himself . . . no end, into a void, into the fog—

And when he awakened, he was outside of the park, with the gates emphatically closed, the sevens integrated back into the decorative iron triangles in the fence so that no one would ever know there were sevens everywhere, with an opaque fog rolling around him, curious, thick and slow.

Money was the elixir of life. If you had it, you could drink from the fountain of all possibilities. If you didn't, you'd die of thirst. Her father had taught her that; in America, they had lived

like that—everything of the best: the biggest house, the best surroundings, imported furniture, important paintings, clothes from
Paris designers, obsequious servants who tended to everything
with the smooth efficiency of an oiled machine. That was how
Zabel expected to live, what he expected his money to buy. What
he had worked for all his life, what he had hoped would pave
over his hardscrabble past.

And his daughter expected no less. It was how she was raised,
what she knew, how life had always been.

But now, she discovered, money was finite. She had taken all
the money she had found in the hotel room, a fairly substantial
sum to have been lying around like that to be sure, but it was a
set amount, and it wouldn't go far enough for her to accomplish
her plan unless she was prudent.

She didn't know how to be prudent. Having the best of everything meant you didn't count the cost. She didn't know how to
count the cost or how to judge the relative value of anything outside the purview of the wealthy.

She knew how to call in a dressmaker to replicate the latest
fashions from the *rue de la Paix*. She knew how to host a dinner
party and how to create a menu. She knew how to be charming
and engage disparate people in a cohesive, all-inclusive conversation. She knew how to flirt, how to make people feel important
and cosseted.

And she surely knew how to pass the bills on to her father.

But—the cost of a hansom cab. The price of a dress at
Harrod's. Where to find the best rooms. How to engage a chaperone. Never had she done these things, and she felt like a tiny fish
floundering around in a great big ocean, with sharks waiting to
devour her.

Never mind that. It must be done. She would just take each
point one at a time, one foot in front of the other, and she would
be fine.

So first she had to find a hansom to take her back into the city,
which took no little time as she hung on fences and traversed unknown streets until one happened by. And then, finally she could
relax for a few minutes and parcel out the details, while someone
else dealt with the fog.

God, it was thick. But it wasn't so much the fog as the feeling of dissonance in the air. As they got closer to the heart of the city, as the coachman fought his way over the bridge near Parliament through the clotted traffic toward Bond Street, she felt an over-whelming sense of heaviness closing in on her.

It was the people milling in the street with haunted eyes; it was her self-imposed and daunting task of finding someone in this misbegotten town that she could stand to be married to for more than an hour. It was her huge disappointment that it would not ever be the bull. And her unexamined fear she didn't really have enough money after all, and would be forced to return to her father and Wroth in defeat.

But that was to be thought about later. For now, she had enough, and she was on her way. A dress, a trunk, some toiletries, a newspaper would help. The best boardinghouse, or the most respectable affordable hotel, perhaps.

Everything was *perhaps* now, when her life had been so certain before. But before there hadn't been a Wroth, or a dissolute bull who looked like a gentleman, patronized brothels and lived like a bohemian.

Not to think about that either.

If only he'd said yes . . .

But he hadn't. And she'd been naïve, and she was well rid of him, and she could do all of this on her own, without him, without her father, without help, without guilt.

What did he have, really? When he totted up the whole experience the following day, there was nothing that sounded concrete, even to him.

Sevens and circles, a dead demagogue whose body was missing, a brothel with moving walls, secret entrances, grown men playing boys' games with secret symbols and hooded robes, mysterious coachmen gone missing, foggy parks, séances with unearthly messages, a vanishing vestal . . .

God, it sounded like a piece of sensational fiction.

He couldn't go to Wyland with it. Whatever he had was as insubstantial as the fog, and there wasn't a thing there that would bring down the incipient movement to canonize Tony Venable.

He heard it everywhere the next day. Whispered in the streets. Talked about in pubs. Proselytized on street corners. It was overwhelming. It clogged the air, as thick and opaque as the fog.

It sounded like the fizzing buzz of bees in his ears.

He had to get away from it, to clear his head in clean air away from the transsubstantial fog of mourning and exaltation.

It was time to go home. Time to put some of this on Lujan, since it had been his suggestion that he pursue it. Maybe Lujan—and it was rather hard to even think this—would have another perspective.

Or some answers?

Lujan?

Well, at the least, he'd be away from London, away from the smoky fog.

And then—there would be Jancie.

And maybe that was the real objective: maybe he just needed to see Jancie.

. . . Maybe it was a bad idea. Seeing Jancie made the schism within him that much deeper. Because as he entered the house, he was stunned that he could also see his voracious virgin equally at home in the drawing room at Waybury, and that was something he didn't expect.

"Well, brother mine," Lujan greeted him, clapping his shoulder, and moving him into the parlor with barely a pause. He was very good at it. When had he become so good at it? "What's to do?"

"That's the question, old man. What is the to-do of the day?"

"Ahhh . . ." Lujan poured the wine. "The Venable thing. They're making him into a saint."

Kyger took a deep, mouth-filling sip. "And apparently he was one. I haven't found a thing"—small lie, he'd found a lot, just nothing that made sense—"I can take to Wyland."

"Then you'll have to look deeper," Lujan said, not tasting from his goblet. "People like Venable, they bury their sins all the way to China. There won't be anything on the surface you could dredge up easily. Nothing as incriminating as Wyland would like to see, and no one expects you could have found anything like that in a month's time in any event. Come, it's dinnertime. Jancie's up with the tot who's been cranky all day. We can talk."

They sat close together at right angles at the foot of the table while the meal was served. So different than the way he remembered; so different from where he'd thought he and Lujan would ever be at this point in their lives—Lujan settled and managing things, and himself the itinerant libertine and idle seeker.

Seeking mysteries, seeking surcease, seeking the kind of love he might have had with Jancie had she not fallen irrevocably in love with the rakehell that Lujan used to be.

And now Lujan was him, the upright, four square country squire, and he had become the voluptuary. The irony was rather jaw-dropping, especially when he thought about himself at Bullhead Manor with the chocolate virgin. Just the kind of thing Lujan had used to indulge in. Virgins for sport, for prestige, for the sheer pleasure of the corruption of innocence.

Jancie had been an innocent . . .

Forget that. Lujan had grown up, and Kyger should be, he *was,* grateful to his brother for sending him on this all-consuming quest. The veneration of Venable's memory was a cancer, a slow-growing, full-body poison that could destroy the country's soul.

But he wasn't five minutes closer to finding out what had made Venable tick, and what it would take to excise *his* poison, than he was the day he'd returned from his travels.

That was the point, not the past, not what could have been.

"So what *have* you found out?" Lujan asked finally, casually, after a half hour desultory conversation over the mutton, and as they were settling back to wait for dessert.

Kyger tipped his wine, listening, as he had since he'd entered the house, for Jancie's footstep, and envisioning instead the chocolate virgin waltzing into the dining room in his mind. He didn't like it, not a bit, that the volatile and unknown Angilee could so easily supplant Jancie in his thoughts, in his family home, in his desires.

Where the hell had she gotten to anyway?

"What have I found out? Not much. Nothing that makes sense." He swirled the wine for want of something to do. "His life on the surface is spotless. I visited the flat. The reverence is astounding. There was nothing there except hundreds of devout believers lined up willingly for hours just for the chance to inhale what was left of him. Everything was sanitized, scrubbed, picture perfect. You'd never guess he was murdered there."

"No. They are good at that."

"Not a scrap of paper . . ." No—wait—there was that pad, with the curious little check mark on it that could have been an upside-down seven—but what could that mean to Lujan, really, when *he* was the one haunted by sevens everywhere . . . "They wanted to open the drawers, the cuboards, the icebox. It was extraordinary."

"He was like that," Lujan said.

"Did you know him?"

Lujan hesitated a fraction of a second. "In passing. He was very magnetic. They are not exaggerating his power to attract in person."

"Or in death," Kyger said dryly. "And then this damnable fog. It's gone on forever. It's like a blanket smothering everything, everyone."

"Exactly. Much nicer in the country. But you know that already."

Dessert was served, a nice selection of tarts, cheese, fruit, pound cake, tea and coffee.

They ate in silence for a few moments, Kyger choosing the cheese and fruit, and Lujan, a tart.

"And how has the mission gone otherwise?"

Kyger cut into the fruit and popped a piece into his mouth. "I find it surpassingly grim that I'm reduced to decadent nights of debauchery at the Bullhead, frankly."

Lujan grinned. "I knew we'd get you there eventually, baby brother. Nothing like it, until a man is ready to settle and spawn. Not your style, though. I can hardly imagine it. Are you searching for something?"

"There *was* a woman," Kyger admitted. But how much to admit? How much had Wyland confided in him? Enough so that he himself was now involved. But—the secrets of the Bullhead? He didn't quite know what they were—yet.

And just why had he obliquely brought up his deflowered virgin?

"Ha!" Lujan clapped him on the shoulder. "I knew it. I knew once you got the hang of things you'd dive right in. A woman. Excellent—"

"What woman?" Jancie's voice from the hallway.

"Ah, just someone he's become acquainted with," Lujan said smoothly as she glided into the room, followed by Emily. "How's the tot doing?"

"Sleeping, finally. And I'm exhausted." She stopped at Kyger's chair to touch his shoulder. "How are you?"

"Escaping London for the moment." He felt her touch down to his bones. He heard a warning *mrrrrr* from Emily, ever protective.

"Escaping that woman, you mean," Jancie said lightly. "Or do you want to?" Now she had seated herself next to Lujan, directly opposite him.

She looked tired, thinner. Still beautiful. Still made him feel like conquering universes, even though her world was Lujan and baby Gaunt. And Emily. He felt the cat rubbing against his leg, almost as if she were reading his thoughts, and pulling him back from regrets and regression.

"I'm not sure yet. She's quite a handful." That was good. "American, by her accent—"

"One of those—" Lujan said dismissively.

"Don't discount the heiresses," Jancie said. "She could lead you quite a chase, Kyger, and I think you need it." She helped herself to the remnants of dessert—a piece of cheese, a corner of the pound cake. Lujan poured some coffee and pushed the pot toward Kyger.

"Quite beautiful," Kyger added, feeling as if he were twisting the knife in Jancie as well as himself. "Very independent. Here with her father; I'm not certain if there is more family. That's all I know."

"Well, hell," Lujan said. "Heiresses don't marry second sons, so my advice is, enjoy her while you can, and give her up gracefully when she gives you the *grand congee*."

"You'll explain, of course, just how one does that," Kyger said with just a touch of irritation. "The graceful part, I mean."

Lujan shot him a look. "You'll know instinctively when the time comes, baby brother. You're a Galliard, after all, you'll do me proud."

Jancie made a sound.

"Exactly," Lujan said instantly. "I'm past all that now. I'll enjoy watching you instead. I won't even give advice. I've forgotten it all anyway." He rose from his chair. "Jancie looks all done in. Excuse us, will you?"

He held out his hand for her, and Jancie took it, touched Kyger's shoulder again, and allowed Lujan to take her from the room.

Leaving him alone with shadows and memories.

How many times had they dined alone here, while Lujan was off screwing whores at the Bullhead? How many times had he wished, had he offered, to marry her? They'd adored each other, just not enough; he didn't have the touch, the magnetism, or enough love to attract Jancie.

Instead he had a rapacious, deflowered virgin offering to pay him to marry her. Hellfire. Close his eyes, and he could see her— her silky skin, her chocolate hair, her fierce response to his possession of her, her even more ferocious iron determination—

So completely and fantastically *his* . . . no one else's before him, no one else's—ever . . .

. . . yet—

Shit . . . he jumped up from his chair, galvanized suddenly. He shouldn't have come here. He should not have just let her go like that. He should have searched for her no matter how long it took, and he should never have come home until the Venable thing had been solved.

He was avoiding everything—reporting to Wyland, the problem of Tony Venable, and the question of the edible virgin—because he didn't know what the next thing was to do—about either of them.

He took the steps two at a time. Jancie had given him his old bedroom, down the hall from hers and Lujan's, and far enough away from the past that memories would not intrude.

They'd redecorated the house anyway. The walls were a soft caramel color with gilt-framed paintings hung above burnished walnut console tables on either side; the woodwork was white now, the ceilings seemed higher, and there was a long Persian runner on the hallway floor.

So different. Even in his room: The walls were a warm color, there were different curtains, new bedclothes, a new mirror, reupholstered chairs. A bookcase that had not been there before with a brass carriage clock ticking off the urgent, passing time.

The bed he had always slept in. His bag on a stand near the dressing room with its new fixtures and freshly papered walls.

Jancie's touch, even in his room, never ever touching *him*.

He felt the impulse to just grab his bag and head out for London right then. It was too hard to be there, too difficult to watch her with Lujan; the loss still was too keen.

Even if it was cut by the thought of the chocolate virgin. But he felt only exasperation about her. And fear that she had gotten deeper in trouble with her indiscriminate offers of money for marriage.

He threw himself on the bed. What the hell was he going to do about her, if he ever even found her again?

What an unholy mess. He knew exactly what was wrong— since he'd been avoiding examining that, too: the goddamned experience at the park of the Seven Sisters had unnerved him. It was too supernatural: the fog, the fence with handholds in the shape of mirror-image sevens, the looming and intimidating faceless statues, the disappearing Samaritan, the ghostly coachman . . .

He still didn't know what to make of it. What to make of any of it. What had it all to do with Tony Venable? On the surface, the mystery of Tony Venable was simple: who had killed a man who was popular, revered, idolized? On the surface, you could list a half dozen potential suspects: a jealous political rival, a woman, a family member, someone from his past, someone out for revenge, someone who just plain hated him.

But that didn't explain the perfection of a life that could not be sullied by anything that was publicly known or the unholy and dangerous escalation of the movement to sanctify the memory and ideology of a man who, under the surface where it was foggy and murky and no one could clearly see, was really a demagogue. And it didn't nearly explain the missing corpse, the ghostly séance and the ungodly message of resurrection.

It didn't explain the sevens.

Sevens everywhere. Maybe that was important. Maybe he was missing something. How many sevens? The whore, tracing circles and lines on his chest, whispering *seven*. The *Sacred Seven*. Venable's address—Seven Park Lane; the number of letters in his name, and in Angilee's—*seven*; the Seven Cups Tavern; the park of the Seven Sisters . . .

What else, what else? So many sevens, leading nowhere—somewhere—? Seven, seven, seven—

The night of the séance—the hotel rooms, all with number seven in them . . .

There was something else; it niggled at him, nipping at the edges of his memory—there were more sevens, more . . .

. . . seven hooded men at the Bullhead . . .

. . . seven, seven, seven—

Precepts. At the memorial service . . .

. . . Venable's seven precepts—what were they? . . . Wait, what *were* they? Something about them which, in his astonishment at seeing Angilee there, he had overlooked. There had been an order to them—a meaningful order? He thought so—because they had culminated in *belief* and—and . . . he had it—*acceptance.* An ascending order of importance to Venable.

But—*belief* and *acceptance*—

Belief in him?

Acceptance of—*what*?

Faith was in there somewhere, too—faith in whom?

Him?

He was unexpectedly drifting off to sleep . . .

A sound at the door which he'd left ajar—hoping, perhaps? He heard it clearly in his mind: *mmmrrrrrow—no hope*—

He'd never stop hoping. *Understand that, cat.*

A scratching sound, as if Emily didn't believe him. He should have expected Emily would come.

Then, a silence. Voices following, crowding his mind . . .

Everybody knows, nobody tells . . .

Right—but what did they know; what wouldn't they tell?

Everyone knew he'd loved Jancie. Forget that.

. . . Something else—damn the cat—why couldn't he remember? He was fuddled by the sevens was what. Too many sevens, meant perhaps to confound and confuse . . . except his eyes felt heavy . . .

Nothing was too extreme to be considered.

. . . *a number, a slash, a fishhook* . . .

Wait—where had he heard those words . . . ?

. . . *fishhook* . . .

—mark that down—

Mark?

No, death *mark*—

I live—

Check.

Right—check—upside down—*seven* . . .

Where? Where? He grasped for the memory—checks . . .

No checks, only sevens.

He was right at the edge, teetering with the certain knowledge that—

The sevens were playing with him . . .

And then he fell—deep asleep . . .

Chapter Ten

She didn't like this. The rooms were small, the boardinghouse in an obscure but respectable part of the city. The landlady was curious and suspicious, but impressed by her resources, even though all the money in the world couldn't buy the comforts she was used to in this place.

But this place, of every hotel and boarding situation she had looked at, was the most genteel and best located of the lot.

God, she hated it. But she could afford it, and by living here, she could afford everything else she needed to accomplish her plan.

She thought she'd gone about it with some degree of intelligence. She'd gone right to Harrod's, and in the course of choosing some ready-to-wear clothes and personal items, she'd unabashedly eavesdropped on random exchanges, struck up conversations with the matrons, patrons, and the salesgirls, and by dint of some clever questioning, she had discovered what she'd needed to know: the best, most respectable, most economical places to live; the exact room rent to pay; where to shop to buy fashionable but well-priced clothes; how to go about finding that all-important chaperone, a so-called social godmother, who was so germane to her plans.

She could do nothing without help, and it galled her now how much she had depended on Zabel to direct everything and keep her comfortable. Now she was alone, she felt as if she were on a precipice and not one inch from falling off.

But that was to think about later.

After her most profitable sojourn through Harrod's, and having charged everything she bought to Zabel because otherwise she would have been distressingly short of money, she had departed with a trunk full of purchases, a cabman at her disposal, and a long list of possible residences to vet. And that had taken the rest of the afternoon with a lot of glib explanations that were only partly believed by the sundry concierges and boardinghouse landladies she had interviewed.

She would have preferred to rent a house, but that, with the influx of the heiresses for the Season, was virtually impossible except in the worst parts of Town, and on top of that, Zabel might be easily able to find her.

So at the end of a wearying day, she was left with three choices: a seedy but well-located hotel, which she immediately rejected; a large bed/sitting room situation in a questionable part of Town; and the suite of small rooms that she had ultimately taken in Camberwell Mansions, an excellent address in the best part of Town.

Two bedrooms, a sitting room with a gas fireplace, a shared hallway bathroom, nice fittings and furnishings, and two meals a day, breakfast and dinner, for an extra fee.

It would do.

The rooms were to the front of the house—that cost extra, too, but still within the amount she could afford—and she had taken the two bedrooms with the idea that her chaperone-to-be would live with her for however long it took to accomplish her goal.

So here she was, in her cozy little flat, thanking the heavens that the salesgirl at Harrod's had been willing to send the bills to Claridge's. She wondered what Zabel would think when he got them. For one thing, he'd know she was still in London. Which was unavoidable, she supposed. But he'd never find her here.

She was somewhat comforted by that.

But now what? She didn't know quite what to do next. She

was used to having someone to do for her. Only since they had come to England had she had to do things for herself. Though Zabel had taken advantage of hotel services like having their clothes ironed and mended, there hadn't been a maid to draw a bath or lay out a dress.

She hadn't even considered she might need to iron the new and neatly folded clothes that were now so tidily packed in her trunk.

How did one iron a dress?

All those mundane things.

And having to find a temporary husband besides. And set aside enough money to tempt some stranger to marry her . . . and live more frugally than ever she had been accustomed to.

How did people do that when there was ironing to be done and meals to be gotten—and a maid usually to take care of those things . . . ?

She resolutely pushed the thought out of her mind. That was to think about later.

For now, her first move was to unpack her clothes. And then read the advertisements in the paper. Though she had been advised to go riding in the Park first thing the next day to see and be seen. To make contacts.

She wasn't so sure she wanted to be *seen* yet. It seemed more prudent to get all her priorities taken care of before making any public appearances.

Especially with Zabel and Wroth prowling around Town.

No, the chaperone was the first order of business, and there needed to be money for that as well, so hiring a carriage for a morning foray with the feckless and fashionable was out of the question right now.

Why hadn't anyone prepared her for all these little details that had to be taken care of?

Don't even think about that. To cope with all these unknowns, she decided, she needed only to focus on one detail at a time—look at what she had accomplished today by following that plan—and the rest could come later.

She settled in a comfortable chair in the sitting room, pulled the adjacent table closer to her, opened the paper to the advertisements, and began to read.

* * *

He dreamt of cats and coincidences, and when he awakened the next morning, there was Emily on the threshold, staring at him with her great golden eyes. *It's time to leave.*

"You can't want me gone more than I want to go," he growled at her as he washed and made a quick change of clothes.

Owwww, Emily said.

"Fifteen minutes, cat."

Mrrrow. Great satisfaction that she'd made her point.

But she didn't move; she just watched him with those all-knowing eyes as he splashed water everywhere and dove into a fresh shirt.

He felt in a tearing hurry to leave—he almost believed he shouldn't have come; he should've gone to Wyland instead, even though his head felt clear for the first time since he'd undertaken this mission.

He didn't quite know why. He had no answers, no explanation for the coincidence of the sevens. But he didn't need one now. This was the part that had come clear to him in his dreams: he had to keep on a straight course to find Tony Venable's Achilles' heel before his followers brought the country to heel.

It was as simple as that, and he couldn't let anything else distract him.

Anything.

He had to get back to London. Waybury felt unexpectedly strange to him, even though he'd been born and raised here and had managed it for years. He was beyond it now, deep into a purpose that was larger than anyone's life except Tony Venable's.

It was the political future of the country.

And it was nothing he wanted to explicate to Lujan as he came racing downstairs to breakfast, his bag in hand. He had, in fact, no explanation or excuse for why he was leaving this morning.

"Hold up, baby brother—" Lujan caught his arm. "What's this? I thought you were spending a few days."

"Changed my mind. What's for breakfast?"

"The usual. Unless you're in such a hurry you want to take a scone or two on the road."

"That would be rude, old son. The least I can do is break bread with you this morning."

They walked into the breakfast room together. Jancie was there, with their son Gaunt in a high chair beside her, and she was feeding him slowly and painstakingly while he played with a crust of bread.

Oh, God, Gaunt . . . Kyger caught his breath. Gaunt . . . the *tot*, Lujan still called him, almost as if he couldn't bear to pronounce the name of his namesake, their doomed baby brother who had been murdered by their father to keep a fortune in diamonds a secret.

The past still haunted them, whether they admitted it or not. As much as Jancie had tried to expunge it, the family history still lived on in the person of Gaunt, bearing the dead child's name, and stigma of his little lost soul.

Not to Jancie, though. As much a part of the story as she was, given her father had been their father's partner and bent on revenge and murder, Jancie bore no such guilt for the things that had happened. If anything, she had brought life to the house, affection to his mother before she died, and her purity and innocence had cleansed the sins of their fathers.

And she loved Lujan with a ferocity that made him sick with envy. She had changed Lujan, remade him, gave him a son, gave him a purpose, gave him a life.

And in the greatest of ironies, he, Kyger, by dint of his mission, had usurped and taken over Lujan's rakehell life, as Lujan had taken over his staid and patriarchal role at Waybury.

The fates had to be laughing.

But these incongruities in no way diminished his mission. Tony Venable, in death, was perhaps more dangerous than in life, and the fact of his missing body was downright sinister, and he was wasting time lingering at Waybury when he should have reported to Wyland yesterday.

Still, he took his time this morning, because he knew instinctively this would be his last morning at Waybury for a long time to come.

Mrrrrrww. Emily again, pacing into the dining room. *I will take care of her.*

Kyger had no doubt: Emily had always been by Jancie's side,

and not even her bearing a child could break the bond between Jancie and her calico.

He touched Gaunt's head, fed him a sip of milk, talked on neutral topics, gazed his fill of Jancie, who was looking a little tired this morning, soaked in the atmosphere of the house where he had once lived a long time ago, and after an hour and a half, he said he had to leave.

"Something's up," Lujan said. "You just weren't this galvanized last night. Something happened."

"No. Nothing happened. I need to report to Wyland, that's all."

"Or that's all you want to tell me."

"Could be," Kyger said noncommittally, "but actually, there really is nothing to tell."

"As you say, baby brother. I have other sources anyway. I'll find out."

Kyger went around the table to hug Jancie. Beautiful, sweet, loyal and true Jancie.

Rrrroww. Emily, emphatically. *I'll watch over her.*

"Take care of yourself," Jancie whispered. "Come back soon."

He wouldn't. "When I can."

"We love you," Jancie murmured.

"I love you, too," he whispered back.

Lujan walked him to the stables. Everything, to his critical eye, looked up to snuff, well cared for, well managed.

"Good work, big brother."

"Well, a man can't trash his legacy," Lujan said. "Can he?"

"I always said that," Kyger responded, as he helped the stable boy saddle up his horse, and he wondered if Lujan heard the slight edge in his voice.

"And you were right," Lujan said easily. "Glad to have you, even for a night."

"Thanks, old man." Kyger shook his hand.

"Come back soon."

Kyger mounted, sketched a salute rather than answer, and nudged the horse toward the stable door and into a trot as he passed through.

Why did he think there was something so final about this visit? He twisted in the saddle to wave to Lujan, who was silhouetted against the stable door.

He saw Jancie, on the front steps of Waybury, holding Gaunt by his hand. It was like a painting, he thought, a picture he'd carry in his mind like a photograph forever; but he was past it now, his future lay elsewhere, and all the years he'd spent here seemed telescoped into an hour, and gone.

Gone.

He turned again to look back at Lujan, who had moved away from the stable door and had started walking back toward the house.

He heard the crisp crunch of the oyster shells beneath his horse's hooves. He admired the swath of well-tended lawn as he cantered slowly down the drive toward the gate, one side of which was swung open, while the other was still in place.

He had seen these gates his whole life, knew exactly what the pattern was; it was as familiar to him as the back of his hand, the wrought-iron chevrons in even rows top to bottom on either side of the gate.

So it had to be that he was hallucinating, because as he came closer and closer to the gate, those chevrons looked to him like two rows of truncated sevens marching up and down, right at his own front door.

"You understand, madam, it's terribly late to be looking to engage a chaperone. All of our best people . . ."

"Yes, I do. I understand." Angilee understood a lot more than that now, after several days of canvassing the papers and interviewing women who were not nearly the caliber of chaperone she was seeking. It galled her that she had been reduced to going to an agency, because they got final approval of *her* rather than the other way around.

But there was no other way. She needed the right woman with the right connections, and she had made that very clear to this dour woman who was interviewing *her*.

"But—I must have someone. My people are stranded in New York—they can't get passage until two weeks from now, and I just arrived here, I'm all alone, and until my father finishes his business in Paris and can return to London, I must have someone. The best someone possible, because I will accept nothing less."

Well, that was piling it on, she thought ruefully, but the best advice was to consult an agency rather than hire someone out of hand, and her foray into the advertisements had proved the truth of that. So she had dressed elegantly and expensively and come to the Streatham Agency on Saint George Street, and spun this spider web of a fairy tale to the disapproving woman behind the desk, who was looking at her through a lorgnette that made her seem that much more formidable a barrier than Angilee's lack of credentials.

"You can certainly make inquiries about my family," Angilee barreled on when Miss Burnham said nothing. "My father is a well-known investor in the States. He sent me ahead to engage rooms and set us up for the Season, and what has happened but my retinue was caught in the influx of the rush to come to London and had to give up their passage to accommodate those who could afford to . . . pay more for their tickets. Well, that leaves me in the lurch, without proper accommodations and without staff. At the minimum, I need someone very well connected who can direct me and see that I comport myself properly here. Now, do you have someone who can meet those requirements?"

Miss Burnham pursed her lips, and looked Angilee up and down once more, and consulted the application she had filled out, which included what she was willing to pay the right person. "I will need to look into the matter," she said finally.

"Then I would be happy to return tomorrow in the hopes that you will have found the exact person I need, and we can proceed from there."

And now what? Miss Burnham would make her inquiries and discover that Zabel was right in Town and Angilee had told her a ringing pack of lies.

Forget about that. If she were meant to have a chaperone through this means, then everything would fall into place. Or perhaps the amount of money she was offering was enough to tempt Miss Burnham to provide the chaperone without checking her particulars, since her percentage of that fee would be rather hefty.

Don't think about it; leave it to fate.

Well, charging her clothes to Zabel had been a big leap into faith and fate, although she supposed he might refuse to honor the bills. It wasn't her problem now, though. The thing she needed most was entrée into those social gatherings that would put her in contact with the kind of man who might consider marrying her for money and a month.

Yes, a month would do. Enough to show Zabel the license, for him to question the minister, to assure himself the union was legal, and to get Wroth out of her life forever.

So now what? She stepped out of the elegant mansion in which the Streatham Agency conducted business and into bustling Saint George Street, which was crowded with carriages, horseback riders and strolling passersby.

Any one of them could be a menace to her, she thought suddenly, because somewhere in the deep heart of this city, her father and Wroth were lurking, making plans, searching for her. They could be passing by in a cab, they could be walking down the street, they could be spying on her at this very moment, or they could have hired someone to find and follow her . . .

Or . . . she could be letting her imagination run away with her.

Which was much more likely. They never could have guessed she'd gone to that . . . that brothel place, or wound up with a hired penis in a house of moving walls.

So what was the likelihood they would think to look for her here?

She was being cautious, that was all, just thinking of all the possibilities no matter how improbable.

She started down the street at a brisk pace. Such a beautiful day today. So different from that foggy day, when the air was so thick, opaque and clogged that she couldn't see a foot in front of her and the bull couldn't see his way to marry her.

Forget about that, too.

Now she was taking steps, firm steps forward that had nothing to do with the hired bull, nothing to do with her father, everything self-directed, and in her own hands, and she could just pretend that misbegotten adventure with the bull at the brothel never happened and go on from there.

She didn't expect the solution to her problem would actually present itself at the door of her rooms the next day. But midmorning, there she was. Her name was Mrs. Geddes, and she was a tiny woman with a slippy gray topknot and a no-nonsense manner who barged into the sitting room and paced around Angilee as if she were a prize cow as she stood in the threshold.

"So, you are Miss Rosslyn." She made it sound like an impossible problem. "Close the door, won't you? Thank you. Now we can talk. Here are my *bona fides*. Let me immediately assure you that Miss Burnham conducted a thorough investigation of your background, and is sufficiently assured of your credentials, despite the Cheltenham tale you told her, to send me to you. So you must tell me exactly what is going on, Miss Rosslyn. I am very particular, and I don't hold with lies or obfuscation, and I will reject the position in the event you choose not to be candid with me."

Well, that was clear, Angilee thought, although she was rather taken aback by this Mrs. Geddes' frontal assault, but not so much so that she forgot her manners. "Won't you have a seat, Mrs. Geddes? Shall I call for tea?"

Mrs. Geddes sat. "That would be nice."

Angilee wasn't quite certain the landlady would agree to make the tea, but she called down to her nonetheless. Mrs. Keck said she would, and Angilee gathered her wits, pulled a table up between her and Mrs. Geddes, and settled in a chair opposite while they waited.

"So," Mrs. Geddes said, looking around her with great curiosity. "This is what we know: There are no servants stranded in New York. Your father is not in Paris conducting business. Rather, he is right here in London, enjoying the rewards of all his connections. It is known his daughter is with him this visit, and he has not reported that she's gone missing, so we must assume there is some reason he'd wish to keep such a catastrophic thing quiet for the moment. So exactly what am I committing myself to, Miss Rosslyn?"

Once again, Angilee was startled by the breadth of Mrs. Geddes' information. "Miss Burnham is very thorough," she said after a moment, "and very quick with her sources. Everything you say is true. I did come to England with my father, and he came, as have many others, with the express purpose of finding a husband for me. However, what I did not know was that he had already contracted an alliance with a man I had never met, and fully expected I would adhere to his desire that I marry this man he had chosen, without consulting my wishes whatsoever."

There was a knock on the door, and the landlady entered with a tray, which she set on the table. "I put out some cookies as well," she said.

"Very considerate," Angilee said. "Thank you kindly, Mrs. Keck."

Mrs. Keck gave her a meaningful glance that said there would be an extra charge for this as well, and withdrew from the room.

Angilee turned to Mrs. Geddes. "Will you pour?"

"Let me see how you pour," Mrs. Geddes said.

Angilee poured carefully, cautiously, Mrs. Geddes nodded her approval, and they sipped for a moment in the silence, and then Mrs. Geddes said, "Do go on, Miss Rosslyn."

Angilee took a cookie just to take a moment to think how she would put the rest. It was inconceivable that she should tell Mrs. Geddes that she'd stolen an unconscionable amount of money from her father, deceived and betrayed him, and left her putative fiancé days before the ceremony was to take place.

She wondered how much more Mrs. Geddes really knew. This was a tight society. When you were absorbed into it, you became public property, and everyone knew everything about you—where you lived, who your ancestors were, how much money your father had, who was designing your wedding dress and who your attendants would be.

What hour you would be walking down the aisle . . .

Had Zabel even planned that far ahead?

What could she reasonably tell Mrs. Geddes?

"I don't want to marry this man," she said finally. "My father refuses to heed my wishes, so I saw nothing for it but to strike out on my own and find my own husband, and to do it as clandestinely as possible until I found the right man." Put like that, it sounded impossibly naïve. Impossibly foolish.

She went on resolutely: "I admit this is unorthodox beyond permission, but I was desperate. My chosen fiancé did not please me in any way, shape or form. He is utterly repugnant to me. And so here I am, having rented my own rooms, seeking the next proper step to achieving my goal of finding a husband of my own choice."

Mrs. Geddes made a sound that might have been acquiescence, or just a noncommittal snort. There was silence for another minute or two, and then Mrs. Geddes said, her tone conversationally mild, "And tell me truthfully, what have you left out of your story, Miss Rosslyn?"

Angilee lifted her cup to her lips and met Mrs. Geddes' razor gaze over the rim. This woman was as sharp as a surgeon, knew just how to cut deep. No glossing over things with her. No hiring her either after she heard the rest. And she would have to tell her the rest. There was no getting out of it, she could see that clearly. This was not Mrs. Geddes' first turn around the block.

Angilee sighed and put down her cup. "I ran away in the dead of night, Mrs. Geddes, and I took a fair amount of my father's—assets—with me."

Mrs. Geddes' eyebrows rose. "A *fair* amount, Miss Rosslyn?"

"He will not try to arrest me for stealing what will be mine eventually," Angilee answered tartly. "He wants this marriage—badly."

"I see," Mrs. Geddes murmured.

Angilee rose. "I'm so sorry to have wasted your time, Mrs. Geddes."

"Oh, sit down, Miss Rosslyn. We're not yet done. You rather interest me, actually. You're no milk-and-water miss like the rest of them, and that's refreshing, to say the least. Your father hasn't yet sent the Yard after you—in fact, there has been not a whisper that things aren't as they should be—so we can assume he's not so much interested in getting the money back as he is having you walk down the aisle with the man he chose for you. A very interesting challenge, Miss Rosslyn, to provide you with proper chaperonage and the introductions that will help you achieve your goal. Very interesting indeed—"

She poured herself another cup of tea and sat back, sipping. "I know many people," she said after a while. More silence, and then, "It will take a little doing to gloss over why you are not sponsored by your father." More silence as Angilee sat with her hands in her lap, waiting for the final *coup de grace*.

More silence. "We could change your name." She shook her head. "No. That would raise more questions than we want."

More silence. Angilee could almost see the wheels turning, and Mrs. Geddes turning over every idea, every option, every possibility that would meet every expectation of propriety.

"Ah. I know. We'll just act as if you are still with your father and he has hired me as your companion. No one need know, because neither he nor your would-be fiancé will tell. Not at first, at any rate. So we'll come to grips with that when we must. If we ever must. Meantime, we must make lists; we must make plans."

She stood up abruptly and held out her hand.

"This is a most delicious problem. Very interesting. I *will* help you, Miss Rosslyn. Oh, and my bags are right outside your door. Would you kindly bring them to my room . . . ?"

The fog had lifted by the time he reached Town late that afternoon; the sun was shining, and it felt as if a new energy had been infused into the atmosphere.

It felt strange. It felt as if the crushing sorrow had lifted with the fog and the air was charged with movement. There were no longer knots of people clustered on the street corners, and the passersby seemed to move as if there was a purpose, a place to go, something to do.

The difference was stunning. What had happened between the time he'd left Town and this moment?

He headed toward the Livery and took care of that, and then set out on foot to Wyland's offices.

Something was different. The sun was lowering, but there was a brightness in the air, as if it had been cleansed of grief and mourning somehow. Something had changed—what?

A moment later he saw exactly what had changed. There were signs everywhere, and the signs held the promise:

Tony Venable's Message of Hope: "I LIVE"

Resurrection and life—? Well, hellfire—the body was gone, anything could be made of that to the willing and gullible.

Tony Venable's Message from Beyond the Grave: No, not the rebirth, not yet—it was too soon to give them his replacement.

No, this was just about the pledge, the one thing they yearned for: the restoration of the paternal Venable, the man who would take care of them, make decisions for them, create the perfect paradise for them, and give them freedom besides.

Goddamn.

And on every street corner, hung from trees and poles, were small baskets with cards in them—palm-sized cards with messages, Tony Venable's message and his precepts, in different combinations on each card.

The first read, *Hope Message Return Patience*

Goddamn.

He went from corner to corner extracting cards.

Faith Belief Live Return

Passersby taking one, reading it, holding it tight, close. Tucking it away to take it out later. Reaching for another one. Reaching for the promise . . .

Testament Believe Love Acceptance

Jesus. Like prayer cards.

Respect Loyalty Return Trust

Holy saints . . . and all overnight—how the hell had they done that?

"Look at this, have you seen this?" he demanded as he was shown into Wyland's office. He tossed the cards down on Wyland's desk.

Wyland picked them up and spread them like playing cards. "They turned up overnight." He got up to shake Kyger's hand. "Just suddenly they were all over Town. Sons of bitches. Pushing that ecclesiastical boundary a little too far on top of the missing body, if you ask me. Not coincidental, by the way. Sit down."

Kyger sat. "I haven't got much to report, and the fact it's been a month and a half since Venable's murder and the veneration of him is escalating like *that* . . . I feel as if I'm failing you."

"These things take time, my boy. I knew that when I brought you into this. No one expects you to do in a month what the Yard and all our investigators haven't been able to do in the two years Venable rose to such power. On the surface, as you see, he's pristine. But you have to scour the surface first to make sure there isn't some telling flaw. So tell me what has happened."

"Another trip to the Bullhead." He was reluctant to even say that much because he had no idea if what they had seen there, he and his vanishing virgin, had anything to do with Tony Venable.

Or the fog, the coachman, or what had happened at the Park of the Seven Sisters.

Or the mysterious and ubiquitous cards, for that matter.

"I found nothing conclusive," he said. Just the chocolate virgin, moving walls, hooded men massed in sevens, the mysterious disc symbol, and the undercellar storeroom which had nothing stored in it. And the coachman who had somehow found his way to the Bullhead from Cheapside.

Nothing definitive at all. Everything as insubstantial as the fog, and the whole sounding like a chapter in a penny dreadful.

"But—its obvious pleasures aside, I think there is something to be uncovered there," he added. "I just don't know what."

"I do, too," Wyland concurred. "But these insidious cards that turned up overnight, something wholly unexpected—and I'm thinking this is another avenue we need to explore. Someone funded those signs and those card pockets all over the city. That's not an inconsiderable amount of money to spend to disperse Tony Venable's message. The timing on this is spectacular. All in the month or so since his death—the growing movement to lionize him, the move to make his house a shrine and center of his ideology, then that séance and the uniform message to his adherents, then the body disappears—nothing on that, by the way, and the Yard is deep into investigating it—and now the signs and cards. Signs and wonders, some might say. We can't let it go farther than this."

"They were snapping them up this morning as I came here."

"It's a brilliant tactic. All in public, and they just won't let him die. I just wonder where the money for this is coming from. And maybe, if we can find some link to the money, we'll find a clue to what will take Venable down. So—by all means, keep following up at the Bullhead—at your pleasure—but now, since the little Season is about to launch, I think we're going to launch you into society as well to see what idle gossip you can pick up.

"You didn't hear me say that, by the way. If the powers above even knew that I'm running this whole operation *not* by the book . . . This is so out of the ordinary, I still don't know quite what to do, or even what you're looking for. Whatever seems out of order, I suppose. What seems anomalous. Whoever might seem to be a great admirer of Venable's ideas and ideology. A boast, a brag. Someone carrying an inordinate number of the actual cards. Or talking about them . . . I really don't know what would raise your suspicions. I just want you to be looking—starting tomorrow. Public places first so you'll start to be seen but not draw attention to yourself. A subtle insinuation is what we're after. But you'll be among the kind of people who might just support Tony Venable's cause. You'll make it a point to ride in the park every morning. Start conversations. Make acquaintances. Go to the museum, play cards at the clubs. Lujan belongs to Heeton's. I'll get you in there. I'll make certain you get invitations to the right dinners and parties, places where someone else might be conspicuous, but because you're Lujan's brother, you'll be welcomed."

Kyger blinked. . . . *because you're Lujan's brother* . . . words he'd hardly ever thought to hear; he was shocked to the core that Wyland was telling him that his big brother had not just been a steeped-in-sin voluptuary who cared for nothing but the satiation of the flesh. That he hadn't just come to Gomorrah for the express purpose of fucking his life away. That something else had happened here, and that he had made the connections and alliances that a man of stature and wealth ought.

"Are you still in Cauldwell Gardens?"

Kyger nodded.

"I think you should move into the town house. It makes a better story—the younger brother back from his year abroad and ready to immerse himself in society—and perhaps find a wife . . ."

"That's a little self-serving," Kyger said. "Even if I wanted to find a wife, there's no time for that."

Wyland shrugged. "It's a plausible story. Lujan has settled down. You've done your world tour. You're well-heeled. You're taking your pleasure at the Bullhead—which any well-bred scion of a wealthy man would—and now you're thinking about marriage. It serves our purpose just as well, my boy, and you'll be operating on two fronts here, and perhaps between the two things, you'll uncover something we can use."

"As you say, sir. I'll open up the house today."

"Good. And I'll infuse your account with the funds you'll

need. Hyde Park tomorrow, then, and dinner and dancing to follow."

"It sounds so frivolous," Kyger said.

Wyland grasped his hand. "Or, of everything we've tried, it just might prove the most fruitful."

Chapter Eleven

A London Season was a proscribed thing, aligned with the opening of Parliament and timed with the end of the sporting season in the country, a grouse shoot having more importance than governance in some quarters.

The first event of the Season, after Parliament convened, the presentation of this Season's debutantes at Court, and Easter, was the Royal Philanthropic Society Charity Ball—the Queen's Ball, as it was known, the most prestigious charity ball of the year. The invitations were the most coveted, the contribution was costly, and this year, because of the upcoming celebration of the Queen's Diamond Jubilee later that summer, it was one of two major must-be-seen-at events this year, and as always, it was the signal for the launch of the Season.

"So," Mrs. Geddes said as they were going over her list of necessities and must-do items the next day, "we must engineer an invitation. You can be certain that your father will have been invited, and probably his invitation included you. And you must be aware that you could see him there."

"Well, then—" Angilee said and stopped short. The prospect of seeing Zabel in that kind of crowd didn't bother her at first thought. The more important thing was the invitation. Immediately it occurred to her that she could just slip into Zabel's hotel room when the maids were cleaning and the door would be ajar, find it and save Mrs. Geddes a lot of trouble.

But she couldn't tell Mrs. Geddes that.

"How do we go about doing that?" she asked finally, already girding herself for the task of returning to Claridge's and instigating a room search. The maids came at noon, she seemed to remember, and probably Zabel would be out at that hour. Although once in a while he did have his midday meal in the room, more often than not, he—they—dined in the hotel dining room.

"You leave that to me, Miss Rosslyn. There are ways. This is a charity event, after all. And it is the Queen's Ball. Money is never refused."

"I see," Angilee said. But what she saw was more money pouring out of her pocket when the simple solution was to extricate her legitimate invitation from Zabel's room.

How hard could it be? Of course, he could have posted guards in the hallway, waiting to pounce on her in his certainty she must return sometime. But surely after a week, he'd have understood she wasn't coming back, she did have money, even if it was *his* money—but he had more than enough money anyway—and that she was not going to marry Wroth, and she was perfectly capable of fending for herself.

What would she do if he had hired watchmen to guard the suite?

She'd deal with that later. The simplest thing was to get to the hotel and get that invitation so she wouldn't have to spend the money to buy one.

"Well, here is the itinerary that would normally be followed during the Season," Mrs. Geddes said finally. "You'd spend the morning riding in Hyde Park, between ten and perhaps noon. You'd have breakfast, and then either begin your round of afternoon calls or go shopping. You might have been invited to receptions, picnics, garden parties and the like, but that won't happen for a while, and so these adjustments have to be made: we will attend public amusements—polo or cricket matches, for example; we'll take an additional afternoon ride in the park, go on promenades, you and I together, go shopping, to museums and to the lending library, and hope to make some acquaintances who will be sufficiently charmed by your father's wealth to include you in a dinner or evening event invitation.

"Meanwhile, I will scour my connections to secure those same sorts of invitations—and I'm assuming you would prefer to attend dances and balls, where there will be a larger population of eligible gentlemen who are not yet attached. The competition is fierce this year, as you know. We need to buff up your wardrobe as well, which is very elegant and trim, but not—quite . . ."

Angilee bridled. She had excellent taste, she knew it, and her newly acquired wardrobe *was* up to the mark for ready-made wear. But—this was not a ready-made society, and wardrobes were looked at through a magnifying glass. "Yes," she said tartly. "My *quite* wardrobe is sitting in my dressing room at the hotel doing no one any good. You must allow me some time to see if I can get hold of it, rather I spend additional funds to reoutfit myself."

"Do you truly wish to do that?" Mrs. Geddes sounded very doubtful. "On the other hand, it would take quite some time to have the dresses made to my exact specifications. So . . . perhaps you ought . . ."

The "ought" part was the scary part. Stealing a piece of pasteboard was one thing, but how she would accomplish the filching of an entire wardrobe from the hotel was quite another. Although a trunk would be helpful. And perhaps buying new undergarments to save some time.

"I think I must try," she said finally.

Mrs. Geddes stared at her. "Well, I have never . . . you *are* an original, Miss Rosslyn, truly fearless in the face of everything that could happen in the course of your attempting this. I will deny backward and forward that I ever had anything to do with you if your father should discover what you're about."

"A wise move," Angilee said dryly. "This is all between my father and myself in any event, and I am determined to come out the victor. And if I need my beautiful Parisian designer clothes to do so, then I will make sure I have my Parisian designer clothes. Just don't ask me how I'm going to accomplish it."

"I wouldn't dream of it," Mrs. Geddes murmured. "I truly don't want to know."

Angilee didn't want to tell Mrs. Geddes that *she* didn't know either, but time was growing short. By Mrs. Geddes' list, it seemed to her she had a vast amount of work to do on her own. She had to make an effort to meet people, and make herself agreeable enough to be invited places, while she cleverly insinuated herself into the mob of British and American heiresses jockeying for the same position in a way that made her distinctive enough to be noticed by some eligible bachelor.

With her father's intimidating presence at any one of the events she might attend, although she was certain he would never make a scene.

But even then, there was no guarantee she would find someone willing to marry her on short notice.

Well, that was for later. Right now, she needed that invitation to the Queen's Ball, and she definitely needed her beautiful new clothes.

She needed a plan of attack.

She needed to know if anyone was watching her father's hotel suite. She needed to know what time the maids came in to clean. She needed some kind of suitcase or portmanteau. She—

BUT—! She'd left with nothing: her suitcases, her trunk, were still in the suite, unless her father had totally discarded everything that was hers.

Would he? She didn't think he would . . . it was too soon—

Was it?

And if he had—? Would he have stored her things in the hotel? Donated everything to a charity? Burned it in the sitting room fireplace?

No, that was an investment of too much money for him to do something as foolish as either giving her clothes away or donating them. He'd store them for sure, if they weren't still in her closet.

She needed to get into the room. She needed to accomplish all of this in the next two days, if not tomorrow.

All right. She squared her shoulders. Tomorrow. First things first. And the rest could come later.

Kyger fully expected to find the town house closed up tight and empty. It wasn't. He opened the door to the warmth of a house that was attended to, that was bustling with servants, that was ready for someone's arrival.

Lujan?

"Oh, yes, sir," the butler, a butler who was new to him, said deferentially. "Mr. Lujan comes about once a month to tend to his investments and the like."

Oh, yes, the investments. His deceased father's unholy, long-lost hoard of diamonds that they—he, Lujan, and Jancie—had all transformed into fortunes that would cushion them for the rest of their lives.

He'd barely touched any of his money since he'd returned. And Wyland was going to finance this little Season, which wouldn't come cheap.

But Lujan—managing his investments? Lujan, in the percents, eking out the best interest, making his money increase, rather than spending it on whores and wine? Lujan belonging to Heeton's . . . ?

God, the world *had* turned upside down, and it wasn't just the foggy mysteries of Tony Venable, the Bullhead, all the coincidental sevens, or those insidious invocation cards.

And being *home,* although he'd never considered the town house his home, really, wasn't much reassuring, because nothing here was what he thought it would be either. Nevertheless, here he would stay, and so he told the butler once he had introduced himself and made clear he would be in residence for the time being.

"I'll write a note to be sent down to Waybury that I will be occupying the town house for the foreseeable future, if you'll see to it—Cryder, did you say?"

"Yes, sir. I'll arrange for a boy when you are ready, and meantime, I'll ring for a footman to take your bags."

"Excellent. If I may—some tea . . . and perhaps dinner to be served early."

"I'll see what Cook can do."

And now what? He wandered into the parlor and threw himself into a chair by the fireplace. A servant could procure him a mount for tomorrow's ride around the park. Tomorrow afternoon, he'd stroll through the Royal Academy's summer exhibition, and later, he'd find a cricket game or something like that. Public, open, lots of opportunity for conversation.

. . . Lujan's brother—you'll be welcomed . . .

All things he'd willingly renounced in favor of life in the country. Look at him now—prowling around brothels in the name of justice, and girding himself for a Season to root out a killer.

God.

He'd given up the rooms at Cauldwell Gardens. A good thing, because his vanishing vestal could never find him again. Couldn't distract him again, couldn't beg for help and importune him to marry her.

She'd left of her own volition anyway. He'd never see her again. And that was to the good—she was just a cheap whore anyway, and he was just lying to himself if he thought otherwise.

So why was she still in his head and on his mind? Why was he still thinking about her? Why did he still feel there was danger surrounding her and that her innocence was no pretense and she really needed help?

And why did the sex of her still suffuse his senses?

It made no sense. He'd never see her again.

He looked up and disengaged from the thought of her as Cryder entered with his tea.

Claridge's was brimful of people at eleven in the morning. All those trim, tight, beautiful *a la mode* young heiresses, fresh-faced, glowing-eyed, setting out just a little later than usual for their morning rides.

It was easy to mingle among them, to waltz through the lobby and the dining room where dozens of families were just finishing up brunch and deciding how to spend the rest of the morning.

There was a palpable excitement in the air: the debutantes had been presented, the invitations had been issued for the Queen's Ball for the succeeding Saturday evening, and the formal launch of the Season was about to begin.

No one noticed her—but Angilee had dressed not to be noticed—as she slipped through the dining room from the lobby to the entrance that was accessible from the guest elevators.

This was the trickiest part: someone could recognize her. Someone her father had hired could discover her. The concierge might remember her.

The elevators were so slow, she thought she would scream. They stopped at every floor. God, there were so many guests, all those fathers, all those families, all those *girls* who were competing with her.

This was an impossible task. Her father would win.

No, he wouldn't.

She positioned herself at the endmost elevator, with her face averted, and waited impatiently for the lift. Time was flying. She could feel it rushing against her face like the wind. She had accomplished so much, and there was such a long way to go.

It all seemed insurmountable suddenly. She felt as if she had thrown everything away and there was no chance to escape her fate.

She felt like a fool. Except she had no time for that. That could come later. Everything else could come later.

For now, she had a mission, and she would push through. She moved aside as a dozen people emerged from the lift, and she slipped in and urgently pressed the button.

One person dove in before the cage door closed, and she held her breath that it wasn't someone her father had engaged. But no, he got off on the third floor. She let out her breath.

A moment later, she was cautiously easing herself out of the lift into familiar territory: the silent, hushed floor of suites—all corner suites—all as huge and luxurious as her father's.

It had taken fifteen minutes to get up here from the time she entered the lobby. And the reception area was empty. There were no guards. There was no sign anyone occupied any of the suites. No sign that maid service had either come or gone.

And she felt a moment of pure terror that there was nothing else she could do, no other plan to formulate.

There was virtually nowhere to hide, unless she crouched under one of the two console tables, where she could easily be seen by anyone exiting any of the rooms or coming off of the elevator.

Other than that, there was a thick, plush oriental rug on the floor, a gilt-framed mirror hanging over each of the consoles, a small, round parlor table in the center, on which mail and messages were distributed, and two ceiling-height potted palms in glazed pots, one on either side of the two bronze elevator doors.

Her frustration was intense. She should have asked at the

front desk about the maid service. Or the concierge. He probably wouldn't have remembered her. She ought to be grateful there weren't armed guards outside her father's suite.

They could, however, be inside.

Everyone could be inside, just waiting for her to make an egregious mistake.

Except, she'd already made it by coming here and leaving herself so wide open for discovery.

She felt her bones turn to jelly as she heard the rumble of the elevator coming upward and saw the brass pointer above swinging inexorably toward this floor.

Oh, God, now what?

She pressed the button frantically, but that was no help—the second car was at the lobby level, and not moving, and the rumble sounded louder and louder in her ears.

She darted to the opposite door and squeezed herself tight against the palm. After all, what could happen? It could be any one of the occupants of the other suites, at which point she really need make no excuses; it could be the maids, and they hopefully would be intent on their purpose, would, with any luck, start on her father's suite of rooms, and wouldn't even notice her squeezed behind the palm.

Or it might be Zabel, and in that event, her mission would be over right then, right there.

She held her breath and wedged herself even more tightly between the wall and the trunk of the palm, thankful she was wearing drab colors, and closed her eyes tight, as the lift made a noisy halt and the door slid open to the sound of voices.

Zabel? Neighbors? Maids?

Another sound, as she thought her heart would explode—wheels. Something rolling. A trunk, a handcart? Room service?

God, she couldn't stand this. If by the grace of fate she was not caught, she wasn't coming back. Whatever she meant to accomplish, she must do today and never return.

She opened her eyes, fully expecting to find Zabel standing there, menacing and *right*.

But no—and she almost dropped to the floor—not Zabel. Not neighbors—luck was with her—it was two women, one of them

at the back end of a handcart with supplies and cleaning imple-
ments, and the other unlocking the door to Zabel's suite.

Oh, dear God . . . she felt paralyzed as she watched them pull
the handcart over the threshold and park it where it kept the door
from swinging shut.

Oh oh oh oh . . . the relief pounding in her kept rhythm with
the pounding of her heart. A minute to catch her breath, to
relax—but she couldn't spare that moment—she couldn't stay
here like this—she had to get into the suite.

She heard the chatter of the maids as they descended on
Zabel's bedroom to make the bed and dust.

Now . . .

She clamped down on her fear, eased herself out from behind
the palm and darted to the handcart and crouched behind it.

Great—that left her wide open to be seen by anyone coming
out from the other suites or the elevator.

Whose stupid plan had this been?

The maids were still in the bedroom. She slipped into the
room and made for the sitting room windows where there were
thick brocade curtains framing the view.

But—the maids might dust and shake out the curtains. Still
they were the safest bet, thick and encompassing like the curtains
she'd hidden behind at Bullhead Manor.

She had to trust . . . she had come this far on gut and guile,
and what else was there for her to do? Her money was limited,
she'd spent too much already on the fees to the agency and on
Mrs. Geddes' salary and the flat.

Money didn't last. It was the hardest thing for her to come to
grips with after the free-spending life she'd led with her father.
Money ran out. It could buy only so much when you were trying
to spread it out over so many different expenses and you had to
pay them.

It was her only salvation, and she had to do everything she
could to conserve it. So there really was no choice: she had to be
as circumspect as possible and get out of the hotel with a trunk-
load of her expensive clothes and that invitation to the Queen's
Ball.

She couldn't afford either otherwise, and she had to go to that ball, and she needed those gowns. It was simple as that, and it was the only plan she had, and she meant to carry it through.

And the rest she'd think about later.

Kyger rode that morning in the Park. This was a pleasant enough exercise on many levels. All the beautiful aristocrats were out taking the air, with the full influx entering the mill around eleven o'clock. There were carriages and horseback riders; there were those who chose to stroll and some who brought a light repast and stopped to have an impromptu picnic.

They all knew each other, or if they didn't, they knew the right people to introduce them to the right people. It was a fabulous quadrille with its own fancy steps, its own intricate pairings, and all of it done with an ease of manner and deceptively clever maneuvering that fooled no one as to its true purpose.

But then, these people were experts at that.

He had hated those games, hated the insincerity, hated the calculated desperation of the marriage mart.

And here he was, the last place he'd ever thought he'd be, secretly seeking the key to a demagogue's downfall, a vanishing vestal, and a financial fountain that could fund a dead fanatic's future.

And no sevens anywhere . . .

He listened in on the snippets of conversation as he cantered past knots of people and slow-moving carriages. It was all the same: wicked gossip about who looked haggard, who looked thin, who was beyond redemption, who was the coming thing.

Derision abounding for the American heiresses, irritation that their turf was being invaded, overrun, penetrated by the enemy. Wagers as to who would wind up with whom. Who was the most eligible, who was the most desirable, who had the most money, who would buy a marriage.

Debutantes did not care about Tony Venable.

Nowhere did he see evidence of the invocation cards. Nowhere did he hear any mention of Venable at all. All the focus was on the coming events of the Season. The Queen's Ball. The exhibit at the Royal Academy. The results at Ascot. The right invitations. The competition. The fashion. With whom to be seen, where to be seen, whom to ignore.

He rather liked being the mysterious stranger among them. He knew they were looking at him. He selectively acknowledged some of them. He heard the whispers: *Who is he? Why don't we know him? Oh, I would like to know him . . .*

Find out who he is—

The first step toward securing coveted invitations—make everyone want you because they didn't know you and thought perhaps they should.

Just in case. Just in case you *were* somebody. Just in case you were fabulously wealthy. And you weren't married. And you were looking for a wife.

He was back to the town house two hours later for a light lunch and a change of clothes. Out once again, on horseback, and over to the playing fields at the Crossway for a well-publicized cricket match between the teams from the Eligibles' Club and Heeton's.

Here he was in the company of men of influence and power, avid sportsmen, who were perhaps rabid about politics. Enough to donate that kind of money to Tony Venable's cause? Hard to tell. They were no different from each other than they were from him.

In the stands, there were a dozen or more women, accompanied by their chaperones and their fathers, who had a betting interest in the game.

The rooting was hot-tempered and fierce. There were no conversations, except about who should be on the playing field, and what the batter's chances were against the next pitch.

On the surface, attending a game was a good idea, but in the heat of a game, no one was discussing politics and money over the consequences of a fielder's inability to make a critical catch.

In the end, he left the game early and took a leisurely ride back to Town and through the Park again, where the late afternoon loiterers were taking another turn themselves in the hopes of seeing or meeting someone interesting.

Then they would ready themselves for the evening's events, which now, in advance of the formal opening of the Season, comprised private dinners, or a musicale, attending the theater or the opera.

None of which interested him. He was more interested in trying to sort things out, to lay out the mysteries and make sense of them. He would eat in and spend the evening at home . . .

—the town house, *home?*—

He wondered if he'd ever had a home. Even when he'd managed Waybury, it had been Lujan's home. This town house was Lujan's home away from home, when he made his now monthly sojourn to Town.

Where *was* his home?

It was strange to think he'd never had one. And he suddenly felt a strong elastic pull to remedy that. And that maybe the purpose of his journey to demonize a demagogue was to finally bring *him* home.

An hour seemed like a lifetime when you were hiding behind a thick muffled curtain on a warm spring day.

The maids, chattering, laughing, efficient, went from Zabel's room to Angilee's, which really ought not have needed any straightening at all, spent ten minutes or so in there, and then back into the parlor and sitting room to dust, sweep the carpet, and swipe the mirrors and metal surfaces with a vinegar-and-water cleaner, and then they were gone.

Angilee took a deep breath to calm her thrumming body and shaking hands, and then she pulled back the curtain from the far side.

Empty. Quiet. Except for her incessantly pounding heart which was so loud, she'd been certain the maids would hear it.

There was no sound anywhere. The walls were so thick no noise could penetrate, not from the reception room, not from outside. She wouldn't be able to hear a footstep, even. If Zabel should return, she would hear the key in the lock, and nothing more. And then she'd have perhaps thirty seconds to hide.

Where would she hide?

Oh, hell, did that matter right now? Under the bed, then, she thought, as she darted into the room that had been hers. Would that fool anyone? She didn't want to try. The thing was to get what she needed in the next ten minutes and get *out*.

Dresses first. Forget the undergarments and accessories. That could come later.

Oh, but her jewelry—maybe her jewelry . . . damn, damn, damn . . . was anything even here? The room was neat. She ripped open a dresser drawer.

Yes! Piles of lingerie. Yes. Yes. Her relief made her knees weak.

No time for that.

She needed a suitcase—or something . . . would Zabel have stored her trunk? The suite was so huge, he really would not have needed to spend that money. There was room enough in the dressing area, which was as large as a bedroom itself.

Let my trunk still be there.

Her clothes were still there, all hung neatly encased in tissue. Oh, thank God. But not the trunk. The trunk was gone.

Now what? Time was flying. Zabel had suitcases. She was certain of it. She hadn't wanted to crush her clothes in that small a space, but the good thing was, she'd be able to manage suitcases, where she might have had to call a bellhop to take her trunk.

All right. Suitcases, then. She went into Zabel's room, into his dressing room. Into the storage cupboard first—yes, there, on the top shelf—everything arranged to give her the most trouble and take the most time—into his bedroom for the chair at the small desk by his bed . . .

Don't look at his bed. Don't smell his scent, which permeated the room. *Don't think, just do . . . just go . . . get the suitcases . . . there*—two fairly large canvas suitcases trimmed in brown leather . . . they would do just fine . . . put back the chair, close the cupboard doors, the dressing room door, his bedroom door, make sure no one had entered while she was taking the suitcases . . . couldn't be too cautious . . . it was just a little after the noon hour by her watch . . .

What *had* Zabel done in the midday hour? She couldn't remember anymore. He was probably at some club, probably with his cronies planning the evening's debauchery.

Don't think about that either.

Into her room, open the suitcases, which actually were fairly deep. And just pile in the clothes. Fold, push down, crushing the tissue, crushing the delicate fabrics—the satins, the silks, the feathers, the lace—in they went, indiscriminately, haphazardly.

She had no idea which dresses she was taking, just enough to fill two suitcases. And when they were piled up with her dresses, she threw in handfuls of the spider-web delicate lingerie, and only then did she close the lids and lock them down.

Only then did she allow herself to breathe. And lift the suitcases off the bed.

Oh, dear God, they were heavy. Heavier than you'd think with those thin silk dresses. She staggered out into the parlor with them. How was she ever going to get out of the hotel with them?

That would come later.

She needed that invitation, and that would be either in the desk in Zabel's room or . . . or—she didn't know where.

Into Zabel's room again. To the desk. Papers on the desk. Nothing that looked like an invitation. Damn. Into the drawer. More papers. It seemed as though there were an inordinate amount of papers for a man who was just visiting.

She didn't care. Just the invitation, that was all she wanted. Nothing in the desk. Back into the parlor, into the sitting room where there was another desk, this one by the window.

Time, time, time . . . nothing on the surface. More papers in the drawer—wait—under the papers, a square vellum envelope.

Open it, hurry—copperplate script—

*The Patronesses of the Royal Philanthropic Society
Request the Pleasure of Your Company . . .*

There it was—it might even be, it probably was Zabel's invitation, but he could easily secure another. Better still, maybe he wouldn't take the trouble to attend.

All right. She could leave.

Except—

Wait—her jewelry—

No—Zabel had probably put it in the hotel safe . . .

A quick look . . . Back into her room—

She always kept her most loved pieces that she wore the most in a small leather case that had a mechanism she could attach to the underside of the lowest dresser drawer, so that the case was far back under the drawer so it didn't catch when the drawer was pulled open.

She knelt beside the small three-drawer dresser next to her bed, held her breath, pulled the drawer, and reached underneath it for the case.

. . . there it was—yes . . . no time to check if everything was there—she had to get out, *now* . . .

She opened one lock of one suitcase and shoved in the invitation and the jewelry case, closed it, and grabbed the two suit-cases.

Oh, God. Staggered out into the reception room, got the door closed behind her. Punched the lift button. Hoped and prayed no one was coming up to this floor—

Hoped and prayed Zabel wasn't returning from some meeting or the club or lunch; thanked the heavens that her father was a man of consistent habits, and that the hotel maid service was timely.

The brass pointer started swinging upward.

Her heart began pounding. That weakening terror suffused her body. The game wasn't over yet. She couldn't assume some-one wasn't in that lift. Couldn't assume it wasn't Zabel . . . couldn't assume her life wasn't over—yet . . .

Held her breath. Wanted to sink into the floor. Felt time stop, heard the grinding, halting sound, and the smooth slide of the bronze door opening into the lift—

The empty lift . . .

She almost fainted. Not quite. Had the presence of mind to drag one suitcase to hold open the cage door, so she could pull in the other. And only after the door closed and the cage clanked tight did she let out her breath and clutch at the grab bar so her legs didn't give out.

Almost over . . . almost . . .

Down, down, down to the lobby—all those people—if she could just get a bellboy now—

Her breath felt tight; her heart felt constricted. She lifted the suitcases and lurched out into the lobby—

"Here, let me help you—why didn't you ring for a bellboy?" It was a gentleman emerging from the dining room, someone she didn't know, an older gentleman with a kind face—*will you marry me?*—it would save so much time and effort, but there was a woman with him . . . "Here—boy—" he called for one who came with his merciful rolling cart, and he tipped the boy, tipped his hat to her, took his lady by the arm and disappeared.

"Where to, ma'am?"

She pulled herself together. "Please, would you secure a cab for me?" The pleasures of having money. She flashed the boy a smile. "Thank you so much."

She followed him out to the carpeted canopy area at the side of the hotel. She was safe, finally. No one would see her here. This was for the arrival and departure of tired and bedraggled travelers, the real bustling heart of the hotel, not to be seen from the elegant front entrance where everyone emerged *comme il faut* and ready for the day.

Almost there. A hansom drew up, the driver and bellboy simultaneously reaching to open the door for her.

One more step to anonymity. Almost there . . .

"Where to, ma'am?"

The driver was young, eager. She gave him the address and climbed into the cab, leaned into the shadow of the cushions and breathed a deep sigh of relief, because now, finally, as the hansom pulled away from the hotel, there was nothing to fear.

Chapter Twelve

"We have three days," Mrs. Geddes said, as they opened the suitcases and sifted through the dresses. So many dresses. Even Angilee hadn't known how much she had stuffed into those two bags. And she surely didn't know the etiquette and subtleties of dress required on this side of the Atlantic.

Mrs. Geddes lifted each dress out and made pronouncements:

A green watered-silk evening gown with chiffon pleating and ruching around the bodice—"That."

A butter yellow chiffon over satin—"That."

The white faille with feather trim. "No."

The mauve chiffon with paillettes. "That."

The purple-and-white taffeta. "No."

The sky blue mousseline. "No."

The ivory silk and chiffon. "That."

A bronze taffeta with matching passementerie embroidered on the hem, waist and bodice. "That."

The dresses fell in a heap to one or the other side of her bed.

An ivory satin and lace. "That."

A dress of black moire. "No."

"Why not that?" Angilee asked, pointing.

196 / *Thea Devine*

"Not with your coloring," Mrs. Geddes said briskly. "Beautiful dresses, all quite *a la mode*. Extremely *quite*. Perfect, actually, but not if they wash out your complexion and make you look drab."

"Oh." Who ever considered such things when on a spending spree?

"Your father gave you *carte blanche*, didn't he?"

Was that a bad thing? "Yes." Obviously it was.

"I knew it." Mrs. Geddes picked up a moss green silk and gold-shot tulle ball gown. "That. Quite lovely, actually. Perfect. I think that one is perfect for the Queen's Ball. And how clever of you to . . . obtain . . . your invitation."

"It was the only thing that made sense," Angilee said, picking up the ball gown and holding it up against her body. It was wonderful—a rich, elegant color that brought up the pink in her cheeks, and the gold flecks made her eyes seem to sparkle.

Mrs. Geddes was right. In this gown, she would conquer society, find that husband, and she would show her father just how much she didn't need him and how independent she could be.

Because he'd be there—he'd find a way; as she well knew. Zabel was a most determined man. He would have discovered by this time that someone—and who else could it have been but she?—had scavenged the suite and taken the clothes and his invitation. But what could he do, after all? What *would* he do, even if he accosted her at the ball? It just wasn't *de rigueur* to strong-arm your daughter in public. Especially at *the* social function of the year. With everyone watching.

She was safe.

Maybe.

"We'll need accessories," Mrs. Geddes was saying. "You forgot the shoes, the gloves, a little bag. The jewelry—while it's not spectacular, I can make it look like more than it is."

Angilee heard very little of that, just this tail-end warning which made her shudder: "So—we will go shopping tomorrow, Miss Rosslyn, and I hope you're prepared to spend some of that money."

It was now one day until the Queen's Ball, and several days previously, Kyger had received the coveted invitation to Heeton's

where he had spent two pleasant evenings playing cards and losing big, which, combined with his nonchalant attitude about the
money, made a favorable impression on his hosts, who indeed
had welcomed him most warmly on learning he was Lujan's
brother.

Conversation around the table that first night was idle, far-
ranging, nonpolitical: they were feeling him out, testing his met-
tle, looking for soft spots, making certain his philosophical
positions were in line with theirs.

He found it was easy to predict what they wanted him to
say—and it was his job to say what they wanted to hear—but
nevertheless, the camaraderie was so seductive once those tests
had been passed, he could see how someone would just fall in
and let himself be enfolded by the sense of community that subse-
quently surrounded him.

The second night things got a little more pointed. Politics now
came into play in a seemingly casual way. Comments about the
queen, the government, the prime minister, and in connection
with that, finally, just a passing reference to the death of Tony
Venable.

"Not such a shame, that," one of the men, Hackford his name
was, commented as he took two cards. "He was getting beyond
himself. Knee deep into that autocratic nonsense. Thought if he
were actually appointed prime minister, it really meant he'd be
king."

"Or dictator," another put in.

"What do you think, Galliard? Heard enough about the ven-
erable Venable to offer an opinion?"

"I've heard some rumblings, of course," Kyger allowed. "Don't
forget—I'm only back in London since mid-March. So I've heard
a lot of talk in the street, a lot of grief, anger, a lot of breast-beat-
ing."

"And all that bogus religiosity, too," Hackford said disgustedly.
"Makes me cringe. Not over yet, either. Did you see those pockets with those cards?" He made a sound. "Sleight-of-hand nonsense. Now, *these* cards make sense. So, where are you, Galliard?"

"Right here." Kyger lay down his cards. "And vengeance is
mine, Hackford . . ."

"Clean and sweet," Hackford admitted, throwing in his cards

and throwing up his hands. "All right. I concede—a man needs to be juiced up by a win every now and again. But this is the last one, Galliard. The next round is mine . . ."

And it was: Kyger made sure he sustained a healthy loss, tempered by a couple of unexpected wins. It was easier that way, too. These men, contrary to how they appeared, were sharks, and they were out for blood, whatever the undertaking. And they were serious cardplayers, and serious money turned over in these games.

They were among the movers of society, and they tended to hide out in the clubs. Some were married, some were looking, some wished the Season and the heiresses would just go away, but they all would be attending the Queen's Ball, along with everyone else in London and beyond.

They would not have supported a city full of those cards of supplication that disseminated Tony Venable's precepts and promises like seeds. Because those words would sprout and grow if they were planted in the proper soil. And someone with money knew—the general populace, those who'd adored Venable, was ripe for the plowing.

Just not these men. They hated Tony Venable, and they saw clearly what he had been about. *Autocrat. Bogus religiosity. Sleight of hand . . .*

Exactly.

At least that was what they said publicly. What did they think behind closed doors? Shit—what was he thinking?

Nothing was exempt from consideration.

Hellfire.

The day before the ball, after an afternoon of bonhomie at an exclusive garden party at which all he heard about was who was the most eligible, the handsomest, the richest, the most desirable, the best catch, the least likely, he realized he hadn't done anything about proper evening dress for the next night.

Well, good—he wouldn't have to go.

No, not possible. So what did the gentleman of fashion do in such a situation? There couldn't be a tailor in London where something like that could be procured at this late date with this many bachelors loose around Town.

However—the thought hit him—he did have a brother who

sometimes came to Town. Maybe he kept a second wardrobe here. Maybe even—a waistcoat and tails.

He rang for Cryder.

"Sir?"

"Mr. Lujan—does he keep some clothes here for when he's in Town?"

"Yes, sir."

Hope against hope: "Formal clothes?"

"Yes, sir."

"I need to borrow them. Would you bring them to my room please?"

Cryder didn't look happy. "Yes, sir."

He had taken the guest room. He hadn't gone into, hadn't even gone near, the room that was Lujan's and Jancie's. The guest room was commodious enough. The guest room wasn't redolent of her scent and their sex.

He wasn't going to think about that. Too much loss in his life, between his mother and Jancie and everything that had happened in between. But those two years away had been good for him, had made him sinewy and strong in ways that he hadn't even counted yet.

Maybe too sinewy to wear Lujan's clothes?

The garments were on the bed when he retired for the night. They proved to be snug across the shoulders, and the trousers didn't break over his shoes at the angle he preferred, but on the whole, the suit fit at least well enough for him to wear the next night.

Small mercies.

But fate wasn't merciful. He found himself tossing and turning all night with the feeling he was missing something, that there was something among all the oddities and coincidences that he wasn't seeing. All those sevens. Those subtle references to *sacred*. The Samaritan. The mystery coachman. The séance. The moving walls.

Check, check and check. He'd been over and around all that dozens of times since the moment he arrived. Wait—check. Right, he'd been on that point sometime in the past few days. Gates with triangles that separated into mirror-image sevens. Chevron sevens . . .

No. That was really stretching things to imagine the equally angled chevron decoration on the gates of Waybury represented sevens. It had been a stunning moment, but—he was letting the idea of the coincidences get totally out of hand.

But there *was* something about a check mark.

Chevrons could look like check marks.

No. No. Something else. Check marks. No—marks . . .

Death mark. There had been, early on, a reference to—where had he heard it? He pummeled his memory with no luck until he finally fell asleep.

The next morning, he went for his now usual morning ride. The day was bright, beautiful, warm with the promise of spring, if not the promise of Tony Venable.

He was amused that the prospect of attending the most prestigious event of the Season that night had in no way deterred the debutantes and bucks from their morning exercise in attracting attention.

They swarmed around and about him like bees, their conversation a lulling buzz enveloping him, and then they were off down the riding track with a verve and vigor he wished he felt.

This was one morning, however, that he was of no particular mind to chase after or listen in on random conversations to try to solve the impenetrable mysteries surrounding Tony Venable.

For once, on this bright spring morning when there was no unsettling fog creeping in around the sunshine, he just wanted to feel its warmth, and look at the flora and fauna in the Park, and let the passing lady-flowers take a good look at him.

As if it all were real. As if he had a place here and the right to be among them, and to choose among them. As if things were normal and, outside the boundaries of the Park, there weren't fanatics trying to make Tony Venable into something he wasn't.

Just for this morning—to enjoy the calm before the storm of the Season really began . . .

And yet, even with all the life springing forth in the Park, trees were dying. Trees that weren't budding out, whose desiccated bark was peeling off in wallpaper-sized strips, whose trunks were bitten into by birds and blistered by lightning strikes . . .

There, ahead of him a huge tree in its death throes, crosshatched, with a huge chunk of it gone. And over there . . . He reined in suddenly, violently. Over there . . . Walked his horse slowly onto the grass to the tree . . . on which there were slashes cut deep into the bark.

They looked like check marks. They looked like upside-down sevens . . .

They had little points on the short end that looked like—

. . . fishhooks . . .

Fishhooks . . .

His blood ran cold. There was the link—the thing he'd forgotten, was missing, couldn't think of. Fishhooks. Check marks.

Death mark. He heard that long-ago, well-paid informant saying it as clearly as if he were behind him. The mark that was on Venable's body. The bloody little cut on his bare chest that was shaped like—a fishhook . . .

The death mark.

Everybody knows, nobody tells . . .

Nobody tells.

But something else struck him as forcibly as lightning as he stared at the slashes cut into the dying tree.

The mark on Venable's body could just as well have been a *seven* . . .

"A ball of this magnitude is a fabulous thing," Mrs. Geddes said, as she arranged Angilee's hair into an ornate upsweep and dotted it with a handful of glittering earrings from Angilee's jewelry case. "Barring, of course, the celebration of the Queen's Diamond Jubilee. But that will be later this summer, and a very different sort of . . . There. Lovely. A simple necklace. Diamond earrings. A bracelet. A wrap. Don't forget your gloves. The carriage awaits . . ."

Angilee slipped her feet into the too-expensive ivory silk slippers they had found in a small shop not far from Bond Street. And the gloves in a matching parchment color . . . they felt like a second skin; their cost alone had skinned a fair amount of the money she'd allocated for the accessories, those details that were oh, so important, Mrs. Geddes insisted, and on which she must not skimp.

She would count it money well spent only if that one man she needed, the one man who would agree to marry her, was among those attending the ball.

He would be. She would go to this ball believing she would meet him there, tonight, and the rest could come later.

Mrs. Geddes, who was attired in stringent black-watered silk, enhanced with lace-and-jet jewelry, had ordered a carriage for the evening.

A carriage that immediately got caught in the crush of traffic approaching the Mayfair mansion of the Duke and Duchess of Shaftsbury, who were the evenings' hosts.

The mansion sat on a corner, four stories of highly decorated stonework, with two arched doorways on the sides that faced the street, which gave immediate access to the reception rooms. The arrival times had been staggered to prevent such traffic tie-ups, but no one ever paid attention to that. One didn't want to arrive too early or too late, and it was considered a good strategy to plan to arrive at eight o'clock, which meant one might hope to be in the ballroom by nine or nine-thirty.

Angilee's pulse began to thrum the closer they came to the mansion. This was it—entrée into one of the most exclusive social functions in Europe. The handsomest, wealthiest, most socially revered men in the country would be here. And after all, she didn't need a duke—a baronet would do just as well.

Or the itinerant son of a diamond miner . . .

Don't think about that . . .

As the carriage crept closer to the entrance of the building, she could see all the flower dresses of the women, the bright blooming colors, the bronzes and yellows, mauves and blues. The brilliant women, dripping in diamonds and sapphires and pearls. The gorgeous men, so tall and formidable in formal dress. The bevy of chaperones clucking after their charges like mother ducks.

It was a wonderful spectacle, and wholly unlike anything she had ever experienced. New York had not been like this, with its stiff, disapproving patronesses, who looked down their lorgnettes at her and her *parvenu* father. And the men and women, who'd known each other since the cradle—no room in there for anyone but themselves.

No, this was so much better. So elegant. So exciting. All those American heiresses who couldn't find husbands at home, mingling with the lords and ladies, and you could not tell who was which.

In a moment, she would be among them, as wealthy and elegantly dressed as they, with as much purpose and need as they, and she would outwit and outmaneuver them all one way or another.

The spectacle had suddenly turned into a battle for her, and she forcibly clamped down on that combative feeling because she didn't want to diminish her pleasure in this evening.

Even waiting to debark from the carriage did not make her as impatient as it made Mrs. Geddes.

"They have never found a way to have a ball and accommodate the conveyances of those in attendance. You would think after all these years . . ."

"And how many years have you attended balls, Mrs. Geddes?" Angilee asked, merely—really—to make conversation.

Mrs. Geddes shot her a look. "Enough to know nothing will ever change and not to complain. At least they have their people directing traffic. That might make things a little less congested."

Still, it was after nine o'clock by the time their carriage pulled up to the door. Even then, Mrs. Geddes preceded her in order to keep a rein on Angilee's impulse to race out of the carriage and into the reception room. Ladies walked decorously and never showed that kind of energy. She needed to save it for the dancing in any event.

"Slowly, stately, decorously . . ." Mrs. Geddes whispered as the footman helped her from the carriage. "Chin high. You're a princess, a queen. Everyone's watching . . ."

And cameras clicking and artists sketching, trying to catch every detail of every gown in a minute's glance. The swelling murmur of conversation. The crowds. The scent of perfume. The stinging rays of light refracting against diamonds. The warmth of so many bodies in one place, pressing to move up the two wide staircases to the ballroom. So many *beg pardon*, *sorry*, *excuse me*, and interested *oh*'s and *well, hello*'s, as gentlemen inadvertently knocked against Angilee and took notice of her.

It could not have been more perfect. She was admitted instantly on extending Zabel's invitation to the attendant at the door, and she drank in every detail, from the huge anteroom set up with refreshments to the smaller room beyond where tables had been arranged for those not inclined to dance to play cards.

In the cloakroom, she gave her wrap to an attendant, took a tasseled dance card and pencil from a basketful set by the door, and was handed a beautiful hand-painted fan, the favor of the evening, as she and Mrs. Geddes entered the ballroom.

Not once did she think about or look for her father. Or Wroth.

They'd never find her in this crowd anyway; and if they did, they'd never make a scene among all these people who valued appearances as much as manners.

Good. She could relax and enjoy herself. Because somewhere, among all these eligible, rich, lovely men, there had to be someone who would be willing to marry her.

Kyger arrived sometime after ten o'clock as he had been advised by his friends at Heeton's. In that way, he'd avoid the crush and the initial awkward partnering for dances by which time the debutantes and spinsters wouldn't be feeling quite so desperate, and fresh food would have been put out in the supper room.

It was an overwhelming affair. Even at ten, people were still arriving in droves, and he had to elbow his way through the loitering crowd who were deep in conversation to make his way up to the ballroom.

There, it was a brilliant scene of color and movement. The floor-to-ceiling windows were wide open to mitigate the stuffiness of so many bodies in one place. There were chairs lining the walls, candlelight throwing a soft glow over everyone and reflecting the frieze-framed mirrors on every wall. The dance floor was burnished to a high polish, and the dancing was concentrated at the end of the room where the orchestra played, even though the music could barely be heard for the hum of conversation.

Along the sidelines, chaperones watched their charges with the eagle eye of an admiral on the foredeck. Nearby, knots of gentlemen discussed politics and business until they were nudged by their wives or mothers to choose a partner for a dance.

Circling around them, a promenade of gentlemen with their dance partners making their way to take some refreshment before attempting the dance floor again.

Here and there, a face Kyger recognized, from the club or from the cricket field. Nowhere, the insidious ghost of Tony Venable.

And yet, he must have attended many functions such as this. Surely someone in this crowd was missing him.

He wandered through the groups in conversation, listening, excusing himself, trying to find a place to get to—the refreshment table, perhaps—that wouldn't require him asking someone to waltz, and would allow him to freely eavesdrop.

Except it seemed as if he'd been taking the verbal pulse of the crowds since he'd come to Town. It was wearing—the whole Tony Venable thing was exhausting, because he was still grasping air.

And it was obvious he wouldn't hear anything of interest here. Everyone was too focused on the charm, eligibility and social standing of every one of the men and women in attendance. Beauty was negligible, depending on the side of the bank account.

Still, he saw them eying him, as if he were one among them. He felt like it tonight, especially when, as he approached the refreshment table, he was hailed by Hackford and a companion he identified after a moment's furious thought as Billington, another of the cardplayers, the silent one, from his evenings at Heeton's.

"Well, you tidy up well," Hackford greeted him. "Have some punch."

He took the delicate cup, marveling at the expense of having enough cups, refreshments and food for a thousand guests. But that was this kind of event. Everything was thought of, everything provided.

Music pounded away in the background. A swirl of dancers surrounded them, and moved on. All they could do was mill through the crowd and watch. Conversation was virtually impossible. Matrons were looking speculatively at him, Kyger realized, now he was in the company of Hackford, with an eye toward getting an introduction and forcing him to dance.

The last thing he wanted.

Was it?

The women were beautiful, really, and it wasn't just the lights and the romanticism of an evening that hinged on meetings, matings and possibilities.

All of that was in the air and more. A sense of excitement and urgency and all of it having nothing to do with sevens, secrets and Tony Venable.

Good. Maybe he needed that, after this afternoon's stunning realization. He needed not to be thinking about any of that tonight.

Something would present itself. It always did.

. . . *what*—? Something played around the edges of his memory, something he needed to know, but then the thought swirled away as several of his acquaintances came to greet Hackford and beg an introduction to Kyger.

Here was the beginning of the end, he thought resignedly. And he would be out on that dance floor long before never.

"Let me present Mrs. Sparks," Hackford murmured, with an evil glint in his eyes.

"Mrs. Sparks."

"Mr. Galliard. So pleased to meet you. We do have the acquaintance of your dear brother, Lujan. And now we know you both. Pray let me introduce you to my daughter, Jacintha."

There was nothing for it but to take Mrs. Sparks's arm and allow her to bring him to Jacintha, who proved to be tall, willowy, and while not beautiful in the common way, rather striking. And deadly dull.

"So pleased," she murmured as he bowed.

"Would you care to dance?" He had to ask. His skills on the dance floor were decent at best, and nothing compared to those who had been tutored by ballroom masters.

She threw a terrified look at her mother, which seemed to indicate she no more wanted to dance with him than he with her. But her mother stared at her in that meaningful way mothers on the prowl had, and she stood up stiffly and said, "Thank you, I should. Like to dance, I mean."

He found a smile. "I won't bite, and I don't dance very well myself."

That did not ease the tension on her face.

It was a waltz. "We'll count the steps together," Kyger said, trying to reassure her. He held out his arm, and together they walked onto the dance floor, and he put his arm around her and gently began to sway and move her stiff, resistant body.

"One, two, three, one, two, three . . ." He kept time as he literally pushed her unwilling body around the dance floor, barely avoiding collisions now and again, and regretting the need to be accommodating and kind.

Jacintha had no feel for the music and no conversation at all. She would never be the first sought nor would she be the last to find a partner, if her dowry was as generous as he perceived it probably would be. Women like her endured mistresses, bore babies and immured themselves in the country, content with their titles and their tenacity at finding a husband.

Round and round they pushed, making their way through the hundreds of dancers in a stolid workmanlike way. He saw the mother, nodding the way mothers did who were parceling possibilities in three-quarter time. He saw Billington, deep in conversation with several other men, he saw Hackford gleefully following them around the dance floor on the fringes, he saw . . .

He saw . . .

No—they were past what he thought he'd seen, past all probabilities, past redemption in this awful pounding partnership of a dance . . . it could not have been—it *wasn't*—because if it was . . .

This goddamned dance was never going to end. Jacintha had started to relax just at the minute his attention had been diverted elsewhere, and now that she wanted to exchange pleasantries, he needed to find—*her* . . .

. . . Imagination? No, it had been *her*, his vanishing virgin— hadn't it?

Round the floor they went, one two three, one two three . . . hell and forever, this dance . . . looking, he kept looking . . . finding a noncommittal word now and again to keep up his end of what passed for conversation.

His mind on *her*—dressed in mossy spring green, fresh as the air, chocolaty hair sparkling like dew . . . vanished again—

Too many people separating the illusion from the reality; it would take this entire night to find her . . . or she could be out the door like Cinderella already . . .

Leaving no glass slipper behind. Just the glassy eyes of Jacintha as the dance mercifully came to an end. And now mercy on his part: "Would you care for some refreshment?"

She stared at him. "Uh—no—oh, yes, please—"

Which then required that he offer his arm, promenade with her to the refreshment table and ensure she had everything she required.

After, he thanked her politely for the pleasure of the dance, returned her to her mother, thanked Mrs. Sparks for the kind introduction, and held his breath as he escaped.

Hackford intercepted him. "Sorry, old man. That was your initiation, having to dance with a chair virgin. You acquitted yourself quite well."

"She was very sweet. She hates to dance, but I wager she'll do well walking down the aisle, and I wouldn't be half surprised if it wasn't with you."

Hackford gave a shout of laughter, clapped him on the shoulder and invited him to the card room.

"You're not fulfilling your God-mandated duty here, Hackford. I, however, consider myself exempt."

"My dear boy—if Lujan can settle down, so can you."

"But I like the wanderlust life."

"From what I hear, you like the life of lust."

Kyger stiffened. *Something will present itself* . . .

Hackford? How did he know? That, he hadn't expected.

"Well, there's someone here tonight I could lust after . . ." *Damn it, I have lusted after . . . I have pinned and pronged and pumped myself into her body and I want her—*

Hackford moved closer. "Tell me who?"

"Saw just a glimpse of her. A beauty garbed in green . . ."

"Oh, that's helpful."

"Porcelain skin, chocolate brown hair . . ."

"Sounds delicious—stop there, or we'll all try to eat her before you do . . ."

"You can but dream, old son. I *will* find her first. I know what she looks like."

Hackford wheeled around, eying every flower dress in sight, seeking those women dressed in green. "That one?"

Kyger shook his head.

"That one . . ."

"Not hardly."

"A lot of green girls here tonight, my man."

"Thank God," Kyger said fervently. *Something* . . . and how did he translate that *something* into something tangible.

Maybe not tonight. Tonight was to find the elusive, vanishing and ever innocently virginal Angilee. Tonight he wanted no help, no camaraderie. And tonight was the one night he couldn't shake Hackford from his side.

Or was that deliberate?

He began prowling around the room, and Hackford fell in step beside him, murmuring, "I'm intrigued."

"Can't find your own flower-lady?"

"No, no—you're not allowed to diminish my manhood. You are, however, allowed to share."

"I am not surprised."

"It's mandated, actually."

"Take your choice, Hackford. You could have any of them."

"Yes, but a virgin with chocolate hair—that's something else again."

Now he was irritating, and Kyger was annoyed. He clamped down on his temper. "Any other friends of friends you'd like to introduce me to?"

"What about that one?" He nodded toward a blonde girl, really a girl, in apple green who moved with gawky steps but with the certain assurance of the wealthy and wanted among the matrons and patrons.

"That girl has money," Kyger said.

"Oh, she has money, and she's ripe for reaming. Just the right age, that one. They're malleable, that young. And grateful."

"It's not her," Kyger said dryly.

"You're a sly one."

"I'm sorry I ever said a word. You'll haunt me now. I've made her into something she's probably not just by calling attention to her. It will hardly be worth the effort to find her now."

"Bored easily, eh? You probably imagined the chit anyway Come on, let's have a round of cards."

They skirted the edge of the crowd, heading toward the supper room, and there, just out of the corner of his eye, Kyger caught a flash of green emerging from the cloakroom. He leapt forward, with Hackford on his heels, his first instinct to grab Angilee's arm—it was Angilee, wasn't it?—and caught himself, and heeded his second, more rational thought to just follow her until . . .

Until what? He cornered her? He coveted her right out in public?

But he couldn't know her; he'd told Hackford he didn't know her. How could he pretend to not know her when she would instantly recognize him?

Or maybe not. She *had* run away from him, after all.

Hellfire.

Now what? Have someone introduce them? Ridiculous.

She'd swirled through the crowd with an expert assurance, moving toward a phalanx of older women who could only be the chaperones. Worse and worse. And Hackford not three steps behind him.

"I say, Hackford—"

Thank God . . . Hackford slowed down and turned to the voice and engaged him in conversation.

Kyger quickly came up behind Angilee and called her name softly.

Even in the din, she heard him, she whirled, and it *was* her— the her he *knew,* and yet, a her who was different, with her worldly Paris gown, her lush coloring, her fresh innocence, her patrician bearing.

What had this *her* sprung from? This wasn't the desperate virgin looking for a way out of a distasteful marriage. Nor was this a woman unsure of herself or her place in society. She looked the part; she acted the part. She was the woman of wealth and breeding she had always claimed to be.

But he also knew she was headstrong, stubborn and singleminded.

And luscious as chocolate.

She gave him a disgusted look. Trust her hired penis to show up just when she didn't need the complication of him around.

She had thought things were going just fine so far. There was as yet no sign of her father or Wroth, and there were hundreds of lovely eligible and potential husbands roaming around the ball-room, any one of whom could ask her to dance at any moment, could ask her to . . .

"You! I thought it was—well, who cares who I thought it was . . . What do you want? You shouldn't be speaking to me anyway without an introduction."

"I'd say we've been—well, improperly introduced."

"You must be imagining it. I've never seen you before in my life."

"Aha!" Hackford, coming up behind him. "Well, hello, and who is this? Do introduce me to your friend, Galliard."

Galliard? Galliard? Angilee didn't know the name, hadn't come across it in the social register that Mrs. Geddes had insisted she read before the ball. Galliard. She rolled the name around in her mind, on her tongue.

Galliard. She couldn't quite connect it to the hired penis in the brothel. This was insane. Him, here. How was this possible, when he was a dissolute libertine who lived in rented rooms somewhere outside of Town?

"My name is Angilee Rosslyn," she said abruptly, preempting Kyger's introduction.

"Ah, American."

"From the South," Kyger put in helpfully.

"And I'm James Hackford." With the obsequiously proper bow.

Kyger could have strangled him, but Hackford went on in his easy way: "So pleased to make your acquaintance, Miss Rosslyn."

"Are you, *Mr.* Hackford? Or is it Lord? Will you marry me?"

That shocked him. He took a step back, absolutely at a loss for words.

"Or you, Mr. Galliard. Will you marry me?"

"Are you asking every man at the ball?" Kyger asked wryly. Hackford looked horrified. "Has anyone said yes?"

"So pleased to make *your* acquaintance," Angilee said through gritted teeth. "Let us keep it that way. Mr. Hackford? My pleasure. Mr. Galliard . . ."

She turned away as Hackford punched his arm. "She's crazy. You're well rid of her."

"Give me a minute," Kyger murmured, hoping his desperation didn't quite show. "I'll meet you in the card room. Five minutes."

It was almost too late. There was a dragon waiting for Angilee with a most disapproving look on her face as Kyger intercepted her again.

"You can't keep doing things like that."

"Like what? Looking for a husband? But that's the express reason I'm here, and if you won't marry me, I need you *not* to be here, so that other eligible gentlemen may have their chance."

"Angilee—this is crazy."

She shot him a sizzling look. "It is the perfect plan. When I find a husband, it will end all my problems. The fact I was damaged goods counted for nothing, so more drastic measures were called for. Let me introduce you to my chaperone, Mrs. Geddes. Mrs. Geddes, I know it's bad form, but this"—*libertine,* she wanted to say, *this bastard,* she wanted to say—"guest," was what she said, "introduced himself to me, and surely it's bad manners to just walk away."

The dragon looked him up and down. "And just who are you?"

"Kyger Galliard, ma'am."

"Galliard—Galliard—the diamond miner who died two years ago?"

"Youngest son thereof, ma'am."

"Well, not an itinerant ne'er-do-well, at any rate," the dragon pronounced. "There was a fortune in diamonds involved, or so the gossip said."

Spread by his brother no doubt, Kyger thought. "So they say."

"And I assume you've been at the family town house since you returned?"

He looked at Angilee, who was pointedly looking at the crowd. "Just returned there, ma'am."

She raised her eyebrows. "Well, a house in Belgrave Square is nothing to sneeze at."

"No, ma'am."

He waited, but the dragon didn't offer him *carte blanche* to call on Angilee. And she had her nose turned up at him altogether.

"Miss Rosslyn?"

"Mr. Galliard?" Her tone was frosty.

The dragon caught it. "A pleasure to meet you, Mr. Galliard. Perhaps we'll see you again sometime during the Season."

"Oh, you may count on it," Kyger murmured. "Angilee?"

She gave him a startled look.

"Would you care to dance?"

He'd raised his voice slightly, too, so everyone around heard his request, and now she was trapped. Mrs. Geddes had dismissed him, and he did not want to be dismissed, and so––she could refuse him, but she was in no position to make a scene about anything. Her father, or Wroth, could be anywhere in the room. She was safer in *his* arms at the moment than sitting with Mrs. Geddes, waiting for someone to ask her to dance.

And it would be rude beyond measure to refuse, and it might deter any other man within earshot from asking her to partner him. She looked at Mrs. Geddes, who was also gauging the temperature of the crowd around them, and she nodded almost imperceptibly.

"I would be pleased," she answered, taking his arm and allowing him to lead her onto the floor. He put his arm around her, and she flinched at his touch, and the feel of him against her, and the memories that instantly flooded her mind and body. *Control that.* "What do you think you're doing, Mr. . . ." She couldn't quite say his name yet. *Mr. Penis. Mr. Took-my-virginity and left me high and dry . . .*

"Dancing with you, as prescribed by custom."

The orchestra struck a note, everyone stood poised, waiting for the swoop of the music, and as it swirled up around them, off they went, in graceful concentric circles around the ballroom.

"If you won't marry me, there's no point to your dancing with me," Angilee whispered fiercely.

"But we've danced before, Miss Rosslyn, hip to hip, body to body, and I haven't forgotten a moment of it."

"That's curious—I don't remember ever having met you, Mr.—" *Bullhead bull . . .*

She felt color rising in her cheeks at the thought of it, of what she'd done in desperation, in the name of directing her own future her way, and in the name of circumventing her marriage to Wroth.

Even now, she felt terrorized by the mere thought that he or her father might be prowling around somewhere in this ballroom. For all her bravado, she knew he still had a score to settle with her, for running away, for stealing his money, for foisting her expenses off on him, for stealing her clothes and his invitation to this coveted event—

But the bull's arms around her were so strong and secure—*why* wouldn't he marry her?—it made so much sense, it wouldn't be forever, and he could have whatever she could afford to give him in the end . . .

. . . except—

. . . had she imagined she'd heard Mrs. Geddes say he had a house in Belgrave Square . . . ? And something about a fortune in diamonds? She hadn't been half listening in her pique, but she surely had heard that . . .

Hadn't she?

"You're wasting my time, Mr.—" Again his name stuck on her tongue. "I could be dancing with a man who *wants* to marry me."

Her single-mindedness irritated him. "You are so fixated on being married. You don't need to marry someone. There are other ways around your problem."

"But this is *my* way," Angilee said, scanning the crowd for some inkling of whether Zabel was there. "And your way was to say no to my proposition. We have absolutely nothing to talk about."

It was true, if she was going to be that obdurate, there was nothing more to say. But he could kiss her into submission. It was tempting to want to try. It was the wrong time and place to want to try, with Hackford hovering around the edge of the circle of dancers, and the dragon standing there with her arms folded eying him as though he was the plague.

Or the second coming, since his fabled fortune in diamonds had been right on the tip of the dragon's tongue.

Damn Lujan's hide.

"Oh, I have lots I want to talk about."

"I don't know what you're talking about," Angilee said as they whirled around to the eddying strains of the waltz. Almost over, almost there. Some prospects eying her with interest.

She smiled brightly, looking just past him. *Galliard* . . . whatever his name was—that could have been a lie—whoever would have thought . . . ? The man she'd paid to take her virginity—the second son of a . . . *bitch*—

Chapter Thirteen

She was a sensation. Once the ice was broken, and someone had taken notice of her, the men lined up quickly to fill her dance card.

Angilee loved the fact there were dozens of them. She felt powerful, beautiful, wanted. And she hated being beholden to her hired penis for all the immediate and gratifying attention. She disliked it intensely that he just stood on the sidelines watching her with a stormy look in his eyes.

She despised herself for having given her body away to a stranger before she had had the opportunity to explore the possibilities of a Season as a means to find a temporary mate.

She loved whirling around the ballroom in the arms of the various gentlemen who were well-bred, admiring, eligible, charming and available.

She didn't like any of them particularly, but it wanted only one of them to be interested for her to move to the next step of her plan.

She made it a point to be extra appealing, accommodating and admiring. She spread Southern charm like it was molasses. She tilted her head beguilingly and smiled at every comment no matter how inane, and complimented her partners extravagantly on the least little thing, even to the way they kept time to the music.

It was tiring. At least with the bull, there had been no pretense. She had chosen him for a reason, one that was up front and nakedly there. And that didn't just go away because she had dismissed him: she was pointedly aware of him as she circled the floor with this partner and that, manufacturing conversation and compliments.

Why wouldn't the bull marry her? It would have saved so much time and energy. It could have been done already. He could have been two weeks into the bargain already, even if he didn't need the money, with the end in sight.

He had no right to pop up like this and make things worse, and make her want something she couldn't make possible. She wished he would go away.

Let him go away . . .

Damn him, damn him, damn him . . .

"You were saying, my lord?" she murmured as she lost track of some point her partner was making.

"Would you care for some refreshment?"

"Oh, I'd be delighted," she answered, whipping enthusiasm into her tone, as the waltz ended and the Honorable Trevor Smythe held out his arm.

The bull was watching still, standing there like marble, unmoving and disapproving.

He had no right to even *look* at her. He'd had his chance; he'd had his turn. He'd had *her,* and none of that was enough to induce him to marry her.

So let him steam and stew. Let him wish and want.

Let him look at all these other men who wanted her now.

She smiled up at the tall and awkward Honorable Trevor, and gave him her hand.

"Ah, she found another pigeon . . ." Hackford, sneaking up by his side. "And that one *is* ripe for plucking. Good luck to her. No one knows who she is anyway. Come along now, we've got a serious game going in the back room and we need an infusion of a thousand pounds of flesh . . ."

Kyger made a sound. The last thing he wanted was to leave the ballroom. Angilee was dangerous with those dark come-to-me eyes, and that curvaceous body that too many men already had held in their arms.

He knew what it was like to hold her, to plumb her, to wring from her a pure, uninhibited sexual response. That kind of physical connection was not that easily dismissed.

She hadn't forgotten, she had power now, which she didn't know fully how to wield, she couldn't be trusted, as well he knew, and she was hell-bent on finding someone to marry her—a combination that was ripe for disaster.

She was in a reckless, dangerous mood, and he wasn't even certain that the dragon would be enough protection for her.

And he didn't have the right. Or the time.

Hellfire.

He didn't care. No, he cared. Shit.

"Listen, you're falling into an abyss, my friend. You need to come with me. This is all a set piece. All the marital arrangements have already begun behind closed doors, except for those wild cards, like the American heiresses. And they're negligible. They'll marry whoever's mausoleum needs to be bankrolled. So it's hard to tell where your goddess over there fits into the pantheon of open purses. Forget her—believe me, there are dozens of willing women—you don't need her, no matter how alluring she is."

"No," Kyger said reluctantly, flatly, letting Hackford lead him away. "I don't."

I do.

They maneuvered through the throng, and it seemed as if it had increased twofold since Kyger had arrived. It was now past midnight, and the attendees acted as if the ball had just begun. There were dozens crowding into the supper room, dozens more on the dance floor. Dozens of women swarming in and out of the cloakroom or the dressing rooms, mending torn hems, fixing their hair, checking their jewelry, stealing out to look over those who had just recently arrived in hopes it was someone fresh and new.

And they were still coming up the steps from the reception rooms.

But back in the card room, things were quieter. Two dozen perhaps, seated by fours at the various tables.

Hackford paused on the threshold for a long moment, scanning the tables, until he found the group he was seeking, and suddenly he relinquished Kyger's arm.

Kyger looked down curiously. Hackford's arm was stiff at his side, with his hand clenched, and then slowly he moved his forefinger to point downward, and his thumb outward.

It was but a moment's worth of movement, if that, and then Hackford grasped him by the elbow and propelled him forward before he even registered that something had happened.

Or had something happened?

"These are old friends," Hackford was saying. "Billington you know. Wambley. Beston. Armitage. Here you go—Galliard the younger, full of push and vinegar and thinks he knows cards. Let's show him, gentlemen, shall we?"

He pulled out a chair for Kyger, and the one next to him. "What's on for tonight?"

What was on for the night was large losses, deliberately large on Kyger's part. And Angilee flirting around the edges of his consciousness.

Forget her.

He couldn't. She looked too beautiful tonight, too beguiling. There was something about her. Maybe it was just her single-mindedness, or the way she flaunted rules. Whatever it was, she was too seductive, and she could not be left to her own devices, and the dragon ought to know that.

Only not from him.

He heard the music faintly in the distance. The dancers had broken for supper around ten-thirty, and the dancing had resumed an hour later. By custom, there would be another dozen or so dances before the ball ended, which meant that many more men Angilee might rashly proposition.

No—he was worried for nothing: the dragon would not let that happen. She hadn't encouraged *him*, nor Trever Smythe. The dragon would protect her, she didn't need a knight-errant, especially one who had taken her virginity and twice refused to marry her.

220 / *Thea Devine*

He needed to concentrate on the cards. On losing. On that curious hand movement. On the mission.

And he couldn't. He was as chained to the table as if he were actually in shackles. At that point, it was easy to lose, because his every thought was centered on Angilee.

He had to find her—sometime tomorrow. If she had a dragon, if she had a proper ball gown and jewelry, if she had entrée into social circles, then she was somewhere in London, if not with her father.

He could find her. It might be too late, but he would find her. And meantime . . .

The game went on. These were baccarat devotees, with a side dish of *vingt-et-un*. They played in shifts, they played hard and steady, and they played to win.

They were winning, and he was going down for the count. But they all knew about and believed that he had a fortune in diamonds stashed away somewhere, and he was ripe for the plucking, and they'd nip and pick at him until he was stripped bare.

And then they wanted to go to the Bullhead.

"Come along, my good fellow." Hackford nudged him. "A good time is to be had by all. It'll be on our chip. Let's go."

And they went, through the still teeming crowd, both in the ballroom and those now slowly making their way to the lower level, and waiting for their carriages.

Angilee and the dragon among them? Damn it, where was she?

Thank God, the multitude moved slowly, engaged in gossip and speculation every step of the way. He had a chance to scan the crowd, to look for the telltale green gown, the elegant posture, and the chocolate hair with glittery drops sprinkled through the curls.

But all this shuffling forward made Hackford impatient, rude, and he wasn't about to wait: he was a veteran of those events; he got them through the crowd in jig time.

There were a dozen footmen, taking names, and a dozen more boys acting as runners. One by one, the carriages were called forward, according to name, from where they were parked on streets adjacent to the house.

Hackford barged up to the front of the line and gave his card.

There was a disapproving murmur behind him, but he didn't care.

"That's the thing about these affairs," he said as they settled into his carriage and it moved forward slowly. "You never can get away fast enough."

But once the carriage was clear of the clog of waiting vehicles, they were off like the wind, arriving at the Bullhead less than an hour later; and in five more minutes, they were admitted into the lush and hushed reception room.

A woman glided out, dressed in form-fitting diaphanous black, which merely emphasized her breasts, her hips, her nipples, her shaved mound. Her hair was pulled back into a topknot, and around her neck she wore a black leather choker with a black leather rose appended.

"My lords?" Her voice was husky as if she had just had sex. Her body was luscious, her nipples tight, hard, bulbous and tempting.

Hackford was tempted. He paced around her, eying her as if she were a prime piece of horseflesh. And then he moved behind her, wrapped one arm around her waist, and encircled one breast with his thumb and forefinger.

Forefinger pointed down, thumb straight . . .

Sliding his fingers down to her rigid nipple tip where he squeezed, hard. "We'll have a night of nipples and fucking. Starting now, Mistress Nipples. Starting with your honey. Spread your legs."

She complied instantly, lifting her hem, spreading her legs as Hackford ripped apart his trousers, and in a moment, he had her backed up against a wall, and he was humping her.

"Good hot wet one, gentlemen," he panted as he spewed. "You next, Billington."

Each of them took their turn with her, Armitage and Wambley in particular riding her hard and rough, lifting her high against the wall, huffing obscenities as they thrust themselves to oblivion.

Kyger last, almost as if he were the initiate. In he went, off he went, like a trigger pulled by mistake—he shot his wad instantly, hard and heavy.

"First course," Hackford said. "She's available for the entrée and dessert. Whom should we ask for?"

"Mistress Nipples will do," she murmured.

"We want nipples," Hackford commanded. "Now."

"Excellent, my lord. Come with me."

Their rooms were on the upper floor, where everything was that much more lavish. Thicker carpet, more elegantly appointed rooms—there were satin-covered beds, satin sheets, piles of plush pillows on which to ride or recline, several thickly cushioned benches, both flat and inclined to accommodate whatever position the client was inclined to initiate.

Here, a beautiful courtesan came to help him remove his clothes and warm up his body for the strenuous night ahead. Kyger felt more like a pasha waiting to be serviced in his seraglio than a randy libertine paying to expend his seed.

The courtesan was naked, but for a veil over her head which obscured her features, and the necklace with the black rose, and her fingers were like fairy touches, patting, stroking, slipping, sliding, caressing . . . and then she offered her body as his vessel, bending over the bench that was inclined, so that his engorged penis, which she had deliberately aroused to the point of expulsion, could empty into her, and ready itself for what came next.

There was no way to avoid availing himself of her nakedly accessible receptacle. They were watching. He would have wagered his fortune on it. There was nothing else he could do, no other choice but to grasp her hips, tilt her body upward, force his way into her soaking wet hole, and take her as quickly as he could manage.

And it was quick. Five hard thrusts and he was gone, almost as if his spunk was so pent up, he couldn't wait to expel it. And that on top of emptying himself in a flood into the first whore.

He wondered if they measured the amount of semen produced in any given night by any given patron, and if that were some kind of test.

He wondered if tonight, *he* were being tested . . .

Because this kind of camaraderie was too much, too soon, even with him being Lujan's brother.

God, he wanted to get out of there. No more anonymous naked bodies. No more slick meaningless couplings with slick meaningless whores . . .

Four women slipped into the room, each one of them veiled,

shaved, and with the ubiquitous black leather rose around her neck. They surrounded him. They reached for him. They took him as he stood, one after the other, hands, mouths, tongues, all over him, in every valley, every cleft, every opening, every inch of his skin, fondled, licked, nipped, between his legs and down to his feet, at which point he had sunk to the floor, and they were all over him.

One at his mouth, two at his penis and balls, and one, somehow, deep between his legs. No words needed to be exchanged. He was their king; anything he wanted, they would provide. And more. They held his hands, his legs; they kept him immobile while they prodded him, played with him, and sucked at his penis and scrotum.

He came. A man had to be inhuman not to sink into the voluptuous handling of four beautiful women whose sole function was to fuck him. He came in a spume of hot semen spraying high and hot all over him, all over them, and they took it and rubbed it all over their breasts and nipples and rubbed it all over him, and licked it like it was vanilla cream, and they made him shoot off even more to massage into his skin, and between their legs.

He felt boneless, as if he would never move again. His body felt sapped and drawn, as if they had taken his lifeblood as well as his semen.

And they were still at him, with their hands, their mouths. They were expert, these faceless courtesans, and they acted as if they were enjoying every nip and bite as they roamed up and down his body, devouring him, inch by inch, eating his penis inch by inch until it hardened into a stiff iron bar of penetration.

And then, one by one, they sat on him. Just eased themselves over him, their legs spread wide to give him the best view of their bare raw nakedness, and they took him, slowly, grindingly, agonizingly, one by one, wringing from his penis every last spurt and drop after he had come three separate times inside them.

And then silently, they left, slinking out like ghosts, leaving him sprawled on the satin sheets soaked with his rich warm semen, and the scent of lust still thick, hot, and arousing permeating the air.

He fell into a deep, exhausted sleep in the thick ensuing silence. A strange sonorous silence, from which he awakened with a jolt, suddenly aware.

It was too quiet. Too dissonant, as if there were a presence in the room. Or the watchers . . .

He swung out of the bed. No one in the room.

The four hungry houris had not returned. Odd.

Everything was odd tonight.

He prowled the room, every instinct on the alert.

Too fast, too soon . . . he couldn't shake the feeling. Hackford had brought him along too quickly for a few days' acquaintance. Even with the losses at the card table. Even with the use of Lujan's name.

Shit. He moved to the door. Thought better of it. They were watching.

Were they watching?

He cracked open the door. Not a soul. Too odd. Not the usual Bullhead menu of on-the-hour pleasure and pain.

Or maybe not this night for him.

Why?

He eased out into the hallway, naked. No hindrances tonight. No clothes. No chocolate virgins to slow him down and impede his progress. No sevens, signs, symbols, or omens.

He wasn't so certain about the moving walls.

The hallway was no different than the one in which he'd been trapped on the lower floor. The dim lighting, the long swath of thick carpeting, the mahogany walls incised like panels, the fitted doors with the brass pulls.

What was different besides the opulence of the rooms? The ominous silence? As if things were going on behind closed doors? Things were, things no decent man wanted to know about. Or be part of.

Jesus . . . he was getting nowhere. The hallway ended at an intersecting corridor, nothing different from the floor below. The smooth walls, the ringing silence, the feeling of walking down the road to Sodom . . . nothing he hadn't experienced on his previous visits.

Yet something was different. It was a different floor of the mansion, a different level of services, a different feeling in the air.

But no different floor plan: at the end of the intersecting corridor, there was no place to go, no moving walls shifting him into secret rooms with secret symbols and secret men playing children's games with their secret rituals, secret silence and their predilection for the prurient.

That was all it had been, what he and the chocolate virgin had seen, he thought suddenly. Just another component of Bullhead's menu of services for the profanely wealthy. This scene, had they watched it play out, would have been the sacrifice of a virgin, perhaps, who would have been placed on that bier, her naked innocence at a convenient height for easy, hard penetration by all the participants in what had probably turned into an obscenity of a passion play.

Enough of that. These voluptuaries lived to spend their seed, in secret and behind closed doors, and the more they expelled, the more they needed the experience heightened by the forbidden pretense of the pornographic.

And the women, the whores, were complicit, everything was consensual, and that was the whole of what the Bullhead was about.

His sensibilities were tame by comparison. He couldn't even imagine what Hackford and his friends were up to tonight. He didn't want to know, nor could he explore any further; he'd been away from his room for far too long, long enough to arouse the suspicions of the watchers or . . . what if Hackford had come looking for him?

It took him two minutes and he was back lolling on the sex-scented satin sheets. Fooling no one, probably. But not a moment too soon because he heard a soft scratch at the door, and Hackford's voice, calling to him.

"Galliard. Come. Mistress Nipples is performing for us."

No time to grab any clothes; Hackford was buck naked in any event, and grasped his arm and pulled him the opposite way down the hall and into a doorway that was marked by a shiny black disc just over the opening.

Inside, the scent of ejaculate and sex was thick and overpowering. There were a dozen other men already there, all naked, all with protuberant erections being attended to either by one of the two veiled courtesans dressed in the leather necklaces with the black roses, or by their own hand.

On a dais in front of them, the courtesan Hackford had named Mistress Nipples was tied by her wrists to a piece of furniture that looked like an ornate hall tree with openwork on the upper half that allowed for her silken bonds to be threaded through, and a seat with crosspieces, which gave the mistress purchase to drape her legs over to give full widespread access to her lush shaved cunt. There was a soft pillow just in front of this where her supplicants could kneel, worship her sex and spill their seed in adoration.

Beside her, there were two men dressed—eunuchs?—in loincloths, each of whom was responsible for fondling one nipple which sent the mistress into a continual writhing belly dance of pleasure as it sent her audience into convulsive ongoing orgasms.

And whenever they felt like it, any of the guests could lick, suck, poke or fuck anywhere on the mistress they were moved to, so that there was also an ongoing pageant of two to three men at her body at any given moment. When any of them wished to suck her nipples, the eunuchs held her breasts and made certain the nipple was tight, prominent, and succulently rigid.

When any of them wished to suck between her legs, the eunuchs lifted her hips to provide the perfect opening for an avid poking hot wet tongue.

If any of them wanted to fuck her, they canted her body at the perfect angle for penetration.

Sometimes there were three at a time working her body; sometimes it was just her sensual fuck-me dance with the eunuchs stroking and squeezing her bulbous nipples. Sometimes there were two sucking her nipples and one kneeling at her cunt.

At all times, the voyeurs stroked and pumped themselves to the rhythm of whatever was going on in the tableau, and coming one after the other or in unison.

"We're keeping score—" Hackford whispered. "How many comes. Look at Armitage. Five by my count, and he's still poling himself. Stupid ass. Obvious stuff. Stupid nipples. You and I . . . we like it just a little bit more refined, just a little bit more . . . of everything. I mean, how different is one naked cunt from the next?"

Shit, this was going places Kyger did not want to pursue, and it was all because of Lujan, and the assumption that he was like Lujan—*only better.*

Not that better. He wasn't immune to the atmosphere of lust and lechery. He was as susceptible as the next man, just as hard, just as high at the sight of a woman's well-worked and pleasure-wracked naked body.

He was a little appalled at the intensity with which he was re-acting to all of this sucking and fucking; and a little leery that the jaded Hackford was going to carry him off to participate in the more *refined* pleasures of the evening.

The servicing courtesans came around to him, and he allowed them to stroke and pump him to a satisfactory climax, and he was stunned he had that much spunk in him still.

An hour or so later, the mistress changed positions—the eunuchs brought out a platform with a thin silk-draped mattress into which was cut a curved opening. The mistress was untied and carried to the platform, placed belly down, with her chest positioned in the opening so that her breasts swung free. Her arms were raised above her head and tied to the platform, and her hips were canted upward so that her cunt was readily available for obverse penetration.

In this permutation, her nipples could not be stimulated by the eunuchs, but there was space enough beneath the platform that any of the voyeurs could slip beneath and suck at her teats to his heart's content.

But the main attraction was the prolonged fucking of the mistress from behind by one after another of the onlookers.

Even that palled after a while. Kyger resisted taking a turn, but he had no clear reason not to. If he were of Lujan's ilk, if he were to be classed as a friend, and among these men for this purpose, he could not refuse.

It was a tricky fine line to walk when he didn't know which way he would fall. Or what he could learn by traveling this road to sinful surcease with them. They were habitués of the manor; they probably came for a nightly dose of debauchery which even he could see was wearing thin.

What could that precipitate but a still more egregious abuse of the whores in order to whip up the kind of multiorgasmic excitement they were coming to crave. They probably poked, pried, pinched, and pronged every hole that crossed their paths.

And this had been Lujan's world.

"Your turn," Hackford prodded him gleefully, his penis still slick with the mistress's juices.

Kyger unfolded himself from his seat and made his way down to the dais and the mistress.

This had been Tony Venable's world. The thought floated up from nowhere; he hadn't considered Venable or his mandate for one moment tonight, and yet here he was at the Bullhead, among those who might have been his cohorts, his supporters, his friends.

And he was experiencing the same level of luxury and lasciviousness as Venable allegedly had done in those last halcyon days before he'd been murdered.

He had inadvertently stumbled into where he needed to be.

The disc over the door . . .

Signs and symbols, and he wasn't noticing because he was too taken up with resisting what he must embrace.

Sex and sin.

He positioned himself precisely behind the mistress. He knew Hackford was watching. They all were watching.

Were they the watchers . . . ?

Nothing was exempt from consideration.

He looked up at the coat tree as he girded himself to take the mistress. And he saw what he missed before—a pattern, an openwork design of circles and triangles . . . which when looked at closely—resembled . . .

Sevens . . .

He hadn't been paying attention. Signs and symbols all around him and he hadn't even noticed. They'd surrounded him with smoke and sex to distract him, and now they were all watching, waiting for him to make full bore use of the current distraction.

Or was he imagining it?

No time to figure it out now.

Hellfire.

And none of those realizations had wilted his ramrod penis. Shit. What the hell was wrong with him? Now he had to perform.

He nudged the mistress's bottom, and plunged himself home.

* * *

Kyger crawled back to the room and fell into the freefall slumber of the depleted and spent. His endurance was wholly tapped out, his body utterly drained of juice, of vigor, of life.

He couldn't take any more. Hackford and his group were still going at it, inexhaustible, unceasing, unendingly galvanized by each new erotic transposition of the mistress's malleable and bottomless capacity to entice them and fuck them.

And it was not enough for Hackford; he had as much as said so.

He slept. The silence was flat and enfolding, verging into the black hole of another ceaselessly carnal night at the Bullhead.

Lujan's life. How had he tapered down all that craving for sex to concentrate solely on Jancie? When did the lust for mindless sadistic fucking peter into something more acceptably manageable and still remain satisfactory for someone like his brother, or someone like Hackford?

The questions came tumbling up into his dreams, into his consciousness, so insistently they woke him.

Or maybe it was the sound of a low-pitched gong somewhere in the distance.

What?

The gong sounded again, barely audible, but the musical note resonated in some unconscious way deep in his gut.

He bolted upright and grabbed for his trousers. He knew that sound. It was a call to order. A summons of the unholy participants, the hooded figures marching by sevens into the mysterious basement room, the bier, the gong . . .

He leapt for the door and eased it open. The gong sounded again, reverberating against the smooth mahogany walls. And far down the hallway, at that intersection, he caught a fleeting movement, as if someone or something had just rounded the corner.

He moved, following quick as a cat, down the hallway in three seconds, and then flattening himself against the corner of the wall, listening.

The gong sounded again.

He peered around the corner.

Seven hooded figures were lined up at the end of the corridor, facing the wall. They couldn't go forward; they could only turn around and come back toward where he was. They stood motionless, waiting.

And on the wall, above their heads, there was the same shiny black disc as the one over the door to the mistress's haven, the same as the one over the door with the symbols in the mysterious basement room.

Signs and symbols.

Hellfire.

He wasn't up for this right now. He was so tired, so enervated. He wanted to fall on the floor and sleep. He wanted . . . to wait, to see.

He waited. The figures waited. They were waiting for something; he was waiting for something. What?

The gong sounded again, a deep resonating tone in the silence. The wall moved.

The wall moved . . . sliding back into itself. The figures moved forward in step. Kyger followed, as close behind as he could as they marched into a black void.

The wall slid shut behind him. The figures had disappeared up a dark stairway. He crept up the steps after them. He heard chanting in time with their footsteps, but he couldn't make out the words. Not yet.

But the closer he got, the clearer he heard them: . . . tion. Preservation. . . . ation. Retribution . . .

And again—as if they were reciting a list of rules—or precepts, except that these rules were not what he would have expected to hear, not the precepts of Tony Venable.

These were something else again; he heard the chant clearly this time: Devotion, Persuasion, Progression, Preservation, Dissemination, Propagation, Retribution.

And they were moving upward, instead of down toward that basement room with the bronze doors.

Up to attics? To places and spaces no one knew about, that were so exclusive a man could hide every vice, aberration and perversion?

The chant went on: Devotion, Persuasion, Progression, Preservation, Propagation . . .

The climb was steep. Who knew that when you steeped yourself in sin and salaciousness, you came that much closer to heaven?

Or hell.

He was well below the robed seven as they came up onto the landing. Here, he could just see, it was exactly the same as below. The seamless incised mahogany walls, the lush carpet, the dim atmospheric light, the onyx disc . . .

And someone was there, waiting for them.

"Brethren."

His voice was deep, compelling, almost inviting in its clarity, its sanity. This was a leader, a commander.

The most dangerous one of all.

The robed figures answered him: "We are the brethren sworn of the Sacred Seven. We preach, we promise, we practice the seven disciplines of Khudama: devotion, persuasion, progression, preservation, dissemination, propagation, retribution. We believe in the supremacy of seven, the power of seven, the wisdom of seven. We follow the disciplines, we revere your word, and swear to take the secrets of the Sacred Seven with us to the grave."

The commander spread his arms wide.

"My brethren. The circle of your vows is unbroken."

The seven answered: "Till death, Revered Ancestor."

The gong sounded. There was a sliding sound, and suddenly there was an opening behind the one they called Ancestor who bowed, nodded, and disappeared inside.

Kyger crept farther up the steps. The seven had lined up precisely, the first of the robed figures holding the pole with the disc symbol.

The unbroken circle; the never broken vows.

They marched into the room in a stately procession. Kyger followed, as close as he could, but he needed to get closer, to get inside that room, in fact, because for certain that door was going to close behind them, and he would learn nothing else.

He dove for the floor, and on his hands and knees he crept after the last acolyte, keeping carefully in line with his robed figure, as he slowly paced his way into the room, and then diving into the shadows when he got past the threshold a moment before the door slid closed behind him.

He was lying belly flat on the floor, half under a sofa, his nose rubbing into the thick Persian carpet. He held his breath, he didn't move. The silence thickened around him in an ominous way. For all he knew, the revered Ancestor had spotted him, and it would be but another moment before he was hauled out and persecuted.

Killed perhaps, if this seven thing was as serious and deadly as it sounded.

But no . . .

"Brethren, we have come to discharge our final duty to our beloved brother Venable."

Venable . . .

Kyger rolled under the sofa and crawled forward so that he could see into the room. It was a luxuriously appointed room. Soft sofas everywhere, small tables, low lights, rich fabrics, doors leading to other rooms on two of the walls.

As Wyland had theorized, had believed, as he himself could never have conceived. The secret seraglio existed. Tony Venable was no saint. He was whoremaster, a procurer, a white slaver.

The seven acolytes were lined up before the robed figure they called the Ancestor, who stood at the foot of what looked like an altar. In front of him were lined up five naked women who were veiled and dressed in the leather necklace with the black leather rose. They all looked alike, the size of their breasts, their shaved mounds, and their identities, their beauty blurred by the veil.

The courtesans who had serviced them this whole evening— Venable's hand-trained sex slaves . . .

The Ancestor went on: "We are in Tony Venable's private apartments—"

. . . that explained it, explained everything.

"—where he selected, tried, trained and subjugated thralls to sell to a list of wealthy and avid clients. These cunts will be remanded to their owners after we thoroughly test them. The fees already paid for the privilege of purchasing one of these prize cunts is hereby donated to the coffers of Khudama to be used at my discretion."

The Ancestor looked around with an air of paternalism. "We all know how thorough our brother Venable could be—and was—in training these bodies to the proper nuances of submission. They earned the accolade of the black rose. They are the crème de la crème of those who apply to work at the manor. But our brother Venable has been gone now more than a month, and his buyers are impatient.

"However, in all that time, there has been no discipline, no controls, no punishment, even though we have put the cunts to good use for our own purposes. But a cunt can get lax, forget who is her master, forget what she owes to her overlord.

"I'm afraid we cannot yet relinquish them to their owners. For our brother Venable's sake and his sterling reputation, we must thoroughly test them. Fuck them until they scream for mercy, my brethren. Make certain they beg for more, or what use are they to their masters?

"Make them earn their coveted black rose one more time. Don't overlook any little thing you can think to do to them or demand of them. That's what they trained for; that's why their owners have paid such exorbitant prices to own them.

"Later, we will determine if it will profit us to continue Brother Venable's tradition of providing cunts for those who wish to indulge themselves by owning one, or whether to train them and keep them for our own private use. You will vote when you are satisfied you have thoroughly reamed them and you feel they are ready to be handed over to their new owners.

"Take your time. Make them work for the privilege of servicing the distinguished men to whom they've been sold. Make them earn the money that has been paid for them."

The gong sounded, loud in the aftermath of the Ancestor's exhortations.

"Make your choice, my brethren . . . make sure you test every single one of them . . ."

Chapter Fourteen

It had been the best night, beyond her every expectation. Angilee was still waltzing on a cloud when they returned to her flat. Still enchanted by the number of men who had danced with her, and begged permission of Mrs. Geddes to call.

"Surely one among them . . . ?" Angilee mused as Mrs. Geddes expertly unhooked her and helped her undress.

"We have a long way to go, Miss Rosslyn. This was but the first salvo. There are negotiations going on behind closed doors even as we speak."

"Do not tell me it is the same here as in America. Like bonding with like, and no one new can get past the door."

"Something like that. But then you Americans have barged in with a flagrant and seductive display of your bank accounts. Of course an impecunious earl or baron is going to look your way."

Angilee didn't like that response, but then she thought the better of it. A titled gentleman who needed money was exactly what she needed, so perhaps this was the very course to pursue. "*Are* there any impecunious barons among those I danced with last night?"

"There might have been."

"Good," she said. "Those are the ones I wish you would encourage to call."

"Hmph," Mrs. Geddes snorted as she lifted the dress over Angilee's head. "This is just the beginning, Miss Rosslyn."

"It has to end soon," Angilee said pragmatically. "My purse is not bottomless, and I need to find a quick solution."

"You could always apply to your father. I daresay any interested party will be speaking with him in any event."

"What?"

"My dear girl, you are too green for words. Of course anyone interested in forming a connection with you would want to speak with your father. Settlements, my dear. Financial assurance."

"Oh." Angilee felt as deflated as a balloon. "Damn."

"Miss Rosslyn . . ."

"But I've told you, he cannot know. I would provide the funds to the gentleman . . ."

"Then he wouldn't be a gentleman if he accepted them," Mrs. Geddes said tartly. "This is not how things work."

"Why didn't you say that in our interview?"

"Because I do wish to help you. You don't want your father to be able to break this marriage apart in any way. But we need to do this properly, Miss Rosslyn. Nothing less will suffice."

"But it's a temporary measure, Mrs. Geddes. I thought I made that clear to you."

"My dear Miss Rosslyn—no marriage is a temporary measure. You cannot go ahead solely with that in mind. You must think of it as a long-term proposition—it could very well turn out to be—where you would be fully fixed for the future, with the proper husband and a very nice situation in the country."

Because there *was* some hope for that, given Angilee's beauty, pedigree and her father's wealth. Mrs. Geddes had made certain of that as she conversed with all and sundry during the ball. Zabel Rosslyn was not, perhaps, as well known as a Vanderbilt, but he had very quickly built up a network of acquaintances who would vouch for him. That said something about his character, and Mrs. Geddes' ability to bring Angilee's desire to be married to fruition.

Of course, Angilee's naïve plan to thwart her father had to be scotched. Mrs. Geddes's own reputation depended on it. She'd tread carefully around that particular point during the interview, thinking that when they were launched into the Season, Angilee would come to see reason. But obviously she had picked the wrong moment to broach it.

"No, I will not think of it like that. I want my freedom, and I want not to have to marry the repulsive viscount, nor do I want to be married myself any longer than it takes for my father to desist his unreasonable demand that I marry the candidate of his choice. Is that clear? Can we proceed on the assumption that somewhere in the vast numbers of gentlemen seeking to marry, there is one in dire straits enough who would be willing to accept those terms?"

And now, she thought morosely, the bull, with his *fortune in diamonds and house in Belgrave Square not to be sneezed at* had to be wholly eliminated from consideration. And he would have been so perfect. No one she could meet subsequent to this would be more perfect.

"You will run out of money before you find him," Mrs. Geddes said. "It is a consideration."

"But it's my money and my risk," Angilee pointed out.

Mrs. Geddes forebore to say that it wasn't, really. "And if you aren't successful?"

"I have another plan," Angilee said instantly. She had no plan. The bull didn't need her money. There was no other plan.

"I hope so," Mrs. Geddes said, as she hung the dress and began unpinning Angilee's hair. "The window of opportunity will not be open that long, Miss Rosslyn. Your father—who by the way *was* at the ball—"

"*What?*" No, he hadn't been, Angilee would have seen him, sensed him, smelled him.

"—*was* at the ball," Mrs. Geddes repeated emphatically. "I know you didn't see him—I think he made certain you didn't see him . . . just be aware that your father will probably be present at most functions you will attend this Season. You're walking a very fine line here. He is known. And now you are known. You can't be at odds with him like this. It will surface, you'll become the subject of gossip and speculation, you'll be considered fast, and it will be very unpleasant in the end. And if you had to elope . . .

well—let's put it this way—you hired me to advise you and help you. And I hate to see you just throw your money away."

Hours. The testing, the naked unfettered-every-which-way coupling, the multiple partner, multiple position orgy went on for hours. His mind could not comprehend what further Tony Venable would have required of these whores that the brethren of the Sacred Seven did not try with them or invent on the spot.

It dulled the senses; it palled like the thickest fog. The room steamed up with the overwhelming stench of sex and semen. They sprayed their scent everywhere, they sucked and fucked and licked and bit at every naked part viciously; they rammed, jammed and crammed themselves into every opening, one and two at a time; and withal, they never removed their robes or hoods, and they just enveloped the whores as they invaded and inundated them.

God almighty. Kyger couldn't even envision it, how Venable seduced these willing whores, when he even found the time to teach, to fine down his impossible sexual standards on a half dozen of them at a time; and how and where he found his buyers and what kind of money changed hands.

Who were his clients? Who was so fabulously, obscenely wealthy that he could pay the price for his own well-trained, personally tutored submissive mistress?

It was so wearing, watching the brethren expel their seed, take a new position and begin pumping all over again. They were all over the floor and the sofas, sometimes not three feet away from where Kyger lay, giving him a full intimate view, an education in sucking and fucking he would rather not have had.

Their endurance was exhausting. They might rest for five minutes, and then they were mounted again, riding to a lather, while two others poked and prodded the thrall from behind.

He was exhausted watching. It was like a bad pornographic novel, with pages and pages of unending repetitious fucking that dulled the senses and made the whole process so unappetizing he never wanted to have sex again.

No point. No emotion. No feeling. No pleasure.

Get it over with . . .

Who decided when a thrall had been tested enough? What

was *enough?* Maybe there was never enough when it came to sex-ing a Tony Venable–trained submissive.

God, he wanted it over with. He was so tired. He felt cramped, utterly drained and dry as a bone. He thought he must be delirious, as two dozen different thoughts assaulted him—puzzle pieces of all the differently shaped clues.

He had some of the answers now. He had found the rooms at the Bullhead where Venable was last seen. He'd stumbled onto what he needed to undermine the canonization of Tony Venable by his followers.

He'd uncovered the truth; Wyland could find the proof.

And he was a witness to the thing *everybody knew, nobody told*—the existence of the Sacred Seven.

That was enough. More than enough for him. Enough to get him killed if any of them even had an inkling he was there.

He wriggled his body a little farther back under the sofa. Now he was cramped and crowded, and for certain he couldn't move if he didn't want to be murdered where he lay.

It was too fatiguing, all of it. And right now, he didn't care about any of it, except how he was going to get out of there.

And the daunting thing was, there was a good possibility that maybe he wouldn't.

It had to have been early morning when the brethren finally were done, and it was only because each of them was completely pumped out and as dry as the desert.

The thralls lay limp, and sound asleep, wherever in the room they had been abandoned.

And the robed Ancestor sat on the altar, nodding approvingly, lord of them all.

"You have done well," he said at length. "They are primed. They have perfect obedience. They are ready to fulfill their duties. We can deliver them with the pride of knowing that our Brother Venable's high standards have been maintained."

Holy hell . . . Kyger shook himself awake. Something was happening—movement beyond the sofa . . . the women being nudged and prodded to their feet, sleepily falling into line before the Ancestor.

The Ancestor rose from his seat and paced slowly around

them, nodding, touching, thumbing the retracted nipples of the first thrall to make them hard and pointed, slipping a hand between the legs of the second to feel her wet, pinching the bottom of the third, poking his fingers hard up into the cunt of the fourth, whereupon she immediately spread her legs and sank onto the hard thrust of them. He pulled the fifth thrall forward to suck her nipples while he fucked the fourth with his fingers until she came in a writhing frenzy.

Or pretended to, Kyger thought cynically.

"Very good," the Ancestor pronounced. "Luscious, in fact. These nipples are as succulent as any I've tasted. I wish these cunts were ours exclusively, but they have been paid for, and we will honor the contract. My brethren—"

The robed figures came to attention and lined up beside the thralls.

"Their masters are waiting."

The gong sounded.

The first of the brethren picked up the onyx disc and slowly paced his way to the door which automatically slid open.

Each of the brethren, but one, escorted one of the five thralls out of the room, and the last of them accompanied the Ancestor as they made a stately, almost ceremonial exit from Tony Venable's rooms.

The door slid shut before Kyger could wriggle himself out from under the sofa and dive out to freedom.

Hellfire. Sunk in the swamp and sex-and-semen perfumed backwash of a night of pure selfish debauchery.

He'd have just as soon gone to sleep just where he was, but the scent was overpowering and time was spinning by and he had the spunk-soaked luck to be stuck in Venable's secret aerie with the golden opportunity to search to his heart's content.

How fortunate could a man get?

But—shit—what if Hackford was looking for him? Son of a bitch—he really had to get out of there. He had to . . .

He had to take ten minutes and search the place, he did. It would probably be fruitless—Venable hadn't been the sort to leave concrete evidence of anything visible, not even in a place where he felt safe as houses. No one was that safe. Not even Venable.

Or he'd still be alive.

Still—he was here . . .

A quick hand search in and under each of the sofas, the tables, underneath in case something had been plastered there, around the altar, which was really a dais with a chair as wide as a throne, and a shelf with some icons on it.

One door was locked, the other gave into what had to be Venable's training room. A mirrored room of racks, benches, chains, locks, whips and an ornate glass-encased cabinet full of sadistic accoutrements that a decent man would never wish to see all in one place and at the hand of one man.

A man who was a devil. Who wanted to be a saint.

Not now.

Not ever.

He needed to have seen this. He needed to tell Wyland, and Wyland needed to raid this place and find these things and bear witness to everything he had seen.

He felt sick looking at all of it. His mind recoiled as his imagination ran rampant picturing it, envisioning Tony Venable, in this room with those women one by one, blackmailing them somehow, dominating them, humiliating them, bringing them to a place where they willingly spread themselves naked and open with no protest, no complaint, where to them it was a privilege and duty to abase themselves for the pleasure of the powerful men—any men—who demanded it of them.

What kind of women were these who would allow themselves to willingly come to this place, in their minds and with their bodies?

It was incomprehensible. What could Venable have offered them that was so seductive they would offer themselves up for that kind of sacrifice?

It was inconceivable. And yet, it was. And Venable had done this in secret, ongoingly, while he preached his brand of tyrannical paternal freedom, maintained a scrupulously blameless public life, and aroused his followers to such a frenzy they would enshrine him and embraced his message from beyond the grave.

I live.

I will return.

Prayerlike cards of exhortation, all over London, in concert with that ungodly séance. He remembered precisely what had been printed on them: *hope faith wait return* . . .

Who? Who had the reach, the power, the knowledge, the money to perpetrate those cards?

The Sacred Seven?

Venable had been one of them. They had to have known what he was about. They had to have tacitly approved his message, even after death . . . or had they?

What did he really know about any of this? Whispers. Insinuations. All those symbols, sevens everywhere. A subtle message? A warning?

Who were the Seven? What did he really know?

One of them was called the Ancestor. They followed something called the Disciplines of Khudama. Their symbol was the eternal circle which they swore loyalty to till death. They did not remove their robes even to fuck.

They lived in the shadows, in secret, in obscurity, within the private and privileged sanctuary of the most public place in all of England wielding a nebulous power that *everybody knows, nobody tells.*

Brazen. Bold. Like smoke. It was there, a scent, a shape, a visible cloud . . . take a breath, blow, and it was gone.

Goddamn.

He was missing something; he didn't know what. He felt it in his gut, his craw, and his fury at the likes of Tony Venable who could get away with abusing women like this.

But did it matter? He'd uncovered Tony Venable's secrets; he had found the thing that would destroy the idol and save the country.

Wasn't that enough?

He looked around the heinous room that was a testament to one man's self-indulgent, greedy, godless, sadistic nature.

Not a man. A corpse.

A missing corpse.

Jesus. And no, it wasn't enough.

There was nothing here; the cabinet was padlocked, so unless he wished to break it and perhaps endanger himself, he could take nothing from this awful room.

And he really had to find a way out of there, *now—*

. . . wait—

This he hadn't initially noticed in his first appalled survey of the room. In the cabinet, among all the cuffs, scourging whips, clips, clamps, ankle bracelets, creams, potions and paraphernalia, there was a little pile of black leather strips—no, he moved in closer to see exactly—they were leather body enhancements: thrall collars, belts, straps for the crotch and bosom, and the leather necklaces he was now familiar with.

And in the midst of all that black leather that looked like a pile of coiled snakes, someone—Venable?—had placed one pristine white leather rose.

Angilee was not happy. Mrs. Geddes was going to make her conform and find a reasonable marriage partner. Well, fine. She could work around that. She could pretend, just as Mrs. Geddes had pretended to get the job, that she had reconsidered, due to everything Mrs. Geddes had made her aware of, and she had come to believe the course Mrs. Geddes suggested was best.

And then, she would just go her own way, using Mrs. Geddes's resources and protection.

And the rest she'd think about later.

It was a plan.

So accordingly, she and Mrs. Geddes went through the cards and invitations that had been left in the days after the ball, some of which honored Mrs. Geddes' connections, as she was not loath to point out to Angilee, and they determined which of the invitations they would accept, and which of the callers Angilee should welcome.

And which of them, Angilee decided, she would privately pursue, as she coyly extracted all the information about each of the gentlemen to see who was in precarious financial straits and might welcome a short-term marriage and some long-term payment to accomplish it.

The next major upcoming event was a dinner and cards at the home of the Duke and Duchess of Beddingford for a select hundred of the most interesting people in Town for the Season.

"You may be certain your father will be among those attending," Mrs. Geddes said. "They generally invite an even number of intriguing newcomers interspersed with old friends, important connections, and social lions."

"That sounds perfect," Angilee said brightly.

Mrs. Geddes looked at her skeptically. "I know you are not above subterfuge, Miss Rosslyn, but rest assured, I will have my eye on you at every moment."

"I truly don't know what you mean," Angilee murmured. Damn it. She couldn't be that transparent. She had to work on that.

But meantime, she would play by Mrs. Geddes' rules for the moment. And if a situation, if an advantage, came to hand, she'd make use of it without hesitation and without consulting her chaperone.

After all, Mrs. Geddes was absolutely right—that was what she was paying her for. Advice and connections. And everything else could come later.

The silence was killing. The door wall was smooth as ice with no discernible way to open it. He was as trapped as a man could be, and by his own devices. Unless someone came, he could die in that horror chamber of a secret apartment.

There were no windows, no other egress. Venable had meant this to be his sequestered chamber of initiation into his sordid rites of bondage and slavery. His secret world. The one the outside world that revered him was never meant to know.

He had to get out. He had to tell them, tell Wyland, get them there, let them find what he had found.

It wasn't possible. This apartment was as tight as a drum, with no exit anywhere.

Unless someone came.

Which could be a lifetime from now.

Or—perhaps the Ancestor . . . ?

All right. He had to keep calm. This was not a life or death situation. There could be other women who wanted testing. Or a new batch who needed tutoring. Someone would come eventually, so the question was how could he increase his chances of getting out the door when that happened without being seen.

He turned and surveyed the room.

The sofa under which he had concealed himself was not that far from the door, but it was still far enough away that he wasn't able to take advantage of the moment the door was open.

So his best chance was to angle it closer, hope no one noticed, and conceal himself until . . .

Jesus—he *was* going crazy if he thought Tony Venable's acolytes would have noticed the precise placement of the furniture and if something were out of line.

Hellfire.

Lord, he was exhausted. From being awake all night, from his juices drained to his soles, from his shock at what he'd discovered, and from his frustration at his inability to act. And his every muscle felt as if it were strained to the breaking point when he thought about Hackford prowling through the mansion looking for him, and him nowhere to be found . . .

How the hell could he explain that?

Maybe he'd never need to—he'd just crawl under the sofa, and they'd find his skeleton there . . .

He felt the skin melting off his bones as he slept. He was certain hundreds of years had gone by, eons had gone by, heaven had gone by when he heard the loud thumping noise that sounded like thunder.

He awakened to find himself whole, alive, and hearing his name, fuzzy, from afar: ". . . Galliard—you in there? Do you hear me? Are you there? Galliard . . . !!"

Hackford!

He shook himself awake, girded himself for the next moment, whatever that would be—Hackford entering, Hackford discovering him under the sofa, Hackford with a weapon sent to kill him . . .

Holy shit. Hackford—or had he expected this?

And then the sound of the door sliding open . . .

Hellfire—

He braced himself . . . whatever happened, it would be close . . .

Hackford stepping into the room. "Galliard—are you fucking here? Where the hell are you? Jesus Christ, man—"

Opening the locked door—Venable's bedroom? Kyger could

see very little from that angle. A massive bed. An oriental rug. Mirrors.

"Shit, man, where the hell have you got to?" Into the training room. "Galliard, you son of a bitch—" Out again before Kyger could react.

Looking around the altar room, seemingly at a loss. And then he made for the door and Kyger moved, sliding out from under the sofa and diving for the door with his hand before it integrated perfectly with the wall.

It closed into his hand. It crushed into his hand. He hoped to hell Hackford was down the steps because he was dead if he wasn't.

The damned thing was as heavy as a stone, and he crawled to it and, with his other hand, pushed hard against the edge. It almost didn't move. There was something in the mechanism that propelled it forward hard and heavy.

It felt like a lead weight had been incorporated into the structure of the door. He needed every ounce of strength, every dead muscle, to push that door back far enough so he could wriggle out from that room.

It took time. More time than he had. Someone else could be coming even as he was pushing his way out of the room. Hackford could return. The seven brethren. The Ancestor. Lord almighty—

He gave one last shove, and the door moved back on its track perhaps a foot, enough so he pushed himself through the narrow opening and rolled clear of it not a minute before it rolled toward him again and slammed shut.

Holy shit. Now what?

There were too many walls without doors in this place. He crept down the stairs to the next level, to the wall where the seven brethren had entered the anteroom to the apartment.

Blank walls. Another symbol. Of the reach and influence of Tony Venable—just when you thought you had something to grab on to, there was nothing but a slippery surface, no catchplate, nothing on which to hinge anything.

He hadn't been paying attention.

He sat down on the lowest step and braced his throbbing arm

on his knee. Trapped again. His hand in fiery pain. His body sapped and depleted. His mind blurry from lack of sleep.

And nowhere to go in this hell of one man's making.

They had entered through the wall. Another moving wall—not a door . . . it had moved inward; the whole panel moved inward.

All right. That was encouraging. No heavy doors to slam back on him. More like the moving walls that had trapped him and Angilee that night, like the one that had given into another anteroom with another staircase leading to another secret ritual room.

Damn and hell. What was this place anyway? A house of fog and illusion?

Maybe . . . maybe—maybe he was groggy as all hell, but it suddenly seemed to him that the point of the Bullhead was not to accommodate well-to-do oversexed men looking for obscene and anonymous couplings.

No . . .

No, what? The thought slipped from his mind. He felt as slick and slippery as the walls that surrounded him. He couldn't catch the thought. Didn't want to. Wanted desperately to find a way out.

Stand up, then. Look over your surroundings. You came in behind the brethren through that wall.

. . . it sounded insane. *I crawled through that wall* . . . No signs and symbols on that wall tonight. Every man for himself tonight. And so they had, all those brethren, all for themselves over those faceless, well-trained, naked bodies . . .

Forget that . . .

He forced himself to stand up and, holding his injured arm against his body, he began feeling up and down that wall. *Like a man feels a woman's body* . . .

Shit and damn—they were getting to him. He was thinking like them. Or he was just woozy from exhaustion; he couldn't even tell which was which at this point.

Wait a minute—there, in the wall, the telltale incised seam. He ought to just push it and let the whole thing collapse—everything would collapse if he pushed—his life, the illusions, the secrets, the lies . . .

Stupid . . . had to protect himself. Had to get out of there in one piece, get to Wyland, get the officials in on it . . .

Had to—

He moved his hand cautiously to the corner of the wall.

Pushed.

A little give there?

Pushed again cautiously. Warily. Anything could be beyond that wall. Death could be beyond the wall. But he had known he might be playing with fire when he started this quest.

He pushed again, and the wall started to separate at the angle.

Holy shit.

He was dreaming. Nothing from this point on could be real.

Another push. And another. Inch by inch he pushed like a blind man until there was an opening just wide enough for him to squeeze through.

And hope no one noticed because there was no way to pull that wall back in place.

Dead man for certain now.

He made his way slowly and carefully down the hallway, turned to the right, met no one, which was either scary or pure luck, even assuming he was back on his room floor.

Which he didn't assume at all given his fuzzy state of mind.

Which room? Was it this hallway? Or had walls shifted and moved and he was totally lost . . .

Hellfire. His head felt like a lead weight.

Wait—

Here?

The doors all looked the same. Why the hell hadn't he counted the doors when he'd first arrived? Some investigator he was . . .

This one looked right.

No—this one?

Fog drifted into his head. He so desperately needed sleep.

Choose one.

Nothing to lose. Either right or wrong, and then he'd bluff it out from there. He reached out to the ring catch on the door in front of him. Pulled. Entered.

Yes? He didn't know for sure. It was empty anyway, and maybe that was all he needed. A nice empty room with a nice empty soft bed.

No—wait . . . there, his shirt, his boots . . . oh, God . . . he shimmied out of his trousers and fell on the bed and into a black void where nothing existed but sleep.

And a massive pounding on the door.

"Galliard, goddamnit—are you goddamned in there? Where the fuck are you?" The door slid open. Or maybe he was dreaming it.

Hackford's voice, laced with fury, came at him like a slap: "Son of a bitch—where the hell have you been? I've been searching the whole fucking mansion . . ." He sounded enraged; he sounded just on the edge of terrified.

Kyger was so groggy, he thought he was imagining it; he could hardly understand what Hackford had said anyway, and he didn't know half of what he himself was saying. He knew he raised his good hand dismissively. He thought he said, with convincing indignation, "What the hell do you mean? I've been in this fucking hellhole the whole night, for Christ's sake."

And he was certain he remembered nothing after that because he sank right back into that deep, welcoming, slumberous void.

Chapter Fifteen

The last thing, then, that he needed was to find an invitation to the Beddington dinner in his mail.

He'd been as certain as stones he wouldn't get out of the Bullhead alive; Hackford was on to him, even if he couldn't prove he hadn't been in his room the whole night, and that knowledge wound him as tight as a Swiss watch. Obviously, Hackford knew everything about the secret world of the Bullhead, but there still was a fine thread of desperation in him when he burst into Kyger's room and began questioning him.

There was nothing to do but bluff it out. And Hackford knew he was doing it and couldn't do a thing about it. But there was something about his questions that made Kyger's nerves tighten up like a bow string.

The danger was real. Hackford was one of them, whoever *them* were.

But he knew something about them now. The *them* who operated in secret rooms behind moving walls in the most exclusive brothel in the country. The *them* with their rituals and their signs, symbols and sevens. The *them* who trafficked in white slavery.

The *them* about whom *everybody knew, nobody told.*

Them. Always *them* . . .

He had to get away from them. And he had virtually no way to affect an escape. Hackford was right outside his door, a merciless sentinel, waiting for Billington, and he had made it ominously clear they all were going to leave the Bullhead together.

Hackford was taking no chances. Hackford was just a little distracted. Hackford hadn't even noticed he was injured, because how would he explain that? Some whore bit him? Maybe that was as good an explanation as any. But he couldn't talk his way out of Hackford's determination to pin him to the post.

And it wasn't over either, so from now on, his tack had to be to deny everything with the same unflappable equanimity with which he dealt with Hackford's initial questions, and they couldn't prove a thing.

. . . maybe they didn't need proof . . .

Maybe it was *fait accompli*. He was a dead man already.

He had that much time—the time between uncertainty and decision—to get away from them. Split seconds. Eternity.

Hellfire.

"GALLIARD . . ." Hackford's bellow. "Let's go, man."

Kyger opened the door.

The two of them were there, like a wall between him and the outside world, and the only place he could wedge himself was between them, as close as a Siamese twin.

They were his guards, escorting him to the gallows.

Where did they execute traitors at the Bullhead? In some mysterious secret room in the bowels of the lower level where he'd be swallowed up whole forever?

Mordant thought. And he didn't think he was being facetious.

No. It wasn't going to happen.

They paced down the hallway, Hackford looking grim as a griffon. No conversation, no trying to dig for details or expose the lie. The verdict had been.

Perhaps by them.

That *them*.

The ones to whom Hackford owed his allegiance.

He had to get away. His hand felt like a piece of meat. The pain was like a deep, dark hum in his body underpinning his supreme sense of pulsating menace. Of life and death.

The hallway was empty. No one around. And again, in this

world of illusion and movement, he had no idea where he was. It didn't matter.

He waited. He watched. For that one moment when their attention was diverted, for that moment when one might speak to the other, or a door would open somewhere, or they might hear a noise . . .

Just one split second was all he needed—and he'd attack them, he'd kill them, he'd break down the walls if he had to.

Again.

But the leeway he needed was provided by the mundane sound of a door opening somewhere far behind them.

In that split second, he acted: he rammed Billington's ribs with his elbow, and almost simultaneously he wheeled and thrust his foot in front of Hackford as he moved to restrain him, and Hackford pitched forward off balance.

Another jot of a second to turn and run toward that sound, with Hackford bellowing behind him: "STOP THAT MAN . . . !"

Down the hall, around the corner, down this endless walled-in hallway, he ran until he rammed hard, shoulder-first into the wall at the end of the corridor, and it folded in and fell over. He ran through that room to the fury of howling occupants, and he rammed down the next wall, and he ran . . . to the next wall, and the next and the next . . .

And he ran . . . leaving everything in chaos behind him, in the precisely ordered world of the debauched and profane.

And now Wyland wanted Kyger to go out for an evening of dinner and cards. Hellfire. Fun and games after what he'd just come through? Light badinage and social chatter after a night of bondage and sadism?

No.

Hell. He was dead on his feet; there was no time to seek out Wyland today in any event. Maybe he'd go. Maybe he wouldn't.

He crawled into his bed, he told Cryder to wake him at five o'clock, and he slept. He was in such pain and so exhausted he just couldn't do anything else.

At five o'clock, he was in no better shape than he had been when he arrived home, but he forced himself to awaken and to contemplate if he had enough energy to attend the event.

There was no way to pretend his hand wasn't useless.

Hell, *he* felt useless. What had he got after all this rooting around among the slick and the salacious? Nothing. Bearing witness was not the same as providing proof.

He was no farther along than when he'd started this quest, except that now he knew exactly what Tony Venable had been about, he knew where to find proof, and he knew his life was on the line.

And there was nothing he could do about any of it. Tonight.

Given all that, he was still on duty for Wyland. They wouldn't try anything in a social situation. He could still troll for conversational clues and information. He wasn't done just because he'd come away empty.

This time.

The thing wasn't over. He felt it in his gut. Hell, the thing was just beginning. The thing was explosive.

And he was just the man to set the detonator.

And he would.

But now—it was time to dress for a party . . .

Angilee in the bronze gown with the passamenterie embroidery was a sight to behold. Just beautiful. Mrs. Geddes wasn't loath to say so either: she felt as if she'd discovered her, invented her. Angilee could hold her own anywhere, in beauty, in style, in graciousness. She was born and bred to graciousness, but she had a very unfeminine will of iron, as Mrs. Geddes was very well coming to know.

They were arguing about the jewelry. Angilee insisted on the gold beaded choker. Mrs. Geddes felt it was too much against the ornate swirls of the embroidery.

Angilee won. She simply put the necklace on and that was that. Diamond earrings the size of dots in her lobes. Nothing in her hair this time. The gloves, the wrap. She was ready.

"Excellent." Mrs. Geddes was in her usual black silk, a different design this time, simpler. Elegant. "They will swarm around you. Trevor Smythe will be there. Perhaps he—"

"I'll be so happy to see him again," Angilee said.

"You did that so well, Miss Rosslyn."

Down they went to the carriage, rented again for the occasion, and off they went to the Beddington house. No crush here. Everything stately, ordered, calm. Footmen opening the carriage door. Velvet carpet on which to walk so as not to soil a hem, a pretty shoe. A helping hand to step up into the house. Respectful bows. Sincere sounding welcomes from the staff who took wraps, directed them to the dressing room to tidy up their hair.

Perfection.

Just what she would want, Angilee thought. Maybe it wouldn't be so bad to think about marrying forever, if she could have a life like this.

A life with a man like Trevor Smythe, who almost immediately came to greet her. Almost as if he had been waiting for her.

"*After* we greet the host and hostess," Mrs. Geddes said gently but pointedly, "I should be happy for Miss Rosslyn to renew her acquaintance with you."

The Beddingtons were not at all as stuffy and stiff as Angilee imagined. They were a couple of a certain age, but they had a certain youthfulness, humor and vigor about them that was very appealing.

They were enjoying themselves hugely because they were such congenial and convivial people, and their sole concern was the comfort of their guests.

They greeted Angilee as if she were an old friend, asked about her father, how she was finding life in London thus far, commanded her to tell them if there was anything they could do that would make things more enjoyable for her, and directed her, on Trevor Smythe's arm, to the refreshment table.

The main floor of the house was lit to a warm soft glow by hundreds of candles. The refreshment table was in the center of the anteroom, beyond that, to the left, was the card room and to the right, the dining room.

There were musicians playing a light air from a balcony in the dining room, and there was a most festive atmosphere among the arrivals.

"I'm cautioning you again," Mrs. Geddes whispered to Angilee as she sipped some punch, "your father most assuredly will be among the guests. You must maintain your composure; you must not let personal matters interfere with your duties as a guest."

"I understand."

"They're pairing off in the card room," Trevor Smythe said. "Would you care to play a hand?"

"I'd love to watch," Angilee said, "if you're quite certain it won't bore you to tears to just observe for a while."

"Delighted," Trevor Smythe said, adroitly concealing whatever his real feelings were. "Miss Rosslyn . . ." He offered his arm. "Mrs. Geddes."

She took the other. He *was* a gentleman, for all his awkwardness.

She slanted a look at Angilee. Angilee nodded imperceptibly, not a little irritated that Mrs. Geddes might be right.

But she didn't have to make a decision tonight. Just soon.

And then her heart sank. Sooner than soon.

As they left the reception room, she saw him. It was only a fast glimpse, but it was enough to ruin her evening, because Zabel had just entered the room.

Bright lights and happy people—there was an antidote to the festering morass that was the menu for a night at the Bullhead.

Coming here, he had decided, was a statement: he wasn't running scared, because for certain, some of the habitués of the Bullhead would be in attendance. Hackford might be in attendance. Billington. Armitage.

Them. The *them* that ruled this world hiding behind rituals and robes.

He came up into the reception area slowly and cautiously. He had had no little trouble dressing this evening because of his hand, which he held stiffly at his side. There was nothing to do for the pain, and he wasn't sure just how convivial he was going to be as the Beddingtons greeted him with the same warmth they displayed to all their guests.

He was impressed with how kind they were, and how accessible, how cordial to their guests, even the ones who were new to their circle, which they made a point of expanding every Season.

They were the kind of people you wanted to know better, and to be included among those they considered friends.

Immediately he headed for the refreshments. Instantly he saw

Angilee, on the arm of Trevor Smythe—oh, he did remember Trevor Smythe—entering the card room.

He veered to the left to follow. This was a calculated risk—Hackford, if he were here, would most certainly be at a table. The gauntlet would be thrown.

Not yet. He surveyed the room from the threshold, and there were just the usual avid cardplayers setting up the usual four-somes. Some were already engaged, hot and heavy; others were standing around talking, greeting newcomers.

Angilee and Trevor Smythe paced around the room, talking to his acquaintances, making small talk. But Angilee was looking around in a most furtive way. Perhaps only he noticed, but he could swear there was a sheeny wariness in her expression. As if she fully expected to see someone she did not wish to encounter.

He watched for a moment or two more, and then he saw him—a stout, determined-looking older gentlemen covertly following her . . . not a suitor—he had to be the wicked warlock of a *father* who wanted to sell her to the vicious viscount.

He eased his way into the card room. The father, if it were he, was not going to accost her—he could see that—he wanted to, but he comprehended it would be bad form to make a scene here.

But he wanted to; his expression was strained, and he kept moving forward as if he were thinking to go ahead and talk to her, and then restraining himself because she was in the company of a gentleman.

And then the dragon moved in.

And that point, Kyger saw Hackford enter the room, and Hackford knew he was there, and as if he was at magnetic north, he was coming toward him, homing in on him. And he couldn't get away from him if he tried without calling attention to the situation.

Hackford's social expression turned menacing for just the beat of a second as he grasped Kyger's arm and propelled him, with what looked like congenial friendship, to a secluded corner.

"Well, old son. Aren't you the clever one. Or are you? Let me make you aware of this: we are all around you, we don't like trai-tors, and we make certain they pose no threat. You don't know who we are or when we'll attack. I'd be very, very careful, if I were you, who you speak to and what you say because we'll be watching, and we don't forget."

He relinquished Kyger's arm, saying in a louder voice, "There you go, Galliard, that's what I needed to tell you. So good to see you."

And he walked off toward one of the card tables as if he had just delivered a message from a friend instead of a dire warning.

Well, hell.

Kyger strolled around the periphery of the room toward where Angilee, Trevor Smythe, and several of his friends were watching a card game in progress, all the while keeping an eye on Hackford as he was dealt into a game, and on the father, who had grudgingly settled himself at another table.

He almost didn't speak to her. He had to speak to her. She was pure melted chocolate in that gown, a pure luscious memory that tantalized him every time he saw her, no more so than now.

Someone ought to have snapped her up already. But he didn't want anyone to want her, to touch her, to . . . do the things they had done together in the name of her thwarting her father.

The sin was, he still couldn't do anything for her, about her, or protect her. So to come two feet near her, and to presume any right to know anything about what was happening, was sheer gall on his part.

He did it anyway.

"Miss Rosslyn."

Angilee looked up at him from under the veil of her eyelashes as Mrs. Geddes swooped down on them. "Mr. Galliard, how nice to see you. I do believe you've previously met Mr. Trevor Smythe."

They nodded at each other like opponents in a boxing match.

"Mr. Galliard." Mrs. Geddes now. "How nice to see you."

"How unexpected," Angilee put in a little maliciously. This was wearing—first her father, now *him*. Thank God, Zabel had chosen the wiser of two courses and was now immersed in a heated game of whist.

But now to have to deal with the *bull* when Trevor Smythe was evincing such particular interest . . .

"Can we have a moment?" The bull.

We've had too many moments, she wanted to say. *You've wasted too much of my time, and you want more?* She looked at

Mrs. Geddes instead. Mrs. Geddes was parceling out the worth of a fortune in diamonds and a house on Belgrave Square. Mrs. Geddes nodded yes.

She wished she hadn't. But Mrs. Geddes didn't know they had met before or under what circumstances.

Under him. Forget about that. It never happened. She had to pretend none of it ever happened and that she had just only met the bull at the ball and he was renewing his acquaintance.

Except she didn't have the patience for it. Unless he had changed his mind . . . ?

She shot him a longing look as they moved to a more private corner. But when he turned to face her, she made certain her expression was cool, calm, disdainful and a bit removed.

"Mr. Galliard. You must know you're taking up valuable time in which I could be speaking with someone more eligible and more willing to marry me."

"Ah, Hackford didn't rush into the breach?"

"Hackford—? Oh, the gentleman whom you were with that night? He's here, is he not? No, he hasn't made an offer. Nor have you. So exactly what do you want now?"

"To kiss you." He was shocked he said it, stunned he wanted it so ferociously, especially in the midst of this crowd, while he was steeped in pain, and on the heels of Hackford's threats.

"I'm afraid not, Mr. Galliard." She slanted a look at him. "Is there anything else?"

"Is that your father at the table over there?"

She threw him a speaking look. "How perceptive of you. Yes, that is my father."

"And the gentleman in question—?"

"Not in attendance." *Please marry me—it would make things so simple. We could deal well together for the time I need to provide my father with proof that we are wed . . .* "Is there anything else?"

He didn't know. He needed to know everything, even though he knew everything that mattered already: her scent, her taste, her nakedness, her response, the way she enfolded him, fit him, rode him, came for him . . .

He could offer her nothing when he wanted to give her everything, and he hated it that he could only stand by and watch her careen into the hazardous world of advantageous alliances and mercenary matrimony and nothing to help her, to stop her.

What could she buy with the bribe she was flashing around? Who could she buy?

Him . . .

No. Except when she looked at him like that, like she wanted him, wanted their sex, their connection, their coupling, their pleasure in spite of the means by which it had happened—then he wanted to throw everything away, and he wanted to give what she—what *they*—most wanted.

Except—*they* could kill him. *They* might go after her. *They* might know everything about what happened between them, and he couldn't risk that, risk her, risk them.

"Mr. Galliard?" He looked as if he were someplace else, thinking about someone else, and Angilee did not like that one whit. Especially when Mr. Trevor Smythe was waiting, especially when there were so many possible connections she could make tonight.

"Yes, Miss Rosslyn."

And then he looked at her—*marry me,* she willed it, prayed for it; she yearned for it—really looked at her. *Help me* . . .

And he said, "No, there's nothing else. I just wanted to be certain all was well with you."

His words were humiliating, washing over her like hot water.

"As you see, Mr. Galliard, I'm perfectly fine. So you need not concern yourself with my well-being in the future."

"Can't guarantee that, Miss Rosslyn."

"Well, *I* will, Mr. Galliard. I'll guarantee that." She sketched a curtsey. "A pleasure to see you again. For the last time, I hope."

He watched her move away, back to Trevor Smythe, back to the dragon who was looking puzzled and a little irritated. Back to pretending to watch the card game, which he'd have wagered she didn't even know what game it was.

Back to the pretense she really had some control of her life when she'd chosen a course where she had no control. She was fooling herself if she thought a wealthy father and her flaunting the rules of propriety guaranteed anything but trouble.

And he'd just put her into further danger by just speaking with her.

They were watching.

And now they'd be watching *her*.

The card pockets were still filled when he made his way through the streets the following morning to Wyland's office. It was another edgy foggy morning that refused to burn off as the sun rose, almost as if it had a will to oppress everything beneath it.

Kyger pulled a card from one pocket, another from a pocket three streets beyond. They were all the same, all different: *believe faith live accept return . . .*

The five-point petition in a handy carry-away form that incorporated Venable's precepts and the resurrecting message of the séance. He lived. He would return. Believe, have faith, wait, accept.

Hellfire.

But it also seemed to him that the keening signs of mourning had diminished. The fury over the disappearance of the body. There were no angry knots of people demanding justice, explanations and revenge. There was an air of resigned acceptance; there was stillness about the crowds in the streets now that was just as disquieting as their grief.

As if they were waiting.

Waiting for what?

For the new Tony Venable. The one who would return, the one who would take his place and take them to the place that Venable had always promised.

God, no.

But—

—when he thought about it . . . the card pockets. The messages. The séance, the manipulation, the Bullhead, the sevens, the death mark—*everybody knows . . .* and the salacious underground life of Tony Venable, secret, sacred and profane.

There was connective tissue in there somewhere, he just hadn't found it yet. Soon. He felt it coming. He was racing toward it— all the answers to all the mysteries—and if Wyland could get into that secret apartment, the thing would be over. The revelations would come.

Wyland listened in silence, sitting there with his fingers steepled and a deep troubled expression on his countenance.

"They indicated he'd sold the women, you say," he said finally when Kyger had finished outlining everything he'd seen and the things he'd deduced. "Trained them as slaves and sold them? Venable?" As if it were inconceivable. As if this were the last thing he expected to hear.

"Isn't it? Isn't it the very kind of thing you need to take him down?"

"It's exactly what we need, if we could show it. If we could prove it. Can we prove it?"

"What if we raided the Bullhead? There's just no other way to get into that secret apartment again now."

Wyland gave it a moment's thought. "I see some immediate drawbacks. If what you say is true, they have mechanisms to prevent discovery of anything they want to hide. They've made certain of it. They've made provisions for it. That means we'd probably find nothing if we go in there out of hand. Which means an embarrassment for the department which, in the wake of this whole Venable debacle, we frankly can't afford. We need something up front and immediate that we can show the grieving public that will prove everything you say."

"And what would that be, short of a picture of the training room. And even then—" Kyger broke off. "Shit—there's nothing to connect Venable to that, in any event."

"That is the genius of Tony Venable. He's as slippery as an eel, even in death."

"One of his women, then?"

"Do you think you could coerce a confession?"

Kyger flashed onto the scenes of two nights previously and shook his head. "Not likely."

"We need either bring him down or bring in his murderer. Those are the options. Both of them impossible. Though I must hand it to you that you discovered the one thing that would blacken his reputation beyond redemption—but how can we do it with what we have?"

"And what do we have?" Kyger said tiredly. "One eyewitness to his venery, a missing corpse, a murderer on the loose, and a house of diversion and distraction."

"And deception," Wyland added dryly.

Kyger grunted. "Not much there to grab hold of."

"And yet you have. You've been persistent, you've made this mission your own, and you've uncovered what we need. Now we just have to . . . make it real. I don't even know how to tell you to do it."

"No, Venable was too smart, too slick. Nothing connects him to that apartment except those who were there, and you can be certain they will be loyal to death. Why shouldn't they? They reap all the benefits, including the continuation of this unprecedented service they will continue to provide to their spoiled, self-indulgent fellow men."

God, he was feeling as let down as a lead weight. Slick was the word for Tony Venable. Like snakeskin. Slithering and writhing away before you could catch him. Speaking with a forked tongue, then striking in secret. Shedding his skin and leaving just the untraceable remnants behind.

"Find one of the women," Wyland said suddenly. "If you could find one of the women he trained . . . we'll find a way to induce her to testify to the truth of what you saw."

He caught the tail end of that, he was so aborbed in his ruminating about the nature of Tony Venable. "Say again?"

"Find one of the women."

Find one of the women? At first thought, it sounded impossible. They had been so dominated and beaten down, they couldn't possibly have a thought or a mind of their own. And the men who owned them would hardly put them on public display.

Where would one find them?

Wyland went on, parceling his thoughts out loud: "You said— the Ancestor indicated the women had already been purchased, that they were honoring Venable's last contract with those clients. That the buyers were waiting for them. Buyers who could conceivably be among the wealthiest men in the land . . ."

"Or not . . ." Kyger interpolated.

"Let us suppose some of them are. The women are here, either in London or the country, hidden away perhaps, somebody's dirty little well-kept secret, one can assume. But somebody knows who the purchasers are. Somebody knows where to find them. If you find that somebody, you'll find the woman we need to break this whole Tony Venable thing wide open. Just one witness—that's all that's wanted."

"Among a couple hundred horny marriage prospects."

"Somebody sells the idea to those women somehow, wouldn't you think? Why would a woman give up marriage, security and legitimacy for that?"

"Not enough men?" Kyger suggested. "Aren't the odds rather staggering—more women than men seeking marriages in any given Season?"

"You might have a point there. If that's so, I feel we're in luck with things just getting into full swing. There must be a procurer of some sort trolling every event. The brethren are not going to relinquish this lucrative business, I can tell you that. We have a real chance to put paid to this cult of Tony Venable in the next month or two. Are you game, Galliard? It means more of the same—keep your eyes open, your senses tuned, your instincts honed. We'll get you into the various events. You see what else you can dig up."

He rose from his chair and held out his hand. "You can access the funds you need in the usual way. Oh—and I wouldn't hesitate to try to get into the Bullhead again. There has to be more answers there. I know you'll find a way."

"That would be a last resort," Kyger said, shaking his hand. "They're on to me."

"Your call, Galliard. Let's meet again next week."

The Season was all about debutantes, heiresses, spinsters taking one last shot at finding a husband, the morning see-and-be-seen rides in the Park, teas, picnics, theater, opera, also for the purpose of being seen and meeting and greeting, dinners, parties and balls, all cascading one after the other toward making the advantageous marriage.

The competition was now getting fierce after the initial sniffing out period. The dresses were fancier, more expensive, more Parisian, more revealing, more colorful. The possessiveness over certain of the more eligible of the prospects became more pronounced. The American heiresses became more aggressive; the English roses became more pliant to make contrast more acute.

And Angilee became more determined. It just wasn't possible she would fail, even against the most persevering of her rivals.

She wasn't without suitors, even this early in the game. Trevor Smythe, for one, was intrigued, and he had come to call.

And that person, Hackford, who had been with the bull. He made her just a little uneasy, but his manners were as impeccable as Mrs. Geddes could have wished, even if the conversation was somewhat stilted.

And then there was Wendham, who was very nice, but not particularly attractive, and Hairston, who just sat and stared at her wistfully.

Each of them eligible, willing, wanting a wife, but not on a temporary basis. And she didn't want any of them permanently.

And she must consider a permanent situation as well as her own desire for independence. Much as she hated to admit it, Mrs. Geddes might be right about that. A woman had to consider the future. And the constraints, which were always present. How the thing looked was every bit as important as how one obtained it.

If only there were someone who was even remotely attractive to her.

There is.

No. She constantly shoved the solution of the bull away, although seeing him at these two successive events had been nerve-wracking. By comparison, her other possible suitors were diminished by him, by her knowledge of him, the memory of his possession of her, and the pleasure of their coupling.

How could that knowledge not be an undercurrent in her every consideration of a husband? She knew more than she ought now, and he had spoiled her for anyone else in more ways than one.

It wasn't fair to have stumbled on someone like that and to have him completely disregard her. She hated it. She hated him. And time was running out, and she was certain to see him again somewhere else, as well as her father, as well as Wroth, and the half dozen men who had been encouraged to call and discouraged by her in the process.

Trevor Smythe, however, seemed not to be disheartened by her cool disinterest. His pursuit was dogged, steady, consistent, kind. She hated him. No, she didn't hate him; she just could not conceive of being in bed with him doing the things she had done with the bull, things she had let him do with his hired penis.

Hired—bought and paid for. She had to keep reminding herself about that, because if she didn't, she fell into the swampy speculation of what if, and why hadn't he. She romanticized the whole situation when, in fact, the reality was she had paid a man, a penis, to have sex with her.

In a brothel.

For whatever motives and reasons. They made sense at the time. And they ruined her forever for anyone else.

It was done. Asked and refused. She had *paid* him. There had been no affection, no caring, some little consideration, but no connection between them, *none*. She just wanted it because it was familiar. Twice familiar.

And she thought that maybe there was something there that could underpin a temporary marriage.

But she'd *hired* him . . .

Stop thinking about him.

She hated him. She hated Trevor Smythe. And Wendham. And Hairston. And she felt just plain leery of Hackford. She had the distinct feeling his tepid pursuit was for some other reason entirely. And she really wasn't interested enough to try to find out.

But he was nowhere in consideration. It only wanted that she be polite to him when next they met.

Forget him.

This whole scheme just wasn't working, and she didn't know what she was going to do.

There was no other plan.

She should just go back to her father, marry Wroth and forget it.

She shuddered at the thought.

The hell with it.

Forget them all.

Chapter Sixteen

She kept going that week—to lectures and musicales, to polo matches and on late afternoon rides in the Park, all with Mrs. Geddes properly pinned to her side—but she kept wondering to what avail.

The round of activities was beginning to feel repetitious. She saw the same faces, the same gentlemen, the same dresses, exchanged the same pleasantries daily with the same people as she had seen the night before, the day before, the hour before.

No one appealed to her. No one came out of the shadows to present himself as a likely candidate to marry her, and she felt the terror of the trapped. Zabel was stalking her like a cat, letting her have her bit of a leash and waiting to yank her back when her efforts failed.

And they would fail, miserably. At none of the amusements had she seen the bull. At all of them, Trevor Smythe had appeared, certain of his welcome, the worth of his name, and his quiet persistent pursuit.

He was fascinated by her beauty, her accent, her flirtatious ways, by her subtle aggressiveness, her curiously American plain-speaking, the fact she was educated, she had *done* things, and been places that girls of his acquaintance had not. And her open purse.

He was one of the ones, Mrs. Geddes finally made her aware, who needed an infusion of vigor into his situation by someone from abroad. It was tidier that way.

"Well, you see how that works," Mrs. Geddes said at one point as they made their way to a polo match at the Burlston Club on a particularly damp day. "All interest must be focused on the one who can do the most for the legacy. And no one has to know. Of course, they all know, but it's neatly tied up, and he's the envy of his friends for the coup of having married an American heiress. Your father, from what you tell me, was not far wrong about that."

"I don't like it," Angilee said crossly.

"And yet it is exactly what you said you wanted. Someone who needs money, who's willing to marry you . . . the catch is, he might not want to divorce you. But how can that be so bad when you will have all the amenities and stature his name and his estate can provide?"

"I don't know. It just is." But she did know. Trevor Smythe was not the bull. He didn't look as though he had anything of the bull about him anywhere on his person, and she despaired of how she could convince herself to both marry him and share his bed. It was inconceivable.

But time was growing short. It must be considered.

She gave herself two more weeks to find a more likely candidate, and then she would—she must—listen to Trevor Smythe's proposal. Which he had already come too close to uttering the day before when he had come to call.

He was almost on one knee before she stopped him, using every ounce of grace and diplomacy at her command to divert him from his purpose and still make it seem natural and as if she hadn't comprehended what he'd been about to do.

Very draining, dealing with a gentleman's finer feelings. And she had to face that she might have to do that her entire married life with him, if she accepted him. Just another kind of discipline forced on her, no different from Wroth's desire to dominate and constrain her.

Damn. Marriage was a quagmire, and only the woman got sucked into the muck.

And she was already in over her head, and she didn't know what she was going to do.

The next evening, everyone turned out for the garden party at Haverdene House. Mrs. Geddes dressed Angilee in a tulle-draped ivory silk gown sewn with sparkling crystal beads around the bodice and hem, discreet diamond earrings, and matching shoes, gloves and wrap.

She looked as tall, proud and elegant as she ever had felt. She could conquer the world dressed like that. There just wasn't any world to conquer.

"Once again," Mrs. Geddes said, "I warn you, your father may be in attendance, and you must exercise even greater caution and restraint if you must deal with him at all."

"Then I'll try not to," Angilee said, although she didn't hold out much hope for that, the way she was feeling right now. Zabel was going to win, it was simple as that. And she was looking at a lifetime of servitude with a venal viscount.

And all for her father's ambition to be included among men of influence and power. What on earth had Wroth offered him that he was so willing to sell his only daughter to him?

She had been so consumed with circumventing him and getting herself set up correctly and with every propriety and concern covered, she hadn't really given this component of the equation as much thought as she should have.

What was it that Wroth had that her father wanted so badly?

What had Mrs. Geddes said about his connections? That they spoke well for him in the short time they'd been there? But they'd only arrived perhaps two, two and a half months ago, and the news of her upcoming marriage to Wroth had been waiting for her. Contracted before they arrived.

She had been so outraged by that, she hadn't thought clearly about the logistics of it, not least, where or when her father had met, or had contacted Wroth. Perhaps there had been some back and forth before they'd even left New York, but if so, Zabel hadn't said a word to her.

As she remembered it, all their focus had been on the trip to England, the upcoming Season, the opportunity to make an attractive alliance with a titled aristocrat.

And so here was the end result of that: a prearranged marriage she didn't want, her decision to give away her virginity which did not deter her would-be husband, and then her desperate flight from her father while stealing his money, and going to great lengths to hire a social dragon to protect her and guide her, while she yearned for a man whose penis she had hired for a night as the solution to her problem.

Oh, there was no redemption for her in heaven. All she had done thus far had sunk her deeper into the quagmire, with not a prospective husband in sight to pull her to ground. And there was no other possibility at the moment but the one at hand: Trevor Smythe.

She would let him propose, she thought, panicking wildly. She would accept him. Tomorrow, when he called.

But meantime, there was a party. On a warm city night when the fog didn't hover oppressively, and everyone was dressed in bright luscious colors, and so happy to be outdoors with music playing and waiters passing food and champagne, while they milled and strutted around a huge swath of lantern-lit gardens that seemed like a fairyland.

Somehow in the soft diffused light, everything looked different and every man looked like a prince.

The Haverdenes had done it up beautifully. Tables scattered around for sitting and talking, an army of attentive waiters and footmen. A string quartet playing softly in the background. A floor set up at the far end of the garden for dancing later.

Everything the same, but something was different. Angilee felt it in her bones as she wandered through the crowd, nodding to acquaintances, stopping to chat now and again with people to whose dinners or parties she had been invited.

The Beddingtons were there and greeted her warmly. Trevor Smythe materialized out of nowhere and took up his usual position at her elbow.

Mrs. Geddes nodded her approbation. Angilee's heart sank a little lower. Into the quagmire. Into the muck.

No sign of the bull.

Feeling as if she were being sucked deeper and deeper into the void.

A swarm of debutantes and her rival heiresses entered together arm in arm, talking and laughing together like the best of friends. Pretending they weren't in competition for the same men, the same titles, the same money.

Was she the only one who was out to buy a marriage? Sometimes it seemed like it.

But then, her father had thought he'd bought one, too . . .

She went on doggedly, mingling with the crowd, letting Trevor Smythe guide her, hand her a goblet of water, pretending to listen attentively as he whispered in her ear.

And then she turned to set the goblet back on a passing tray, and caught her breath. Worse and worse. Wroth had just entered the garden, and a step behind him, she could just see her father.

This was the first time she'd seen Wroth at any of the social events she'd attended. She had been so hoping he'd gone back to his home, wherever that might be, hopefully hours, days, away from London. But there he was, surveying the scene, his cold gaze resting now and again on a passing woman, with a hard assessing look that made Angilee shudder even as far away as she was from him.

Zabel said something to him. He shook his head, and the two of them proceeded down the steps into the garden.

Angilee just wanted to flee. She was shocked by her reaction. Her emotions boiled into pure fear, and a kind of loathing that seeped up from her bones. She had to get out of there because if Wroth found her, he would not observe the social niceties, she was certain of it.

He just was not that kind of man. And he was looking for *her*. She felt it in her heart, in her gut.

Mrs. Geddes murmured, "Your father has arrived."

"I know."

"And the man with him?"

"Wroth."

"I see." Mrs. Geddes threw him a covert glance. "Yes, I see."

"Exactly."

"Stay calm."

That was impossible. Zabel trailing her around a card room

was one thing, but Zabel and Wroth together, cornering her, each from one side, was something altogether devastating.

They were coming at her. Not after her. At her. As if they would attack her and hold her up to the multitude as some kind of example. And they wouldn't hesitate to do it either, because Wroth didn't care, and her father was so single-minded about fulfilling their contract that he'd endure any humiliation, especially if it was hers, after all she had put him through.

Her body went boneless. Her dress felt as if it was weighted, pulling her down, into the quagmire, into the morass of Wroth's punishing expectations.

She couldn't breathe. She felt as if the blood were draining from her body; she felt time slow down. In her mind, she heard Wroth's voice detailing all the little disciplines he would impose on her once they married.

Her knees went weak.

"Are you all right?" Trevor Smythe, as punctilious as ever.

She swallowed hard. Someone had stopped Zabel to say hello, presumably one of his good newfound connections. "Could we—? I need a breath of fresh air. Could we move someplace where it isn't quite so crowded?"

He took her elbow, took command as she had hoped he would and turned her away from the threatening approach of Wroth, whose step faltered, as if he hadn't expected this defection, as if his mere presence alone would have turned her to immobile stone.

It didn't deter him, she knew it wouldn't, but it gave her a moment's respite from the threat of him accosting her, as Trevor Smythe and she threaded through a crowd in which Wroth could not in good manners try to apprehend her or make a scene.

"Just keep walking," she whispered to Smythe. "There's a most unpleasant gentleman who wishes to speak with me knowing that I would not wish to exchange even a word with him."

"Of course." He didn't ask who; he didn't ask why. He just acted, keeping them moving, keeping them out of Wroth's way politely, graciously, unobtrusively.

He was so tall, so strong, so unusually assertive tonight that she thought perhaps she should take another look at him tomorrow, because maybe—just maybe—he *was* the one . . .

* * *

So here he was again, outfitted in Lujan's too-tight tux, his hand in screaming pain with nothing to be done about it, which had been the concurring diagnosis when he finally went to see a doctor, and now he must gear himself up for another evening of lighthearted diversion.

And look for a panderer while he was at it. Wyland's assignments were not easy. It could be anyone. It could be one of *them*, the *them* who were all around him, waiting to attack if he wasn't careful about what he said.

He was a dead man with a dead hand, and he was playing a deadly game with people who did not gamble.

Kyger knew it even more now because in these two or three intervening days between his visit to Wyland and this next invitation event, he'd done some research into the identity of the Khudama whose disciplines were so revered by the brethren.

It had been a quick trip to the British museum after his visit to the doctor, an idle thought as a way to get his mind off of the torturous throbbing of his hand. It had just been a way to pass the time.

He hadn't expected to find anything. And so he found something.

Khudama was real—an ancient scribe who had invented a system of governance and order that had been adopted over the years by military organizations—and others.

It was the *others* that caught his eye.

It was a fluid system of rank—it presupposed an organization, or community, would be formed into a world state with a leader who was to be known as the Patriarch, and each state would be divided into provinces, each governed by an Official, and with a descending order of deputies within each community which he designated as citizens, followers, aspirants, and enforcers.

It sounded so very much like the new world order that Tony Venable had advocated, preached, and sold to his adoring followers that it was stunning.

But how that had been corrupted into an overarching secret organization coded with sevens, a number, he came to find out, that signified supremacy, power, intellect, arrogance, and secrecy, was still a mystery to him.

And it proved nothing, except there was some underpinning to the signs and symbols that seemed to haunt him at every turn.

But the connection . . . ? Venable had reconfigured the disciplines of Khudama to suit his own philosophy, his own ends.

And the Sacred Seven seemed to be something quite apart from that, except insofar as Venable had been one of them.

A revered one of them. Deep on the inside with the robes, rituals and a secret life, of which they all were a part, with vices that were such a tremendous financial resource for the brethren, they were contemplating continuing his program of recruitment and corruption.

And yet he had died.

No, he was murdered. And with a symbol that could have a seven carved in his chest.

Murdered by whom?

It didn't make sense.

He was one of them.

Except that the disciplines to which the brethren pledged themselves were not the precepts of Tony Venable.

Think about that for a moment. And about how dangerous Venable had become with his autocratic vision of a benevolently patriarchal society.

There was something there—something he couldn't quite catch on to yet—again. The connective tissue . . .

Hell, what about his own connective tissue which was like raw meat in his hand. Cryder had to help him dress, and between them, they rigged up an unobtrusive sling, so that his arm had some minimal support.

He stared at himself in the armoire mirror. Nothing elegant here. The collar was too tight, the vest barely buttoned, and the trousers were just that little much too short. Add the sling to that . . . and his limp hand—he looked like a boxer who'd taken a fall.

He flexed his fingers, made a fist, let his hand dangle—no lessening of the pain, even with the support. How was he ever going to get through this evening . . . ?

. . . wait—something in that movement caught his attention.

What? Wait—

He curled his fingers into a fist again, and then draped his hand and watched in fascination as his thumb and forefinger involuntarily formed a right angle . . .

Not a right angle—

. . . in the mirror, right before his disbelieving eyes—a reverse *seven*.

Holy shit.

Holy hellfire . . .

Where—? Where he had seen that . . . noticed that—?

He wracked his mind. Where in the name of holy seven had he seen that . . . ?

Hackford . . .

Holy saints—

. . . entering the card room at the ball—

He closed his eyes, thinking back—

Hackford, holding the whore's breast that night . . .

He'd thought nothing of it at the time, just that it had been Hackford's way of fondling a whore—

Except it hadn't. It had been something else entirely, and right under his nose.

Too much to call it a secret signal . . . ? Or—was it *that* simple—? And that covert and subtle and discreet?

God.

In a crowded room, who would notice?

In the heat of a whore's seduction, who cared?

Unless someone was watching, unless it was mandatory a signal be given . . .

He tried it with his right hand, exactly as he remembered Hackford had displayed it.

In the mirror, reflected back to him—a right side *seven*.

Christ.

Sevens everywhere. Secret seven, Sacred Seven . . .

The clock struck seven—

It was time to go to a party . . .

Knowledge was an interesting thing. It wasn't that he was looking for signs, symbols or sevens. But now he was aware of the hand signal, he saw it everywhere. And it scared the hell out of him.

From the moment he stepped into Haverdene House, he thought—*thought*—he read the signal flashing everywhere.

And that was the thing. He might just be hallucinating. He was probably imagining it. The pain in his hand was making him delirious.

Maybe . . .

He stepped into the elegant, burnished entry hall of Haverdene House, presented his invitation and was escorted to the rear hallway and the gardens.

He paused between the two columns that framed the steps that led down to the garden pathway.

From this vantage point, the gardens seemed like a land of enchantment, with the soft lights, the colorful gowns, the happy buzz of conversation, people turning and greeting each other and those newly arrived, raising a hand with fingers slightly curved in, and the thumb and forefinger pointing out and up . . .

. . . *seven* . . .

No. *Yes.*

Kyger stood for a moment watching. He wasn't imagining it, it was there. The hailed greetings. *Seven.* Someone holding out his hand to take another's. *Seven.* Casually strolling down a pathway, a hand pointing downward as one guest passed another. *Seven.* Gesturing in conversation. *Seven.*

This was insane. Sevens everywhere? *Everyone?*

He shook himself. Forced himself to focus on the meandering guests rather than their gestures. Saw the Beddingtons, the Haverdenes. Saw a lot of familiar faces he couldn't identify, faces from parties, from cricket matches, from riding in Hyde Park.

And he kept seeing the hand movement, endlessly, covertly, discreetly, done and gone. Saw it everywhere.

Kept denying what he was seeing. And finally in the distance he saw something that made sense: Angilee.

Vanilla and chocolate, eminently edible and regal as a queen.

Angilee. Who was doing just fine without his interference, judging by the two gentlemen by her side. He recognized one of them from the ball, but the other was a stranger. However, the dragon was very properly hovering nearby. Angilee had no need of his protection.

He stepped down into the garden and paid his respects to the Haverdenes before proceeding deeper into the crowd.

He felt like a lion in the jungle, surrounded, wary, edgy, as if there was unseen danger at every turn. Every one of them aligned with the *seven*. There was no other conclusion; enemies everywhere, or else he was sleepwalking through some kind of deadly dream.

No, it was real. He distinctly felt the stem of the goblet he picked up off of a passing waiter's tray. Felt the champagne bubbles tickling his nose, and the crisp liquid tingling on his tongue. Not a dream. Just signals and sevens everywhere.

Hellfire.

Keep away from Angilee.

Easy enough. There had to be five dozen attractive young girls milling around, looking for someone to talk to, to latch on to, to marry.

He could pretend.

"Hello, I haven't seen you before."

The speaker was young, beautiful, shy, even though she had accosted him.

"Hello." He bowed. "And you are?"

"Oh." She looked around her almost as if she were afraid she was committing some impropriety. Then she smiled. Anyone else would call her beguiling. "I'm Irene. Who are you?"

"I'm Kyger."

"Kyger—" She rolled his name around on her tongue, liking the sound, the fit.

"Would you care for some refreshment?" It was the requisite thing to say. She would say yes, he'd get her a glass of something innocuous unless she preferred champagne, and they would exchange a few flirtatious words until someone more likely came along.

"Thank you." She smiled again. Absolutely fetching, like a shy colt, eager and fresh and new. "Champagne would be fine."

"Truly?"

"We won't tell," she whispered.

A man could fall into those eyes and get caught in those long fluttering eyelashes. He looked for a waiter. She turned to speak to someone. He followed a waiter to pick off a flute of champagne for her, a warrior hero returning to his Queen of Troy with the prize.

And he stopped dead in his tracks.

She was standing with her back to him. She was wearing, properly, a lovely demure virgin white gown with little embellishment except for one telling decoration. At the small of her back, where the draping was gathered, there was a rose.

A white rose.

He came up behind her with the champagne flute and touched her there to make her aware he was behind her, and then he handed her the flute, his hand still at her back.

On the rose. The same kind of rose he had seen in the display case in Tony Venable's training room: a pristine white *leather* rose.

And all he had to do was look closely, and he saw there were more. There was a white leather rose pinned on the backs, shoulders, bodices, the belts of the gowns of every girl who was dressed in white.

It was stunning, all at once, all of this evidence of Tony Venable's influence everywhere, even in death.

Those roses were no accidental detail. Someone was procuring these girls. Someone at this party, someone with connections to Venable and the Sacred Seven.

Who, among them, all of them, who had made that discreet hand signal, recruited the girls?

They must have started at the onset of the Season—perhaps before—singling out likely candidates. But what kind of girl did they look for among the preening aristocracy that was so certain of its place and its customs . . .

And why would any girl even agree to it . . . to be marked and set apart and made into an object of domination and dependence. It was just inconceivable, but all the signs, symbols and clues were right here before his eyes, in one of the most socially public places yet . . .

"Irene—"

She turned, tilted her head, fluttered her lashes and gave him a speaking look out from under them. "Yes, Kyger?"

"That's a lovely dress. And that rose detail at the back . . ."

She smiled, and it was the smile of the Mona Lisa, infinitely knowledgeable, mysterious, self-aware.

He was on very strange footing, but he pressed on, even though he felt as if he were in quicksand. "It catches a man's eye. Makes him look closer."

"Yes," she whispered. "Exactly."

Now what? Mention that he noticed the other girls? Not politic. And there was something in her eyes, the glittery, sheeny look of someone whose expectations had been met. And she was looking at him encouragingly.

He stared back, deep into her eyes, into those innocent, worldly eyes, that beautiful young face, that expression that said, *ask me.*

He didn't know what to ask.

She helped him. "Do you like what you see?" she whispered barely above a breath.

"Who wouldn't?" he said gallantly.

She waited a beat. "They said you could ask now." Another breathy whisper as if she didn't want anyone to hear her encouraging him.

"Did they . . ." he murmured.

"I'm in training, you know. I promise, I'll be so good. I'll do just what you want, anything you want." She sent him another deep speaking look. "Anytime you want."

Somehow he kept the shock from his face. Somehow he looked past her compelling eyes, looked around him, and suddenly perceived what this party was about.

All around him, in little conversational knots, the girls in the white gowns with the leather rose detail were soliciting their potential masters.

Not the procurer, whoever he might be—the girls themselves.

Holy hellfire.

And here was the sweet little Irene, enchanted by the idea he might want her, he might buy her, and she would have the privilege of servicing him the rest of her youthful life.

Good God.

By invitation only. Signal you're one of us and you will be discreetly approached.

All those sevens. All these men. All these dewy young girls . . . marked already by the white leather rose.

"Well?" There was just a thread of impatience in Irene's voice. He hadn't leapt at her offer; she was ready to move on.

What to say? "I would love to in other circumstances," he said gently, "but I have someone."

"Well, why should that matter?" Irene asked petulantly.

"It does."

"Is she here?"

Kyger shot a look over to where Angilee was still deep in conversation with Trevor Smythe. She was an out, an escape; he could make his way over, say a few words and get out of this slave market.

"She is. Over there."

Irene looked *over there*. "Oh," she said. "Well. Then you'll want to rescue her."

"I think I do," Kyger said. He didn't have to make a polite withdrawal—Irene just turned away and hooked herself onto the next passing gentleman.

Jesus. And all around him, negotiations were going on, or the girls had had no success and were moving on to the next prospect.

After all, that was why they were all here.

And the sociable, accessible Haverdenes—they were involved, too?

It was a web of invisible strands tightening around him. The only thing that made sense was Angilee. And the whole thing with her had never made any sense.

Nor did it tonight. He ought to just leave. He was feeling queasy enough at the situation. He felt as if he was a sojourner in a different kind of hell.

He eyed the situation with Angilee. She looked restless and uncomfortable, but there really was no reason to approach her other than Irene might be watching to see if he had told the truth or if he had just been looking for an excuse to reject her.

Hell, was this whole damned pornographic world watching?

He moved slowly toward Angilee, still undecided. Her gaze kept covertly sliding to one side, and when he looked in that direction, he saw why she was so edgy.

Her father wasn't ten yards away, hovering, waiting, engaged in impatient conversation with a tall, cool, ascetic-looking gentleman who was also staring tightly at Angileee, and it seemed as if both of them were just waiting for the right moment to swoop down on her and corner her.

To do what? What could they do in this company, where every move was suspect and everyone closely watched?

His gut tightened. There was danger all around, for him, for Angilee.

That man with Angilee's father—there was something ominous about him—the way he was looking at Angilee, as if there was a volcanic fury in him, and he couldn't wait to take it out on her.

. . . or was *that* the one her father had wanted her to marry . . . ?

Hellfire.

If he even got near her . . .

He moved closer. The father and his friend moved closer.

Angilee saw them. She put her hand on Trevor Smythe's sleeve. The other gentleman bowed and excused himself, and the father and his friend moved closer.

Angilee looked panicked. She said something to Trevor Smythe, and he shook his head.

Kyger moved closer, and noticed that the dragon was nowhere around. The dragon had discreetly left Angilee and her potential suitors alone, hoping something would happen.

And something was going to happen: she was wide open for her father and her would-be fiancé to approach her and prevent her from gracefully withdrawing.

And that man was itching to get his hands on her. Kyger could see it clearly, and he was closing in on her fast.

Time for action.

In this sick, slick foggy world of sevens and sin, where he had no clue and no control, he could do something about this.

It felt good to move forward with a definite goal, something concrete, something real.

Angilee watched in dread as her father and Wroth, who had now separated, circled around her. She was lost now; they'd been watching her for the good part of a half hour, waiting for the exact moment, and now—this was the end, they'd get at her, they'd take her away, they'd make her marry Wroth . . .

. . . maybe even tonight . . .

Trevor Smythe was useless; all he could do was stand there and eye them suspiciously as they came closer. He couldn't challenge them, he didn't know them or the threat they represented, and he didn't have the grace and skill to whisk her out from under them.

She was trapped—it was over . . .

And suddenly, it wasn't—

Coming through the crowd, strolling between them before they could converge on her—oh, God . . . the bull.

Oh Lord, oh Lord, oh Lord—

She crossed her fingers. She saw her father first, just within hearing distance . . . good—

Should she? Could she? . . . this was the biggest gamble of her life, right now—the bull was her only hope, her only chance . . .

Her heart pounded so hard she thought she'd die. She made herself rise up from the bench where she'd been seated, made herself move forward to greet the bull with both hands outstretched, made herself say loudly, liltingly, "There you are, darling! You're just in time."

She grasped Kyger's hands hard.

Help me.

She looked up at him, pleading mutely.

Help me . . .

And then she turned to the thickset man who had come up beside him.

"Daddy—" Was that her voice, so light and carefree? The bull hadn't said a word. He looked a little dumbfounded, but he hadn't said a word.

She rushed on, "I'm so glad you're here tonight. I want you to meet my new husband."

Help me.

He didn't say a word.

"Kyger—" She was breathless now, racing to get it done before he could deny it. "—my father, Zabel Rosslyn. Daddy—" Her father looked murderous, but there was nothing he could do right here, right now. "Meet my brand-new husband, Kyger Galliard."

Chapter Seventeen

Trevor Smythe gaped.

Zabel stared at her for a moment, his face like stone. And then he said in the softest, silkiest tone, "And just when did the happy event take place, and why was your father not notified of it?"

Help me . . .

He couldn't refuse—maybe he didn't want to. And there was Mrs. Geddes edging up to the group, consumed with curiosity because Zabel had deliberately kept his voice ominously low.

"We eloped," Kyger interpolated smoothly. "Three days ago, at my brother's home in the country."

"Really? Well. I should like to have some proof of the particulars," Zabel said tightly.

"And I'll be happy to call on you this week with all the proof you could require," Kyger said in kind, fully aware of the malevolent presence on the other side of him that was listening avidly to the exchange, and damned sorry one hand was so useless—a fact that wasn't lost on the man beside him.

"Wroth," Angilee said tinnily, turning to him. "You heard our good news."

"I heard someone got married," he said edgily, "but anyone

could say that. *I* could say that. I could claim there was a prior contract." The threat was there, hard as a punch.

Kyger looked at him. "Disappointments sit hard, it's understandable, but it's none of *our* concern," he said at length. "Angilee—?" He offered her his arm.

"I was only waiting for you," she said in a cooing voice, taking hold of him as if he were a lifeline, and ignoring Mrs. Geddes' covert gestures and indignant expression.

"Don't rush," Kyger whispered.

"I have to talk to . . ."

"No." He threw a quick look over his shoulder. They were all standing there, still dumbfounded. He saw Rosslyn say something to the dragon, and then Wroth say something to him, and Mrs. Geddes responding to both of them, but what could she tell them, since she didn't know them—nor they her, as far as he knew—

. . . but . . . nothing was exempt from consideration . . .

And then, the thought was gone as they mounted the garden entrance steps, and he turned his attention toward getting them out of there without incident.

No luck there.

The Haverdenes appeared suddenly. "Leaving so soon?" Mrs. Haverdene asked sweetly. "Is anything wrong?"

"No, no," Kyger said easily. "Lovely party. But—we're newly-weds, you see."

Mrs. Haverdene looked startled. "Oh. I see." She didn't see. She hadn't expected that explanation, and it showed clearly on her face.

"Exactly. So we're rather in a hurry to . . . well, you understand. So thank you so much for the invitation to this lovely evening, my lady. It is time for us to go."

Angilee looked at him uncertainly. Why did it feel as if Mrs. Haverdene was not happy about them leaving? As if they both were there to detain them?

But her presumptive *husband* wouldn't let that happen, she was certain of it, just as he had heroically prevented her father and Wroth from wresting her away from the party.

Kyger shook Mr. Haverdene's hand, bowed over Mrs. Haverdene's hand, and then grasped Angilee's arm.

"My dear—" He propelled her forward around the Haverdenes, who were standing like sentinels at the gate, whispering, "Just keep going, we'll sort everything out later."

He had come by horseback; she and Mrs. Geddes had come by hired carriage. He made the instant decision to appropriate the carriage, tie on his mount, and get her to Waybury House as fast as possible—tonight.

And that with his damned useless hand. Shit—just to make things that much more difficult.

He should be used to it—nothing about this bedamned mission had been easy, so why should his escape with Angilee into the void of the night be anything but difficult?

Getting the carriage, setting up his horse, acclimating himself to the one-handed feel of the reins, wrapping them around his left leg so that he had some balance, leverage and control. Using his injured hand nonetheless, because he just had to until such time as he could give the horses their head.

Angilee didn't question him, and he wasn't after explaining anything until they were well on the road. And it was already after ten o'clock.

Hellfire.

He drove the horses cautiously through the empty streets, thankful that the clatter prevented any conversation.

And what was there to say, after all?

Everything had come full circle—his chocolate virgin was getting exactly what she'd wanted when she first accosted him: that legitimate marriage for which she could present proof to her father so that whatever the contract existed between him and the wretched Wroth, it would be nullified.

What on God's earth could Wroth have offered him that was so extraordinary he would sell his only daughter to that man?

He wheeled the carriage around a corner and down toward the empty street toward Westminster Bridge.

God, it was dark; except for the intermittent gas lamps on the bridge, and along the street, there was no light anywhere. There was no moonlight; there was no fog.

For some reason, he had expected that oppressive supernatural fog would come settling down on them at some point so that they couldn't progress another mile.

But tonight, no fog. Or maybe—if the fog were as sentient as he sometimes thought it was—it had spread over the *other* bridge, the one it would have been more likely for him to take.

Perhaps he had outwitted the fog.

He did not think he'd outwitted Wroth or the Sacred Seven.

He pushed the horses harder, using his injured hand to painfully pick up the slack. They had to go faster now, to get out of the environs of London sooner than soon. Her father could be following, or Wroth, or any of them.

There had been something so insidious about this evening. So unnerving. The white virginal whores in training. The Haverdenes stopping them by the door. They were all involved. They all knew, they tacitly participated. They all had a secret. Every one of them.

All of them? Which secret? Buyer? Seller? *Brethren?*

Nothing is exempt from consideration . . .

Holy hellfire.

There was something niggling at him about that, but he needed all his energy focused on keeping the horses in line and on track as he drove them still harder into the suburbs of London and onto the turnpike out of London.

They hadn't said a word to each other in all this time. He hadn't wanted to talk, and Angilee couldn't think of one thing to say that would explain her behavior—she'd told him all of it already, and there really was nothing more to say.

Surely his meeting Wroth made clear why she had been so desperate to escape him. But now that she had forced the very thing she hoped Kyger would volunteer to do, she was deep in distress that he had done it, as they barreled down the turnpike and into the deep, dark mysterious night.

She hoped he knew where he was going. For some reason, the night void was comforting, so dark it was like velvet, and she felt as if they were wrapped in a cool black buffer against the evil that pursued them.

And Wroth *would* come after them; he was that kind of man.

She huddled in the corner of the carriage and shivered. She had no wrap, no clothes, no ring, no license, no assurance that the bull would even follow through on his promise to present proof of their union to Zabel within the next few days.

What if, when they arrived wherever he was taking her, what if he backed away? What if he felt tricked and trumped? What if he hated her for coercing him so blatantly?

He was driving so recklessly, she thought the carriage would overturn a half dozen times, because his one hand was limp, and his whole body was straining to simultaneously control the horses and whip up their speed.

She thought he hated her; she felt as if he couldn't wait for them to arrive where they were going so he could get rid of her.

She hung on, crouched low, and kept quiet, letting the night air wash over her, and hoping for the best.

They came to the gates of Waybury as the first fingers of dawn light streaked the sky. They had stopped twice to rest the horses, never with a word, as if any sound breaking the dark silence would unleash the unspeakable evil.

He had to despise her for what she'd done. And she had to trust him.

Did she trust him? A hired penis who frequented a brothel and allegedly had a fortune in diamonds and a house in Belgrave Square?

Did she trust him? She'd longed so hard for him to provide the solution to her problem that now it was a fact, she didn't quite know how to feel. She knew how he made her feel, in bed, between her legs, mounted over her and riding her hard. But that wasn't the same kind of trust—or was it?

But really, it was too late to think about trust when the thing was already done and he was slowing the carriage down as they approached an iron fence centered between two stone columns. He turned in through the gate and onto the crackling oyster-shell drive and closer and closer to the looming dark shadow of Waybury House.

"My brother's house," Kyger said. His voice sounded rusted even to him. His hand was a fiery mass of nerve endings, and every muscle ached from the strain of controlling the horses.

But they were there; they were safe.

"It's so early," Angilee murmured. She still was at a loss what to say. This man was going to marry her. Be her husband. Stand up to her father. Defend her. Take her to bed. Make love to her.

She shuddered. The end was coming. She just never expected that it would be in a dark carriage in front of a dark house in the middle of a dark nowhere with the dark man she'd paid to take her virginity and tried to bribe to marry her.

No bribe needed after all. Just imminent danger compounded of an angry father and a thwarted would-be fiancé.

She'd have to remember that for later. After the divorce.

Kyger came around to her side of the carriage. "Let's get you inside."

"But we'll wake them . . ."

"That's why there are servants."

Oh, she liked that comment. She allowed him to help her down from the carriage and to the front door. One peal of the doorbell. A moment later, the door opened.

"Mr. Kyger." A deferential footman. A beautiful entrance hall. Maids scurrying immediately to turn on the gaslight, light the fireplaces, and welcome them into the parlor.

Kyger settled her on a sofa near the fireplace.

A few moments later, the butler—Phillips, was it?—appeared with a tray of sandwiches. "Tea is imminent, Mr. Kyger. And I've sent for Mr. Lujan."

"Thank you, Phillips. And a blanket for Miss Rosslyn as well, please."

Phillips returned with that in moments, with Lujan hard on his heels, and Emily pacing curiously behind him.

"Jesus, baby brother, what the hell—?"

"Good morning to you, too, old son."

"So what's to do? Did Phillips go for tea? Good. What happened to your hand? Hold on for a minute—I'm starving. You can't wake a man up in the middle of the night, for God's sake, and expect—well, I don't know what you can expect . . ." Lujan bit into a sandwich just as Emily said, *mrrrowow*.

"Blasted cat. Jancie's coming, honest to God."

Emily paced over to where Angilee was sitting. *Oww*. Short, sweet. Approval? Disdain? No way to tell: Emily was reserving judgment, settling down on her haunches to wait and watch.

"All right. Ah, here's Phillips. Clear the table. Right there, then, my man. Excellent. You might get a cold compress for Mr. Kyger's hand. And perhaps your guest will pour?"

"If you'd stop babbling for three minutes," Kyger said dryly. "This is Angilee Rosslyn. We are married."

Lujan started, nearly dropped his sandwich.

"Or will be," Kyger amended. "I need your help."

"And *I* need some tea. How do you do, Miss Rosslyn. I think you're crazy. He's as unreliable as a sieve. Pour the tea, would you?"

Angilee poured, at a loss how to take that comment. The two of them were doing just fine without her response, handing off quips like they were music hall comedians. And they looked so alike, especially around the eyes, but it was obvious Lujan was the voluble one, the one to whom everyone would gravitate in any social situation.

He just had a knack. He made her feel immediately at ease, and as if she'd known him for years. He grinned at her, and she smiled back.

"Very nice, brother mine."

"This," Kyger said dryly, "is, if you haven't guessed, my reprobate older brother, Lujan."

"How do you do," Angilee murmured.

"The question is, what can *I* do for you?" Lujan asked.

"Here's the thing," Kyger said. "Angilee is in a situation where it would be better if she had been married three days ago. Legally and legitimately. To me."

"Oh. All right." Lujan took another sandwich. "So we'll do that."

Kyger looked at Angilee. "There you go. All right and tight. And when can we get that done?"

Lujan waved his sandwich. "Elsberry will do it. This afternoon. I'll arrange the rest."

"Perfect."

"What's perfect?"

Jancie, standing on the threshold of the parlor. Something within Kyger constricted. Beautiful just-out-of-bed Jancie probably doing exactly what he imagined she had been doing with Lujan . . . that was her life now, and he had loved her, and he wasn't going to feel guilty for bringing Angilee home to marry her.

Emily got up and walked toward Jancie. *Mrrrroooww. He's going to marry her.*

Jancie looked at Angilee, all wrinkled perfection in a Parisian gown of tulle, silk and crystals, and she didn't know what to say. She looked at Kyger, who in her eyes was the same wonderful brother-in-law that she had relegated him to be, and he looked just a little sad, because he'd have to let go of the past and make a future with Angilee if he truly meant to marry this gorgeous creature.

His gaze caught her eyes. And she saw the truth: he meant to marry the creature. Whatever the reason was.

She suddenly felt rumpled, tousled and disheveled in her robe and gown. But so would the creature if she had just been summarily awakened from a deep sleep.

And she herself had no room for any feelings of envy. She had what she had always wanted—Lujan, a home, a family. She shook herself out of her reverie and extended her hand.

"Hello. I'm Jancie."

"I'm Angilee."

Now they heard the soft, slurred American accent.

"Oh, my," Lujan said. "I thought there was a story, but now I see that there's a *story*. Sit down, stop pacing—you, too, Jancie. This we have to hear."

"I'll give you the short version: Angilee's father, an American investor from the South, contracted an alliance with a titled gentleman here in London which turned out to be totally repellent to her. She needed a husband to forestall the would-be fiancé's claims, and I volunteered. Last night, we were at an event where the same said gentleman and her father were about to corner her in a most unpleasant and public way and force her compliance, so we told them we were already married. Which we will be this afternoon, by your word."

"Oh, that's excellent, baby brother. Concise to a coin. What are you leaving out?"

"Everything else," Kyger said.

That made Jancie smile.

"Nothing important," Kyger amended. "More importantly, Angilee is about to fall over. She needs a bed, a bath, fresh clothing, which I know Jancie will help her with, and Lujan and I need to make some plans."

"Of course," Jancie said.

"Too kind," Angilee murmured. "I *am* tired."

"And there's so much to do," Lujan said briskly. "Take her off, my dear. Take the cat. I'll take my brother, get that hand fixed up, and then we'll figure something out and we'll reconvene here for late breakfast—ten o'clock, let's say—to see where we are by then."

Lujan was a miracle worker. They came down for breakfast to find a sideboard groaning with everything from broiled grapefruit, oatmeal, toast, three kinds of eggs, bacon, ham, and kippers to kedgeree, beefsteak and kidney pie, biscuits, muffins, scones, jams and butters, fruit, tea, chocolate, and coffee.

And plated at Kyger's place at the table was the marriage license dated three days before, and a handwritten invitation on a parchment card to the wedding of Miss Angilee Rosslyn and Mr. Kyger Galliard at three o'clock that afternoon at the village church, the Vicar Elsberry presiding.

"Nice, big brother," Kyger murmured, turning the card over in the fingers of his *good* hand. "So we munch and marry."

"And munch some more," Lujan said. "Mrs. Elsberry likes nothing more than to hold receptions for Galliard weddings." As she had for him and Jancie when they were wed in the church garden nearly three years before. She was busy even now cooking and baking, up to her elbows in food, flour and flowers. "Jancie?"

Jancie turned to Angilee. "I hope you won't mind—the seamstress is altering your gown to make it more appropriate for a wedding."

Angilee blinked back tears. "I don't mind." The words nearly stuck in her throat. *Mrroww.* Emily was there suddenly, rubbing against her leg reassuringly.

Jancie bent down to rub her ears, and Emily jumped up on her lap. *Owww. Hungry.*

"That damned cat is always hungry," Lujan said goodnaturedly, nipping off a piece of the kedgeree and feeding it to her. "That's it. We're all set. Jancie and I will stand up for you, and the whole thing will become legal as lunch not long after. So—eat your breakfast, children . . . we have a long day ahead and a lot to do."

He was like a general marshalling his forces. Kyger needed

that crumpled tux taken care of. A good bath. To soak that hand.
A nice two-hour nap. A ring—perhaps there was one among their
mother's jewelry, all of which had come to Jancie in the end.

Angilee, meantime, needed more sleep as well. A hot refreshing bath. And, Lujan said with a wink, the leisure to reflect on
this horrible mistake she was making, marrying Kyger.

Everything else, he and Jancie would take care of.

So that at two-thirty that afternoon, it was he and Kyger who
drove over alone to the church while Jancie helped Angilee with
her gown, and Mrs. Ancrum, the housekeeper, took charge of the
toddler, Gaunt.

The dress makeover was sublime. The drape of chiffon had
been removed to fashion a veil; the crystals had been reworked
into a band to hold the veil, and the dress reconfigured so that
now there were longer sleeves with just a hint of crystal sparkle at
the wrists.

Jancie's feelings were in absolute turmoil as she fastened the
long line of silk buttons down Angilee's perfect back and smoothed
out the gown.

The creature looked even more beautiful, if that were possible.
This . . . this Angilee . . . would be Kyger's wife within the hour.
And all because of a situation. What situation? A situation with
her father and a man she didn't wish to marry? Why should
Kyger have gotten involved in that?

And she hadn't heard a word about love. Nothing about caring or connection or feelings.

Why hadn't she questioned that more carefully this morning?
Said something. Held them back from doing something that
sounded as if it would turn out disastrously. Marriage was hard;
loving someone was hard. So to just walk into it recklessly because of a *situation* . . .

This was *Kyger;* she loved Kyger. She should *say* something to
Kyger.

Emily sat down right in front of her. *Mrrrooww. Don't be
foolish; don't say anything.*

Jancie let out a deep breath. So, so wise Emily. She knew
Jancie's secrets; she knew the feelings that Jancie continually suppressed.

Owww. Better that way.

Probably so. Emily knew best; she always had.

Ooowww. It will be fine.

She had to believe it would be. Emily knew.

"There—I think we're ready now. Are you ready?"

Angilee looked down at Jancie, who was still smoothing and patting the skirt of her gown. How nice she was, and how kind. Not judgmental. So deeply in love with Lujan. And maybe just a little wary of this sudden and unusual marriage.

She had a right to be. Because now the moment was at hand, Angilee was scared out of her wits she was doing the wrong thing.

Mrrrroooowww. Emily, most emphatically, as if she were saying *stop it*. Emily, staring at her hard, with her bright golden eyes. The message was clear—get on with it.

"I'm ready," Angilee said, with a tremor in her voice that she hoped only she heard.

Jancie smiled and held out her hand. "Then let's get you married."

It was a real ceremony in a real church with a real groom and herself, a real—dressed like a real—bride. The vicar was real and so kind, and his wife a gentle soul who adored Jancie and loved to host a wedding.

Angilee could not have felt more welcome or wanted by any two people as Lujan escorted Kyger down the aisle, with a church full of neighbors looking on, and she and Jancie—and Emily—followed.

The sight of Emily made her smile: her regal walk as she paced down the aisle, her elegance, the way she knew to move to the side, the emphatic way she sat herself down to watch, pinning Angilee again with those knowing golden eyes, as if to reassure her that everything would be fine.

"Do you take . . ."

". . . lawfully wedded . . ."

". . . I do . . ." Kyger—his voice strong, certain.

". . . I do . . ." Angilee in a whisper. She held out her hand, and Kyger slipped on a ring. A beautiful diamond ring.

. . . a fortune in diamonds . . .

Oh, God—what had she gotten herself into . . .

"... now pronounce you ..."

"... kiss your bride ..."

And then Kyger loomed over her, tilted her face up to his, slanted his mouth over hers, and then slowly and deliberately took her kiss, took her lips, took her tongue ... took her forever just in that brief momentous kiss.

She felt a moment's shame for how this had started, because in the end it turned out real. It should have been real. It was as real as it could be for the short time he would keep her as his wife. And then it would end, and all the real would evaporate into illusion ... because that really was what it would have been.

And now, the celebration. Of the illusion and what might have been. All the kind neighbors, who'd known Kyger forever, wishing them well, eating the food, making conversation about small things, country things. *Real* things.

And thinking this union was real.

Kyger, with his injured hand held carefully, being fed by Jancie from the long lace-covered table full of a selection of salads, cold meats, cheeses, fruit, cakes, and a big bowl of wedding punch. Lujan, lord of the manor, greeting the neighbors, so kind, so sociable—no class differences here, at least at a wedding.

Angilee drank it in, wishing it were real, and that it was she and Kyger who would be returning to Waybury. Forever. For real.

But instead, they would spend the night, whatever the night would turn out to be, and in the morning, with all the proper documentation and papers in hand, they would return to London, and to Kyger's life there that she had so precipitately disrupted.

She knew nothing about his life there except that he frequented the Bullhead and he turned up at all the right social events.

Social events—

Oh, God, Mrs. Geddes, whom she'd just left standing there with her father and Wroth—the worst bad manners ever, not to have said a word, not to have gone back and—

And *what?* Nothing she could have said in the aftermath would have made it right ...

And then—and then ... her clothes, the money—oh, dear God—everything she'd left by just running off with the bull—not the bull now, she had to stop thinking of him like that—

. . . and for all she knew, Mrs. Geddes was at the flat now, fuming and fussing about her betrayal, and searching all over for that little fortune with which she had been going to bribe someone to marry her.

She had turned everything upside down in that insane moment of panic that had led to this insane moment of union to Kyger Galliard.

She had a lot to answer for in her insanely determined quest to foil her father and countermand his wishes.

And she would. As she looked around her at everyone participating in the joyful celebration of her marriage, she knew she would.

Angilee was exhausted, and Kyger insisted she just go to bed and that everything else could come later.

That, however, was so much her way of thinking that she was shocked at her feeling she wanted everything resolved now. Even the things she couldn't do anything about: Mrs. Geddes, her father, Wroth. The mistake of this marriage.

"We'll sort things out later," Kyger said again. "You need sleep, I need to talk to Lujan, and we both need not to be pressured by the circumstances. The thing is done. We made sure you were safe first; everything else can come later."

He was too kind, and Angilee was feeling too guilty. His family was too kind, and she was a self-centered schemer, and she had to atone. "We'll start divorce proceedings immediately . . ." she started to say, and he shushed her.

"Tomorrow. We'll take care of all that tomorrow."

He meant it, too. He meant to protect her, he'd always wanted to protect her, and now, after all his resistance, he finally could. His chocolate virgin was his, as legal as the law and church could make it, and he was content to just savor that fact and not think of the ramifications beyond it.

Or the things he had learned and things he must connect to finally fulfill the mission.

Everything later.

He looked up to see Jancie at the door, which he'd left slightly ajar.

"Is everything all right?"

"Absolutely. I think some hot chocolate would be good"—*for my chocolate virgin*—"and . . . is Lujan around?"

"In the library. I'll see to the chocolate." And as Jancie turned from the doorway, Emily walked in, jumped on the bed, and settled down beside Angilee's left hand.

Mrrrrowww. I'll stay here.

Angilee stroked her ears.

She slanted a look up at them with her golden eyes. *Oww. You all can go now.*

Jancie and Kyger withdrew. Jancie said, "Angilee will be asleep before I get back with the chocolate."

"I know." Kyger touched her shoulder. "Thank you."

She grasped his hand, perhaps for the last time. But she wouldn't think about that. "No thanks needed. I'll get the chocolate."

Kyger nodded, and went downstairs to the library where Lujan was lounging in one of two recently purchased leather chairs with a leather account book.

It was a strange picture. Lujan, who had never cared five farthings about Waybury, and had spent years living in a debauched fog in London, was now the meticulous and scrupulous gentleman farmer, taking over the running of Waybury House and its farms as though he had been born in the fields, and watching every ha'penny like a mother hen.

Thank God, he'd reformed for the love of a good woman, or where would Kyger be now? Still running the estate, resenting his brother and still being the one that Jancie could never love.

God, why think about that now?

"So, baby brother . . . congratulations."

"Thanks for your help." Kyger settled himself into a chair opposite his brother. "I could not have done it without you."

"Oh, now, you could pull the same strings," Lujan said, setting his account book aside. "A country town is a country town. You don't stop being a son of the soil just because you defected to London."

"I guess not." That was for sure, judging how they had taken to Lujan after the fact. Kyger closed his eyes to blot out the memories. There were too many in this house, in this room.

Maybe they'd never get over the exposure of the secrets and betrayals of their fathers. Maybe things like that lived in the soul of a house. Whatever it was, he felt something sitting in that room, and all the new paint, new wallpaper and new furniture could not suppress it.

"Jancie's with the tot," Lujan said. "I don't know. They reach the age they can walk and just about talk and you'd think that would make things easier. Cute little fellow, though. A man should have a son." Lujan thought about it a moment. "At least one. If not—oh, a half dozen."

"Like you?" Kyger murmured.

Lujan sighed. "A man can reverse a reputation."

"And so you have," Kyger said generously.

They fell into silence for a few minutes. And then: "You can tell me now, old son. What's the real story?"

"The real story about what?"

"You and Angilee."

"Pretty much what I outlined to you."

"Didn't say where you'd met her."

"No, I didn't," Kyger said.

Lujan waited for the confession, but Kyger wasn't giving one. "Who's the father, then?"

"I doubt if you'd know him." Silence on Lujan's end, and Kyger gave in. "An American investor named Zabel Rosslyn."

Did he imagine it, or did Lujan recognize the name?

"Oh, yes," Lujan said. "Yes, he's been introduced around in certain circles. I know the name. A little bit too fast and forward for most people's taste, given the caliber of wealth that's hit the shores this year. Not quite in the Vanderbilt class, Mr. Rosslyn, but very ambitious. Don't know it's going to take him anywhere, but—is Angilee the only child?"

"Yes."

"Then I take it he's not a happy man tonight, given you wrecked up *his* plans pretty thoroughly."

"I wouldn't think so."

Another silence. And then: "You're a credit to the Galliards, baby brother. I could not have done better myself."

"Exactly what I thought," Kyger murmured.

A beat. "What about Wyland?"

"Doesn't know yet."

"Anything to tell?"

"Not much. The probem of Venable is still a slippery slide with not much to grab on to."

"Still? I would have thought you'd uncovered something by now."

"Didn't say I hadn't. Proving it is the sticking point."

"Anything you can tell me?"

"Not yet."

"But you're close—"

"Close."

"Good."

That was too self-satisfied a comment for Kyger's peace of mind. "And why is that, big brother?"

Another silence.

"I have some news myself," Lujan said at length.

Kyger opened his eyes. "Good news?"

"I think so."

"All right, then—"

A beat. "They've asked me to stand for Parliament."

Kyger jolted upright. "Well, hell . . ."

Another beat. "Venable's seat."

"*What?*"

"You heard me."

"*Who?*"

"What do you mean, who? Who do you think?"

Oh, he knew who he thought—it was obvious: Venable's followers, his faction, his idolators . . . Goddamn—his own brother—being used by those fanatics . . .

He jacked himself out of the chair. "*Who?*"

"God, stop that—you're like a madman. Wyland's people, who did you think?"

Kyger stopped dead in his tracks. " . . . *Wyland?*"

"Wyland. It's time. He's been dead long enough."

"That's debatable," Kyger threw in bitterly.

"What? Oh, the body—well, nothing to be done about that that Wyland isn't doing. The point is—they've got to get someone favorable to them in there, and not some half-baked demagogue.

Simple equation—it's been nearly three months, the furor hasn't died down, and someone of Venable's faction will snap up that seat if Wyland doesn't get someone viable up in opposition *now*. So . . . baby brother—it's going to happen, so fix the idea of it in your mind right now—you're looking at Lujan Galliard, M. P."

Chapter Eighteen

Lujan an up-and-coming M. P., and the chocolate virgin, his wife, in his bed—? There were two impossible things before breakfast, and yet both were no illusion. Both were real in the way that things that seemed upside down really proved to be right side up when you looked past the fog obscuring the details.

Or had he fallen down a rabbit hole?

No. The chocolate virgin was there, in his bed and sound asleep, and just as beautiful and luscious as when she'd first bluffed her way into his room at the Bullhead.

And now she was in his room at Waybury House.

Back around in a circle, nearly where they had begun.

And he hadn't come very far since then. He'd made headway by inches, and the end result was this—he had very little to take back to Wyland except his incredulity that Lujan was about to be their candidate to stand for Venable's seat.

Upside down. The last thing he ever expected to hear.

How could it make sense that he'd actually offered to wed the woman who'd tried to bribe him to marry her, and his brother was suddenly on the verge of a political career after a lifetime of libertine lassitude?

Reality, obscured by the fog of illusion. A rabbit hole.

And the vanishing virgin, as if by magic, reappearing in his life, and in his bed.

That should be his focus, not the fog, not the illusion. *She,* of everything, was the most real. The question was how real did she want this marriage to be?

Not real. Not as real as he was thinking he wanted . . . but then, he wanted even now to sink himself into her. His body tightened, hardened and elongated just looking at her sprawled in his bed.

Now he was avid to have everything because he had nothing—no home, no family, no love, no answers. But he had her for as long as it would be, and he had in her everything a wife embodied: the sex, the connection, the companionship and, in the most abstract way, a home.

But what did she want? He knew some of it: independence, freedom, the ability to live her life how she wished and with whom she wished, but those were all theoretical ideas and ideals that weren't possible with all the constraints that would be put on her.

So what *did* she want? What would she settle for?

Him.

Right now—him.

Because he wanted her no less than he had from the moment she barged into his brothel bedroom. There was something about her—that iron strength, that indomitable nature, that quality of innocence in a woman of some small experience, his unholy and overwhelming desire to protect her . . . all those things still infused his feelings about this woman who was now his wife.

And that was over and above his pure naked desire to fuck her—endlessly, forever.

Right now.

Not *right* now. The chocolate virgin slept.

And he might never have a good night's sleep again.

He slept, he didn't expect to fall asleep, and he was dreaming . . . or was it a dream? There was Wyland saying, *find the woman,* but he'd found the woman. Didn't Wyland see that? Right here, next to him. *The* woman.

When had he gone to London anyway?

Wyland: *No, the woman . . .*

Oh, the woman. He remembered, circles, signs, signals, the party, the white rose . . . that woman. What was her name? Find her, bring her to Wyland—she could testify, and then it would be over; they'd bring Venable down—Wyland had distinctly said, that was the way . . .

He jolted awake. Holy hellfire. He had almost let that slip by him.

Find the woman. He'd found her. Or she'd found him. The woman with the white leather rose. Irene.

And all he had to do was take her to Wyland and the whole Tony Venable thing would be over . . .

Simple. No complications. *That* was the way . . .

Angilee had felt shunted off into the bedroom too soon and for specious reasons, but she'd fallen asleep so fast and so deeply that she could not be irritated at the fact she'd been that tired and they really all wanted her to get some sleep.

Getting married was tiring, after all.

Married. It sat strangely in her mouth and on her tongue. For real. Forever. That was what Mrs. Geddes had counseled, and now she was, and to the only one of all them with whom she could reasonably foresee staying with for any length of time.

But every time she thought about what had happened at the garden party, she felt mortified at what she'd done. To have forced Kyger Galliard to acknowledge her as his wife. To have abandoned Mrs. Geddes to her father and Wroth like that. To have disregarded her every piece of advice, her every caution, her every admonition and to do it right in front of her—it was beyond bad manners, beyond impropriety.

She owed Mrs. Geddes so much, and she owed her an apology and something more, which would probably take monetary form in the end. But still and all . . .

And yet, she had what she most desired: the bull had agreed to become her husband, and her father could do nothing about it. Weigh that against anything she'd done to upset Mrs. Geddes, and she might owe Mrs. Geddes nothing.

Well, they'd go back to London in the morning, and she would straighten it all out. All of it. From that town house in Belgrave Square.

Really? Did she believe any of that was true?

She believed one thing only and that was her husband was deep asleep beside her, she had defeated her father, and victory was hers.

And her husband's. Irrespective of whether he had any personal fortune in diamonds, or that town house, it was nothing compared to the Rosslyn wealth, and she *was* her father's only heir.

Unless he'd turned everything over to Wroth in exchange for those introductions to men of influence and power.

Oh, God.

But if he had done that, why would he need or want to force her to marry the man? No, she didn't want to know the answers now. Or ever. Wroth would never be a factor in her life again.

She had what she wanted—the bull. And the rest she'd think about later.

But in the early hours of the morning, when everything was diffused with the soft early glow of rebirth, she felt him touch her, and she turned to him, and into his touch, and she was reborn.

At that hour, when time was suspended, the past was as if it never had been. His kiss was gentle, his touch like silk, sliding over her body with reverence and care, rediscovering all those hollows and valleys and mysterious places that made her who she was and who he wanted her to be.

It was such a tender exploration, she felt her bones melting and her body unfurling, opening wide to let him seek, explore, examine each and every crevice, her softness, her darkness, the unending elusiveness of her—all of that she gave into his hand, in trust and in marriage.

And he gave to her his body, his heat, his penetrating hardness that took her with a forcefulness that made her swoon. Here was the moment of truth and trust—this was what she never would have achieved with any other man, this communion, this coupling, this joining into one.

So slow, so sweet, so impossibly deep and filling, so gorgeously naked and raw, the way she cradled him between her legs, the way he fit her, the measured rocking of their bodies in sensual cadence.

The silence, the dark, the deep, the need, all of it played on her senses, made her vulnerable and needy in ways she had never thought of herself. Made her sink into the billowing pleasure that mounded up between her legs, made her push for more and more of the feelings, the pleasure, the peak that she could only sense beyond the pleasure.

It was coming, coming, coming . . . she resisted it, she wanted to pull it out like a long, thick string of taffy—pull it, and stretch it and elongate it until she couldn't bear it anymore, until her body was tight with it, taut with it, explosive with it, to the point that one more thrust would detonate the blast.

It was there, oh, it was there—she spread herself wider, she hooked her legs over his thighs to pull him deeper, she lifted her hips in a primitive dance of enticement, and still, still it wasn't enough.

What was enough? There would never be enough. She didn't want it to end, this mindless, seamless burrowing into her body. She pressed him tighter, harder, reveling in the rigid voluptuous feel of his penis driving between her legs.

It was torture, it was pleasure, it was unspeakably carnal, it was wholly and irrevocably theirs . . . and she wanted it always, forever. She had committed to always and forever . . .

She reached for it then, for the peak, for the crest, the hard rock ridge on which she could break her fall, and hot pinwheels of pleasure came whirling out of nowhere, dilating through her body wildly, recklessly down her body between her legs, lodging there, coalescing there, becoming the breaking point on which her orgasm spiked and exploded into a long, hard rhythmic culmination.

He let go a moment later, blasting into the backwash of her pleasure, his body primed, hot, volcanic in its eruption and in his ultimate claim on her.

And done. For now.

Forever . . .

And now he was content to just root in her, nestled between her legs, rocking against her, rubbing his pubic bone against hers, enjoying the rough feel of being mounted on her, enfolded by her, embedded in her . . .

This was enough. Just this, his elusive virgin finally pinned down, wedded, bedded and physically bound to him.

Tomorrow would be the beginning of the end. He would head for London. He'd find Irene, he'd take her to Wyland, they'd take down Tony Venable, and he would have fulfilled his mission. And then he'd deal with Angilee's father, and the insidious Wroth, too, and get them out of her life forever.

So many forevers when time was so short and there seemed as if there could never be enough of it.

But he could wait for that. Time was at a premium right this minute. He'd been so haunted by Tony Venable's sins, and he still had things he must do to end that fully and finally. All of that would take time, and he had so very little of it to squander.

He had what was left of tonight, and he needed to use this precious time to *not* think about Tony Venable or his brother's shocking announcement.

Right at this minute, the night seemed to stretch into a timeless void. Tonight all things were possible, and nothing was exempt from consideration.

Not even a future with Angilee.

Tonight, he had the advantage: he had her sinuous edible body tucked tightly beneath him, and he never had to leave her. He could just wedge himself there forever. Push at her gently, thrusting lightly, tightly, sensually. Keep her ripe, wet, hot, wanting.

Simple. All he needed was time.

He moved in her, feeling the urgency to fuck her building in him again, because time really was fleeting. He felt her body give as he pushed against her, felt her soften, widen, brace herself for his first forceful thrust.

Felt himself go wild as he propelled himself into her like a piston, as he felt himself just lose control, of his penis, of his body, of himself, of the moment. There was nothing else, just her heat, his hardness and the galvanic and elemental drive to own her body.

She held him at bay, undulating to entice him still further in her own primitive dance of invitation, pulling him deeper and harder into her body, taking him to the hilt and pushing for more.

He gave her more, pounding into her in a long, hard steady rhythm that made him crazy with wanting to come—but he held on and held off, playing with her, tormenting her, fucking her until she could take it no more.

Her body seized at the last culminating thrust; her body melted all over his engorged penis, bucking and writhing and taking it, taking it, taking it until he burst wide apart and spewed a flood of his hot fertile seed deep into her shuddering core.

And he couldn't stop. He pushed to stay, wanting to wallow in the feeling of his thick hot semen engulfing her, and to submerge his still engorged penis inside her soaked hole. He wanted to fuck her all over again and drown her in his seed. He wanted her naked the whole night in his arms, he wanted her naked forever. He wanted—

He wanted morning not to come, and morning came too soon.

He made her stay in bed as he rummaged in his closet for some old clothes, packed the wrinkled clothes he'd gotten married in and readied himself for the long ride back to London.

And it was as if the night had never been.

"But I'm coming," Angilee protested.

"No, I think you're not. I have some things to do that it would be better if I knew you were here, safe, with Lujan and Jancie."

"But . . ."

"We can take care of everything else later." That didn't much reassure him or her for that matter.

"That's what you always say," she muttered, knowing full well it was how she had always operated.

"I'll be back in a day or so. I have some things to take care of, and then I'll be back."

This sounded so suspiciously like what he had said to her after they'd escaped the Bullhead and returned to his paltry rooms in Cauldwell Gardens, that it gave her pause.

"Men always have things to take care of. I have things to take care of, too."

"Like confronting your father?"

Oh, she'd forgotten about that. Who cared about her father now?

"Like apologizing to Mrs. Geddes."

"Mrs. Geddes can wait."

She supposed Mrs. Geddes could, but—"Maybe you could—"

"No. No time for Mrs. Geddes."

"A note to the agency, then."

"What agency?"

"The Streathem Agency, Miss Burnham. That's where I found her. Just say . . . damn, I don't even know what I would say."

"You went off and eloped with a stranger against all best advice, and left your dragon in the lurch. It can wait, Angilee."

She took a deep breath. "I suppose it can."

"Isn't it enough you've—we've—sidetracked your father's plan to marry you to Wroth?"

It should have been enough. It *was* enough. After last night, it was more than enough.

"Yes," she said forlornly.

She was almost too much to resist. Especially after last night. Kyger pulled his kit together roughly to mask his feelings.

God, it was damned hard to leave her. He had to leave her. He had to wind the thing up with Wyland. It would only take a day. Maybe two. Possibly three.

He didn't even know. He didn't want to leave.

He bent over their rumpled bed, and touched her chocolate hair, her ear, her face, cupped her raspberry-tipped breast. "Then just let me finish up my business in London, and we'll go on from there."

Business in London. Men always had business in London. Angilee would bet Lujan had the excuse of business in London, too. She'd have to ask Jancie.

And anyway, Kyger was adamant that he didn't want her to see him off. He'd be back before she knew it. She should stay in bed and rest, after last night. Like she was porcelain or something.

She was the least breakable person she knew.

She jumped out of bed—stopped . . .

No clothes. For God's sake . . . *no clothes.* Nothing. Her wedding gown and underclothes in a heap on the floor. Nothing else.

That was her business in London. Damn it. The last thing she wanted was to borrow something from Jancie, but almost as if Jancie were aware of her distress, she knocked on the door softly and asked if Angilee was awake.

Angilee dove back into bed. "Come in."

And there was Jancie with a shirtwaist and skirt in hand. "I thought these might do temporarily. Men never think of these things."

"No, they only think about business in London," Angilee said tartly. "Does Lujan ever have business in London?"

Jancie thought a moment. "Now that you mention it, yes, he does. About once or twice a month, he goes off to London on some business or the other."

"I knew it," Angilee murmured.

Jancie was curious but didn't question that comment. "Someone will come help you wash and dress in a few minutes, and I'll send up some tea."

"Thank you," Angilee said.

"My pleasure."

It seemed to be. In no time at all, little Mary with her efficient hands and her country brogue was entertaining Angilee as she helped her nip and tuck the clothes to fit her, and fixed her hair.

"There you go, miss. They're waiting for you down in the dining room."

Angilee made her way down to join Lujan and Angilee at yet another bountifully laid out breakfast. "This is too much. Surely you don't have this every day?"

"Do we?" Lujan looked at Jancie.

"Well, perhaps we don't eat quite this luxuriously day to day," Jancie said.

"There, you see—it's all for you, Angilee. And for my baby brother, if he had stayed. He does have a massive appetite in the morning. As you'll learn, I'm sure."

"He had business in London," Angilee said.

"Of course," Lujan agreed, grinning at her. "Men always have business in London."

Lujan completely understood. Angilee loved Kyger's brother even more just because he understood.

"Exactly," she said, helping herself to some toast and eggs while Jancie poured her tea. "Why don't women have business in London? *I* have business in London, but Kyger wouldn't let me come."

"Interesting you say that," Lujan murmured. "I happen to be going to London tomorrow—on business. I'd be happy to take you in. I mean, Kyger gave no strict instructions that you should be immured here until he returns. If you'd like to spend the day, we could arrange to meet and come home late this afternoon."

Angilee blinked. "I would."

"Then it's done."

God, she loved Kyger's big brother. He completely understood.

Kyger had formulated a plan as he rode back to Town, the first objective of which was to find Irene. Which meant seeing if there were invitations to a party or dinner she might conceivably attend.

He came back by the London bridge and into tight mid-morning traffic as he made his way to the town house.

London looked strange in daylight. London looked . . . normal. Nothing preternatural. Everything calm, the atmosphere quiet, with the usual sounds and movements of the early day.

There was none of the sense he'd had of Tony Venable's death dominating things, although there were card pockets still pinned everywhere. Some were empty; some still had cards in them.

He took one: *love faith future return . . .*

The ghost of Tony Venable never gave up. But now the ghost would be trumped—by the reality of who he was and his secret pornographic life.

If he could find the mysterious and accommodating Irene.

If he could offer her enough incentive to talk.

But that would come later.

First to the town house, where Cryder was surprised to see him return, and sent the maids in a flurry to see to his room.

Kyger took his mail to the parlor and asked for sandwiches and tea while he settled down to go through the invitations and see what was viable.

There were a half dozen visiting cards and three invitations. Dinner and cards. A small private party. And a reception tomorrow night for a minor visiting royal who was in Town for both the Season and the Queen's Diamond Jubilee at the end of June.

The reception seemed the most likely. There would be a crush and a crowd, and everyone loved meeting a royal no matter how far down the line of succession he might be.

But—it would be a very formal event. So he had to lay out

that crushed and wrinkled suit to be cleaned and pressed. He needed to write out an acceptance for the reception, which he did right then, and that went on the hall table to have a footman deliver it.

And he decided over his sandwiches and tea not to report to Wyland just yet. It was a calculated decision. He wanted to have something concrete to tell him; he wanted that proof—he wanted to convince Irene, if he could find her tomorrow night, to talk to Wyland. To tell him why she had been at the garden party.

Just that. If he could do that, it would be over, they'd all be free, and he could think about some kind of future with Angilee.

He liked the sound of that—a future. A wife. A home. Children? Something of his own.

Not quite yet. There were still things to do: visit that Streatham Agency that was so important to Angilee, see her father, get that proof of marriage business settled. Find Irene.

Make one last trip to the Bullhead . . .

What? Why was he even considering that? He wasn't. That would be suicidal. It was tantamount to putting himself right in the enemy's sights. And what could he possibly discover there that would prove anything?

He needed Irene. Or someone like Irene, now that he knew what to look for and what it meant. Someone who'd be willing to tell the truth about the significance of the white leather rose.

Now that he knew the secret of the sevens.

But don't forget—they know you know.

Jesus. It was too easy to forget that, too. He'd been so immersed in getting Angilee out of harm's way, he wasn't thinking about *them*.

And they'd be watching him. Hackford had warned him. Wyland had cautioned him. He had known it from the moment he caught on at the garden party and the Haverdenes had tried to outmaneuver them.

It wasn't over. The danger was still there.

Venable lived. As he wended his way the next morning toward St. George Street, where the agency was located, he saw the card pockets all around, all refilled with Venable's message of resurrection. He saw people taking them, reading them reverently, almost as if those cards were their daily scripture.

It wasn't over. Someone was going to take over. Someone was going to come forward with the same message, the same ideology, and his followers would organize and swell in numbers and . . .

How the hell was Lujan going to deal with that if he got Venable's seat?

Never mind that now. He mounted the wide stone steps at the elegant address of the Streatham Agency and tried the door.

Locked. Strange.

He peered in the frosted glass window of the door, but that was useless; he couldn't see anything. Odd that a business would be closed at this hour of the day. He rang the bell, and banged on the door, feeling conspicuous as hell on this busy street.

It took a while, but finally a very starchy and disapproving middle-aged woman answered the summons.

"Yes?"

"The Streatham Agency? Miss Burnham?"

She looked at him as if he were a lunatic. "Who? What? There's no agency here, no Miss Burnham. You have the wrong address."

She slammed the door, and he didn't feel inclined to pursue it further.

But how was it possible? Angilee wasn't crazy—she had been quite definite that she had hired Mrs. Geddes through that agency. And Angilee just wasn't someone who'd make a mistake about an address.

And yet she had, and now he'd have to track it down.

But as he waited for Zabel Rosslyn in the lobby of Claridge's, he felt on firmer ground: the place was like a parlor in someone's home, with sofas, comfortable chairs, tables, a fireplace, a grand piano, a thick oriental carpet, and wonderful molding on the walls, ceilings and fireplace surround.

Just the place to discuss the legitimacy of a marriage.

But Zabel was strangely late. He couldn't find the bellboy he'd sent to summon Zabel anywhere. People came and went the way they did in hotels, and he was starting to feel extremely uncomfortable to the point where he finally went to the desk.

"Zabel Rosslyn? I sent the bellboy . . ."

"Let me check for you, sir." The desk clerk rifled through the register and checked the key slots. "Are you certain, sir?"

"What do you mean?"

"There's no one by that name registered . . . not now, not anytime in the last six months."

A rabbit hole.

Filled with secrets and lies.

He felt the strength of the power of the mysterious *they*—the Sacred Seven—all around him.

They were watching; they had got Rosslyn out of the way. They had closed down the agency somehow. They knew what he was up to.

They were waiting for him.

He was ready for them. He felt the fury of the righteous. Venable was not going to win. He would bring him down, he would destroy him, destroy all of them, and all of *it* whatever and wherever *it* existed.

He knew this much—the locus was the Bullhead.

That was the thing. And viscerally he knew it, and he knew he had to go back there.

Better by daylight.

It was such an unprepossessing house by daylight—just a big half-timbered country house of sun-softened stone sitting in a well-tended park of emerald lawns dotted with bushes and beds of flowers. It could have been any man's home, his home; it was so like Waybury in some respects, it was frightening.

Frightening that home and life as the common man knew it could be so corrupted, and transmogrified into something so venal, so prurient, so obscene.

He tethered his mount in a copse of bushes near the road. So much easier to skulk on foot, but no one even seemed to be around.

It made him queasy, how quiet things were, as if danger were hovering high above him like fog, or simmering deep underground.

The air felt oppressive. He felt as if he were walking into a nightmare. As if they were waiting. As if they had always known he would eventually come back there.

He moved closer to the house, crouching low, and under the view out the windows. Fake windows in nonexistent public rooms. Someone was watching. That was the word. Someone was always watching, and he couldn't take the chance someone wasn't watching now.

Whose perverted pornographic vision was this place anyway? Who had bought and fitted out this house of prostitution and debauchery?

Try for the front door, or that secret basement entrance through which Angilee and he had escaped? No time for that now. There were probably a dozen secret ins and outs to the Bullhead, but a frontal assault seemed more efficient.

And it was too quiet. He hated how quiet it was.

They were waiting . . . he could feel it, taste it . . . the sin, the sex, the danger, the rage—he flattened himself against the front wall and moved slowly toward the door.

He had to know. He just had to know.

Up the front steps to the burnished front door. So quiet. So deadly. His heart pounding. His life on the line . . .

He reached for the brass doorknob. Touched and retracted his hand as if it had burned him. Grasped it again and turned it. Pushed his way in.

Darkness. No gaslight. Just the north light pouring in through the door. Enough so that he could see—

The place was empty.

Wholly empty. Not a stick of furniture. Not a curtain, a carpet, a chair, a wall. Just a big empty blank space in front of him. As if the house had been gutted.

As if nothing had ever been there at all.

Chapter Nineteen

The reception was held at Gorsenor House, a gala event only slightly less glittering than the Queen's Ball, which had inaugurated the Season.

Everyone was there; everyone wanted to be seen, and hopefully to be mentioned in the morning papers as among those feting that minor royal from that small European country that was such a friend of Her Majesty's.

The aristocracy was there. The Prince of Wales was there. The heiresses were there. The novices wearing the white leather roses were there. Kyger saw them all instantly in one sweeping glance as he entered the elegant marble-floored foyer just outside the ballroom.

But surely they wouldn't be soliciting here.

Nothing seemed impossible to him anymore if *they* could empty a whole house and disperse a small lifetime of lechery in the blink of an eye.

He watched for the hand signal; he looked for Irene. He spoke to acquaintances whose faces looked familiar but whose names he could not quite recall. He moved through the crowd feeling invisible among all the high-powered government officials, earls, dukes and diamond-encrusted duchesses milling around.

He did not see Zabel Rosslyn, when he fully expected to see him, and Wroth.

He drank champagne, he nibbled on hors d'oeuvres, he looked for Irene. He saw a dozen or more white-gowned girls with leather roses pinned in their hair, at their waists, on their bodices. He saw no sign of seven, at least any that were overt.

And he felt a great frustration, as he wandered through the crowd, that he was missing something. That there was something in the stripping and gutting of the Bullhead that was meant to be a message.

He listened in on conversations.

". . . breaking in new staff is just impossible . . ."

". . . was hoping against hope that he would choose to go up to Oxford this term but—"

". . . all the preparations for the jubilee—I don't know how I let myself agree to . . ."

". . . do you like what you see . . . ?"

He stopped short at that familiar question.

The speaker was a dark-haired girl dressed in white, her back to him, with a leather rose fastened at the break of satin buttons down her back.

Irene?

He moved closer, hearing the same solicitation Irene had made to him, almost as if they had all be given a script to follow. The same script. For the same gentleman. The same kind of gentleman who would always pay the price for the kind of submissive service these girls would be trained to give.

Subtly he moved around to see her face, and he was deeply disappointed to find it wasn't Irene. It was another quite beautiful and naïve young thing already in the throes of the Tony Venable brand of sexual education.

And the gentleman to whom she was earnestly speaking shook off her detaining hand.

She didn't like that. Her expression turned vindictive for the merest breath of a second, and then she immediately turned to Kyger and smiled.

"Hello. I'm Alice."

"I'm Kyger." Now he was at a loss, and had to resort to the same lines from the same script. "Would you care for some refreshment?"

314 / *Thea Devine*

"Oh, yes," she murmured. "Champagne would be fine."

He got them each a flute, and they sipped, and he wondered just how to approach her to get the information he needed. "I see a lot of girls wearing that same white rose," he said at length.

She sent him a coquettish look. "Do you know why?"

"Should I?"

She smiled that Mona Lisa smile. "Don't you?"

"Say that I don't," he said carefully.

"It's nice to meet someone who doesn't, actually. They're all so jaded. They've sampled everyone, you know, and there's hardly anything you can offer them that they don't want perverted somehow. Do you understand?"

"I think so. But why don't you tell me more."

She looked around them and lowered her voice. "It's very seductive, but you have to understand that if you take the oath to get involved, you can't renege. Although, why anyone would want to . . .

"Anyway, the thing is, there are more of us than there are available men, so of course some of us won't marry this Season, and maybe not the next or the next. So the idea is, we can have all the benefits of a wife without the onerous duties of managing a house and servants, or dealing with unpleasant relatives, or bearing children.

"We who make the decision not to marry can have the best of that world anyway—our own homes, a monetary settlement, jewels, clothes, luxuries—all that without all the burden of being married.

"Which, after all, is merely a license, a ceremony and a notation in a church registry. For myself, I can't wait. I have a choice from all the available men in London, married or single, instead of just one. The white rose assures them that I'm in the process of being trained to perfectly service them. When I've completed my training to the satisfaction of my tutors, I'll be given a black leather rose to signify I'm ready for all the gifts my lover-to-be is waiting to shower on me.

"It's perfect, it's the best of both worlds. The most influential and wealthy men at my feet. Every advantage after I'm chosen . . ." She looked at him as if daring him to say that any woman wouldn't want that. "A devoted man to whom I dedicate myself . . ."

He was appalled. She didn't know. She really didn't know just what *perfection* meant to those sadistic voluptuaries. They'd put her to work first; they'd bring her down so low she'd be grateful to be sold off to anyone who would pay for her. And she'd be offered only to those who desired a true, fully whipped-into-shape submissive.

"We take an oath, you know, when we first commit to honor our promise. To be loyal to the ideal of the white rose. To have faith in our instructors. Respect for ourselves. To trust in those who will be our patrons. Belief that this is the right course for us. And to accept whatever the future may bring . . ."

Jesus. He knew that litany: it was Tony Venable's precepts, perverted into a hedonist's creed.

I live.

His ideas, his ideology, his precepts would never die.

I will return.

He'd never left. His body might be gone, but he'd never left. His presence was everywhere. His followers, his brethren, his legacy had made certain of it.

And he, Kyger, was wrestling air.

All he had was the corrupted precepts coming out of the ingenuous mouth of a beautiful young courtesan in training.

What could she tell Wyland that he would believe? She had no idea this was an outgrowth of Venable's secret sins.

No idea there was any connection at all.

Except . . . who were these tutors . . . ?

"Who are the tutors?"

This time she hesitated. "Just . . . people who have our best interests at heart."

He wanted to ask how, but it seemed like a superfluous question. She had been so thoroughly inculcated she wouldn't understand. She really believed that she had chosen wisely and well to hand herself over to masters who would subvert her into a prostitute.

"Is this what you really want?"

She looked indignant. "Of course. Isn't it what you're looking for? The perfect woman, trained to be your perfect accompaniment. Someone outside your marriage and your life, who is trained to devote herself totally to you?"

"What man wouldn't," Kyger murmured.

"Exactly. It's even noble in a way."

"A calling," Kyger said.

"Maybe it is. Maybe only certain people are . . . are meant to live like that."

"And you're one of them."

"I can't wait," she said. "Would you like to make an offer? We can ask, you know."

He knew that. Irene had said the same thing. "What would that entail?"

"You tell me, I confer with my tutors, we make a decision whether you can have me."

Oh, she was not as innocent as she seemed; polished to a high gloss, and counting every crown as she spoke to him.

But maybe this was the way to get at the Venable poison. Maybe . . . maybe this was what he could take back to Wyland. He named a sum that made her eyes widen.

"Oh, my goodness," she breathed, awed.

"Talk to your mentors or whatever you call them," he said. "Meet me at noon tomorrow for lunch—at Claridge's. And I hope by then you've made your decision."

Something wasn't right, and he couldn't quite grasp it. All the way home to the town house he wrestled with it. Was it that sweet Alice was so forthcoming? Perhaps *too* forthcoming with all that information, every bit of information, in fact, that he needed, and not a thing he could present as proof?

Or was it that everyone at the reception was a potential customer, as it was at the garden party? And the solicitations were made early in the game so that each submissive in training could be expressly fashioned to the taste of the one who would own her?

God, that thought was worse than abhorrent, but there was no denying the thing was real. The girls were looking for patrons. Actively inviting them to make bids for them. It was all proscribed, it seemed to him. There was nothing there that hadn't gone on for years under Venable's direction.

It made him feel as if he was operating in some parallel world where everything was the mirror image of reality.

The rabbit hole.

The agency that didn't exist; the father who wasn't there; the brothel that had disappeared as if it had been wiped clean by the hand of God. The whoremonger who was dead still selling his whores to the wealthy and elite.

Why did he feel as if all of them were connected?

He got back to the town house well after two in the morning, feeling strangely disquieted.

It was the Venable thing. It was as insidious and insubstantial as air. And yet it was there, and people were still breathing in his ideas and living for and on the promise of his dream.

How did you destroy life-sustaining air?

It was time to meet with Wyland. Before his lunch with the disingenuous Alice. He'd take Wyland with him, and that way he wouldn't have to coerce Alice to go to him with her story.

He would tell it, she could confirm it, and that should be enough proof for Wyland.

And he'd pay Alice the money anyway.

The house was preternaturally quiet. The door was open, and the lamps were lit low, in anticipation of his return. There were shadows everywhere, and it seemed to him that the damned house was too dark.

He didn't like dark houses. He didn't like these foggy mysteries that surrounded him. He wanted an end to the mysteries, to Venable, to the sevens, to everything.

And there wasn't a servant around. Not a sound.

He felt as though he ought to tiptoe up the steps. Instead, he poured himself a brandy on the way to his room.

He wanted his life back, and he had this mordant feeling he'd probably get nothing back in the end. And what he was doing in London when he should be with Angilee back at Waybury, he couldn't for the life of him understand right now.

And that damned tight tux—he threw it on the bed.

That conversation with Alice had been too disturbing; she really believed it, the whole unbelievable myth they'd sold her.

But who? Who was this procurer who had made up this fairy tale to beguile innocents so uncertain of their allure and their power they would give up every legal right for the opportunity to be a doormat and receptacle for some horny, wealthy aristocrat?

It gnawed at him as he lay propped against the headboard sipping his brandy. And the more he thought about it, the foggier everything became.

He knew this now: that there was a cabal, the Sacred Seven, whose leader they called the Ancestor, and that Tony Venable had been one of them. That he had been murdered, and the sign of seven had been cut into his chest.

And it *had* been the sign of seven; there was no other explanation now that he knew the things he knew.

And the government, always wary, then became apprehensive that Venable's philosophy and ideology would catch such hold of the public imagination that he would be elevated to a place where the government could never recover from his influence.

Which was nearly happening.

Thus, they had arranged for the impartial, unknown investigator—him—to find the thing that would demolish the legend of Tony Venable in the public's eyes, so nothing could be traced back to them.

And even though he'd found it, he still hadn't moved three paces from where he had started three months ago. Venable was revered even more, his secret life would stay secret, his secret business would continue as a resource for the brethren, and the Bullhead would rise again, probably in some other stately home, with the same whores, the same masters, the same services.

Nothing he'd done, nothing he'd discovered, would change any of it.

And Alice's story might have no effect at all on the public perception of Tony Venable.

And everything else had just been a distraction.

Even your marriage to Angilee?

Oh, God—he moved restively, kicking the tuxedo onto the floor as he set the brandy snifter down on the table beside the bed—don't even add that into the morass. Keep it apart, keep it pure in spite of how it all started. Keep it sacred . . .

Don't think about it.

He picked up the tux. What was it but a symbol of the unadulterated luxury-loving, pleasure-bent life of the sybarite. Better in Lujan's room than his.

He padded down the hallway and then paused at the door. This would be the first time he'd entered this room since he'd left London. Since Jancie and Lujan had spent time there after the deaths of their fathers.

But he wasn't going to think that way.

After all, the maids cleaned and aired every room at least once a week. Everything would be tucked and tidied, and there wouldn't be any trace of anything in that room.

Not a scent, not a breath of anything of Jancie in that room.

He turned up the gas lamp just inside the door. No, nothing in that room that spoke of Jancie or Lujan at all. It was perfectly neat, perfectly decorated, perfectly bland.

It was as if strangers lived there.

So he'd just put the suit in the dressing room and have done with it. There was a lamp in there as well, and he turned that up to reveal something that surprised him: an unusually full closet.

Holy saints, Lujan had a damn lot of clothing in Town. How the hell often had he come to London anyway in the two years he had been gone?

It looked like every week, by the number of suits and shirts that were crowded in there. It looked like his whole wardrobe.

It looked like another life hanging there.

He pushed aside a dressing gown to make room for the tux . . . and pulled back. The material of the gown felt too coarse to be a garment someone would wear naked after a bath.

It felt too coarse to be something Lujan would own.

Curious. He took out the gown and held it up to the light.

And froze. It wasn't a dressing gown by any means.

And it was the last thing he expected to see: it was a hooded robe, and it looked just like the ones worn by the brethren of the Sacred Seven.

No.

Just—*no.*

. . . *SHIT* . . .

He lay awake all night. Was every damn fucking body in the whole of London involved with the Sacred Seven?

He had to see Wyland. It was imperative he see Wyland and

then talk to Lujan. This just wasn't possible. Lujan had reformed, Lujan had changed, Lujan loved Jancie, he loved his child. He loved his new life, and he had put all of his past behind him . . .

He *had*—

. . . had—a roomful of clothes in Town. Still coming to Town often, by the evidence. Had led the most hedonistic, indulgent, carnal and dissolute life imaginable for all those years he'd lived in London. He'd practically lived at the Bullhead, fucked every whore in the city five times over and every willing woman in the country besides; and hadn't given a shit about anything before he fell in love with Jancie . . .

And maybe he didn't give a shit about anything now.

What else could it mean, this robe among his clothing?

And who had brought him to Wyland to begin with?

Hellfire and shit . . . goddamn it to . . . he felt as if everything he'd ever known had melted into a thick viscous wax. All he had to do was just pick it up and reshape it any way he wanted, because that could just as well be the way things really were as the way he *thought* they were.

He didn't know anything anymore. He was sliding down that rabbit hole again.

He had to see Wyland. This was crazy. This was what he got for poking around where he shouldn't, and he should have learned that lesson a long time ago after trying fruitlessly to pin down something corrupting in Tony Venable's life.

He'd learned *nothing*; he'd learned that malevolence lived beyond the grave, that there was no way to suppress it and that it had a self-sustaining life of its own.

A mobility of its own. And no one could stop it.

Especially not him.

He was out the door by nine o'clock on his way to Wyland's office. He walked into a crisp, clean, clear and sunny morning, the kind of morning that burned off any form of oppressive fog and made you happy to be alive.

He wasn't happy. He didn't like what he was thinking. He didn't like the idea that somehow Lujan was involved in all this.

Lujan was not involved.

Hellfire.

None of this made sense. Not from the beginning.

He had naively thought he was so close to the end.

And then—son of a bitch—Wyland was in a meeting.

"I'll wait," he told the secretary tersely.

But it was a long, aggravating hour before Wyland appeared and summoned him into his office.

"Sit." Wyland motioned him to a chair. "Tell me what further you've discovered."

Everything normal, everything the same. Wyland's kind and encouraging expression. His fatherly manner. His faith, his hope that Kyger had finally found the one thing that would subvert the cult of Tony Venable. He believed Kyger could do it, he wanted him to do it, he was waiting for him to do it.

And Kyger didn't want to disappoint him.

"I found the woman," Kyger said flatly.

Wyland looked pleased. "Did you?"

"Or rather, I found *a* woman. And I found there isn't anything tangible to attach to Tony Venable. Except for one thing."

"Which is—?"

"The promise these virgins commit to, which is in essence the list of Venable's precepts reconfigured to apply to their situation. Except I don't think my informant knows that."

"I'll be damned," Wyland said.

"I made her an offer."

"My dear boy . . ."

"It seemed like the only way; I didn't think she would have come here, so I arranged to meet her for lunch today after she consulted her *tutors* about my offer, and I want you to come. I want you to hear what she told me, and I want to know if it's enough to discredit Venable, because there's nothing else."

But there was, there was something else, but this seemed more important now, more urgent.

"What was it she told you?"

"The precepts, as applied to her *training*."

"That could be enough," Wyland said, steepling his hands. "Anything that would relate back to Venable . . ."

"What about the body?"

Wyland shook his head. "It's the damndest thing . . . can't trace it worth a damn. Have fifty detectives on it, and no one can find a thing.

"But this now, that you've uncovered—the precepts . . . yes, we can work with that—I can see the headline in the *Tatler*—an intimate peek into Venable's school of sin and scandal . . . it's perfect; it's just what we need. I do want to hear this woman's testimony . . ."

Kyger got up from his chair. "Then I'll meet you at Claridge's at noon . . ."

"But first," Wyland said, as if he hadn't said a word, "I need to arrest you—for the murder of Tony Venable."

Chapter Twenty

He froze.

He sensed movement behind him. He heard Wyland say, "Come in, my dear. You, too. Come."

He couldn't move. *Arrest you for Venable's murder*—what the hell?

"Well, baby brother, you *are* in a fix . . ."

Lujan??

He wheeled around. Lujan.

And Alice.

Alice???

Holy hellfire—

"Sit down, sit down," Wyland invited them, as if he were hosting a party. "That's it. You, too, Kyger."

He watched through narrowed eyes as Kyger sank slowly and disbelievingly back into his chair.

"This is the end game, my boy. I don't make any apologies—this was something that had to be done. The timing was fortuitous—it just happened you were the one who came on scene at exactly the right moment."

"Let us say," Lujan put in, "that *I* was the one who saw his possibilities."

"As you wish," Wyland agreed with a note of weariness in his tone. "In any event, you're under arrest, Kyger Galliard, for the murder of Tony Venable. We successfully set up his downfall; we have his killer. We have the new candidate for his seat in Parliament. I think we're all set."

What? *What?* Kyger blasted out of his chair, and Lujan grabbed him.

"Hold it, baby brother. There's nowhere to go. Hackford and Billington are right outside the door."

This was Lujan holding him so tightly by his shirt; his big brother, his nemesis, his adversary, his foil. His—enemy? In perfect consensus over this mad idea to arrest him for Venable's murder?

Down the rabbit hole again.

"I should explain a few things," Lujan murmured. "Not that any explanation needs to be had, but—well, it *is* my brother. I do feel *some* compunction about setting him up this way."

"So kind," Kyger spat through gritted teeth. He sent a scathing look at Alice.

"I do like to think you really would have offered that amount for someone like me," she said sweetly. "But what you will *give* is infinitely more valuable."

"That is to say," Lujan interpolated, thrusting him back into his chair, "your life."

Jesus God. "You've always been one of them," Kyger growled.

"Always," Lujan said, as if he ought to have known. "Here's the thing, if I may be permitted to explain it—?" He looked at Wyland. Wyland shrugged. Kyger had the feeling Wyland always gave in to Lujan on the small matters.

But the big ones?

"This is what it's all about: it's about loyalty, about an elite class that helps and boosts each other, which includes freely giving money, jobs, promotions, help for whatever one of the brethren might need—and all of it guaranteed right to the top so that slowly and carefully, we position one of our brethren in every level of government, every industry, every business, in every corner of Her Majesty's empire, until the brethren are in a position to take over and rule."

"The brethren is one organism," Wyland said, "with one mind, one heart, guided by the Sacred Seven and allegiance to their disciplines, and united in the desire to promote and promulgate the agenda of the brethren.

"And yet there were those among us who took it upon themselves to step outside the foundation of the brethren, who thought that they were above the rules and could disregard the disciplines. They sought to set new parameters for what's permissible and what would be supported."

"Venable," Kyger guessed, hard put to keep the irony out of his voice.

"Had to go," Wyland affirmed. "He was getting too powerful, too dangerous, too autocratic. We called the Sicarian—Lujan, our enforcer—it was taken care of. But he couldn't excise the cancer that was Tony Venable, or the deification of him.

"So we came up with the idea of finding an outside party, whom we would ultimately charge with Venable's murder, to rummage around in Venable's pristine life to dig up the dirt we already knew was there. Thus, Alice and Irene, specifically planted for you to find. It legitimizes the whole thing because a brethren would never be disloyal to another brethren. That's why we needed someone outside, someone wholly unconnected with us. Someone without a wife, a life, or a purpose."

"Someone," Lujan added silkily, "whom, as it happened, I needed to be gotten out of the way—permanently." He smiled beatifically. "All those diamonds, you know. Am I not the sole legatee of my wife *and* my brother? I did enjoy watching you chase down all the clues until we decided the time was ripe to catch Tony Venable's murderer. That is to say, *you,* baby brother."

So the tiger they thought was tamed had never changed its stripes, Kyger thought bitterly. It was all about what it always had been about: the corrosive appetite for and pursuit of power and money with no conscience, no morality, no sanctions except their own.

"Someone who could stand trial, be convicted, and whom the adoring populace can see hang for Tony Venable's death."

"Someone disposable," Kyger spat.

Wyland looked vaguely sympathetic.

"I am really sorry you married Angilee Rosslyn, my boy. I was hoping you wouldn't, because you were chosen to be the sacrifice for the good of the brethren, and that is written in stone."

He really did look sorry. And then his expression changed, and his tone hardened. "It's time."

Lujan hoisted him up. "Let's go."

He reacted instantly, ramming his elbow into Lujan's gut, pushing Alice aside roughly with his injured hand, grabbing for the door and opening it to find . . . Wroth.

"Well, well. Who have we here?" He pushed Kyger backward into Wyland's office, and Lujan grabbed his arms and wrenched them behind him.

"It's time to go," Wyland said.

"But we haven't delivered the *coup de grace*," Wroth said, pacing around Kyger and looking him up and down as if he were an insect. "Not only will you hang for Tony Venable's murder—although his followers might feel they want to take the law into their own hands—but your wife will pay the ultimate price as well. Yes, dear Angilee, who was to have been *my* wife. I'm beginning to think things have worked out very much for the best. She'll be much better off servicing one of our brethren with more patience than I have.

"We're taking very good care of her, I can assure you. We've initiated her into the sisterhood of the black rose."

He saw black, white, red. Blood. He felt turned inside out. He wanted to kill, maim, destroy—

They had Angilee . . . shit shit shit—and he'd left her alone with Lujan—with Jancie . . .

Oh, God, Jancie . . . !!

He felt Lujan propelling him out the door, heard the door close, felt Hackford take his one arm, Billington the injured, good, loyal soldiers of the brethren that they were.

They hadn't taken five steps down the hallway when they heard a shot within the office.

"Done," Hackford murmured with a certain satisfaction in his voice.

. . . who—?

The door opened, and Kyger twisted around to see Lujan and Wroth emerge.

"It's done," Wroth said coolly. "The Ancestor is dead."

More shock. *Wyland? The Ancestor? Dead?*

Kyger reacted—violently, viciously—pulling, twisting, kicking Hackford and Billington simultaneously, fruitlessly.

"Take him," Wroth said. "Sit on him if you have to. We have to end this now so we can take over."

Wroth in charge? And Lujan not making a move to stop him?

"I'll make certain the papers get the details." Lujan. "Cooperate, baby brother. Things will go better. And don't forget Angilee . . . you do want things to go better for Angilee?"

His heart sank. *Angilee*—with the pigs, with the black rose, with the orgies . . . oh, God—he had to get away from these madmen.

"What about Jancie . . . ?" he growled.

Lujan made a face. "Always Jancie. You never quite got over Jancie, did you? She'll be fine. She won't know. Things will go on just as they always have . . ."

Oh, God . . . Kyger could see it in a flash—Lujan at Waybury, spending his time pretending to be the meticulous gentleman farmer, getting more babies on Jancie, and then . . . then—once a month, twice—into town, into sin and sex and . . .

. . . *everybody knows*—

And Angilee . . . whatever future they would have had—babies they would have had . . . damn it, he'd wanted babies, if he could have convinced her to stay in the marriage—and now she'd be the submissive plaything of some jaded and merciless aristocrat—

Oh God, oh God, oh God . . .

He felt his whole life sliding down the rabbit hole into that netherworld of mirrors and fog. Always the fog. Always the seven.

And now Wyland was dead. The one person he'd thought was sane . . .

They were out of the office building now, and they had surrounded him, and Wroth had his pistol jammed right into the small of his back.

Wroth wouldn't miss, either. Wroth wanted him dead anyway because of Angilee. Wroth was a merciless, vengeful man.

The sun burned his eyes, the bright happy sun of this horrible day.

He had to get away.

"They love the cards," Wroth said.

"Worth the money," Lujan said. "Keeps it all alive in a very subtle way, doesn't it? I say it's a nice touch, even if I came up with the idea."

Lujan. Another shock. Had Wyland known? He couldn't have, he had seemed as mystified as anyone, but then—he'd known all along that Kyger was going to be the scapegoat—

God, what a betrayal . . . what an actor . . . he felt that killing anger wash over him again . . .

And Wyland had been the patriarch presiding over the orgy in Venable's apartment at the Bullhead . . .

Jesus—he couldn't believe it—what a bastard . . .

. . . this was so unreal, these meglomaniacal sons of bitches . . .

Angilee . . .

He couldn't give up.

Angilee—

He had to stop them . . . but their tentacles were dug so deep into the fabric of society—how, how, how . . . ?

. . . *nobody tells* . . .

It would be a sensation if he could expose it, if he could prove it—

No—he had to stop Wroth, absolutely, because Wroth seemed to have taken over as Ancestor. Wroth seemed to have some kind of strategy in hand—none of this was random, not their abuse of him nor Venable's death, nor anything that had happened in conjunction with that . . .

. . . *keeps it alive*—

Lujan had said that. He himself had thought that so many times. They wouldn't let Venable die—and he'd thought it was the public, the people who loved him, and all the time it had been Wroth and the brethren keeping him alive . . .

Alive until . . . no—not Wroth . . . oh, dear God, not Wroth.

But why not? It could have been anyone who firmly believed

in patriarchal socialism and had the backing, the wherewithal, and the charisma to step into Venable's shoes.

Once his murderer was put to rest, Tony Venable could be reborn—

—as Wroth . . .

Oh, God.

And tomorrow, they'd announce they'd apprehended Venable's murderer . . .

Three months from Venable's death to a new leader with another corrupted vision of a new world order.

He had to get away; he had to bring down Wroth . . .

And he felt the gun in his back, prodding him on.

They were taking him to the town house. Another shock—that he'd been living there for these few weeks and he'd had no idea—no idea in the *years* he'd spent time there—

. . . and—what? Cryder was . . . one of them? A brethren or a Venable adherent?

Up to the bedroom floor, into Lujan's room, into the dressing room. And there, behind the closet stuffed full of clothes was a secret room.

"Lots of secrets and tricks, baby brother," Lujan said gently. "You'll be fine here. I promise, we want to keep you alive to stand trial, because it's the only way the public will be satisfied."

They nudged him into the space, which might have been five feet square, and stuffy as hell. No ventilation. No light. Bags of clothes everywhere, Lujan's discards. A gun pointed at his head, giving him no options. That close, as he had heard, Wroth was a dead shot.

And he'd be dead anyway if he was confined so closely.

"It will be a day—two at the most," Wroth said. "We expect the public outcry will precipitate a fast trial, and an even speedier verdict. I'd say get some sleep, but you'll have eternity for that."

They stood there, all four of them, like a wall, waiting for him to duck and crawl inside the space.

He gauged his chances. Not bloody good, worse because his hand was still in such rough shape.

But they wanted him to die. And he wanted to live, and taking the chance on that was better than taking a chance he'd survive two days in the attic space.

"All right—in you go," Lujan said, reaching out to push him to his knees.

He went on instinct, still facing them, and jackknifed himself right into Wroth's genitals. Wroth pitched forward over him, howling. Lujan pulled at his left arm as he scrambled under Wroth's weight and between his spraddled legs.

Hackford reached for his right arm as Billington climbed over them to block him at the dressing room door. He wrenched his right arm away and pulled his brother with him as he hauled himself out from under Wroth's writhing body and launched himself into Billington exactly the same way.

It wasn't quite as effective—he didn't have the momentum with Lujan painfully pulling him back, but Billington was caught off balance and fell back awkwardly, and Lujan was half caught under Wroth's hips, still holding on to Kyger's arm.

The pain was indescribable; he thought it was dislocated altogether, and he had about one second to make good an escape while Billington was picking himself up, and Hackford was helping Wroth.

He gave one last mighty wrench, and Lujan let go, and he scrambled over Billington, who latched on to his left leg and pulled him back. He flailed at him with his right leg, hammering Billington's knee hard with the toe of his boot as Billington wrestled to get him in control.

But the knee gave under the pressure of all that force, and he let go suddenly. Kyger crawled over him with Lujan at his heels and the shadow of Cryder hovering at the door of the bedroom.

He saw red again, blood red, so suffusing he knew nothing else but the primitive need to destroy these people. They were ciphers, symbols, sevens—

He launched himself at Cryder with a howl and Lujan right behind him. Cryder went down, Lujan leapt on top of him and the butler, and Kyger levered himself upward abruptly and, using that moment of surprise, rolled him onto the floor.

Up and over Cryder's struggling, prone body. Out in the hallway with Lujan right behind him, thundering down the steps with Lujan grabbing at him, catching him and the both of them toppling down the final half dozen steps and rolling into the hallway in a heap.

Lujan was under him, struggling to get the advantage. Kyger reared back and punched him, in the nose, under the chin, in the throat, until he gagged. Then he hooked him one more time under the chin, and his head hit the floor, and he was out.

Now what? Now what? He had to excise the cancer—he had to stop them all long enough to rescue Angilee. How? How? He heard them coming.

He raced into the parlor. What? What? Gaslight . . . on the wall—flame—they were coming . . . he took off the shade, grabbed a pillow from the sofa, lit it, threw it on the sofa, took another pillow, already aflame, and threw it at the curtains . . .

And then he dove out the window as a wall of flame erupted as Lujan and Wroth came racing in.

She was naked but for a braided leather rose necklace, chained to the wall, and surrounded by men in hooded robes who were walking around, assessing her.

"She'll do, brethren," the one who seemed to be in charge said. "Quite nice. She'll sell high, once we suppress all that fire and independence. And won't we enjoy doing it. She must learn that gentlemen don't prize that kind of self-assurance."

She knew the coward was speaking as much to her as to his brethren, and she hated him, she hated them, she hated the moment still when she'd realized that Lujan was not her friend and that she had been as gullible as a goose.

It was the worst thing, not to have seen what was coming. Just like with her father. Just like with . . .

She felt like an utter fool. Like she had walked right into it, her eyes wide open with genuine admiration for the man who was Kyger's big strong brother.

How stupid could a woman be? That stupid.

Well, it was too late for any of that now. They had her, they had Kyger, if anything Lujan had explained to her was anywhere near the truth, and neither of them were going to survive this.

No, she was going to survive this. She understood it all hinged on how compliant she became. It couldn't be too sudden or too fast. It had to be gradual until they trusted that their methods were working and that she saw the wisdom of their way.

The problem was their methods. She already didn't like their methods, even without being able to look into their eyes. Their stripping her, chaining her, claiming her with the leather rose—all of that was part of the method. They wanted to break her of her antiquated thinking about her role and raise up to the new philosophy of obedience and to yearn for the honor of servicing the needs, the whim, the sexual proclivities of one man, one master who was to pay for the privilege of owning such a creature.

All right. She could pretend. She would do whatever it took to keep herself alive. She wondered, as they paced around her, how long it took to break and remake a reasonable woman.

Maybe never.

She couldn't stand this; she didn't have the patience for this. These ghouls were imitations of men, hiding behind their hoods and their rituals. They were children. They were . . .

She pulled back on her fury. That would get her to a certain point that could sustain her, but any show of it would kill her chances of surviving and maybe get her killed.

Compliance, that was the key. What was her body after all but a shell, a vessel. That was what they thought. That was how they were going to treat her—like an object for their use, their pleasure.

Fine, she could be an object. Just remove herself from the equation and wait for the moment . . . whatever moment that would be . . .

The town house burned. The flames soared high as Kyger raced toward the boulevard. He heard the clanging of bells; he saw people racing toward the square as he ran the opposite direction, cradling his injured arm and feeling a desperation he had never known, both at the loss of the town house and the loss of Angilee . . .

Angilee . . .

Where would they have taken her? Where? They had totally abandoned the Bullhead. What would Wroth have done with her if she and Lujan both had been at Waybury earlier today?

. . . or was it Wroth who had taken her . . . ?

Holy shit . . .

He had no other solution. And besides—there was Jancie . . . oh, Jesus, Jancie . . . at the very least he could—

What *could* he do? Tell Jancie that Lujan was a traitor, a liar, a killer . . . he didn't even know what Lujan was anymore—

But he was thinking as he ran—they wouldn't kill Angilee. They'd toy with her first, they'd humiliate her, they'd shame her, they'd use her, and maybe in the end, they might think they could sell her. But they wouldn't kill her—not right away.

So he could take the chance of going to Waybury. At the least, he could assure himself that Jancie—oh, God—and the boy . . . Gaunt—God—he had to go—it was the first best thing to do, and if all was reasonably to hand there, then the Bullhead on the way back to London . . .

Which would all shoot him into the evening and the night, obliterating any possibility of answers . . .

Shit, shit, shit, shit . . .

He grabbed a passerby on horseback who was gunning toward the square. "I need your mount. I'll pay you."

The man hesitated because he saw a wild-eyed madman with a limp arm. "What kind of money?"

Kyger dug in his pockets and pulled out a handful of silver and a thick wad of pound notes. "Here you go."

The rider gaped as Kyger thrust the money into his hands. "Yes?"

He slid down from the saddle. No use arguing, there was hard, hot desperation here, and a lot of money. "Take it."

Kyger vaulted on, straining his left arm badly all over again as he took hold of the reins and spurred the horse on.

The growing crowd flowing toward the square blocked the streets. He worked his way toward the back streets, out of the way, out of the line of the fire in more ways than one, as the noxious scent of smoke followed him until he was over the bridge.

Waybury had its secrets. A hidden fortune in diamonds, a murder buried for years, a father seeking vengeance, and an ocean of tears.

But none of that accounted for the thing that Jancie had seen today: Lujan, leaving Waybury with Angilee that morning for his usual *business in London,* and skulking back not two hours later in a way that was furtive and suspicious.

At the moment, every feeling of dread and dissonance washed over her, everything she had intuited, that she had felt, that she had ignored, everything she had not wanted to believe because she wanted to believe that Lujan had changed, was happy, really loved her.

He loved her. She had no doubt of that. But *this*—? Lujan sneaking back into his house . . . with Angilee?

Dear heaven. She waited, because for certain they had had an accident or something had happened that made him turn around and come back home. Hadn't it—?

Not a sound. Not a step. He had disappeared somewhere behind the house, and somehow the house had just swallowed him and Angilee up, and everything went silent. Strange. Eerie.

Emily appeared as she was looking out the window for the hundredth time. *Mrrroww. Not there.*

She whirled. "How do you know?" Her voice was shaking. This just wasn't like Lujan.

It *wasn't*. But something about it scared her. Really scared her. And as usual, Emily was there.

"Mama . . ."

She jumped. Gaunt! Oh, God . . . Gaunt. She ran toward him, grabbed him up, hugged him.

Mrs. Ancrum appeared to announce that lunch was ready.

"Would you kindly feed Gaunt, and I'll be taking him out for a little ride this afternoon." She thought she sounded normal; she didn't think the tension was audible.

Ooww. Calm down.

Mrs. Ancrum didn't indicate she noticed anything untoward. "Very good." Off they went, as usual, although normally she accompanied them. But now—she had to plan . . . because if something was going on, she wanted Gaunt out of the house. Away from the house.

Ooowww. Wise move.

What did Emily know?

She paced around the house, upstairs and down, with Emily following her, waiting for Lujan to appear.

Nothing. No sound. No footstep. Her heart started beating erratically. Emily rubbed against her leg. *Mrrrow. Get Gaunt away.*

"You're right." She felt cold, breathless, helpless.

Mrs. Ancrum reappeared. "The darling ate well this afternoon, Miss Jancie."

"Excellent. Now, I wonder—would you be kind enough to take him to the vicarage—? I promised Mrs. Elsberry we'd visit for an hour or so, but I'm not feeling up to it."

"I'd be happy to, ma'am."

She wondered if her face was as flushed as it felt. She waited, containing her impatience, until Mrs. Ancrum and Gaunt went trotting down the drive in the donkey cart.

And then . . . there was still no sign of Lujan.

"What now?" she whispered.

Mrrreuwww. Where else?

Jancie felt frozen. "The basements. The wine room. Why would he secretly go down there?"

Oww. Let's find out.

Jancie couldn't move. She had to move. She didn't want to know.

She had to know.

"You're right," she whispered finally, "let's find out."

Down in the bowels of the house, there were storerooms and root cellars, canning shelves, and the wine cellar.

Hugo Galliard had embraced the life of a gentleman full force for a man who had spent most of his life scavenging in diamond mines. But when he and Jancie's father found their major strike, it was the beginning of a long string of events that had led to his abandoning his partner, marrying a woman of means, and taking on the guise of a man who had always enjoyed the finer things in life while he kept secrets almost to the grave.

The end result was a well-stocked cellar which had become Mrs. Ancrum's and Lujan's purview.

Jancie never went down there. It was filthy down there. It was dark down there, and mysterious and evil.

But today—today . . . she was scared to death of what she would find down there, and she didn't think it would be buried bodies. She armed herself with one of Lujan's hunting rifles, even though she'd never fired one in her life.

The heft of it was reassuring. Comforting. She felt as if she had some power. But she wouldn't find anything there; she was almost sure of it.

She took a kerosene lamp with her, and she had Emily beside her.

It was just—opening the door. Forcing herself to walk down the steps. Holding the lamp up high so that she could see.

There wasn't much to see. A narrow passageway, doors to the left and right, and straight ahead the storage area and the wine room.

And wasn't there a door out to the garden?

Was that how Lujan . . . ? But why—what? Why hadn't he come up and told her he was home? And where was Angilee?

Her stomach knotted. This wasn't good. She wasn't hallucinating. She had seen them, clear as day.

She heard something, a low thrumming sound.

Her heart stopped. A hum transforming into words she could just understand, just hear.

Devotion. Persuasion. Progression. Preservation. Dissemination. Propagation. Retribution.

Oh, God—someone was in the wine room.

Some*one?* Many ones . . . *voices* repeating the litany over and over.

Lujan?

Mew. A peep from Emily right beside her. *No.*

She crept closer to the wine room. She had only been down there a half dozen times, but she remembered it being a large room with the storage areas tucked into the walls.

But what on earth were voices doing in there?

The voices became more distinct.

Jancie eased to the door, her whole body boneless with fear. She cocked the rifle, her hands shaking so badly, she was certain she'd done it incorrectly. And then she turned the knob and pushed the door open a crack.

From this awkward angle, she saw several things. Disturbing things. Things she didn't want to know about but were there, right in her own home: robed men kneeling and chanting. And a woman, naked and writhing, and chained to the wall.

Angilee . . . !

But nowhere did she see Lujan, which was the worst thing of all.

She didn't know what to do . . . Angilee, naked and humiliated like this. These strange anonymous men reciting some ritual chant before—before what?

Whatever it was, she had to stop them. As long as Lujan was not among them, she didn't care.

But the angle was awful. She'd have to aim low to avoid hitting Angilee, and even then, given her inexperience with firearms, there was no guarantee.

Her hands iced up. Nausea attacked her. But the robes were moving, rising up, in preparation for . . .

Euw . . . Emily—*Be brave* . . .

She aimed, following the movement of the bodies—maybe one shot, maybe if she scared them . . . if she just got them out of the wine room, out of the house, away from Angilee, from Lujan, from her life, her love, her heart—if . . .

She squeezed the trigger blindly, and she heard a scream above the booming sound of the shot:

"DON'T SHOOT—ONE OF THEM IS MY FATHER . . ."

Kyger couldn't get to Waybury fast enough, and as fast as he pushed the horse, it wasn't enough. As hard as he rode the poor burdened horse, he could not go any faster, and he had the feeling everything was sliding out of his grasp and in the end there would be nothing there and he'd never know anything for sure.

He spurred the horse on. He was close now, closer than he thought, within distance now, within the boundaries moments later, within sight of the gate . . . the house—

He wheeled the horse tight into the gateway turn and drove him up the drive, dismounted before the poor animal came to a halt and raced into the house.

Into a flat dead silence, and the scent of acrid smoke permeating the air.

Oh, God, was Waybury on fire, too?

Where?

He followed the scent—this was crazy—where was Jancie, the servants . . . Mrs. Ancrum—the tot?

The smoke—he sniffed . . . gunpowder . . .

Holy hell—

He ran down the hallway toward the kitchen. Stronger here. Recently fired, too . . .

. . . where the fuck was Jancie?

Where was the damned smoke coming from?

Wait—the basement—stronger here . . . He pulled open the door, and it hit him in the nose. And the sound of anguished sobs.

OOWWW. He looked down. Emily was sitting there, and he had stepped on her tail.

She turned up her nose. *About time.*

She turned and stalked down the steps, and he followed slowly.

God—it smelled of smoke and blood; it smelled like a massacre.

Owww . . . Emily, leading the way in the darkness. There was soft diffused light ahead of him, though, the wine room as he remembered. And the scent of smoke thicker here.

He pushed open the door.

He saw bodies; he saw Angilee.

Five bodies on the floor. Angilee, naked, sobbing, cradling one of them . . .

He made a sound, and she looked up, her face blurred with tears.

"Help him."

He ignored the rest, and ripped off his jacket and covered her, and then knelt beside Zabel to feel for a pulse, a movement, any sign of life.

Zabel's eyes opened just for a moment. "Oh, it's you."

There was so much blood. Kyger ripped his shirt and stuffed it against the wound.

"So Lujan wins." Zabel coughed out the words.

"Lujan could be dead," Kyger said tersely. "And Wroth, and their whole damned plot to turn Wroth into another Tony Venable. Hold still."

He pressed harder against the wound as Zabel coughed again, or maybe he was laughing.

"You fool." He barely got the words out. "Not Wroth." He coughed again. "It was Lujan they were grooming. Lujan who believed all that Venable crap, Lujan who wanted it more than life . . . so he killed him—he killed Venable . . ." He spit up again. "Your brother—he had that power . . . *power*—and everyone liked him . . . not like Wroth . . ."

Kyger remembered: all those men in high government positions with whom Lujan had been acquainted . . . how it had stunned him. He was stunned now. Or not, knowing what he knew.

But Lujan—the political savior the Tony Venable faction was waiting for, praying for? Lujan, the enforcer for the Sacred Seven? Oh, God, dear God . . .

"He's not dead," Zabel said suddenly, clearly. "You'll see—"
What?

But Zabel was gone, his head lolling against Angilee's naked breast, and her tears washing away all of his sins.

And Jancie was gone, vanished off the face of the earth, as far as Kyger could tell, as he ransacked the house looking for her. Even Angilee didn't know—just that she'd burst into the wine cellar, blasting away until everybody was down on the ground, had unchained Angilee, and together, they had seen to Zabel, knowing already that it was too late.

"And then she left. She said she had to go. She said Emily would stay with us, and she would come back for her—someday." Angilee was dressed now, in some of Jancie's clothes, and somewhat more composed.

It had been a harrowing afternoon. All those deaths, and the revelation that the four other men were men of distinction and worth—all brethren—Haverdene, Beddington . . . every perception of them smashed in the face of the profanity of what they had been about to do to Angilee.

And then, the anguished Mrs. Ancrum coming back to Waybury with the news that Gaunt, whom she had brought for a visit to the Elsberrys, had totally disappeared, and they couldn't find him anywhere, and they searched for hours.

"Miss Jancie came and took him," Kyger assured her.

"I don't know that, I can't know that, and what will I tell her if she comes back and he's not here?"

"I'll tell her. I know she came and took him."

Owww, Emily said. *Listen to him.*

Emily's assurance didn't lessen the tension, however, and there was so much to be done, the authorities called, the explanations, the interrogations, none of which satisfied the inspectors. And then, the disposition of the bodies which were taken back to London.

The end of the story.

If it ever got public, it would be a sensation.

But what was the end of the story?

Even Kyger didn't know. He did know they were not staying at Waybury any longer than these three days, and accordingly the following morning, he called for a carriage, and they went back to London, with Emily cuddled in Angilee's lap.

"She left Emily for me," Angilee whispered.

Mrroww. Yes she did, Emily affirmed.

They drove past the ruins of the town house, which was a mass of stone, brick and smoldering debris. That beautiful, beautiful building—

"More questions about that," Kyger murmured. There would never be an end to it, and maybe this was Lujan's legacy—that he would never be rid of him, that Lujan would always haunt him, always be a part of his life, always on the edges waiting to strike.

The house *was* on Belgrave Square. Angilee felt reassured by that, but not by the notion that she now was a very wealthy woman. They could rebuild the house; they could go anywhere in the world to get away from everything that had happened.

Funny she was thinking in terms of *they* . . .

Or she could divorce him as she had originally planned and live her life the way she wanted to.

She didn't know what she wanted to do.

She wanted to go to the flat she had rented. Her *business* in London. How ironic that seemed now.

When Kyger halted the carriage in front of the building, she felt as if she had lived there a lifetime ago. Kyger helped her out, and she walked up the steps slowly. "Don't come in."

"Why is that?"

"This is another chapter in my life I have to close," she said, but in truth it was because she thought Mrs. Geddes might still be there.

She mounted the steps reluctantly. Stopped. Thought to call Kyger, and then didn't. Knocked on her own apartment door. Waited. Heard noise behind the door, a scurrying, and then the door was opened.

"Well," Mrs. Geddes said. "It's about time. I'm leaving."

"I should hope so," Angilee said.

"Wroth is dead you know—it was in the papers. They found his body in the Galliard town house."

Why was Mrs. Geddes telling her this? "Did they?" Why was she feeling so strange about her?

"So the thing is, he owes me a lot of money."

"Does he? How is that, Mrs. Geddes?"

"Why, he set it up so that you would hire me, of course, and paid me to keep an eye on you and make sure you didn't accept a proposal from any other man."

Angilee's heart went reeling. "Did he? How clever of him. How nice he's dead and out of my life. How do you figure that *I* owe you anything?"

"Well—you're a rich woman now. Really rich. And I know where some bodies are buried."

What an awful rat of a woman. How could she have hired her, trusted her . . . this was such a nightmare . . . "I'm certain you do, Mrs. Geddes, but I think we're finished here. You've had free rent for many weeks. I'm certain you've ransacked my belongings and taken whatever is of worth there. And it may well be you've found my money, and so with all of that—as of this moment, you're trespassing on my property, and if I call the authorities, I will accuse you of theft—you can be certain that I'm the one who will be believed . . ."

"Well, when did you get claws and a backbone . . . very well, Miss Rosslyn. You may or may not be correct in your assumptions, but I'll leave. Just be aware I'll always be here . . . watching . . ."

And she took her hat, she took her suitcase which was at the ready at her feet, she took her coat, and she marched down the steps in high dudgeon.

Angilee closed the door. Went downstairs. Found the landlady and paid her a month's additional rent.

And then she closed the door on that part of this awful nightmare.

Angilee insisted they go to Claridge's and stay in Zabel's suite rather than try to find rooms in one of the hotels that were crowding up in anticipation of the Queen's Jubilee. And that in spite of the fact that Kyger had been told that Zabel was not registered.

"No. Not possible. Watch me." She approached the desk. Introduced herself as Zabel's daughter. Explained the situation, which was that her brand-new husband had been mistakenly told that her father was not registered at the hotel, which had to be a great big mistake, because he was paying great big money for that great big suite he'd rented in February, a month before they'd even come.

The clerk was wary; there were a hundred stories from a hundred people desperately trying to find a room for the upcoming festivities.

"Well, something must have changed. I need to see the manager, please. It may be that my father owes this hotel thousands and thousands of dollars because you see—he . . ."

Thousands of dollars was a language that everyone understood. The clerk immediately felt he had an obligation to investigate Miss Rosslyn's claim and called the manager, and together they went through the records and ultimately found, buried in the paperwork of a hundred other confirmations, a record of her father's reservation, his check, a letter detailing everything he wished to have ready on his arrival, and a note from him latterly, asking that the reservation be switched into another name.

Ah.

Her mother's name, Angilee saw.

Oh.

And no one had claimed the room yet.

Well.

Could she at least see, and they could come with her, whether her father had removed his things? Money changed hands, and they all went up to the suite, and there they found that all of Zabel's possessions were still intact. His papers, particularly.

The manager could see a hundred problems stemming from the fact that the suite had been empty all this time and staff had had access to it.

There was no other claim on the suite, and Angilee and her husband were free to occupy it for as long as they wished. At the same room rate, and the manager would correct the record and issue new keys.

"Of course," Angilee said graciously. They'd be honored, she and her husband.

The word sat strangely in the air.

But it was done.

That part was done.

Nothing else was done.

And suddenly they were strangers, with a meddling meowy cat between them.

They sent for room service.

Ooww. Good idea. I'm hungry.

"There is so much to be done," Angilee said despairingly, ignoring Emily rubbing against her arm. "The lawyers, the funerals, getting money, clothes, your town house, if I want to stay, if you want to go . . ."

"There's nothing that has to be done," Kyger said. "Not this minute. It can all come later."

"I'm very very rich now," Angilee said.

"Me, too," Kyger said.

"Really?"

Mrroow, Emily said. *He is.*

"Really. There really was a fortune in diamonds. It's all in the bank. I didn't marry you for your money."

Angilee sniffed. "I can't believe this . . ."

"Don't. Right now, it never happened."

"But we're married."

"Yes, we are."

"You don't want to be."

"Maybe I do.

"Why? You're not in love with me."

"Damned close. Always wanted you. Couldn't get enough of you. Always wanted to protect you, which I didn't do a hell of a good job of."

Angilee sniffed. "Me, too."

"All right, then. So let's not do anything about it yet. Let's just be married."

"Do you think . . . ?"

He shushed her. "I'm not going to think for at least a year. We have enough to keep busy, enough to deal with. We have time to come to grips with everything that's happened. We've had terrible losses. But we have each other, too, and now we have a shared history. That is not a bad foundation, Angilee. I desperately want a foundation."

Mrrrrooooww, Emily said emphatically. *Me, too. But what about Jancie . . . ?*

"What about Jancie?" Angilee asked.

"I don't know. I think we have to find her. But I think we have to give her some time. That's why she left Emily with us. She'll come back for Emily. Just let's give her time."

They didn't eat dinner when it came. Instead, they climbed into bed together, *her* bed, not Zabel's, and Kyger held her, as Emily nestled nearby. And she cried, and he wondered about the journey that had brought them together and to this place.

He thought about his father, about Jancie and Lujan, and if Lujan were really gone like Jancie, and he thought, if they were gone for good, he'd know it, because they both would have accessed their share of the diamonds.

He wondered if he wanted to know.

He didn't want to know. Not now. Maybe not ever. Maybe it was safer that way.

But for now, he felt safe holding Angilee. This moment was his, now and forever; he had a wife, he had a future, he had vanquished the evil, even though evil still lived.

Evil never died.

And they *would* bury the past, he'd make sure that they kept looking toward the future, and they'd take tomorrow as it came. And he wanted that—a hundred tomorrows that weren't tainted with the ambitions of their fathers, and the sins of their sons.

That was what he wanted. A clean slate, a bright clear future—with Angilee.

His beautiful, amazing, indomitable Angilee.

His *wife*.

Slowly, in the depths of the night, they moved toward each other. Slowly, they moved into the magical touching and kissing and caressing that was the slow mounding prelude to that hot naked connection they both yearned for; slowly and tentatively they came together, as if she didn't know him and he'd never made love to her.

So luscious, so edible—he didn't have to rush now, he could take his time, he could savor every moment, every lick, every nip as he explored the alluring hollows of her body. As he sucked lightly at her raspberry nipples, ran his tongue in the valley between her hip and her belly, as he tasted her everywhere, end to end, top to bottom.

And when he finally nuzzled his way between her legs, and insinuated his tongue firmly into her slit, he could have sworn he tasted chocolate.

Please turn the page for an excerpt from
"Natural Attraction,"
a Susan Johnson story in
STRANGERS IN THE NIGHT,
a December 2004 anthology from Brava.

"Where are you going?" Against the first light of dawn, Jasper took in the delicious sight of Nicky struggling to pull her chemise down over her plump breasts.

"To work. It's early. Go back to sleep."

"I'll come with you," he said, throwing aside the covers.

"That's not necessary. How do I say this politely? Last night was lovely—more than lovely, stupendous and blissful—but I really have to go to work. So thank you for everything, and pleasant dreams."

He'd never been dismissed by a woman after a night of sex or given his congé by a woman for *any* reason. It gave him pause—for the briefest of seconds—before his well-honed self-interest came to the fore. Rising from the bed, he closed the small distance between them, tugged her chemise down for her, and straightened the batiste folds with a flick of his fingers. "I don't know how to say this," he murmured in gentle parody, brushing her cheek lightly. "But last night was beyond stupendous for me, and with that memory still newly fresh, I have no intention of letting you go. I hope you understand."

"Don't be ridiculous." She gazed at him from under her lashes. "You are, you know."

He blew out a breath. "Probably. But I'm coming with you."

"And do what?"

"Whatever you do. Give me orders." He smiled. "You're good at that, as I recall."

"This isn't a seduction, Priestley. I'm tired as hell and not in the mood to put up with this foolishness. Weren't you going hunting?"

"I was until I met you."

"You don't understand. I have no time to be polite."

"You can't work every minute."

"Very nearly. I don't indulge in a life of leisure like you."

"Let me put it this way. Tell me you really don't want to come ten or twenty times tonight, and I'll go hunting for whatever Harry feels is in need of being hunted."

The fact that Jasper was standing very close, his erection at full mast as usual, made it almost impossible to avert her eyes from its splendor. Be sensible, she told herself; don't surrender to Priestley as diversion. There were hours and days, perhaps weeks of work ahead before the balloon was restructured for higher altitudes. "I'd prefer a polite good-bye. I'm sure there are legions of women who would be delighted with your offer."

"Why are you being difficult?"

"Because I'm really busy."

"Then why don't we just say I'll be available whenever you're *not* busy." He ran his fingers up the length of his upthrust penis. "Like now, for instance, if you could spare a few minutes."

"I can't" she said hoarsely, clearing her throat to quickly add, "Really, Jasper, I have to go." Not that her body was in agreement; the hard, steady pulsing between her legs accelerated, her sexual appetite permanently ravenous in close proximity to the viscount's glorious cock.

"Why don't I see if I can change your mind," he murmured.

"No!" She backed away.

"Give me five minutes of your time, and I'll buy Lunardi another balloon. Ten minutes, and I'll buy him two."

She hesitated.

His cock took notice, swelling higher.

"Damn you," she croaked, sorely tempted.

"Think of it as advancing science. I'm sure Lunardi will be grateful."

She'd contributed a good deal of her fortune to Vincenzo's project; another affluent patron—in this case, an influential English one—would be helpful to Lunardi's cause. Damn Priestley for his casual wealth—and impertinence.

Although, if she were honest with herself, refusing Jasper's offer of sex was difficult even without his generous incentive. Nearly impossible, she thought, gazing at the huge, engorged object of her lust.

She shifted in her stance as though so slight a movement would negate the fevered demands of her throbbing flesh and the small voice inside her head whispering, *Think of the gluttonous, sensual pleasure.*

She resisted a second more before deciding, the word *capitulation* faithlessly leaping into her mind a second after that.

As sop to her independence, she decided a quid pro quo would be necessary. She was not so lost to all reason that she would join the ranks of Priestley's paramours without due compensation. "I will agree to your offer, but you'll have to wait until evening. Vincenzo's expecting me to arrive on time."

Out of jealousy, Jasper almost said, no, you must do it now. But in that portion of his brain still functioning outside the tidal wave of unquenchable lust, he understood how much her work meant to her. He understood even better how pleasing her would ultimately be his gain. And perhaps, at base, he refused to acknowledge the concept of jealousy. "You have yourself a deal," he agreed pleasantly. "I won't interfere in your work. I'll stay out of the way. Harry will be there, no doubt. He can allay my boredom."

"As I said from the beginning," she declared crisply, "you should remain here."

"Let me rephrase that. I don't wish to be a hindrance. But if I can help in any way, please, by all means, tell me."

"If that's double entendre, I don't appreciate—"

"You misunderstand. I meant it sincerely."

"Hmmm."

"You needn't be so suspicious. I'm capable of controlling myself."

She smiled for the first time that morning, recalling the astonishing extent of his control. "I stand corrected, Priestley. You definitely have control."

"I suggest we keep our conversation devoid of sexual allusions in an effort to, in my case, tame the wild beast."

Easier said than done, she thought, taking in the splendid sight before her eyes. But she understood duty and responsibility. "I agree," she said, with the same attempt at composure as he. "I'll have Jai bring me work clothes. You may use the dressing room first. How would that be?"

She wouldn't care to hear the truth. "Whatever you say."

Halfway to the door, she turned and looked at him, her expression testy. "I hope you won't pout all day."

He was at a loss as to why he put up with her damnable temper. Then again, a roisterous night of the hottest sex he'd ever experienced might be good enough reason. "I won't pout if you don't," he said pointedly.

She opened her mouth, then shut it again.

"Exactly," he murmured. "And there's more of that tonight if you wish."

"I should send you packing," she snapped, turning around and flouncing to the door.

"If it wasn't my suite, you could," he drawled.

Swivelling back, she leaned against the polished oak and met his amused gaze. "You're too good to give up, Priestley. Not that you don't know it. But, just for the record, I never take orders."

There was no point in arguing; he could dominate her a hundred ways to Sunday if he wished. "Fair enough," he said politely. "Should I ring for breakfast?"

She smiled. "No argument?"

He shrugged. "What's the point?"

What was the point indeed, when you could order the world to your liking, she thought. But contrary to Jasper's opinion, she could be as agreeable as he, especially when he would make it worth her while tonight. She smiled. "Well said. I'll have coffee and scones. Two eggs and bacon." Turning, she opened the door and gave her instructions to a waiting Jai.

Careful to keep their distance, for reasons of insatiable lust, they took turns washing up in the dressing room and by the time Jai returned with Nicky's clothes, Jasper was dressed, breakfast had arrived, and they were about to sit down.

After a quiet conversation at the door, Nicky sent Jai away.

Looking up from the paper, Jasper lifted his brows. "Will he actually leave?"

"He feels I'm safe when I'm at work." Taking her parcel, she disappeared into the dressing room and emerged short minutes later, attired in breeches and shirt, her hair pulled back in a queue.

It was going to be a very long day, Jasper thought, quickly averting his gaze from Nicky's curvaceous form boldly displayed in the tight breeches and shirt that clung to her breasts rather more than he would have liked. He would definitely have to see that Harry found him something to keep him busy at the laboratory. If he were forced to simply watch Nicky all day, his manners would be sorely taxed.

There were limits even to his self-control.

We don't think you will want to miss
Alison Kent's new five-episode series.
Here is a description of all five books.

Meet the men of the Smithson Group—five spies whose best work is done in the field and between the sheets. Smart, built, trained to do everything well—and that's everything—they're the guys you want on your side of the bed. Go deep undercover? No problem. Take out the bad guys? Done. Play by the rules? I don't think so. Indulge a woman's every fantasy? Happy to please, ma'am.
Fall in love? Hey, even a secret agent's got his weak spots . . .

Bad boys. Good spies. Unforgettable lovers.

Episode One:
THE BANE AFFAIR
by
Alison Kent

"Smart, funny, exciting, touching, and *hot.*"—Cherry Adair

"Fast, dangerous, sexy."—Shannon McKenna

Get started with Christian Bane, SG–5

Christian Bane is a man of few words, so when he talks, people listen. One of the Smithson Group's elite force, Christian's also the walking wounded, haunted by his past. Something about being betrayed by a woman, then left to die in a Thai prison by the notorious crime syndicate Spectra IT gives a guy demons. But now, Spectra has made a secret deal with a top scientist to crack a governmental encryption technology, and Christian has his orders: Pose as Spectra boss Peter Deacon. Going deep undercover as the slick womanizer will be tough for Christian. Getting cozy with the scientist's beautiful goddaughter, Natasha, to get information won't be. But the closer he gets to Natasha, the harder it gets to deceive her. She's so alluring, so trusting, so completely unexpected he suspects someone's been giving out faulty intel. If Natasha isn't the criminal he was led to believe, they're both being played for fools. Now, with Spectra closing in, Christian's best chance for survival is to confront his demons and trust the only one he can . . . Natasha . . .

Available from Brava in October 2004.

Episode Two:
THE SHAUGHNESSEY ACCORD
by
Alison Kent

Get hot and bothered with Tripp Shaughnessey, SG–5

When someone screams Tripp Shaughnessey's name, it's usually a woman in the throes of passion or one who's just caught him with his hand in the proverbial cookie jar. Sometimes it's both. Tripp is sarcastic, fun-loving, and funny, with a habit of seducing every woman he says hello to. But the one who really gets him hot and bothered is Glory Brighton, the curvaceous owner of his favorite sandwich shop. The nonstop banter between Glory and Tripp has been leading up to a full-body kiss in the back storeroom. And that's just where they are when all hell breaks loose. Glory's past includes some very bad men connected to Spectra, men convinced she may have important intel hidden in her place. Now, with the shop under siege, and gunmen holding customers hostage, Tripp shows Glory his true colors: He's no sweet, rumpled "engineer" from the Smithson Group, but a well-trained, hardcore covert op whose easygoing rep is about to be put to the test . . .

Available from Brava in November 2004.

Episode Three:
THE SAMMS AGENDA
by
Alison Kent

Get down and dirty with Julian Samms, SG–5

From his piercing blue eyes to his commanding presence, everything about Julian Samms says all-business and no bull. He expects a lot from his team—some say too much. But that's how you keep people alive, by running things smooth, clean, and quick. Under Julian's watch, that's how it plays. Except today. The mission was straightforward: Extract Katrina Flurry, ex-girlfriend of deposed Spectra frontman Peter Deacon, from her Miami condo before a hit man can silence her for good. But things didn't go according to plan, and Julian's suddenly on the run with a woman who gives new meaning to high maintenance. Stuck in a cheap motel with a force of nature who seems determined to get them killed, Julian can't believe his luck. Katrina is infuriating, unpredictable, adorable, and possibly the most exciting, sexy woman he's ever met. A woman who makes Julian want to forget his playbook and go wild, spending hours in bed. And on the off-chance that they don't get out alive, Julian's new live-for-today motto is starting right now . . .

Available from Brava in December 2004.

Episode Four:
THE BEACH ALIBI
by
Alison Kent

Get deep under cover with Kelly John Beach, SG–5

Kelly John Beach is a go-to guy known for covering all the bases and moving in the shadows like a ghost. But now, the ultimate spy is in big trouble: during his last mission, he was caught breaking into a Spectra IT high-rise on one of their video surveillance cameras. The SG–5 team has to make an alternate tape fast, one that proves K.J. was elsewhere at the time of the break-in. The plan is simple: Someone from Smithson will pose as K.J.'s lover, and SG–5's strategically placed cameras will record their every intimate, erotic encounter in elevators, restaurant hallways, and other daring forums. But Kelly John never expects that "alibi" to come in the form of Emma Webster, the sexy coworker who has starred in so many of his not-for-primetime fantasies. Getting his hands—and anything else he can—on Emma under the guise of work is a dream come true. Deceiving the good-hearted, trusting woman isn't. And when Spectra realizes that the way to K.J. is through Emma, the spy is ready to come in from the cold, and show her how far he'll go to protect the woman he loves . . .

Available from Brava in January 2005.

Episode Five:
THE MCKENZIE ARTIFACT
by
Alison Kent

Get what you came for with Eli McKenzie, SG–5

Five months ago, SG–5 operative Eli McKenzie was in deep cover in Mexico, infiltrating a Spectra ring that kidnaps young girls and sells them into a life beyond imagining. Not being able to move on the Spectra scum right away was torture for the tough-but-compassionate superspy. But that wasn't the only problem—someone on the inside was slowly poisoning Eli, clouding his judgment and forcing him to make an abrupt trip back to the Smithson Group's headquarters to heal. Now, Eli's ready to return . . . with a vengeance. It seems his quick departure left a private investigator named Stella Banks in some hot water. Spectra operatives have nabbed the nosy Stella and are awaiting word on how to handle her disposal. Eli knows the only way to save her life and his is to reveal himself to Stella and get her to trust him. Seeing the way Stella takes care of the frightened girls melts Eli's armor, and soon, they find that the best way to survive this brutal assignment is to steal time in each other's arms. It's a bliss Eli's intent on keeping, no matter what he has to do to protect it. Because Eli McKenzie has unfinished business with Spectra—and with the woman who has renewed his heart—this is one man who always finishes what he starts . . .

Available from Brava in February 2005.